SENTINEL

THE BATTLECRY SERIES - BOOK TWO

EMERALD DODGE

EMERALD'S MAILING LIST

To receive the latest freebies, sneak peeks, news, and more, visit www.emeralddodge.com to sign up for Emerald's mailing list.

ALSO BY EMERALD DODGE

The Battlecry Series

Ignite (Prequel Novelette)

Battlecry

Sentinel

Mercury - Available Fall 2018

Enclave Boxed Sets

Of Beasts and Beauties

*This book is dedicated to the memory of
Gregory Buck Welch
6/30/1994 - 2/14/2013*

*And God shall wipe away all tears from their eyes: and death shall be no
more. Nor mourning, nor crying, nor sorrow shall be any more, for the
former things are passed away. - Revelations 21:4 (DRB)*

Ora Pro Nobis

1

The lions had come out of nowhere.

One minute my team and I had been corralling skittish deer and chattering monkeys back into their enclosures, and then the next we were running for our lives from the Saint Catherine Animal Park's main attraction, the pride of five full-grown lions.

I'd seen them earlier as we'd canvassed the zoo with tranquilizer guns in hand; they'd been sleeping peacefully in the shadows of the enormous rocks that dotted their enclosure. None of us had thought to double check the bolt on their gate. After all, if the malicious wag who'd set the other animals loose had wanted to liberate the lions, the lions would've been freed.

But it seemed the ruckus from the other animals had woken the pride, and in short order we'd all been scattered across the zoo.

The pride had stopped chasing my teammates, apparently deciding I was the tastiest-looking prey. They herded me through the zoo's main entrance, over the turnstile, and across the street. My teammates had shouted my codename, Battlecry, a few times before they were distracted by other animals.

Now it was just the lions and me on the dark street, illuminated by the pre-dawn moon and Christmas lights from nearby yards.

I perched on top of a beat-up sedan and watched the pride slink toward me, their unblinking gazes never leaving my face. They were quiet, almost unnaturally so. My sensitive ears picked up the faint padding noises of their paws striking the pavement, but I heard no rumbling beginnings of growls, no snorted breaths, nothing.

Just the sound of five killing machines drawing closer.

The male, a magnificent beast at least six feet long, sauntered ahead of the others. Though I knew little about African fauna, I knew that lionesses were typically a pride's hunters. Why was the male leading?

The gentle breeze billowed their scent toward me. Beneath the musky, sweaty smell of cat lingered the unmistakable aroma of death. The lions had killed recently.

I drew my largest knife from its sheath on my thigh and held it up. "Firelight, tell them I'll kill them if they don't stop!"

Even if my telepathic teammate Firelight, whose real name was Ember, didn't hear my distinct words, she'd know to tune in.

Indeed, a second later, her wispy mental voice filled my head. *What's up, Jill?*

Tell the lions I'll kill them if they don't stop.

I felt Ember slip out of my mind, then back in. *I can't sense them. I couldn't reach them before, when they were chasing us. I thought it was because there was so much chaos. But I can't sense them at all. It's like there's nothing there.*

The hair on my arms stood up. Without Ember's ability to control animals, I had to rely on my powers alone to defeat the pride. Fast, strong, and agile as my powers made me, I was mortal and had faced death enough times to know when I needed to fold. This fight was better suited to Reid, my earth-moving second-in-command, or Marco, who could redirect the sun's heat and light.

However, they were still entangled with animals inside the zoo. I needed to make a decision, fast. My tranquilizer gun had been lost during the frantic scramble to safety, and for the first time in my life I found myself wishing superheroes were permitted to bear proper firearms.

The male stepped aside, and a lioness tensed to spring.

I took aim and hurled my knife. It sunk to the hilt between her eyes.

Instead of dropping, she bared her fangs. I might as well have thrown a kitchen sponge at her.

I leaped off the car and sprinted back toward the zoo's entrance, the image of my knife's hilt sticking out of the lioness' forehead seared into my mind. I'd fought some formidable enemies during my time as a superhero in Saint Catherine, but none of them would've survived a knife in their brain.

Whatever this situation was, it required a team effort. The zoo's entrance was just ten yards ahead—

One of the lions pounced, slamming me to the ground so quickly I couldn't even shriek. My nose broke from the force of the impact, and hot blood gushed out of my face while searing pain licked up my cheeks. Large paws on my shoulder blades pinned me down.

Ordinarily, I would've pulled out my shoulder knife and slashed at the lion's legs, but I doubted that it would do any good to a beast that could survive a knife between the eyes. All of my combat knowledge was founded upon the assumption that my opponent could die.

Suddenly, the lion standing on top of me stepped off. A rough tug on my hair bun lifted my head, forcing me to face the male.

I pushed myself up, my hands scraping painfully against the bloody pavement, and stared at the enormous cat. His white-rimmed eyes were vaguely cloudy, obscuring my pale-faced reflection. Was he blind?

The lion leaned in as if he were studying me. The stench of death and decay became overpowering. His jaws were inches from my face, and I wrinkled my nose at the smell seeping from him. What did the zookeepers feed these things? And what was he doing?

To my right, one of the lionesses took the knife's hilt into her jaws and pulled it out of her sister's head. Instead of a spurting shower of blood, or even a steady flow, a single congealing drop of blood pooled at the bottom of the red slit left by the knife.

Realization sunk in.

I slowly leaned back from the dead lion in front of me.

"Who are you?" I whispered, my skin crawling. "Why are you controlling the lions?"

The carcasses were puppets. I'd never seen anything like this before, but I had no other way to explain how five dead lions were able to move and operate. Clearly some higher intelligence was behind their actions, but what was the goal? Why chase me down the street and knock me down, but not kill me?

As fascinatingly bizarre as the situation was, I could not ignore my gut feeling—the person controlling the lions meant me serious harm. I had two options: try to fight the lions and probably be mauled to death, or somehow alert my team that I needed backup and try to contact the puppet master in the meantime. Clearly, he or she was waiting for something, or the lions would've killed me already. Instead, they stood around me in a circle, never taking their eyes off me.

As I weighed my options, the male gazed up at the zoo's entrance. There was a moment of silence, and then the five lions opened up their mouths and roared.

I clamped my hands over my ears but couldn't help but feel a twinge of hope. The roars would get my team's attention.

I planted my foot on the ground to push myself up, but the male swiped a paw at me, shredding my arm above the elbow. I gasped and doubled over while the other four lions moved in around me, low growls ripping out of their fangs. I pressed my hand to my arm and looked up, heat coursing through my cheeks.

I didn't care how many lions this unknown person was controlling —I wasn't going down easily.

Jill, what's going on? Ember's concerned voice cut through my fury. *Get the team and get out here now. Look for the lions.*

She slipped out of my mind and I glared into the white murkiness of the male's eyes, sensing he was the main avatar for whomever controlled them. "Come out and fight me yourself, coward."

The lion shook its head, its teeth bared in a hideous feline grin. He raised a paw. There was a flash of fur, and pain exploded across my other arm. Blood dripped from my new wounds down to my elbow and pooled on the ground.

Without thinking, I grabbed a fistful of the lion's mane and jumped on him, leapfrog style. Before he could buck me off, I pulled my shoulder knife free, twisted around, and gouged one of his eyes.

In the corner of my vision, I saw a nearby chain-link fence at the edge of a small neighborhood playground. If I could make it there, I could climb it and leap onto a low residential roof to safety.

Without pausing for breath, I jumped off the lion and fled toward the fence, the pounding of paws close behind.

I made a wild, running leap onto the fence and clambered to the top, ten feet from the ground. The lions snapped and snarled below, but I was a good two feet out of their reach. Unwilling to risk falling while walking along the narrow rail of the fence, I gripped the metal and waited for help.

In the distance, Reid and Marco ran toward me. Ember and Benjamin, my fifth and final teammate, were not with them.

"Don't destroy them!" I yelled to the men. "Just trap them!" I didn't want to damage the connection to the person controlling them.

Reid's eyes glowed white, tiny pinpricks in the faint morning light. The ground rumbled, and a depression appeared beneath the lions, sinking six, seven, eight feet below the surface of the street.

Before I could yell my thanks, the fence wobbled and collapsed. I crashed down eighteen feet in a painful heap of loose dirt, metal fence, and cold lion corpses.

I braced for the inevitable mauling.

It never came.

When I realized that I was still alive, I tested my limbs for breaks. Finding none, I pushed myself up and shoved away the portion of fence that had fallen in, still bleeding from my arms and nose.

The lions were limp and inanimate on the ground around me, no more dangerous than rag dolls. I dusted myself off and peered up at the edge of the pit above me.

Marco's light brown face appeared, amusement and worry

battling for dominance in his youthful features. Reid's significantly paler face appeared next to him.

Reid winced as he looked down at me. "I'm so sorry, Jill... Battlecry. Give me a second and I'll raise the pit again."

Reid's slip-up by almost calling me by my real name hinted at how upset he was. We were all more than used to the real-name-code-name flip flop in battle. Though we privately thought of and referred to each other by our real names, in battle Ember was Firelight, Marco was Helios, Reid was Tank, Benjamin was Mercury, and I was Battlecry.

I waved dismissively. "No, don't bother. I don't want to give them a chance to get free. Throw me a rope or something. I'd climb out myself, but my arms are busted."

Marco frowned. "Let me get that useless medic." He disappeared from the edge. "Hey, Mercury! Your girlfriend is bleeding to death! Get over here!"

Reid stifled a laugh. I put my hands on my hips. "Useless medic? What's he sore about?"

"Mercury threw a punch at one of the animals, but he hit Helios instead. It was the funniest thing I've seen all week."

"It was not," Marco snapped from somewhere unseen. "Firelight fights better than Mercury, I swear to God."

I heard someone—probably Ember—smack Marco.

A whooshing sound heralded the arrival of Benjamin. His lovely face appeared above me and he grinned crookedly. He extended a hand down. "You look like you need a medic. Tank, give her a little boost and I'll grab her." Beneath his humor lay the tenderness he reserved just for me.

I raised my hand to grab his, a real smile spreading across my lips.

A horrible growl from behind made me spin around.

There wasn't time to scream as four lions sprang, their teeth sinking into my arms, legs, sides... anything they could bite. My vision colored white, black, and red.

Agony, almost unreal in its intensity, seized my entire consciousness. It was hot, it was freezing, it was liquid and everywhere, it was needle-like and specific.

I was being torn to pieces.

Growls around me mixed with shouts above me, and then I was on the ground, the lightening sky mixing with swirls of purple, red, and green.

In the sky, a bright star twinkled like the crystal on the necklace Benjamin had given me two days before. It was such a lovely necklace, very... very...

I smelled cooking meat.

I heard the thud of boots hitting the ground.

Warm fingers grasped my cold ones.

Electricity surged through my hand and up my arm, down through my abdomen, and into my legs. Skin and muscle sewed itself together. Bones mended. Aches and pains evaporated, leaving wholeness in their wake.

My dull vision, formerly swimming with little dots, came into sharp focus, and I saw Benjamin kneeling next to me, cradling my hand to his cheek.

Marco, Ember, and Reid stood next to the severely burned lion bodies, no doubt Marco's doing. Ember looked nauseated.

I gave my head a little shake, droplets of blood flying everywhere. "Thank you."

Benjamin didn't let go of my hand. "I thought the lions were dead. I don't understand how they just jumped up and attacked you." Painful confusion was in his eyes.

I pulled my hand free and stood, my shredded tunic hanging off me like rags. I beckoned the rest of my team to join me while I kneeled down next to the least-burnt carcass. Marco's blast of heat had scorched most of its fur off, revealing a tiny bullet hole in the skull I'd missed before.

I pointed to it. "They were dead when we arrived at the zoo. When we passed them earlier, I thought they were sleeping. Someone killed them and was controlling them like puppets, but I don't know how. Firelight said she couldn't hear anything in their minds."

Ember tapped her temple. "Well, yeah. If they were dead, there'd be no mind to hear. Whatever was controlling them isn't telepathic. Or at least, it's not like any telepathy I've ever encountered."

Wisps of dirt rose up from the ground and flew into Reid's palm, where they made beautiful, delicate little patterns. He wiggled his fingers, and the dirt clumped together to form small lion-shaped figures that prowled around his hand. "Maybe it's more like my power. I manipulate earth. This person might be able to manipulate dead tissue."

I had a sudden image of being attacked by a flying steak. Ember visibly fought a laugh.

Benjamin stared at the tiny dirt lions without blinking for several seconds. Finally, he looked at me. "Wasn't there a break in? Captain Nguyen said someone robbed the aviary, right?"

"Oh, right." In the morning's furor I'd forgotten that we'd been called in to investigate a far more mundane situation. "Tank, get us out of here."

Reid's eyes glowed soft white and the ground shook. The floor of the pit began to rise, and within seconds we were at street level again.

I nodded toward the zoo's entrance. "Mercury, Helios, Firelight, you go ahead. I'll stay behind with Tank to make sure the lions' bodies are secured so our tissue manipulator can't make a comeback."

"Got it," Benjamin said. "Come on, guys."

The three of them began to walk toward the entrance.

The sight of Benjamin's codename on his back filled me with awe. The five of us had come far in the last half year, but he'd come the farthest. As far as I knew, he was the only reformed supervillain that had ever served on a superhero team, and as he'd just demonstrated, he was arguably the most valuable one of us.

I took a moment to appreciate the emblems we'd chosen to sew onto the backs of our uniforms beneath our codenames, something no other team had ever done. Marco's dark purple tunic bore a stylized yellow sun. Ember's emerald green tunic sported a dog's paw print. Benjamin's gray tunic displayed the unmistakable sign of a medic: a red cross.

I turned to ask Reid if he could make some kind of earthen cage for the carcasses but saw that he was examining his feet. "Hey, what's wrong?"

"The lions were able to maul you because I screwed up." He wouldn't meet my eyes. "I should've assumed the fence would fall in. That was an amateur mistake."

I carefully chose my reply. "Have I ever punished anyone on this team for mistakes in battle?"

"No, but—"

"You just said it: no." I put my hand on his shoulder. His muscles tensed, becoming as hard as the rocks he could move with his mind. "Reid, relax," I whispered. "I'm not Patrick. I'm not going to hurt you."

"I deserve—"

"We all deserve to go home and have breakfast." I gave him a little shake. "We're not doing the eye-for-an-eye thing, remember? If it makes you feel better, I'll let you do the dishes this morning, but for Pete's sake, forgive yourself. I'm fine. We're all fine."

"You almost died. I watched you get torn apart because I trapped you with lions."

"Of course I almost died. We're superheroes. We can't go a week without someone shooting at us or pulling knives on us. It comes with the territory. Stop hating yourself."

He gave me an unreadable glance but nodded once.

I pointed to the corpses. "Let's get the lions back inside the zoo. I doubt the zoo officials want them in the middle of the road."

He held up his hand and dirt from a nearby yard flew to the lions to form small, hard planks beneath them. The lions rose on their little platforms and followed us into the zoo.

Reid went ahead of me, allowing me to see the white-capped mountain on the back of his red tunic.

Once inside the zoo, stone cages sprung up around the bodies. Reid directed the cages to the lions' former enclosure, then dusted off his hands. We hurried toward the aviary, a low building decorated with a mural of brightly-colored parrots and other tropical birds.

Inside, the three others were huddled around a spot on the wall and running their hands over it. The bird house wasn't nearly as noisy as I expected it to be; the birds lived behind thick glass that muffled their calls.

"I know who we're dealing with," Benjamin said without preamble. "This was the Rowe twins."

"Who?" I recognized the surname, but I didn't know the individuals.

Benjamin dragged a finger down the wall again. The stone looked...weird. I was reminded of my favorite photo editing software on my phone, in which I could swirl and warp pictures. The bricks appeared as if someone had swirled them slightly, little curves and whorls appearing where there should've been straight lines of mortar and rock.

"The woman who broke into the aviary was Alysia Rowe. She's our age. She and I played together when we were kids, though I wouldn't call her an old friend. She coined the nickname 'Bleeding Heart Benjamin.' When we were five or six she killed my pet frog because she thought it was funny when I cried."

I already hated her.

"What caused the swirling?" Marco asked.

"That's the calling card of her power. She walks through solid objects, but it's not a clean job." He pointed toward a pane of glass across the dim room. It was droopy and swirled in the middle. "She came for the Socorro doves. According to the plaque on the exhibit, they're extinct in the wild, so they must be extremely valuable." He ran a hand over the bricks again. "A hired thief. She's all grown up now."

"Any idea who hired her?" I asked.

Benjamin shrugged. "Could've been anybody. My family must've contracted with three dozen private parties over the years, and that's not counting the corporate accounts. I'm sure the Rowe family works for people I've never heard of. There are lots of rare bird collectors who would pay Alysia to steal the doves."

"Who's her twin?" I asked, studying the odd patterns on the wall.

Benjamin grimaced. "Will Rowe, my brother's best friend. We called him a necromancer. He can't manipulate human corpses, for some reason, but like you all saw today, animals are no problem for him. I suspected we were dealing with the twins when Reid mentioned tissue manipulation, but I didn't say anything because I wasn't sure. The swirls confirmed that it was Alysia, and I've never met anyone else who can do what Will can." He glanced at Ember. "I'd suggest you do a mental scan for him in one of the nearby houses, but no doubt he beat feet as soon as we went back into the zoo."

Marco gestured toward the Socorro dove exhibit. "Why did they set the animals free if this was a robbery?"

Benjamin ran a hand through his hair. "Yeah, um, about that. I can guarantee you that Mom has told everyone in my old circle that I defected to the heroes. I'm not sure, but I'm guessing Alysia and her brother did this just to be brats and cause problems for us. It's really not supervillain style to deliberately draw attention to our... their crimes. Not unless they're paid to be terrorists like my Uncle Mike usually is. You guys know him as The Destructor." Benjamin sighed. "I think we can expect a lot more stunts like this."

I pulled out my phone. "I'm calling Captain Nguyen. Tell him what you just told me. I'd like to see the frog killer and her brother behind bars, and if you're anticipating Super attacks, the police are going to want to know."

I dialed the police liaison and gave him the all clear. A few minutes later a squad of police officers arrived at the scene, flanked by zoo officials.

One of the zookeepers dissolved into hysterics when he saw the dead lions, but upon seeing my shredded and bloodstained uniform, tearfully admitted that perhaps we'd had no choice. I didn't bother explaining the truth about their deaths.

Marco, Reid, and Ember gave their statements and left the bird house one by one. I stayed behind while Benjamin talked to Captain Nguyen about his suspicions regarding the twins' motives. The Captain nodded and took notes, grim-faced.

Finally, he flipped his notebook shut and pocketed it, then shook Benjamin's hand.

Benjamin joined me at the doorway. "Home? I'd kill for a shower."

I winked at him. "You couldn't kill someone even if they were trying to kill you. Bleeding Heart Benjamin, remember?"

Hurt flashed in his eyes.

I shook my head. "The difference between me and Alysia Rowe is that unlike her, I love that bleeding heart."

"You *love* it? That's some pretty heavy language, Miss Battlecry."

"Oh, stop. Let's not go there."

He chuckled and walked past me, and I took a deep breath before I followed. We joined our team by the zoo gates and walked down the sleepy residential streets of Saint Catherine toward our headquarters.

Half an hour later, we stumbled through the front door of our new headquarters. Without so much as taking off our boots, we trooped up the stairs, down the hall, and into our separate bedrooms.

I heard the sounds of four bodies falling into bed as I peeled off my destroyed uniform. My emblem, a five-pointed star containing the city's seal, was barely distinguishable beneath the bloodstains. I threw the rags in the garbage and crawled under my heavy quilt.

The last thing I saw before I went to sleep was my calendar hanging on the wall, and that day's date circled, with a little sad face drawn in the corner.

2

———

I pushed the sizzling vegan sausages back and forth in the frying pan with my spatula. Even though I'd done everything Reid had told me to do, they were still charred and shriveled.

Sighing, I tipped them onto the plate lined with a paper towel and placed the plate on the table. The toaster beeped, and four pieces of toast popped out at once.

After putting the pan in the sink to soak, I grabbed the toast and prepared the pieces to order: butter and cinnamon for Marco, peanut butter and a buttload of honey for Benjamin, peanut butter and flax seeds for Reid, and mashed avocado, tomato slices, and ground pepper for Ember. I set a bowl of melon and containers of almond yogurt on the table.

Though the meal comprised breakfast foods, it was half past twelve.

The digital clock on the wall displayed the date. Every time I looked at it, my stomach lurched.

"Food's ready," I called to my team in the living room.

While they settled into their seats around the table, I poured glasses of water and tossed the bottle of multivitamins to Ember, who doled them out.

"Hey, Jill, where's your lunch?" Marco asked through a bite of toast.

"I'm not hungry." I sipped my water and swallowed my vitamin. The glare of the clock almost made me throw it up.

"Is this because of what that idiot online said about you gaining weight?" Benjamin asked. "It's winter. Everyone gains weight."

I looked away. "No, it's not that. I just don't have an appetite right now."

They continued to eat and chat, but Ember gazed at me while she ate her healthy meal. *I know today is hard for you, Jill. If you want to talk about it, I'd love to listen.*

I'm okay. I tipped my glass back and forth, swirling the water around. *A little sad, I guess, but way better than I was last year.*

Regular smooching does tend to soothe heartache. Ember's mental tone was teasing, and she glanced at Reid, who was watching a heated discussion about sparring practice.

"—so no, the only reason you can't beat Reid in a sparring match is because you *suck* at sparring. Muscles have nothing to do with it." Marco crossed his arms and scowled at Benjamin.

Benjamin looked affronted. "First, I do not suck. Second, Reid has about twenty more years of experience than I do."

"Dude, you were two feet from that deer but somehow you still hit me. You suck."

The squabble turned into name-calling, but I didn't bother breaking it up. Their brotherly argument only served to increase my unhappiness.

I turned back to Ember. *I'll take you up on that offer right now.*

We excused ourselves and left the room, stopping at the stairs. I sat down on the bottom step and rested my face in my hands.

Ember joined me and put her arm around my shoulders. "I know what you're thinking, that it shouldn't hurt after four years. But grief doesn't work like that."

"Everybody dies, though. Why does his death still hurt so much?" My voice broke on the last word. "I've lost three baby siblings. Why does Gregory's death hurt the most?"

Ember squeezed me. "Maybe because you knew him better, had a relationship with him. Maybe because you didn't have any closure. Perhaps if you'd had a chance to bury him..."

I nodded, and then the sobs began.

My little brother Gregory had been murdered on December twenty-seventh four years ago, the worst day of my life.

Not only had the Westerners attacked Chattahoochee camp that day, but each subsequent year something terrible had happened on the day to compound the memories. A year ago, I'd found out that I was being released into public service in Saint Catherine, to Patrick's team, though it took me a few weeks to appreciate how unfortunate I was to serve under him.

Marco exited the kitchen. He saw Ember and me and hurried over, kneeling down next to me. "Hey, hey. Is this about what happened with the lions?"

I shook my head and wiped my eyes. "Today's December twenty-seventh."

Marco froze, his eyes taking on a distant look. "Oh." He stood up and held onto the banister, then walked into the living room and collapsed on the couch. "Oh."

I dried my eyes and joined Marco on the couch, where we sat in heavy silence for a few minutes.

Dishes clinked in the sink, then Benjamin and Reid came out. Benjamin sat down in the last empty spot next to me. "What's going on?"

"Gregory died four years ago today," Ember said.

I rested my head on Benjamin's shoulder. He patted my hand and stroked my hair. "Tell me about him. He was important to you, so he's important to me."

"Gregory was the best," Marco said, his voice airy with nostalgia. "He was always telling jokes and coming up with crazy plans to build these huge forts in the woods, or trick people into believing something stupid. When he was ten, he managed to convince Elder St. James for three days that he could see the future. When we told Elder the truth, he was laughing too hard to be mad."

"Gregory was the good one," I grumbled, not raising my head off Benjamin's shoulder. "The rest of us Johnson siblings are jerks, but he was sweet."

Benjamin continued to stroke my hair. "I have to disagree with that. You're not a jerk."

"What happened four years ago?" Reid asked. "The Westerners, right?"

My hand curled into a fist. "They broke into the camp. Gregory was on watch with Elder. Gregory got into a fight with one near the big creek that runs through camp. The creek was swollen from all the winter rain, and the Westerner punched Gregory. Gregory fell into the creek and..."

"He never resurfaced," Marco finished. "We searched every inch of the creek bank, but his body was gone. He wasn't the best swimmer, and the creek is ridiculous this time of year. He probably drowned in less than a minute." He sighed. "He was fourteen. Fourteen-year-olds aren't even old enough for watch, but Elder thought Gregory's power was ideal for the job."

Reid placed a comforting hand on my knee. "I'm so sorry. I know exactly what it's like to lose loved ones to the Westerners."

"Who *are* the Westerners?" Benjamin asked. "They never bothered my family while I was growing up. What kind of monsters just pick off kids like that?"

I raised my head off of Benjamin's shoulder and wiped my nose with my sleeve. "They're the worst kind of Supers—they believe they're superior to normal people and that it's insulting for us to serve the country as superheroes. They hate us so much for it that they're willing to kill. They killed my cousin Christiana, too."

"And Hank Theodorakis," Marco said. "He was from the far side of Chattahoochee. His mom died from grief. He was sixteen."

"My mom's friend Lisette Monroe," I said, remembering a story my mom had told me. "She was thirteen."

Benjamin laced our fingers together. "I'm sorry. I'm so sorry."

We sat in the quiet living room, and eventually the conversation turned to lighter subjects. Marco picked up his latest knitting project, a winter hat in vibrant blues and yellows.

The clicking of his needles was relaxing, and I repositioned myself on the couch, my head in Benjamin's lap and my legs draped across Marco's.

Ember and Reid sat at the desk across the room, speaking in low voices. Curious, I focused on what they were saying.

My stomach clenched. They were making a packing list for tomorrow's road trip. I had actually managed to not think about it for several hours.

"Sweetheart, you're green," Benjamin said, stroking my cheek. "Do you feel sick?"

"Tomorrow," I groaned. "I don't want to go."

Marco snorted. "That's a one-eighty from the speech you gave us when we got the summons. What happened to all that confidence?"

What had happened was I'd had a month to ponder my own question: what's the worst they could do to me? Reid, Marco, and Ember had offered various possibilities, namely removing me from service, branding me like an animal, or marrying me off to whomever my father chose. Possibly all three in that order. Marco had suggested the last one, dropping the name of my one-time "suitor," Matthew Dumont, as a possible threat.

That idea was almost funny—I hated Matthew and the feeling, I was sure, was quite mutual—but the point still stood. My father had the right to contract with any camp boy's father and get rid of me.

But I wasn't afraid of those suggestions, finding them all a tad melodramatic. The real threat lay in being moved to a different team.

I was a rabble-rouser. According to our laws, I'd led innocent, pure superheroes down the path of destruction. I'd declared myself the leader of the team despite being female. I'd even welcomed a reformed supervillain into the fold, though I'd eat my own arm before I confessed that to the elders. As far as they were concerned, Benjamin Trent was dead. Benjamin "Corsaro," on the other hand, was alive and adapting well to his new life as a superhero.

The elders would see me as an upstart who needed a firm hand from an established, capable leader. I could be sent to any team in the country, but I'd probably be moved far away from Saint Catherine, the scene of the crime.

I absolutely had to plead my case in such a way that they'd see my side. But would Elder Campbell believe our account of his son's violence and treachery? Could any man who'd raised the likes of Patrick Campbell have pity on anyone? I expected nothing but judgment from him.

My best chance was to appeal to the goodness of Elder St. James, and Elder Lloyd, Reid's elder. Elder St. James knew me and had a history of fairness. Moreover, he was Marco's uncle. Maybe he'd be kind to us. And Reid had spoken highly of Elder Lloyd. He'd lost his only child, Eleazar, to battle more than twenty years ago, and had apparently assuaged his grief over the years by being a father to trainees instead. Maybe he'd be a father to Reid at the tribunal.

But I was not comfortable depending on "maybe."

The events of the summer had seemed so natural and justified when they'd happened. I'd run off, Patrick had gone berserk and tried to kill everyone, and then I took over the team.

We'd operated flawlessly since then, overseeing a reduction in crime across the city. Civilians approached us all the time to express gratitude for saving them from this and that. Some well-meaning graffiti artist had spray painted a mural of the five of us on a wall downtown, though it had been painted over a few days later. My official position was that I didn't approve of graffiti, but I thought the artist had captured Benjamin's good looks quite well.

My favorite picture-sharing app had crashed when I'd posted a group photo of us on the beach, laughing with abandon. Apparently, the app couldn't handle tens of thousands of well-wishes in thirty minutes.

The elders wouldn't care. I wasn't allowed to lead, but I'd assumed leadership. It was as simple as that. Therein lay the dissonance that had chipped away at my happiness for six weeks.

If I returned to the camp to answer the summons, I was implying that they had the authority to summon me. If they had the authority to summon me, then they had the authority to dictate how my team should operate, and how I should be punished for violating those rules.

My presence at the tribunal could easily be perceived as a public admission that I was in the wrong... *if* I could not justify my actions on their terms.

I respected the elders. They'd taught me how to be a hero. Though I did not agree with their prohibition of female leaders, I would return to the camp to explain myself. I could be reasonable.

Besides, if I didn't answer the summons, there would be consequences.

So what would they do to me? Nobody had ever done what I'd done.

I gazed up at Benjamin. "I'm scared," I whispered.

"You fought lions." He tweaked my nose.

"Lions can't take me away from you and make me serve on another team."

"Why do you have to go back? Why not stay here?"

I covered my eyes with my hand. "They'll send a strike team to remove me, if they have to. I might know how to fight lions, but I'm not prepared to take on an entire team of trained fighters, half of whom would probably be my relatives. I know for sure that my cousin Kyle is on a strike team."

Benjamin leaned down and placed a soft kiss on my lips. "Whatever happens, whatever they decide, remember that we're all with you to the very end."

"Got that right," Marco murmured.

I smiled a little. "I'm going to go take a bath," I said, sitting up. "I suggest you all get to bed early, because we've got a long day tomorrow."

I kissed the top of Benjamin's head and tugged on Marco's ear, then made my way upstairs to the bathroom Ember and I shared, closing the door behind me. I turned on the water and let the loud rushing sound fill my ears, blotting out the sadness and worries of the day. Though it was only mid-afternoon, I was drained.

What is the worst they can do to me? The insidious question wedged itself into my brain.

I slipped out of my shirt and pants and looked down. I liked what I saw, though my positive feelings were a recent development. I was confident that Benjamin liked what he saw, too, though he'd never seen this much.

My deep brown hair, which hung a little below my shoulders, was thick and lustrous. I ran a hand over my toned bicep, slightly in awe that only hours before it had been shredded by claws. Thanks to Benjamin, it was as strong and smooth as ever. My lacy undergarments highlighted my feminine curves.

I removed the undergarments and examined them, my finger tracing the patterns on the intricate lace. Before I moved to Saint Catherine I'd never imagined that such beautiful underwear existed. Beautiful items were few and far between at Chattahoochee camp.

I'd been led to believe by several people in my life that I did not possess any natural beauty. Though my accomplishments and attentive boyfriend had vastly improved my self-image, I was aware that one part of my body was still quite ugly. I turned and craned my neck to see my back in the mirror.

Dozens of white, pinched scars crisscrossed my pale flesh, mementos of December twenty-seventh two years ago. I reached a hand over my shoulder and touched one of the scars, then shuddered and pulled my hand away.

Gregory had been dead for two years. I'd been nineteen, Marco had been sixteen, and we'd been convinced that we could find the Westerners and avenge my brother's death. I never discovered who found out about our plan, but our fathers were waiting for us at the gate, their faces furious.

Marco's parents yelled at him for twenty minutes, denied him dinner for a week, and made him personally apologize to Elder St. James.

My father dragged me to the middle of the camp at noon the next day, ripped off my shirt and bra, and caned me in front of everyone, yelling that I was a horrible excuse for a daughter while I screamed in terror and pain.

Elder St. James finally had to step in and tell him enough was enough. Marco had run up and given me his shirt, then helped me to my feet and led me away.

I'd sobbed for hours while he dabbed at my bleeding back. Because the wounds had healed long before I met Benjamin, his power could do nothing to remove the scars that remained.

I stepped into the steaming bathtub, but the usual contentment found in bathing eluded me. I was going back to a place without indoor plumbing, without thick walls to keep out the December winds, without a kitchen for Reid to fill with delicious smells.

What's the worst they can do to me?

I didn't know the answer.

All I knew was that I was going home, and I was scared.

3

"Can I drive?" Marco put on his seatbelt and leaned forward, gazing in open longing at the driver's seat. Reid sat behind me. Ember was squished in between them.

"Do you have a driver's license?" Benjamin didn't look up from the dashboard gauge he was checking.

"No."

"Then you can't drive."

The camp allies had given us a pickup truck for the trip and assured us it was roadworthy, but Benjamin had insisted on checking everything himself. He'd explained the various parts and their purposes to me, and I'd made a mental note to check out a book on auto mechanics from the library when I returned. *If I return.*

Marco sat back and stared out the window, already lost in clearly-troubled thoughts. Inspiration struck, and I opened my door and dashed back into our house. I grabbed his knitting needles and blue yarn from the brown wicker basket next to the couch.

After one last check that all was well, I slammed the door shut and locked it, then typed in the security code. If anyone broke in, the police would be alerted.

When I was back in the passenger seat, I turned around and

handed Marco the needles and yarn. "How about you knit me a new bracelet? I lost the old one at the zoo, and I'd like to have another one to wear at the tribunal."

Marco sighed dramatically but took the knitting supplies from me and hooked the yarn onto the ends.

Benjamin started the truck and entered an address into the GPS. Neither Marco nor I could recall the way to our childhood home, having left it only once, in the middle of the night.

I reviewed our packing list and mentally checked off that we'd put everything in the bed: a duffel with our food, clothes, toiletries, and blankets, as well as cardboard boxes of canned foods, toys, clothes, fresh groceries, camping supplies, toiletries, and first aid kits for the rest of the people at the camp. Our backpacks lay at our feet, filled with spare uniforms and personal items. I wasn't sure what was in Marco's faded green backpack, but I suspected it was handmade gifts for his little sisters.

We pulled out of the driveway at exactly zero six. Captain Nguyen had known for two weeks that we'd be out of town. Father Kokoski from the church next door had agreed to collect our mail. We'd mailed witness statements and articles about Patrick's crimes to the camp, via the allies, and I couldn't think of anything more to do before we left.

Resting my head against the window, I watched the early morning activities of our beautiful coastal Georgia city as we drove by.

The signs of Hurricane Ben's damage were subtle, but present. Faint water lines marked many buildings, eight feet high in some places. Old neighborhoods, many with homes on the National Historic Register, were dotted with new structures, bright and bold against the softer lines of antebellum architecture.

We slowed to a stop at an intersection downtown, next to a street sign that had flowers and teddy bears strewn around the base. I'd learned that while my team and I were holed up in the storm shelter, an entire family had drowned near here.

I closed my eyes, hoping for sleep and relief from the feeling that I should've saved them.

Several minutes later, the sound of the wheels on the road changed from low to high, and I opened my eyes. We were on the bridge that spanned Blackbeard Creek's largest branch, uniting Saint Catherine to the rest of the United States. The last time I'd been here I'd climbed over the safety rail, intent on ending my life. I could still remember the sweat dripping down my face, mingling with my tears.

I'd just found out that my new friend Benjamin was a supervillain. I'd decided that since my life was forfeit, I might as well end it all. Now that I thought about it, I probably could've just saved myself the jog to the bridge and stabbed myself in the heart, but I'd subconsciously chosen to die as Gregory had.

"I'm glad you didn't," Ember said from the back seat.

"Didn't what?" Marco asked.

"Thank you," I grumbled. *Can't you just talk to me like this?*

"Oh, I think we should all talk about this. In case the tribunal doesn't go our way—"

"But it will, so we're not worried," Marco cut in.

"—I want everyone to promise that we'll respond like the levelheaded people we are, and not do something dramatic."

Benjamin laughed. "What on earth brought this on?"

"Jill can tell you."

I pictured hitting her with a dictionary.

"Nice try. Start talking."

Apprehension rose in me at the thought of my teammates knowing about my weakest moment. I considered lying, but with Ember in the truck, that was pointless. "Um, in June, after I found out that Benjamin was a criminal, I almost killed myself. I was going to jump off the bridge."

There was a long silence.

We were back on the highway, the bridge disappearing in the distance behind us. Instead of saying something, or even looking at me, Benjamin pulled over to the side of the highway and put the truck in park.

He turned to me. "You were going to kill yourself?" His hazel eyes, normally friendly, were hard from worry.

Heat crept up my cheeks. "Yes. I wasn't in the best frame of mind that night. I told you about the pills, remember? But I decided against suicide and went home, and then all that stuff with Patrick happened. I haven't thought about killing myself since."

December twenty-seventh of every year was the worst day of my life, but that warm summer night six months ago was a close runner up.

Marco shook his head. "You are the most overdramatic person in the world, I swear. *Oh, my boyfriend is a supervillain so I'm going to jump off a bridge,*" he said in falsetto. "Damn, Jill."

Benjamin gave him an icy glare.

"I was scared of Patrick, you idiot! Remember him? Tall, terrifying, enjoyed beating the crap out of us?"

Marco stopped knitting and looked up at me, then away, shame faced. "Yeah, I remember," he mumbled. "Sorry."

"But Patrick's dead now," Ember said. "And that's the point, isn't it? You thought your life was over, but Patrick turned out to be a temporary problem. If you'd killed yourself, you wouldn't have ever defeated him, and we'd all be stuck with Patrick."

"Or he would've killed us," Marco muttered. "Or we would've killed ourselves."

"Stop," Benjamin growled.

"Let's just all agree that suicide is not the answer to any of the elders' decisions over the next few days," Reid said. "If the worst happens, we'll find a way to deal with it. We always do."

I let out a long-suffering sigh. "I promise not to kill myself."

"Me too," Marco said.

"Or us," Ember said, taking Reid's hand. He beamed at her.

Benjamin continued to look at me, his eyebrows knit together. "You were going to kill yourself because of me?"

I rubbed my eyes. "I've told you how superheroes feel about the forbidden six families."

Benjamin rested his arm on the wheel and pinched the bridge of his nose. "First of all, there are way more than six supervillain families, but that's beside the point. I just... I knew you guys hated supervillains, but... you were going to *kill* yourself?"

"Well, yeah. You were bad, Patrick was scary, and I was hopeless."

Benjamin reached out and cupped my cheek, his thumb rubbing under my eye. Then he pulled me closer to him and kissed me softly. He rested his forehead against mine. "You have to stay alive," he whispered. "Don't hurt yourself."

"I promise," I breathed. My heart swelled with an emotion I refused to name.

Marco cleared his throat. "Since we've got that out of the way, can we get back on the road now? We've got six hours to talk about our feelings."

Unlike Marco, Ember and Reid were peering out the window, politely pretending that the people in the front seat weren't having a moment.

Benjamin gave his head a little shake and checked the rearview mirror. "Can do." When there was a break in cars, Benjamin pulled back onto the road and we accelerated up to highway speed. "So, who can I expect to meet today?"

"My family!" Marco burst out. "Mom, Dad, and my sisters Isabel, Caroline, Adora, and Melissa. I haven't seen them in a year."

He put down his knitting needles and grinned, lost in his memories of my favorite cousins. I was sure they were fiercely proud of their heroic big brother.

"And my family," I said with a sigh. "Fun."

"Mason and Allison, right?" Reid asked. "I believe Mason visited my camp two years ago during a courting swap and hit it off with my friend Emily Begay, but it didn't work out."

I snorted. "Yeah, her dad didn't like my dad. Big surprise."

"Is there *anyone* you're looking forward to seeing again?" Reid asked, exasperated.

"Stephen," Marco teased in a sing-song voice. "Did you ever tell Benjamin about him?"

I twisted around in my seat and swatted Marco. Stephen Monroe had merely been my first girlhood crush—hardly someone to make a big deal out of.

"Actually, yes, she did," Benjamin said calmly. "And since he's a combatives instructor, I did some soul-searching and decided that I won't challenge him to a fight for breaking young Jillian's heart."

"Broken heart? What?" Reid asked in good-natured confusion.

I smiled and shook my head. "It's *nothing*. I was twelve. He was the nineteen-year-old assistant combatives teacher. When he got married, a whole bunch of the girls took it really hard. Someone in this car *might* have cried about it."

The four of them cracked up.

I patted Benjamin's knee. "What I really wanna see is Matthew's face when he meets you. You still going to fight him if my dad makes me marry him?"

I pictured Matthew's horror at hearing that he'd been paired up with the "most unsubmissive, brazen, foul-mouthed hussy" he'd ever met. *I should put that on a business card.*

Benjamin nodded, solemn. "I'll pound his face in. Reid, Marco, you can be my backup."

"You're not going to need backup against Matthew, believe me," Marco said. "He's a beanpole. You might suck at sparring, but you're better than him, I guarantee it."

The conversation immediately devolved into a front seat, back seat argument about Benjamin's sparring skills.

I leaned against the window again, relieved that my shameful episode on the bridge was no longer under discussion.

4

When we were deep in the Georgia countryside, we stopped for an early lunch at a tiny barbecue restaurant nestled in between endless, rolling horse pastures. Far in the distance, the mountains of northern Georgia jutted out of the horizon.

The restaurant was really more of a shack, but the food was delicious. We sat at a picnic table beneath a leafless tree and enjoyed the sweet tea, pulled pork sandwiches, coleslaw, and cornbread. Ember refused the meat and only accepted slaw and cornbread.

Benjamin rubbed my shin with his foot under the table, but we kept our faces straight.

An old truck with two farmers pulled up and they climbed out, chatting about a football game the night before. Beneath their truck, a small stream of black liquid dripped onto the gravel.

I waved toward them to get their attention. "Hey! Y'all got an oil leak." I was proud that I'd paid enough attention during Benjamin's explanation of car mechanics to know what the problem might be.

One of the men peered under the truck and scratched his head. "Now when did that happen? Thanks, darlin'."

Benjamin bit his lip, obviously trying to stifle a laugh.

"What? His truck's leaking."

"What kind of leak does he have again?"

"An oil leak."

"When Reid made cake for Marco's birthday, what did he make the batter in?"

"Um, a bowl."

Benjamin snickered. "In most parts of the country, 'bowl' and 'oil' don't rhyme." He wiped his hands with his paper napkin. "I meant to talk about this with you guys at home, but never got around to it. What are we going to do about my accent?"

"Your accent?" I repeated. "What's wrong with it?"

I loved Benjamin's brisk northern accent, especially how he said my name—he didn't drag out the vowels in "Jillian," instead giving it a crisper sound than I was used to. His accent sounded like Reid's a little bit, but somehow different. I chalked this up to them being from vastly different parts of the north.

Benjamin nodded toward the oil spill. "I think I might be accepted a little more easily if I acted like I was from the Deep South, like you g—like *y'all*." He stretched out the final word. It sounded bizarre coming from his mouth.

Ember snorted tea out of her nose. When she'd composed herself, she said, "Kindly don't say that again. Just use your Maryland accent. You're not pretending to be from a Georgia camp, so why bother faking one?"

I was suddenly self-conscious of how we might sound to Benjamin. I hoped he thought my accent was as attractive as I thought his was. It made him sound so unlike all the men with whom I'd grown up. Ember, and formerly Patrick, had an even thicker accent than Marco and me.

"What is your story gonna be, anyway?" Marco asked. "Wanna practice lying to us?"

Benjamin stuck out his hand, purposefully rigid. "Hi, I'm Benjamin Corsaro. I met Jillian when Patrick attacked the library. We've been dating ever since. I'm a descendant of one of the Supers who wanted to be normal way back when, but I'm very happy to serve the citizens of Saint Catherine as a superhero. By the way, I'm a healer. How may I heal you?"

Reid started to laugh so hard he had to put down his fork. "Oh my God," he wheezed. "If you gave me that speech in Idaho, I'd kill you for *so clearly* being a Westerner. Try to make it sound like you haven't been practicing it in front of your mirror every night."

Benjamin waved his hand dismissively. "That's the gist of it, anyway. I'll improvise when I have to."

"Don't say you're 'dating' Jill, though," Marco said through a mouthful of coleslaw. "Nobody there is gonna care how you feel about our relationship practices. You're courting, or nothing."

"I am *not* saying 'courting.' Ugh, I mean, 'courtin'.' That's how you guys actually say it, you know. Can't put the 'g' at the end of anything." He elbowed me. "Though I do like when you say 'kissin'... and 'fightin'...." He smiled mischievously. "I could listen to you talk all day."

I blushed and looked down at my empty plate, then up at his beaming face. "Don't worry about making people love you," I said, stroking his arm. "You do that naturally."

He brightened.

I stood and grabbed my paper plate and utensils. "I'm going to get more tea. I'll see you guys in the truck."

After hopping back into my seat, I stared out the windshield at the steel gray mountains in the distance. There was every possibility that I'd never have a happy lunch with my team again.

I laid my head against the window once more.

5

"God, was it this long of a drive when we drove to Saint Catherine?" Marco threw down his knitting needles and tossed a blue bit of yarn at me. "Here, I'm done. Try not to have it torn off by lions, will ya?"

I tied the yarn bracelet around my wrist and admired it. "Thank you. And yes, it took this long. We were just happier then."

The blue of the yarn almost perfectly matched the blue of my uniform's tunic, which itself matched the deep azure of a summer afternoon sky. I decided that I believed in the lucky powers of Marco's bracelets.

A few minutes later, a little after noon, Benjamin turned off the highway onto a country road dotted with potholes and tree roots. We were in the mountains now, and conversation stopped while we jutted and jolted up and down the tree-lined two-lane road. Our seatbelts prevented us from being thrown from our seats, but twice we had to stop to resecure boxes in the bed with bungee cords.

The road wound through the mountains into deeper forest. In spring and summer, the woods would've been thick with shadows and life, butterflies flitting from bud to bud, but now the weak winter sun beat down through the skeletal branches, illuminating every-thing with a gray light.

There's no place to hide. The strange thought passed through my head before I could stop it.

"Here's the turn off," Benjamin said suddenly, turning the GPS off with a tap.

The screen didn't display any indication that there was a road coming up, but the truck rumbled to a stop in front of an unpaved single-lane road that disappeared into the trees and over an enor-mous hill. It was more of a path than a road, only distinguishable from the surrounding forest by two grooves made by cars in the past.

Where the unpaved road met the paved road stood a simple metal gate. The sign on the gate read "NO TRESPASSING".

Marco scratched his head. "You'd think Chattahoochee camp's entrance would be a little more, uh, impressive. That wouldn't scare off anybody."

Benjamin studied a print-out from a government website. "It's not the entrance. It's the beginning of the road that leads to the entrance. Jill, can you move the gate?"

I hopped out of the cab and walked over to the end of the rail, giving it a little push. With a rusty creak of protest, it moved out of the way, swinging back and allowing the truck to pass. After Benjamin had driven the truck a little way up the road, I moved the gate back into place and ran to catch up.

We drove for miles on the narrow lane, which went over a wide, swift body of water that I thought might be Gregory's final resting place. The trees clustered so thickly in places that they were able to blot out the sunlight for long moments, casting us into darkness even though it was midday.

Nobody spoke.

After thirty minutes of tense driving, Benjamin pointed ahead. "Look. There's the parking area."

The truck rolled into a muddy gravel lot carved out of the trees and surrounding mountainside. Though there was evidence of recent vehicles in the dried mud, we were the only people there.

We all hopped out and searched for signs of life.

"Where's camp?" I asked. Marco and I had left camp from a smaller entrance on the north side of camp. I assumed we were going to the main entrance on the south side.

Benjamin lowered the tailgate and started passing out boxes. "Now we start walking."

I shouldered my backpack and grabbed the box with the canned goods because it was the heaviest. I hated that Benjamin knew more about getting to my old home than I did.

Marco picked up the box of toys and let out a long sigh. "Let's get this over with."

A beaten footpath at the far end of the lot led off into the trees. We fell into single file and began an arduous, awkward journey that took us up towering hills, down into creek beds that Reid had to build bridges over, and through briar patches.

The whole experience was ridiculously uncomfortable, which I supposed was the point. Nobody would walk down the footpath unless they had to reach the end.

Just as I was about to turn around and ask Benjamin if he knew the length of the hike, I heard a sound that made me stop in my tracks: a baby's cry, high and thin, in the distance.

My team couldn't hear it, but they stopped next to me and squinted ahead. They were familiar enough with my powers to know why I'd stopped.

"Let's go," I said, hurrying forward. Now that I was so close, I didn't want to linger and put off the inevitable. We stumbled up a part of the path that was cluttered with fallen logs, our boxes throwing us off balance.

The trees cleared, the sun came down a little brighter, and we skidded to a halt and gazed up at the forbidding sight in front of us.

The steel wall of Chattahoochee camp, the seat of power of every superhero in America, loomed above us like a metal curtain. Curls of razor wire lined the top of the wall, and I could hear the electric hum of the charge that ran within it. Speakers were placed strategically every fifty feet, used to blare the warning siren, should the Westerners attack.

Directly ahead of us, two large doors in the wall bore a white sign with black lettering.

ENTER AT YOUR OWN RISK
TRESPASSERS WILL BE KILLED ON SIGHT

Marco dropped his box. "Welcome home, kids."

I put down my box and walked up to the doors. How were we supposed to announce our presence? There was no doorbell, knocker, or little squawk box in which to speak. I hesitated, then knocked on the door a few times.

Silence.

I swore and stomped over to my box, sitting down on it and crushing the cardboard a little bit. "Anyone have any ideas?"

Marco raised a hand. "I can melt the doors."

I grabbed his wrist and lowered it. "I don't feel like being killed by the watch, thanks."

Reid gazed up at the top of the wall. "We could fly over on a piece of earth."

My shoulders drooped. Reid's idea was the most sensible. Now I had no reason to say I couldn't come to the tribunal.

Benjamin put his hand to his chin, thoughtful. "You know, Eleanor once told me that in college there's this rule about professors who show up late to class. If they don't come within fifteen minutes of class starting, everyone gets to go home."

I liked that rule. I pulled out my phone and flipped to the stopwatch. "Good ideas like that are why you're on our team. Our fifteen minutes starts... now." I pressed the green start button. I looked over at Reid. "No need to go to all that trouble. They summoned us, so they can let us in. Or not."

Ember dropped her box and rubbed her forehead. "I'm trying to find someone to contact, but there's something... here."

I glared at her. "Stop trying to contact people."

Ember squatted next to a tree stump. She placed her hand on it and let several ants crawl onto her hand. She raised them to eye-level, her head tilted quizzically. "Whoa," she breathed.

"What? Are the ants telling you some wild story?" Marco asked with a snicker.

"Sort of." She sounded almost awed. "Someone else is controlling the ants, like I can, but their power is greater than mine. He or she isn't controlling each individual ant, though. They're tapping into the colony's collective mind. Even I can't do that."

I knew exactly who was controlling the ants. I jumped to my feet. "*Mason!* Open the damn door! I know you're there!" My team flinched at my sudden outburst.

Reid crossed his arms. "He's just messing with us, isn't he? My brothers pull this kind of stuff all the time."

As if to answer his question, one of the metal doors slowly swung open.

Standing in the doorway was a tall, dark-haired man in his mid-twenties: my brother, Mason Johnson. He threw me a baleful look. "Oh, look, it's you. Welcome back."

6

"Why the game?" I asked, glaring at Mason's back while we walked through the grassy field toward the center of camp.

The dead grass crunched under our feet. A sharp, cold wind blew, chapping my hands and lips. Ahead of us, Fort Mountain loomed tall and imposing. In a few hours, it would cast its shadow over the entire camp, plunging us into a premature nighttime.

"Because he's a dickhead," Marco muttered.

"I was hoping you'd take the hint that you're not welcome here," Mason snapped. He hadn't offered to take any of our boxes, even though Ember was visibly struggling with hers after carrying it for so long.

I doubled back and let her place it on top of mine.

I suppressed the urge to roll my eyes. "You're an idiot."

"This is coming from the woman who was summoned to a tribunal for playing dress-up in Elder Campbell's son's clothes. I should slap you for humiliating our family."

"If you do, I'll break your arm for striking my leader," Benjamin replied coolly. Mason stopped in his tracks and stared at Benjamin, who remained unperturbed. "The third heroic character trait: loyalty. Or have you not heard?"

I couldn't hide my surprise. He'd known the principles and traits since July, but I'd never heard him quote them, not once.

Mason looked Benjamin up and down. "Who are you? You're not from around here."

"I'm Benjamin Corsaro, and I won't stand for threats against my teammate, nor do I particularly care if you're her brother. So shut up and take us to the camp." His voice had taken on a steely edge.

Mason wasn't the only one who was speechless. I knew Benjamin had a strong center in that bleeding heart of his, but I'd never heard him speak so sharply to anyone, much less a relative of mine.

Ember gave me a sidelong look. *I wish you could hear what I hear right now. Benjamin is trying to play nice to make us happy, but he already hates this place.*

So, his mention of loyalty had been sardonic. Oh well. I was still grateful for his righteous indignation on my behalf.

We walked the final quarter mile in silence. I took in the details of the camp, looking for changes.

A twine bracelet peeked out from underneath Mason's sleeve, indicating that he was engaged. If we'd had a better relationship, I would've congratulated him.

The square garden plots were fallow and bare, with brown, bent stalks leftover from the fall harvest. Mason hadn't lost weight since I'd last seen him, so it must have been a bountiful year for the gardeners.

We passed one of the many training areas for future superheroes, or as we called them, the trainees. Boards and foam dummies stood in neat rows near a mulch sparring arena. Around the edges of the arena, a handful of small children no older than ten watched in respectful silence as John Theodorakis, the head combatives trainer, and Stephen Monroe, his assistant, demonstrated a roundhouse kick.

I put down my boxes and walked over to them. "Hi, John. Hi, Stephen."

I couldn't help but feel lighthearted when Stephen's eyes crinkled as he greeted us. Hazy, happy memories of my younger self rolled over me, recollections of more innocent days when I'd been smitten by the then-teenager's wavy brown hair, piercing blue eyes, and unusual kindness as he'd demonstrated combatives to us. I'd even gotten into a fist fight once with my childhood rival Berenice over whether he preferred me or her.

Looking at Stephen was like looking at the wild dreams of youth.

"Jillian!" John said. "Children, this is Jillian Johnson, who fights as Battlecry. She entered service a year ago."

Upon hearing my codename, the children all bobbed their heads in respect, though their round eyes implied that they'd heard about me. What were their parents saying?

I kneeled down in front of a smaller girl with pigtails and no front teeth. Like all future heroes, she wore the blank gray shirt and pants I'd worn from ages three to twenty, with a black sash around her waist to indicate that she wasn't a future leader. Only two boys in the group wore the red sash.

"Trainee, what's your name?"

"Ma'am, my name is Heather Harris."

I couldn't help a smile—here was another girl named after a famous, dead hero. The original Heather Harris, Ember's aunt, had been on Elder Lloyd's son's team, and died with him during that terrible gang battle in the slums of San Diego, California, only a week before my birth.

"What are you learning today, Heather?"

"Ma'am, we're practicing kick attacks. After lunch, we will practice our blocking."

Stephen pushed a dummy toward me. "Perhaps Battlecry would care to demonstrate a roundhouse kick for us? She was one of our best students."

Benjamin and the others joined the children.

Mason stood to the side, grimacing and looking anywhere but at me. He'd never received fight training, and I'd always suspected he resented not only that I had, but that I'd excelled.

"Of course," I said, facing the dummy.

I quickly explained my stance to the children, and how my hips and legs moved in preparation for the kick. When I was satisfied that the children understood, I fell back to the first position, pretended the dummy was Patrick, and executed a perfect roundhouse kick, breaking the dummy cleanly in two.

The children cheered. I gave them a theatrical bow.

We resumed our walk to the main camp. Showing off my technique had improved my mood somewhat, and I focused on the happier memories of the surrounding area.

We passed by a blackberry thicket from which Gregory, Marco, and I had once loved to pick fat, juicy berries in the summers.

Far in the distance, older trainees were scaling a high wall at the obstacle course. When they were finished with the wall, they'd have to traverse a Jacob's ladder, crawl along ropes, and keep their balance on an extremely high beam.

A little beyond that, a small tree was broken in two, its top half touching the ground. Years before, Berenice had aimed a punch at me, but I'd dodged it and she'd broken the tree. I'd laughed so hard I'd nearly wet myself.

The memory of my almost-accident reminded me to point out to Ember, Benjamin, and Reid the areas we used to relieve ourselves. Little outhouses constructed of thin boards were tucked behind trees. "But of course, you can use the woods," I said, elbowing Benjamin, who made a noise of disgust.

"Where are all the people?" Reid asked, looking left and right. "I thought this was supposed to be the biggest camp of them all."

"Just wait. We're almost there."

A few minutes later, the field gave way to spread-out trees with crude shelters underneath—huts of boards and tin, all windowless, and sometimes doorless. Few contained any furniture other than storage chests.

Each hut had a campfire in front of it, and people were sitting by them, warming their hands or cooking meals in pots. As we passed, they looked up and stared, some with interest, but others with hard disapproval. I recognized several of the people: the Dufresne family, Morgan and Jeffrey Saur, Ella St. James, the Granthams.

Everyone was bundled in odd assortments of secondhand clothes. Many women and girls wore both dresses and pants, or skirts and pants. Mismatched shoes were the norm, their partners usually having been lost or destroyed. Thick sweaters were more common than proper coats. Ragged scarves and hats completed the winter gear. Everything these people wore had come from the charity truck.

The path widened and branched off as we reached the edge of a meadow in a small valley. In April and May, it was lush and green, full of tiny flowers of yellow, blue, purple, and white that children braided into elaborate flower crowns.

Now it was dead and yellow-gray, but the amount of people milling around gave it a distinct cheer that had been missing from our walk through the camp thus far.

Children of all ages chased each other around and through huts, screaming with abandon as they tagged their friends and played games. None of them wore the gray outfits and sashes of future superheroes, indicating that they possessed powers of no value in combat, such as Mason's ant telepathy. They would grow up and marry, hoping that perhaps one of their own children would bring honor to the camps as a superhero.

Men chopped wood on large stumps and stacked the logs in neat rows, while women tended to children, prepared meals, and did various chores.

A group of women about my age sat around a large fire, all of them nursing infants while gossiping. A teenage boy and girl stood in the shadow of a tree, holding hands and staring into each other's eyes. They both wore twine bracelets, and I was pleased to see that theirs was probably a love match. A large stack of stiff cardboard boxes in the center of the meadow bore the logo of a large civilian charity—the charity truck had been by recently.

"Marco?" A high, sweet voice called my cousin's name. I didn't immediately recognize the voice. "Marco! It's Marco! Mommy, it's Marco! Adora, get Daddy!"

All at once, three little girls sprinted toward Marco and tackled him, their thick braids bobbing against their backs. His box of toys went flying and the contents spilled out; several curious children ran over to inspect them.

The rest of us watched in amusement as Marco struggled to get up from beneath his three youngest sisters. All of them shared Marco's light brown skin, large eyes, and wide grin.

The smallest, Melissa, had grown several inches in the year since I'd last seen her. She smothered Marco's face with kisses and squeezed his neck.

Adora, the next eldest, sat on his knees. She was tall and thin as a rail, with eyes that sparkled from joy.

Caroline had started puberty in my absence—her body was taking on a womanly form, and she was already nearing Marco's height. She was very pretty, and I wondered if some camp boy's father had made her parents an offer of betrothal.

The fourth and eldest St. James daughter stood a little distance from the fray and watched with a veiled expression.

Isabel, now fifteen, was my favorite female cousin. I'd given her my beautiful doll in the yellow dress when I'd turned thirteen and declared myself too old for such childish trinkets. She wore an old pink sweater that I also recognized as a former possession of mine, probably given to her by my mother. Her frizzy black hair was held back in a tight braid and decorated with a large pink bow.

I placed my boxes to the side and waved.

Instead of throwing herself on her brother, she walked up to me and gave me a hug. "Welcome home, Jilly."

"It's good to see you again, Bells."

She stepped away and looked at her sisters, who were tugging on Marco's sleeves now, shouting about presents. "You three! Let him go, *now!*"

The three girls instantly let go of Marco and attacked his backpack, fishing out the contents. As I suspected, they were knit presents for them: a long pink-and-white scarf, a little knit doll, the blue-and-yellow hat he'd worked on the day before, and a hat and glove set in purples and yellows.

Marco shrugged and wandered over to Isabel. "Hey, you."

"Hey, yourself," Isabel said, but she was smiling.

Marco and Isabel hugged, and he kissed her forehead. "You been good while I've been gone?"

"Someone had to keep the wild animals in line."

As she spoke, Melissa and Adora got into a slap fight over the scarf. Caroline stuffed the hats, gloves, and doll under her shirt and sprinted in the direction of the St. James homestead. Her sisters didn't notice. Ember, Reid, and Benjamin sat on the ground and watched it all, shaking with silent laughter.

"How are Mom and Dad?" Marco asked, sober.

I scanned the meadow for my aunt and uncle but couldn't see them anywhere.

Isabel heaved a sigh. "They're okay, but everyone's worried about the tribunal. Dad got into a fight with Uncle Johnson." She glanced at me. "About you. I don't know the details, but I got the impression that they disagree about how severe your, uh, *crime* was. Our moms just want everyone to calm down. I've been busy keeping the girls away from other kids with big mouths."

My heart pounded. "What's the general consensus?"

"Hard to say, because there's about five different versions of events going around. Some people think you killed Elder Campbell's son and declared yourself queen of the city. Other people think nothing happened, and Elder Campbell is mad at Elder St. James for something. Most people believe something in the middle."

"That Elder Campbell is a jerk, but I did something bad." It wasn't a question.

"Yeah, pretty much. I figured that whatever happened, it was your best judgment. You're not stupid." She paused, then reached toward my neck. "What's that?" She pulled out my necklace, a Christmas present from Benjamin.

It was the first and only Christmas present I'd ever received, having never even heard of Christmas before living in Saint Catherine.

"That's, um, a gift from a teammate," I said, unhooking it so she could inspect it more closely.

Isabel gazed at the silver J that hung at the end of the delicate silver chain. The swirly J, which Benjamin said was a "cursive" letter, contained a sparkling crystal in the middle.

It was the most beautiful item in my possession, and I rarely took it off. If I kept it tucked under my uniform, it didn't pose a threat in battle. I liked to think that if Marco's blue bracelet gave me luck, then my new necklace protected me.

Isabel stroked the pendant. "It's so pretty. You're courting, aren't you? Is this a kind of betrothal token? Is it from one of the other men that came with you?"

I gently took the necklace from her and put it back around my neck. "It's from my teammate Mercury, but it's not a betrothal token. We'll talk about that later. Don't tell anyone, okay?"

Marco smirked, but Isabel nodded. "I didn't see anything." She looked over my shoulder. "But I do see our parents coming."

I took a deep breath and turned around.

Walking toward us through the trees were my parents, Gemma and Toby Johnson, flanked by Marco's parents, my Uncle Harold and my mother's sister, Aunt Grace.

Aunt Grace kept shooting fearful glances at my father, whose fists were clenched. My mother exuded exhaustion with every step. Uncle Harold kept his eyes ahead, no doubt searching for his children.

Ember tapped Reid and Benjamin on the shoulder. The three of them stood up, alert.

Uncle Harold and Aunt Grace caught Marco's eye, rushing toward us. She embraced her son and kissed his head. "Marco, I'm so glad to see you."

Uncle Harold shook Marco's hand. "It's good to see you again, son." His words were gruff, but I saw the emotion in his eyes.

Marco grinned. "I've saved all the best stories for you, just like you asked."

Uncle Harold pulled his son into a rough side hug and squeezed his shoulders, then went to collect his other children. As he passed me he tilted his head toward me in greeting, but his eyes contained no mirth.

My heart hammered in my chest as I squared my shoulders and

walked toward my parents. A few feet from them, I bit my lip and waved half-heartedly.

"Hi, Mom." There was a bluish bruise on her right cheekbone.

She lifted her hands as an invitation for a hug. "Hello, sweetheart."

Before I could accept her embrace, my father crossed the distance between us.

The moment seemed to break down to its individual parts: his hand coming toward my face, the sharp sting of his skin on mine, the loud collision of his hand against my cheek, the automatic tears in my eyes, the impact of my body as I fell to the cold ground. My cheek smarted. Stupid, stupid me; I'd fallen because I hadn't braced for the strike. That was as dumb as not expecting Patrick to hit me with the bottle all those months ago.

My mother was wringing her hands. "Toby, please don't do this here."

"Shut up, Gemma."

My mother pursed her lips and backed away.

I looked up into my father's face, not sure what to say. "I'm sorry," didn't quite fit, because I wasn't. "Please don't kill me," didn't work, either, because he couldn't.

Benjamin saved me the trouble of having to choose a response. He appeared at my side in an instant and helped me to my feet. After brushing me off, he touched my cheek, which cooled, no doubt sparing me the same bruise my mother had.

He stepped between my father and me. "I'm Benjamin," he said to my father. "I'm on your daughter's team. I've heard a lot about you."

That wasn't true. I barely ever talked about my mother; I never talked about my father. What was he doing? Wasn't he afraid of my father, too?

My father crossed his arms. "Have you now? I'm sure my daughter has told you some highly unlikely stories about—"

"She's told me about how understanding you were when she wished to avenge your youngest son's murder. I've always admired how mild you were when you sat down with her and discussed how unwise it is to sneak away in the middle of the night to go after dangerous people. I'm sure you took into consideration her youth and grief."

I'd never told Benjamin how I'd received the scars on my back. The only person who knew the full details was Marco, and maybe Ember, if she'd overheard my thoughts.

I glared at them, and they were suddenly absorbed in conversation.

"What are you talking about?" my father asked.

"Exactly," Benjamin snapped. He put his arm around my shoulder. "Let's go, Jillian."

My father's jaw dropped. "Who are you to lecture me about how I discipline my children?"

Benjamin pulled me away, his jaw hard.

We'd walked nearly two hundred feet into the trees before he stopped and faced me. "You're shaking."

I was. I was trembling all over, nauseated, and drenched in cold sweat that made me shiver in the winter air. The other three joined us and formed a small circle around Benjamin and me.

"I'm going to be sick," I groaned, before falling on all fours and throwing up.

Everyone jumped back, but then kneeled near me and put their hands on my back while I retched.

I'd been doing so well. John's enthusiastic welcome, Stephen's smile, and the cheering children had given me hope that my time here wouldn't be so bad. With Isabel and my team near me, I'd let my guard down, allowing my father a chance to strike.

All desire I had to talk to people at camp had vanished, replaced by the primal need to curl up in a cave. I hadn't felt that desire since Patrick had broken the bottle across my head.

"Reid," I gasped. My stomach was still in painful spasms.

Reid rubbed my back. "Don't talk right now. It can wait."

I pushed some of my loose hairs out of my face. "Build a shelter for us. Away from everyone. Please."

Reid stood up. "I can do that. Where would you like it?"

Marco pointed up at Fort Mountain. "How about at the old lookout? Nobody lives up there. We'll have lots of privacy. Can you fly us up?"

Reid nodded. The ground rumbled, and then we were flying up the side of the mountain to a stony outcrop near the summit. Marco gave directions, explaining where to land.

We landed with a rocky *whumph*, all but Reid tumbling off the rock into dead leaves. Benjamin helped me to my feet.

I was now clammy and shivering from the vomiting. "Marco, get kindling for a fire."

Reid walked to a clear spot and examined the rocks sticking out of the mountain's face. "This is good," he murmured. "Lots to work with. Okay, guys, stand back." His eyes glowed white, and then the thick stones began to shift. Rocks flew here and there, forming a small structure built into the mountain's face that would be cramped, but livable. Reid squinted and flexed his fingers, and loose dirt in the structure compacted with a muffled sound.

The glow faded from his eyes and he gave the ground a little stomp. "Did you know that there's a small cave system beneath the mountain? I can feel it."

"You're not allowed to alter the terrain. Tarps only."

The deep, masculine voice came from the trees. I knew the speaker.

We all spun around.

Time slowed as I took in the sight of Elder St. James coming toward us on the path, tall and stern. My stomach, which had just settled, began to quake again. Why was he here? Was he going to punish me right now? Did he know that Benjamin wasn't from Corsaro, but Trent?

I worked to keep my breathing even. "Um, we'll break it down in a minute, Elder."

I needed to keep this man happy above all other people, even my team. I was sure they could handle some mid-December camping. Elder St. James studied me. I felt tiny.

The wind shifted, blowing his scent toward me. I knew that scent well.

Too well.

"Damn it, Matthew! Get out of here!"

Elder St. James's middle-aged face melted away into the smug features of Matthew Dumont.

He burst into laughter, clutching his stomach. "You should've seen your face when you saw me, Jill," he said, giving me a vicious smile. "It's good to know you can still feel fear." He walked up to me and brushed my cheek with his finger. "And boy, do you have reasons to be afraid."

7

I kneed Matthew in the groin.

He fell to the ground, tears pooling in his muddy brown eyes. "You're a devil woman," he moaned, before spitting at my feet.

Benjamin took a step toward us, but Marco held him back.

"I wanna watch this," Marco whispered. "Jill always does something funny when he's around."

I put my hands on my hips. "That was for tricking me, Dumont. And for touching my face. We've had this conversation before: you do *not* touch me without my permission, got it?"

Matthew scowled and climbed to his feet. "Yeah, yeah. Whatever. I just came to see if you're still psychotic. I'm not disappointed."

I tossed my hair. "Now that your curiosity has been satisfied, get your skinny ass out of my campsite."

"What are you going to do, make me?"

"You're awfully cocky tonight, Matt. You've obviously forgotten the last time you couldn't keep your hands to yourself."

"You're oversensitive. You didn't need to break my hand."

"You groped me, idiot."

"Who cares? We were engaged."

"We were not engaged. We were courting."

"We *were* engaged, and that's practically married. I didn't need your permission."

"Did our dads ever shake on it? No. We weren't engaged, and you're delusional."

"And *you're* a nasty little—"

Reid cleared his throat.

Matthew turned to look at my teammates, who all shook their heads. The men had their arms crossed, exposing their impressive biceps. Ember's fingers danced on the handle of her knife.

The color drained from his face, and then he looked at me again. "See you around." He hurried off down the path, toward the main camp.

Benjamin cracked his knuckles. "Don't tell me that was the big, bad Matthew Dumont. I can definitely beat that guy up. I think I'd be doing a lot of women a favor."

Marco and Reid clapped Benjamin on the back and went to check out the newly built shelter.

Before following, Benjamin came to my side. "Are you okay? You told me he was nasty, but I didn't know he was *that* nasty."

I pecked him on the cheek. "I'm fine. Go with the guys. I'll be there in a minute."

After one last hard look in Matthew's direction, Benjamin joined them.

Ember walked up to me and placed her hand on my shoulder. "Hey, why don't you get some rest? We've all had a long day. You'll be better able to handle everything with some sleep."

Matthew's jibe about the groping incident was the latest in a long line of unpleasant trips down memory lane.

He'd tried to feel me up, I'd yelled at him and broken his hand, and we'd gotten into a screaming match. He'd spilled everything: how his parents had made him court me to make me feel better, that he hated how headstrong I was, and that he hoped someone would beat some sense into me one day.

I put my hand on hers, still staring after Matthew. "I hate this place, Em. I want to go home."

Ember turned me around to face her and gazed into my eyes, taking my hands in hers. "I don't know if everything is going to be the same, but we all want you to know that we're here for you. Since we got the summons, I've heard you go from your usual self to, well, someone who's afraid all the time. I want to see the Jill who stepped between Patrick and me and said he couldn't harass me anymore."

"I was so angry then," I said, closing my eyes. "I don't want that."

"Better righteous fury than fear."

"Em, the tribunal—"

Ember placed her hand on my cheek. "*Look.*"

My vision swirled, and then I was no longer in front of her on the top of a mountain, but in a small classroom at James Oglethorpe High School, looking through the memory-eyes of Ember.

I heard my voice, but it didn't sound like how I heard it in my head. Instead, it sounded how Ember heard me—a little higher than I was used to, and strong. Confident. I stood to her right, staring at Patrick with fierce hostility. I felt Ember's appreciation and admiration.

The memory shifted, and we were sitting on trash cans at the mouth of an alley. Ember was relieved I was with her, chatting the hours away. The vision changed to a little later, while she watched me taunt a mugger. *Fearless...*

I was standing in a drenched library, holding a wire and ordering Patrick to surrender or die. He sank to his knees and I smiled.

We stood in a dingy living room in front of a knife-throwing target. I placed a knife in her hands and patiently corrected her stance.

I hung my head and apologized for trying to sneak books into the house and hide them from my friends. My shame was written all over my face. Ember could hear my thoughts, all my self-abuse and doubt.

I waved while Ember and Reid flew away in a Coast Guard helicopter. Though I grew smaller in the distance, she could hear my relief that my team was safe.

As quickly as she'd entered my mind, she was out. We were back on the sparse mountaintop, the men none the wiser about what had just happened.

I shivered, though not from cold.

Ember squeezed my hands. "I want to see that Jill again. That Jill had plenty to fear, but she *faced* those fears, and she defeated them." Her brown eyes glistened with the vehemence in her words. "You're Battlecry. That's a rallying shout before waging war. Fury and boldness are built into your name."

"No, it was an allusion to my grandmother's power. She had an ultrasonic scream that could shred metal."

Ember just shook her head and pecked me on the cheek. "Get some rest, and then think about what I said, okay?" She let go of my hands and walked inside the shelter.

She might as well have asked me to drink the ocean.

Marco ducked out of it and began collecting dry twigs and branches. I joined him.

Marco peered toward the deep pink western sky. "The sun's going down. Benjamin's going to have trouble tonight, even with the blankets. Has he ever spent a night outdoors in winter?"

"I... Crap. I don't know." We had plenty of blankets, but even I knew that outdoor living took some getting used to. Benjamin, tough and strong as he was, was in for a long night. "Just keep the fire going, and I'll make sure he's warm."

"Oh, I bet you will." Marco snickered. "Cuddled up under the blankets, who knows what will—"

I whacked him on the head with a stick. "Go soak your head in the creek." I turned on my heel and walked back toward the campsite, warm under my collar.

Ever since Benjamin and I had officially started dating in July, we'd always kept our physical relationship fairly chaste; kissing on the couch in front of a movie was the extent of our "activities." However, when I'd developed a nasty cough on Thanksgiving, he'd been all too eager to give me a check-up in the sick bay.

I'd been led to believe all my life that civilian men, having grown up without the principles and traits, were wild, almost animalistic, in their sexual behavior. One visible bra strap would drive them into a frenzy. Benjamin had only been a superhero for a few months, so I expected him to seize upon any opportunity for fooling around.

Yet, when I coyly asked him on that Thanksgiving afternoon if he wanted me to take off my shirt so he could listen to my heart with his stethoscope, he'd paused, cleared his throat, and told me that I was going to be fine. He'd left me in the sick bay, confused and humiliated.

The next day I'd pulled Ember aside and asked her, with my hands in my pockets, if Benjamin was really attracted to me.

"Are you... Are you *serious*? You're really asking me this?"

"Well, yeah."

"Jill, if you could see what I've seen in that boy's head, you'd... No, I'm not even going there. Yes, he's attracted to you. When I was dying on the floor at the convenience store, he healed me, then actually took the time to admire your chest." She glared at Benjamin's door.

I'd thought about asking her what his fantasies were, but backed away when I saw her face.

So, I knew he was attracted to me, but why had he turned me down?

Perhaps it wasn't a flaw in my physique—I had to admit, I looked good in my underwear—but a flaw in my personality. Plenty of boys in this very camp had said as much. I'd gotten into yelling matches with my father, mother, cousins, and Matthew plenty of times over the years. I'd challenged the other trainees to competitions of strength, speed, and agility just to watch them curse when they lost.

Or maybe Benjamin found me intimidating? I was nearly six feet tall, built like an ox, and had nearly beaten my former leader to death. Benjamin had practically hyperventilated when I'd straddled Patrick and aimed blow after blow to his bones and organs, deliberately drawing out his death.

It was probably a combination of all of those.

I dropped my sticks and twigs into a heap by the shelter and started to look for rocks to make a fire circle. I'd considered every possible reason Benjamin could've rejected me. Each reason sat in my chest, heavy as the rocks in my hands.

What had gone wrong over the last few months? We'd all been so happy. I'd been so happy. Ember was right— something was off about me. I used to be so... so...

A hawk soared overhead, circling for a meal. I put down the rocks and followed it until I reached the overlook.

Northern Georgia stretched out before me, visible for fifty miles in all directions.

The lights of the campfires in the valley flickered like stars, beckoning me toward their warmth. The various meadows and training areas seemed so small from my vantage point, like pieces in a grassy patchwork quilt. The large obstacle course, tucked in its own meadow, looked like a set of structures for dolls.

The voices of my fellow campers, occasionally audible on a still day, were lost in the roar of the December wind as it whipped through the mountains and stirred every tree as it went.

Beyond the ugly wall, the hazy lights of Chatsworth, Georgia winked at me. The first question I'd asked the man who drove Marco and me to Saint Catherine had been the name of the town I'd seen from my lofty perch for so many years. I loved to hike to the overlook. Marco, my eternal shadow, had often joined me.

Our last sunset in the camp had been spent at this very spot, speaking in wonder of what life in a civilian town would be like. We couldn't conceive of a true city, as none were visible from Fort Mountain.

I closed my eyes and breathed in deeply, inhaling the smoke, moisture, bark, decay, and unnamable scents of the moment. The wind raised each hair on my arms, teasing me with its strength. For all the adventures I'd had in my sunny seaside home these last few months, it was here on the jagged peak of a mountain that I felt truly alive.

My city was eternally on my mind, but my heart was a mountain range.

I stepped back from the edge and ran into the woods. A few

minutes later, I finished building the fire circle and arranged the kindling in the usual little stacked formation.

A gust of wind nudged the smaller twigs and caused a shiver to shoot down the back of my neck. We needed to get the fire going. "Marco! I need you!"

Silence.

Sighing, I stood up and poked my head into the shelter, where the others were arranging blankets and backpacks to form a makeshift bed. Benjamin was in the process of putting on a thermal undershirt, giving me a glimpse of his flat abdomen, with its light smattering of hair that I liked so much. I grinned.

Ember gave me a look of exasperated disbelief. "Whatever gets you smiling."

"I'm going to go find Marco. Who wants to come with me?"

They all agreed to come, and we flew on the rock toward the main meadow, which was now dark and lit by the jumping, ghostly glow of dozens of campfires.

Marco was sitting with his parents and sisters, talking with great animation. The younger two girls hung on his every word. I focused on his words and gathered that he was sharing a story about an armed robbery he'd foiled. When he reached the part about the robber pointing a gun at his head, Melissa hid her face in her mother's shirt.

People everywhere were cooking dinner over their fires. Warm aromas of soup, vegetables, and meat wafted under my nose, reminding me that I hadn't eaten in hours. When we returned to the shelter we'd eat some of the food we brought in the duffel. The boxes of supplies had been left with the ones from the charity truck.

My team dispersed and wandered away from me. I searched around for a friendly face with whom I could visit.

At the far end of the meadow, a few teenagers danced around a fire, holding hands and singing an old song about the first superheroes. I watched their feet move in the intricate, quick movements I knew well.

While I watched the happy dancers, a large gust of freezing wind caused every campfire to gutter and throw burning embers high into the air, where they lit up the night sky like glowing, fiery confetti. Like sparks from a flint.

Without consciously deciding to move, I walked toward the dancers. As I neared the group, they stopped and stared at me as I approached.

One of them, a boy in his late teens, wore the red sash of a future leader. I recognized his face, but I couldn't recall his name. I stepped into the circle. None of the teenagers moved or spoke. Instead, they watched me, the planes of their faces lit up in ghostly oranges and yellows.

"Ma'am, how can I help you?" the future leader asked politely.

"Trainee, what's your name?"

"Noah St. James, ma'am. When I enter service next year, my code-name will be Python."

"It's nice to meet you, Noah. I'd like to dance with your group, if you don't mind."

Noah faltered. "I... I don't think that's allowed, ma'am. I don't think we're supposed to fraternize with the teams who came for the tribunal."

I held out my hands to the girls beside me. They hesitated, then took them. I looked Noah in the eye. "You're a future leader. You're going to dance with heroes like me whether you want to or not."

Noah's brow furrowed as he tried to work out the meaning of my words, but he joined hands with the boy and girl beside him. The girl to my right flashed me a shy grin and began to sing again.

I closed my eyes and let the old tune carry me away, away from the tribunal and the judgments, away from cold and hunger. We sang about great teams of the past who'd sacrificed their lives to keep innocent people safe, and when the music swelled we raised our hands above our heads to clap twice, I opened my eyes and smiled at the stars.

Mercury shone above us, beautiful and bright in the darkness.

Another gust of wind threw an ember into my eye.

With a cry I fell to my knees and covered my eye with my hand. It wasn't agonizing, but my reflexes wouldn't let me open it. A burning, prickling pain spread across my lid—I'd have trouble seeing for a while.

Everyone stopped dancing. Noah kneeled down next to me. "Ma'am, what should I do? I can get a wet cloth for you, if you want."

"Get my teammate Mercury. Tell him his leader needs him."

Noah stood. "Mercury! Your teammate needs your assistance!"

Benjamin was there in the blink of an eye. "What's wrong?"

A few people gasped. Before I could answer, his fingertips brushed my cheek. The burning faded into nothing, and I let go of my eye.

"You're a healer? I mean, sir, you're a healer?" Noah asked. "And you can run fast?"

"This is Noah, a future leader," I said to Benjamin. "He doesn't think he's allowed to dance with me."

Benjamin glanced at Noah, clearly unimpressed. "Yeah, I'm a healer and I can run fast." He paused, then relaxed. "Cadet, go find every person in the meadow with an injury, and tell them to come to me."

Noah nodded quickly and ran off toward the rest of the people in the meadow. The other teenagers crowded around Benjamin and me.

"Sir, how long have you been in service?"

"Sir, what camp are you from?"

"Sir, what's your family name?"

Benjamin held up his hands to shush them. "I'm afraid I don't have time to answer all your questions, since I'm sure Red Sash will be back soon with a crowd in tow. Please refer all questions to my leader, Battlecry." He gave me a warm smile. "She's the reason I'm a superhero." He walked off toward Noah, who'd already found half a dozen people who needed healing.

The teenagers turned their attention to me, and I began to tell them the tale of how I'd met Benjamin Corsaro, the man who'd been born with fabulous powers, but had never had a chance to learn how to be a superhero.

As word of Benjamin's ability spread around the meadow, a large throng began to form around him. I fell back and watched Benjamin work his wonder, and the thrilled reaction of the crowd each time someone shouted to the sky that they'd been healed. Several people burst into tears when their oozing wound, hideous burn, or severely fractured limb was made new.

A man from the far side of the camp, Mr. Mukai, came up to me and pulled me aside. I'd played with his daughters Lillian and Rosie when we were small, before they'd died of illness in the same year. His only surviving child, Florine, was fourteen. "Jillian, what family is that man from? Is he courting?"

I covered my smile with my hand. "I'm sorry, Mr. Mukai, but Benjamin and I are courting. And he's not from any camp. He's from one of the obscure families, the Corsaros."

Mr. Mukai balked. "How did you find him?"

I watched Benjamin heal a preteen girl with a patch over her eye by pressing the tip of her nose. She collapsed into hysterical giggles, then pulled off the patch. "It doesn't hurt anymore!"

"We were at a café at the same time. He met a girl there who'd been injured in a bomb blast. He healed her and thought I wouldn't notice." It occurred to me that Mr. Mukai wouldn't know what a café was.

"Jill!" Isabel's voice came from behind me.

I excused myself from Mr. Mukai and hurried toward her. She was sprinting toward us, clutching a stitch in her chest.

"What's going on? Are you okay?"

"Ran... too fast... Mr. Dufresne is... setting up... the watch." She finally caught her breath. "I ran to get the other injured people from the south end of the camp. Caroline is going to get the people from the west side."

"What happened with Mr. Dufresne?" Sidney Dufresne was the watch commander.

Isabel beckoned the rest of us to come closer. "I, uh, overheard him talking to Elder. There's going to be another trial before yours. I don't know who's in trouble. But the big news is that they're putting you guys on the watch bill at weird times. I think they want to keep you apart. Benjamin's on watch tonight. Marco, Jill, and Reid have watch tomorrow night after the tribunal. Ember, you're going to be on the hunting team all tomorrow, except when you're testifying."

I swore. "What are they worried about? Do they think we'll start trouble?"

Isabel nodded fervently. "Yes. They think you'll fight their judgment at the tribunal."

"That sounds like they've already decided," Reid said, his eyebrows knit together. "They haven't heard Jill's defense."

"How did you hear all this?" Marco asked sternly. "Have you been eavesdropping again?"

Isabel gasped. "Of course not."

Her wide-eyed innocence fooled nobody.

"Isabel St. James, what have I told you about listening in on conversations?" Marco said, his voice suddenly deeper. "One day you are going to get into serious trouble. Elder will not be understanding if you're caught spying on him."

"How do you spy on the elders?" Reid asked.

Isabel flashed an impish smile. Her light brown skin, black hair, and pink clothes faded into the darkness, making her nearly invisible in the low light of the night. My sharp eyes could make out her reedy figure in the air, but to an average person who wasn't looking for her, she would've been practically invisible.

"Wow," Ember and Reid said in unison.

Isabel reappeared. "Okay, yes, I've been listening. But a lot of weird things have been happening lately, and I want to know why. For example, some men in a white truck came a few nights ago while I was on watch. They gave something to Elder, who put it in his house. I've never seen that truck before."

"What did the truck look like?" I asked.

"Forget that. Elder gets stuff all the time. Why were you on *watch*?" Marco asked, a deep frown twisting his features. "You're fifteen."

Isabel blinked at him. "You were seventeen when you left, weren't you? They decided I was old enough to be on watch. I don't mind doing it. I get a lot of time to think and stuff. And I can talk to Timmy when we patrol together."

Marco launched into a full interrogation of Isabel about "this Timmy guy," and I knew my part in the conversation was over.

Reid and Ember wandered off hand-in-hand to watch Benjamin heal the ever-growing crowd. I sat down on a tree stump, trying to ignore the clawing emptiness in my stomach.

I watched the ebb and flow of the people flocking to Benjamin. Every few minutes he had to turn away someone with sickness, and in the glow of the firelight I could see the genuine regret in his eyes when he explained that he could only heal injuries.

I marveled that Benjamin was from a forbidden family. Though my understanding of the world had widened to accept that the camps could produce villains and that villain families could produce heroes, it was a mystery to me how he had sprung from two parents who murdered and robbed.

And now that I thought of it, how had Eleanor turned out so well? Wherever she was, I was certain she was the same happy, chirpy person who'd locked her brother in a room with a superheroine so they'd have to make up.

"Hey."

Matthew's soft voice made me twist around on the stump.

"Oh, go away. I was actually starting to feel better."

Matthew stopped walking a few feet behind me. He was carrying a small bowl, steam curling up from its contents. My stomach growled.

He held out the bowl to me. "I brought you dinner."

"Why? What's in it for you?"

His shoulders slumped. "I want to start over."

"Did it ever occur to you that it's a little past way too late for that?"

Matthew settled next to me on the ground. "I know you hate me. I know I deserve it. I just...I guess I got in the habit of being a turd to you, you know? That's the game we played for so long that when you came back today, I didn't even think about it."

"When did you grow up?" I snapped. I was staring at the bowl. My mouth watered at the smell of beef and vegetables.

"Around the time I heard that my sister Justine and Mason were betrothed." His words too flat to be anything but true. "I realized that I was jealous, and that I'd messed it up between us."

So Mason was engaged to Justine Dumont. That explained his twine bracelet.

I supposed I shouldn't have been surprised; my parents had always gotten along with the Dumont family, who were as traditional as they were. It was pure coincidence that the Dumont children were all close in age and the opposite sex of the Johnson children, but it made courting easy. Allison had married Samuel Dumont last year. I hadn't seen her since coming to camp; she was probably at her new campsite.

"Yeah, you did mess it up," I said. "You said nasty things to me and you touched me even though I said you couldn't."

Matthew appeared to be thinking. "That was wrong of me," he said finally. "And I understand why you broke my hand. You were right when you said that we weren't engaged, and that I had no right to touch you."

I studied him, searching for the hidden intent in his little speech. Matthew wasn't bad-looking, per se; dark hair and eyes, full lips, and a strong jaw all added up to a pleasant face. Some of his muscles had filled out since we'd had our weird courtship years before. He wasn't Benjamin, but he wasn't repugnant, either.

"I'll take that soup."

He handed it to me and I sipped from the bowl. I missed Reid's cooking. "So what did you come here to say? That you're sorry for everything? Or just today?"

"How about both?"

A thousand replies rushed through my head. Half of them were pure invective, an instinctual response to his presence. The other half were borne of gratitude that he'd finally admitted to wrongdoing. Matthew's smooth lies—that I was the most beautiful woman he'd ever met, that I was special, that I was smart and funny, that only I could make him happy—had eaten at my self-esteem for years. After all, if he'd had to lie to me, how could I believe that anyone would ever mean them?

But then again, unbelievable as it was, Matthew was apologizing and admitting that he'd been a jackass to me. The least I could do was forgive him and let the both of us move on. The twenty-seventh principle, virtue, demanded moral excellence.

I took a deep breath. "I accept your apology. And your friendship, if you're offering it. But I won't be courted by you."

Matthew pursed his lips, thoughtful. "Are you courting someone else?"

I pointed to Benjamin in the distance, who was now explaining how to clean wounds. "Benjamin Corsaro. His codename is Mercury." Affection spread through me, warm and comforting as bath water. I pulled out my necklace, which sparkled despite the firelight. "See? He gave me this."

Maybe Matthew and I weren't enemies anymore, but I wasn't above showing off gifts from another man.

Matthew stared at the necklace. "That's... fancy," he said, a little stiff. "That was very generous of him. He must really like you."

"He does."

"He's a healer and a runner, right?" Matthew ran his thumb over the J. "Can he fight?"

I shrugged. "Yeah, some. He doesn't have the training that normal camp boys have, but that's not really his job. He's on the rear line with Ember."

Matthew tucked my necklace back under my collar, and his hand brushed the tops of my breasts.

I glared at him.

"Sorry," he murmured. "I really didn't mean to do that." Matthew stood up, still staring at my chest. "I have to go. I'm on watch tonight." He left as quickly as he'd come.

I sat on my stump, trying to work out what had just happened. A slow smile spread across my face as I realized the truth: Matthew was *jealous*.

I ate my soup, laughing quietly every now and then. At least one good thing had happened today.

8

At twenty-two hundred, Ember, Marco, Reid, and I sat around the crackling campfire. Benjamin had been called away by Mr. Dufresne to hear the basics of watch duty and had promised to return soon.

Reid and Ember huddled together under a thick blanket, no doubt speaking telepathically. Every once in a while, the corners of Reid's mouth would quirk, and Ember would nuzzle against his cheek. He'd steal a quick kiss and she'd giggle.

If they kept that up, Ember was going to have to take a year off from crime fighting to have a baby. I'd miss Ember on the battlefield, but I liked the idea of them starting a family.

Ember and Reid had been in love as long as I'd known them; it was only a matter of time before they got married. Leaders were allowed to perform the ceremony. I pictured binding their hands with ribbon and saying the brief, simple vows that would unite them.

I stopped watching their little game and nudged Marco, who didn't need a blanket.

He was staring into the fire without blinking, the flames reflecting yellow and red in his eyes. He hadn't spoken for a while.

"Hey," I said, my voice low. "What are you thinking about?"

"Tim Spivak is courting Isabel." His lips barely moved. "Mom and Dad really like him."

I couldn't remember ever meeting Tim, but I knew a few Spivaks. They were a cordial, industrious family from the far side of Chatta-hoochee, where the Dumont family also lived. Lark Spivak served in Baltimore alongside Reid's brother Reuben and Berenice.

Perhaps Tim had been one of the many little boys running around when I'd visited the other end of the camp, usually to deliver a message or, for a brief time, visit Matthew.

"If your parents like him, he can't be bad," I said gently. "I know she's only fifteen, but Isabel is a sensible girl. She'll want to wait until she's older to get married."

"That's not it." He was still staring hard at the fire. "I'm... I'm just..." His large eyes filled with a bottomless sadness.

Marco looked up at Ember and Reid, who were now sitting with their eyes closed, their heads bowed together.

Serenity poured from them like the fragrance of a rose bush in bloom, filling the whole area with their happiness. There had been a time when their happiness had sickened me—what had changed?

The answer, of course, was Benjamin. He lavished me with affec-tion. I wore a sign of his feelings around my neck.

I put my arm around him. "Do you want a girlfriend? Is that it?" I mentally tabulated all the girls around his age that I could think of.

"No, I don't want a girlfriend. I'm just... I'm tired of being alone." He dropped his head. "Greg died, then you found Benjamin, and even Isabel is paired up. I'm sick of this." He hurled a twig into the fire. "I just want everything to go back to the way it was."

Ember opened her eyes and looked at Marco, then stood up. "Reid and I are going for a late-night walk." Reid grinned and followed her as she led him by the hand into the darkness.

"Aren't they subtle," I muttered.

Marco's mouth twisted. "Whatever. I'm going to bed." Before I could say anything he stood up and stormed into the shelter, leaving me alone by the fire.

The chilling breeze whipped my hair around. I pulled a blanket around my shoulders and stared at the flames as Marco had.

In twelve hours I'd be at the tribunal, pleading my case in front of the three elders of the people involved. Would they have compassion on me and say I was innocent? Would they find me guilty of something abominable, and order my hair to be shorn off before I was flogged?

Possibility after possibility pricked at me, and I hugged my knees. Ember wanted a braver Jill, but I couldn't summon the confidence I felt when I'd faced Patrick. He'd been wrong, and I'd been convinced of that.

But the elders weren't Patrick. They weren't beating me, abusing me, or misusing their power to oppress and torment me. They hadn't done anything to me.

Now that I thought about it, Elder St. James had actually helped me in the past. He'd intervened when my father had caned me, yelling at him that stripping and publicly beating his grown daughter was an inappropriate punishment for what Marco and I had tried to do. He'd been kind enough to honor the friendship between Marco and me by allowing Marco to serve when he was underage.

He was a stern, remote figure in my life, but overall, I had to say he was a positive force. I couldn't speak for Elder Campbell or Elder Lloyd, but I felt better about Elder St. James. He was a good man.

The sound of crunching twigs and leaves distracted me from my thoughts. Benjamin traipsed up the trail, shadows visible under his eyes. He sat down next to me, shivering lightly.

I inched closer to him and tossed the blanket around his shoulders. "Here." I tugged the blanket close around us. "I'll help you warm up." I remembered Marco's teasing from earlier and bit my lip, trying not to giggle. Now that Benjamin was here, it didn't seem so absurd anymore.

He kissed my cheek. "Thanks. How are you feeling?"

"Worried. But I think Elder St. James will take my side tomorrow. I don't want to talk about it, though. How was watch training?"

"It's not hard, but I'm so beat right now, and I've got watch in two hours. I've been up since four, which means I'll have been up for twenty-six hours by the time I get off watch. And then the tribunal starts."

"You should get some sleep while you can." I gestured to the shelter. "I'll stay up and wake you up for watch."

"Nah, I'll just stay awake. I'm so tired that waking up for watch would be torture."

I nudged him. "If you're ever kidnapped by supervillains, I think you'll find that they'd disagree with your definition of 'torture.'"

Benjamin stared off into the dark. "I'm so glad I met you, Jillian," he said finally, his quiet voice edged with sadness. "You freed me from that life."

I rested my head on his shoulder. "Did you ever torture anyone?"

The thought of Benjamin ever deliberately harming someone in that way was so ludicrous that it didn't bother me. His brother Beau, on the other hand, was cut from different cloth.

"No. But there were times when I ran with a crowd that did. If I never saw them again, it would be too soon."

"You're part of a better crowd now. You'll never have to worry about watching one of us doing something as heinous as that." Guilt pricked at me; I'd essentially tortured Patrick before he'd died. "Anymore," I added. A shooting star streaked across the sky. "Make a wish."

"I wish I won't be tired tomorrow for the tribunal."

I sat up. "If you're so worried, just go get some sleep. Seriously, your bed is right over there."

Benjamin pondered that for a moment. "Or I could stay up with you." His hand found me under the blanket and he entwined his fingers with my own. "Sleep or alone time with Jillian? Decisions, decisions." He moved his face closer to mine. "We never get to be alone at home."

"I don't want to sway your decision-making," I whispered, enjoying this turn of events. "But..."

I cupped his cheek and kissed him, my hand leaving his and resting on his firm waist.

Benjamin inhaled and tangled his fingers in my hair, kissing me with such passion that when our blanket fell, I couldn't feel the cold. Instead, I felt quite a bit hotter under my uniform.

I found myself half-sitting, half-kneeling in his lap. His hands moved up and down my back, sometimes tugging lightly on my hair and other times resting on my hips.

I gripped his muscular arms, imagining them unclothed, holding me tight. The thought made me ache.

For the first time in many weeks, I wasn't afraid of tomorrow. I was dedicated to *this* moment, to *this* happiness, and I didn't care one bit about what the elders were going to do to me. I was pressed up against Benjamin, the man I... I...

"Benjamin," I whispered into his lips.

He groaned in pleasure. "I love it when you say my name."

I leaned back a little and, without breaking eye contact, took my shirt off, revealing the lacy blue bra underneath. Benjamin's eyes widened and he froze, his eyes locked onto my chest, which was just inches in front of his face. I slipped a strap down my shoulder.

His face was shocked, but I knew for a fact that he was pleased by what he saw.

"I—J... Jillian..." He was still staring at my chest. "We... We sh—"

I pressed a finger to his lips. "I want to show you how I feel about you. I want to show you how you make me feel. Please let me." I slipped the other strap down.

Benjamin grabbed my shoulders and pushed me off him into the dirt. He scrambled to his feet and hurried a few feet away, then leaned against a tree, facing away from me.

I pulled my bra straps up and tugged my shirt over my head, blushing furiously. "What?" I demanded, my eyes itching. "What is it?"

Benjamin didn't face me right away. When he'd finally calmed his ragged breathing, he turned, his face scarlet. "I can't sleep with you. I just can't. I'm sorry." He hung his head. "What happened was my fault. This is all my fault. Please don't feel bad. Please."

I wrapped my arms around myself. "Oh, I'm not supposed to feel bad because I was turned down flat by my boyfriend for the second time? That I feel like a slut because I keep trying to get you to sleep with me?"

"That's it. That right there." His voice was hard. "*That's* why I can't sleep with you."

I gasped. "Because I'm a slut?"

The tears spilled over. I'd tried so hard not to call myself that after he'd turned me down in the sick bay. I'd never imagined *he'd* actually feel that way about me. But now that he'd said it, I chastised myself for my naiveté. Of course he felt that way—I'd practically thrown myself at him.

But Benjamin slapped a hand to his forehead. "No! It's because you equate wanting to have sex with being a slut! And all the other stupid crap you guys believe about sex and relationships and hair and education and *everything*!" He pounded his fist into his forehead. "God, I'm saying 'slut' now. I hate that word. This place is so backwards, can't you see that, Jillian? Can't you see how messed up this cult is?"

"Stop calling us a cult! We are not a cult!"

"Yes, you are! You guys can't even go to a freaking doctor when you get hurt because your stupid elders want to control every single damn thing in your lives. I wanted to leave this place ten seconds after I got here. I'm playing nice to keep everyone happy. But I'm tired of it. I'm so damn tired of watching you cower when... when your father or whatever walks by. It's like I'm looking at the girl in the café again. I'm sick of watching what you put up with because of what your oh-so-holy elders tell you."

"I... I do not cower," I growled, balling my fists.

He narrowed his eyes. "Earlier today, when Matthew was here, what was your big objection to him groping you?"

I reeled from the subject change. "What?"

"Matthew! The skinny freak who showed up today to harass you! Why were you so angry when he groped you?"

"Because I hadn't given him permission! What does this have to do with anything?"

Benjamin slammed his fist into the tree. "No! You were pissed off because he groped you without permission when you weren't *engaged*! That's what bothered you! Not that he'd molested you, but that he'd molested you when he supposedly wasn't allowed to! My God! Did it ever occur to you that Matthew is *never* allowed to touch you without your permission? That if we ever got married, I wouldn't have sex with you without your permission?"

Once again, I was knocked off course.

"But..." I rubbed my forehead. "That's... That's not... What?" Marriage implied consent. That's what my parents had always taught me.

Benjamin made a noise of disgust, his face an unattractive grimace. "I cannot ethically have sex with someone who thinks that there's ever a time when she can't say no to me. That goes against *my* principles."

I unclenched my fists. "I...I do not cower."

"Your father literally knocked you down as a greeting and you just stayed there. What are you going to do when the elders do the same thing? Are you going to be the meek little mouse they want, or are you going to stand up and *fight them*?"

"I can't fight the elders!"

"You can fight anyone you want to!" he roared. "You're a super-hero! The only thing stopping you *is you*!"

I burst into tears. "You have no idea what you're saying! If I fight the elders and somehow manage to get away from camp with my life, I'll be a rogue. Don't you *get* it? I'll have no contact with my family or friends, I'll be cut off from the allies and their resources, and any other superhero can kill me." I clenched my fists. "Without this 'cult' you hate so much, I'd be nothing. Yes, it sucks, but this is my life, Benjamin!"

He gave me a look of deepest disgust. "No, this is cowardice."

"Go away," I said through my tears. "Just go away."

He let out a long sigh and rubbed his eyelids. When he was done, he opened his eyes, and his face had softened. "Oh, Jillian. I'm sorry. Please don't cry. Look, we're both tired. I shouldn't have yelled." He held out his arms. "Come here, sweetheart. Let's start again."

I faced him, tears still falling. "I said go. I don't care where. Leave this stupid cult camp if you hate it so much. Just stay the hell away from m-m-me."

A fresh sob overtook me, and I stomped into the shelter and threw myself onto the hard earthen floor. I was already freezing, but I didn't go outside to get a blanket in case he was still there. I didn't hear the crunching of leaves, so I assumed he was brooding in front of the fire.

"Screw you," I muttered into the darkness. "I hope you freeze out there."

"Wha?" Marco mumbled. He'd slept through the whole fight.

I curled up with my arms around my knees. "Go back to sleep."

Marco turned over and began to snore.

Eventually my tears stopped, and I drifted in and out of sleep. In the middle of the night, when the fire had died down and no longer cast light into the shelter's open door, I jerked awake to see Ember and Reid had returned, resting peacefully. I stared at them for a moment then put my head down again.

I wasn't cold. Someone had put my blanket on me, and the air smelled like Benjamin, spicy and sweet. For a second I wondered where he was, but then I remembered he was on watch.

I laid in the dark, thinking about our fight. I didn't understand much of what he'd said, and we needed to talk about it. The more I thought about the fight, the less angry I was.

I hoped he was dressed warmly and didn't trip over anything in the dark, and that the other people on watch would treat him with respect.

One thing he'd said still bothered me, though.

"We're not a cult," I mumbled. I pulled the blanket around my shoulders and closed my eyes, but I was still awake when the morning sun peeked through the trees.

It was time for the tribunal.

9

Benjamin still hadn't returned to the campsite at zero seven, a full hour after he was supposed to return from watch. Reid and Marco had gone off in search of him, leaving Ember and me to get ready.

Half an hour before the tribunal, I pulled on the cleanest, least-wrinkled uniform I could find in my backpack. Ember and I brushed each other's hair and arranged it in elegant rolls called chignons, which we'd discovered months before on the internet. Not only did the chignons make us look more dignified and respectable, it hid the true length of our hair.

She straightened the hood of my tunic for the third time. "Remember what I said yesterday. No matter what, we'll be there for you. We all love you."

I caught her hand. "I know." Ember chewed on her inner cheek and said nothing, so I embraced her and asked her what she never had to ask me. "What are you thinking?"

"I'm thinking I might lose my best friend." Her voice cracked, and she hid her face in my shoulder. "I'm thinking that they're going to be horrible to you. I'm thinking they might hurt Reid or Marco."

She began to cry in earnest.

I held her for a long time, searching for the words that would comfort her. What could I say to her if I myself had the same fears? What would make me feel better if she were in my shoes?

The best thing I could do was shut down the irrational fears.

I rubbed her back. "I'm the one in trouble. We all know that. I left the team. I took up leadership. I fought Patrick. We all have to testify, but I'm the one in trouble. So don't worry about Reid or Marco, and certainly don't worry about yourself."

She sniffled. "But they might take you."

"No matter what they'll do to me, you'll have Reid, and Marco and Benjamin. Benjamin and I had a fight last night, but I know we'll make up and he'll stay on the team. Even if the worst happens, you'll have the guys."

"I don't want to be the only woman on the team!" she wailed. "I've done that twice!"

That was true. Ember had served as the lone woman for months alongside Reid and Patrick, before Marco and I were assigned to Saint Catherine, and then again when I'd abandoned the team. I hadn't given much thought to how she felt about it, but now that she had brought it up, I wagered that my presence was desirable.

"But these'll be nice guys," I reminded her. "No Patrick. You'll know them, you'll like them, and they'll look out for you. And you never know, if I'm removed from the team, they might replace me with another woman."

"Oh, yay, some dumb rookie."

I let go of her, a twinge of heat in my stomach. I'd been so afraid of the elders that I hadn't considered that Ember might be afraid, too.

"There's no guarantee I'll be removed from the team. But listen to me. You're all going to be okay." I put my right hand over my heart. "They can do what they want to me, but I swear to you, I won't let them do anything to you guys. I'll die before that happens. You want me to be brave and confident again? This is it. I will *not* let them hurt you." I breathed in through my nose, then exhaled slowly out of my mouth. "So don't be afraid."

Ember's wan smile made it all feel a little less bleak. We walked out of the shelter, past the smoldering fire, and down the rocky path toward the meadow.

The main meadow was filled with people from all over Chatta-hoochee camp. They arranged themselves in neat lines and rows, awaiting the entrance of the elders. There were at least two hundred people in attendance.

Off to the side, away from the main crowd, were three dozen trainees, ranging in age from five to late teens. They stood up straight and tall, their faces blank.

As I passed them I pulled my shoulders back and made eye contact with every one of them. Though I was facing disciplinary action, they all bowed their heads a fraction in deference to the active superhero who'd acknowledged their presence.

Ember craned her neck. "Where are the guys? There are so many people here that I don't want to listen for them. Talk about a headache."

I stood on my tiptoes and scanned for our team. They were at the far end of the meadow, huddled under a tree in deep conversation.

Ember and I ran to them. As we approached, the man I thought was Benjamin turned.

It wasn't Benjamin, but rather a young man in his mid-twenties who looked a lot like Reid. They had the same strong jaw, light hair, tall frame, and gray eyes. He wore a sharp uniform that comprised a snug thermal top and khaki trousers, like my own.

Was this one of Reid's brothers? If so, what was he doing here?

He turned, allowing me to see the codename stitched in neat letters over his breast: Obsidian.

Yep, this was Reuben Fischer, from the Baltimore team. I assumed his codename was a nod to his superpower, which Reid had once told me was the ability to manufacture and manipulate a mysterious "shadow" substance, which could be crafted into weapons and other shapes.

"Hi there." I held out my hand. "You're Reuben, aren't you? I'm Jillian, your brother's leader."

I expected him to tut at me or roll his eyes, but he gave me a firm handshake. "It's a pleasure to meet you, ma'am. I've heard a little bit about your accomplishments. I'm so happy that Reid can serve with a decent commander." As he said 'commander,' he shot a dark look toward the crowd.

Ember offered her slim hand. "I'm Ember Harris," she said shyly. "Your brother and I are courting. I've heard a lot about you."

Reuben smiled, but it didn't reach his eyes. "It's a pleasure, Miss Harris. Reid was just telling me about you."

Reid sighed. "But you still haven't told me why you're here."

"I said you'll see. I don't want to have to explain myself twice today."

So Reuben was here to "explain" himself. Isabel had mentioned another tribunal—what the heck had he done? Was his whole team in trouble?

"Is the rest of your team here?" I searched the crowd for familiar faces. "I haven't seen Lark or Berenice in years."

"They're in Baltimore. It's just Peter and me."

Marco let out a derisive laugh. "I hate that I share a last name with that guy. You have to be a special kind of weirdo to call yourself Imperator. 'Hi, I'm the commander, so I'm going to call myself Commander. Latin makes it cool, though, right?'"

Reuben didn't join our laughter. "Don't let him catch you making fun of him. He's a sensitive little boy."

I had a feeling that Reuben and I would have been good friends if we were on the same team. His sardonic air reminded me a little of Benjamin. *Speaking of whom...* "Hey, where's Benjamin?"

Marco made a pained face. "I don't know what you said to him last night, Jill, but he was a pissy little brat this morning."

Reid nodded. "Marco's not exaggerating. We went to get him as he got off watch, and he told us to buzz off and that he didn't want to see you. When we reminded him that the tribunal is today, he said he didn't give a, uh, *crap* about what the elders decided, and that he hated this place."

I rubbed at my gummy eyes, not allowing myself to cry in front of my team or Reuben. I struggled to comprehend that once again Benjamin and I were at odds over my upbringing.

We'd had our disagreements before, and I'd admitted that the elders hadn't dealt fairly with us and our educations, but was he really so disgusted with us that he was skipping the tribunal?

Half a dozen rowdy men walked out of the woods behind us. Ember whipped around and groaned. "The hunting team is looking for me. Damn it, I *hate* hunting." She pecked Reid on the cheek. "I'll be back to testify later."

One of the men waved at her. "Hey, Harris! They said you're with us today!"

I heard her mutter a stream of curses, but she waved back. When she joined them, she turned around gave me one last sad wave, then disappeared into the woods.

A few seconds later, the clanging of cowbells around the meadow announced that the tribunal was about to begin.

Reuben's complexion turned sickly, but he held his head up high. "Let's go."

As we walked toward the center of the meadow, we passed a large post with two iron cuffs on each side, and a large campfire with a long metal rod sticking out of it.

Reuben shuddered when he saw them, and his hands began to tremble.

Though I did not know what his crime was—and he had obviously committed a serious crime—I put my hand on his shoulder.

He shrugged off my hand. "Don't worry about me. Be a good leader and look after your team."

10

Elder St. James entered the meadow first.

Garbed in black, he strode up to the middle of the three wooden chairs and sat down. His face, so similar to Marco's father's, betrayed exhaustion. His black hair had turned dark gray since I'd seen him last, and his dark brown skin was lined with more wrinkles than I remembered. Had the last year been so terrible? He looked like he'd aged a decade.

Immediately after Elder St. James had taken his seat, two men also dressed in black appeared from the woods.

I took an instinctive step back.

Elder Campbell bore a resemblance to Patrick that was so striking, it was as if my former leader had been resurrected and was coming to exact his revenge on me for usurping him.

Though I'd seen him before on the recorded speeches we'd had to watch, I saw now that the similarities went beyond mere facial features. Elder Campbell had the same haughty air, the same scowl, the same raw power oozing from him. He would never take my side.

Elder Lloyd, leader of Coeur d'Alene camp in Idaho, had a quiet air. He was tall and balding, with light eyes that showed his unhappiness. He appeared to search the crowd.

When his eyes fell on the Fischer brothers, disappointment became evident on his face. He'd traveled all the way across the country to hear testimony from not one, but two of his camp's sons, and Reid's camp was even stricter than mine.

"There will be silence during the tribunal!" Elder St. James bellowed.

Complete silence fell on the crowd.

Elder St. James put his hands on his knees. "Peter St. James, come forward."

Peter St. James, one of the many St. James family members, stepped out of the crowd. Though he and Marco shared a surname, they couldn't have been more different.

Peter was tall and white, with neatly-combed light brown hair, a pointy face, and a heavy brow that gave his stare a permanent intensity. His uniform was identical to Reuben's, except for the name stitched on the breast: Imperator.

Elder St. James leveled a coolly distant expression at Peter. "Peter St. James, you requested judgment today from the tribunal regarding your teammate, Reuben Fischer. State your case."

Peter took a deep breath. "Earlier this year I found out that Reuben was seeing a civilian woman in a social way. I confronted him and told him that I knew about his behavior, and I told him that he had to stop seeing her."

So there it was: Reuben had been visiting with a civilian.

What he'd done was bad, but not the end of the world by any means. When I'd still believed Benjamin to be a non-powered civilian, for a little while in the café, I hadn't given too much thought to breaking that rule, because it was commonly broken. Patrick would've gone berserk, of course, but most leaders would've given their teammate a slap on the wrist.

The real danger lay in being caught having sex with a non-powered civilian. We were supposed to be paragons of virtue; being caught in bed with a member of the public was a serious crime.

Elder St. James all but rolled his eyes. "I assume something else happened to warrant this tribunal. We're not interested in minor infractions that can be handled within the team."

Score one for Reuben—even Elder St. James didn't want to hear Peter's whining about such a minor quibble.

Peter fidgeted. "I caught him again. I followed him when he was supposed to be on patrol. He went into the house of the same woman and stayed there for several hours."

The crowd gasped, but Reuben's face remained a smooth mask. I felt a surge of judgment, but then I remembered that I'd intended to seduce Benjamin the night before. Maybe I couldn't condone a sexual relationship with a civilian, but I wasn't in a position to condemn him, either.

"And then what happened?" Elder Lloyd asked quietly. "I assume you confronted him."

Peter's demeanor changed. His shoulders slumped and he gazed at Reuben, shaking his head. "I did. I told him that I was going to send him to another team to get him away from her because she was obviously a temptation. And then... and then he said..."

Reuben stiffened. "Say it," he growled.

"He said they'd gotten married."

There was chaos in the meadow.

Men and women pointed at Reuben, screaming that he was perverted, a traitor, a deviant, and a disgrace. Someone yelled, "Punish him!" and then the chant began: *punish him, punish him, punish him, punish him...*

Reid tried to shield Reuben from the crowd, but Reuben gently moved his brother aside. "I don't want your protection."

I waited for the revulsion and betrayal to come. Reuben had removed himself from our gene pool. It was one of our most absolute laws: we could not marry non-powered people. Marriage was for the begetting and training of children, who would hopefully have a power that could serve either the public or the camps.

How could a child born of such a mismatched union possibly grow up in an edifying environment if one of their parents was a civilian?

Reuben's crime was a very serious crime indeed. He'd be flogged.

But I served alongside a reformed supervillain from one of the forbidden families. I'd also committed a crime worthy of the whip.

The elders yelled for quiet, and the crowd settled down.

Elder St. James stood up. "Reuben Fischer, step forward."

Reuben threw back his shoulders and strode to the middle of the meadow.

"What do you have to say for yourself?" Elder St. James's voice was a low rumble.

"I love Gabriela. We were legally married a year ago and I have no intention of leaving her. I wish to leave service and live as a civilian. I told Peter that, but he insisted on a tribunal." Reuben threw a cold look at Peter, who stared straight ahead at the elders.

The crowd tittered, and Elder Lloyd held up his hand. "Leave service? Is that your final statement?"

"Yes."

Elder St. James nodded. "We will retire for deliberation and return in half an hour. Peter, Reuben, you are not permitted to leave the tribunal site. Everyone else not involved in today's proceedings is ordered to go to the south field. The public portion of the tribunal is over."

Elder Campbell and Elder Lloyd followed him into the trees. Their crunching footfalls grew fainter and fainter, until they were so far away that I would not be able to overhear.

Peter retreated to the far side of the meadow. Nearby, at the edge of the tree line, a lone fox sat watching in the shadows.

I waved, and the fox dipped its head once. Ember was a wily woman.

The enormous crowd moved south, toward the main gate.

Marco, Reid, and I dashed forward and grabbed Reuben, pulling him into the tree line.

"What the hell, Reuben," Marco whispered, checking to make sure that nobody was listening. "You married a *civilian*? Does she have powers? Please tell me she has powers."

"No, she doesn't have powers. But yes, I married the woman I love." Reuben spoke without inflection. "People do it every day."

"Superheroes don't marry civilians every day," Marco shot back, rubbing his temples. "Oh my God, they're going to kill you. They're actually going to kill you. It's happened before."

"No, they're not," Reid said. He steepled his hands, tapping his index fingers together. "I think Elder Lloyd is going to fight for you. I mean, what can they do to you, right? You're married. It's done. You're legally bound to Gabriela. That's her name, right?"

Reuben's eyes took on a faraway, dreamy look. "Yeah, Gabriela. My wife." He breathed in deeply and closed his eyes. "My *wife*. I love that I can say that now. We had to hide our relationship for so long."

Reuben radiated the happiness and peace that Ember and Reid had the night before. I didn't know how I felt about Reuben's decision to marry a civilian, but I knew that his love for her was real. I could respect that.

"Tell us about her," I said.

Reuben gazed into the distance for a long moment, then held out his hands, palms-up. A wispy, black, shadowy substance materialized and swirled into the miniature shape of a curvy woman standing in the center of his cupped hands.

He lifted her to his lips and kissed her head with breathtaking tenderness, then sighed in contentment.

"Gabriela Mendez is the most incredible woman I've ever met," he said softly.

For the next thirty minutes Reuben told us of his meeting and courtship of the civilian who held his heart.

While he talked, my sorrow over Benjamin's anger turned to resentment. Reuben was a far better husband than Benjamin was a boyfriend at the moment. Reuben was facing severe punishment for his marriage, but Benjamin couldn't even show his face when his girl-friend—heck, his whole team—was about to testify about events that he'd been a part of. He hadn't received a summons, but the very least he could do was show up.

The clanging of the cowbells interrupted Reuben's retelling of their tiny church wedding, in which only the priest and two of Gabriela's friends had been in attendance.

Reid patted his brother's back. "It's time. Remember, I'm your brother, and I support you."

"So do I, if that means anything," I said. I'd never forget how lovingly he'd kissed his little Gabriela figure.

"Me too," Marco said. "I like you."

Reuben nodded and stared at the post and fire in the distance. He swallowed hard.

I put my hand on his cheek, the intimate gesture already feeling natural. "Don't think about it. There's no guarantee."

"Reuben Fischer and Peter St. James, come forward for judgment," Elder St. James ordered, his voice carrying across the meadow loud and clear. He pointed to us. "And you three, also."

Reuben and Peter walked forward until they stood in front of the elders, who hadn't taken their seats.

Marco, Reid, and I joined them, though I was unsure of what was going on. Why were we involved in this? And now that I thought about it, why was the judgment private if the trial had been public?

Something about this situation was off.

Elder St. James pulled a small vial of clear liquid out of his pocket. It was no bigger than my thumbnail. Four tiny pins stuck out of its cap.

"Reuben, do you know what this is?"

"No, Elder."

"This is a gift from the Bell family. They've long contracted with our people, since the days of Christina St. James. The Bells work hard to make sure that our needs are met. They provide you with all your medical supplies, for example."

I knew the name. Before everything had happened with Patrick, my team and I had taken a minute to ponder why supervillains were attacking Bell Enterprises' buildings. Benjamin and his brother were robbing the Bell Enterprises Industrial Complex when we'd had our almost-fatal encounter.

I hadn't given the mystery any thought since that day, though.

Running away from my team and taking over as leader had completely diverted my attention.

"What is it?" Reuben asked casually. But his eyes were locked on the vial.

Elder toyed with the vial, though he took care to not touch the pins. "This is called JM-104. It's a special compound made solely for the use of the elders," he said calmly. "We order it before tribunals in case we hear testimony like yours, but we haven't had to use it in years. I'm beginning to think we should use it more as a warning."

I didn't trust what was in that thing.

Elder St. James continued to turn the vial over in his fingers, his expression turning sly.

Elder Lloyd looked away, while Patrick's father crossed his arms, his face blank.

"Roll up your sleeve and hold out your arm, Reuben." Elder St. James's voice had become hard. A shiver raced up my spine.

Reuben hesitated, then rolled up his sleeve to the elbow before holding it out. Elder St. James placed the vial's needles on the underside of Reuben's wrist, on the blue vein.

There was a click and a hiss.

Reuben screamed and fell to his knees, clutching his wrist. He looked up at Elder St. James with tears streaming down his face. "What... What *is* this?"

His whole body quaked and he doubled over, his face nearly touching the ground.

"*That* is a three-month dose. Reuben Fischer, the elders find you guilty of attempted desertion, public disobedience of your rightful commander, and unlawful contraction of marriage. Your punishment is to be given a three-month dose of JM-104, flogged, branded as a deserter, and removed to another team. If you speak with, or otherwise contact, the civilian woman again, you will be killed."

Reuben tried to lunge at Elder St. James, holding out his hands in an odd way—like he was holding a sword, maybe. He froze, staring at his hands, then at Elder St. James. "What happened to my powers?"

Elder St. James smiled. "Three months."

THEY MADE us watch Reuben's punishments.

Reid kept his composure when his brother, cuffed to the pillory, endured lashing after lashing from Peter.

However, when the small red-glowing D—for Deserter—touched Reuben's cheek and he screamed in agony, Reid fell to his knees and vomited.

11

Peter led Reuben away after the branding. Reuben was barely able to walk, sometimes having to lean on Peter.

Reid watched them leave, his face white. Marco kept rubbing his eyes.

When Reuben and Peter had disappeared from view, the elders took their seats again. The sun was high overhead.

He picked at a piece of lint on his sleeve. "Jillian Johnson, come forward."

I took a few steps closer. "I'm here, Elder."

"All of you are here to testify about the defection and disappearance of Patrick Campbell as well as your...*assumption* of leadership."

"But... but Ember isn't here." I looked around for her.

"My niece is needed on the hunting team," Elder Campbell replied smoothly. "I trust that her testimony wouldn't be any different from yours, considering that you serve together."

"I think you'll find that her testimony is the most important, once you know exactly what your son did." My words were almost a growl. I steadied my breathing. *Keep it together, Jill.*

Instead of replying with a nasty remark, Elder Campbell looked away, thinking about something. "Be that as it may be, we will proceed without her. If we determine that her testimony is necessary, she'll be called."

"Start at the beginning," Elder St. James said.

I began the ugly tale of how Patrick had abused his teammates from the moment we'd begun serving in Saint Catherine. I didn't have to change any details about his behavior as I recounted my first six months of service. When I described the beatings he'd given me—tossing me around the room, pulling my hair out of my scalp, punching my stomach—Elder Campbell winced.

I brought the story to June of that year, when I'd met Benjamin.

At that point in my testimony, I began to fudge a little bit, removing any hints of the Trents. Benjamin was merely a superpowered civilian whom I'd happened to meet one day. We'd struck up a friendship, he'd healed my battle injuries, and then he'd proven his good nature by saving Ember. I never mentioned the warehouse.

I did, however, tell them that I'd made a poor judgment call during a fight because I was intoxicated by painkillers—painkillers I took to stifle the pain in my head from Patrick's bottle.

"Elders, on my honor, I was too afraid of Patrick to tell him that I couldn't patrol that night. I would've rather patrolled while high and face death on the streets than tell my leader that he'd injured me. And that night, during a fight, I decided to chase after a criminal instead of stay with Marco like I should've." I put my right hand over my heart. "I know that was a bad decision, but I swear, I wouldn't have made it if my judgment hadn't been compromised by those pills."

Elder Campbell nodded. "I understand, Jillian. Please continue."

I described how I'd finally snapped when Patrick had moved to hit me for leaving Marco, then how I'd run off and decided to be a superhero on my own, which wasn't allowed.

"I didn't know if I was allowed to come home, and I swore to protect the city. I couldn't just leave. It would've been against the principles."

The elders exchanged little side glances among themselves.

I wrapped up the tale with a slightly altered version of events that didn't include Benjamin's family: Benjamin and I fought Patrick, who fell into the floodwaters and drowned.

Elder Campbell hid his face for many seconds as I described his only child's death.

When he'd composed himself, I gestured to Reid and Marco. "But before you make any judgments, you need to hear what happened while I was gone from base camp."

Elder St. James nodded toward Reid. "Reid, we only need your testimony. Speak."

The smell of Reuben's burning skin still lingered in the air. Reid took a labored breath. "When Patrick discovered that Marco and Jillian had saved the hostages, he confronted Ember and demanded that she tell him where they were hiding. Ember heard in his thoughts that he planned to ambush and kill them. When she refused..."

Reid pressed his fist to his mouth, and I knew he was reliving the memory.

"Go on," Elder Lloyd said.

Reid dropped his hand. "When Ember refused, Patrick attempted to rape her, to terrorize her into talking. He would have succeeded if I hadn't pulled him off her." Reid's hands clenched and unclenched. "Ember told me later that Patrick had often used the threat of rape to keep her in line. Elders, I don't care how much my teammates, male or female, disobey their leader. Patrick had no right to prey on her that way. It's a violation of everything we stand for as superheroes."

"I completely agree," Elder Campbell said, his voice heavy with grief.

I did a double take. Since when was he reasonable? Everything I'd heard about him had added up to a despicable man.

Elder Campbell turned to the other elders. "Gentlemen, there are two issues at hand. The first issue, which is the defection and death of my son, primarily concerns my son and niece, so I will issue judgment."

Elder Campbell stood up while the others remained seated. He took in our faces: my open mouth, Reid's hard eyes, Marco's suspicious squint.

"Before everything, I must apologize for my son's actions. He was cruel and angry from childhood. He never should have been released into service, much less leadership. When I sent him to Saint Catherine, I believed that responsibility and hard work would cure him of his problems. I was mistaken, and for that I am deeply sorry."

Too little, too late. My bitter thought echoed around my head.

"I sent my niece with him for the same reason, I believe, Elder St. James sent Marco with you, Jillian. I understand that you two are close and find comfort in each other's company. I knew that my son was fond of Ember... or so it seemed to me. I see now that his feelings for her were not pure, and that I sent Ember into a dangerous situation. For that, also, I am deeply sorry.

"Because of my severe lack of judgment, my son was able to abuse the four of you, and I do not blame you for leaving by any means necessary. I expect that you thought I would insist on punishment for my son's death, but I officially release you from blame or guilt."

He sat down.

The three of us were frozen, too stunned to speak. Elder Campbell wasn't angry. We were not going to be punished for defying our leader.

That was a gift so unexpected, I didn't know how to process it.

But as Elder Campbell had said, there were two issues at hand. The second issue, that of my leadership, still had to be addressed.

However, I no longer felt the keen sting of fear. Though Reuben had been dealt with harshly, we'd been shown incredible lenience by Elder Campbell. I dared to hope that the elders would show lenience again. After all, if they could condone the team's actions as a whole, surely they could support my position as a leader.

But Elder St. James looked at Elder Lloyd, who nodded, his face grim.

Elder Lloyd slowly stood and faced Reid. "We've spent several weeks discussing what we are going to do about your inaction."

My eyes flickered to Reid. *What the hell?*

Reid blinked rapidly. "I don't understand."

Elder Lloyd pointed to me. "That young woman felt she had to take up the mantle of leadership. As you know, women are not permitted to lead. We had to ask ourselves why you, the oldest fully-trained male superhero, didn't take responsibility when you should have."

Reid's eyes darted back and forth between Elder Lloyd and me. My heart began to pound.

Elder St. James removed a newspaper clipping from his pocket. "This is an article from *The New York Times* about how Battlecry has made history by being the first female leader in half a century. They anticipate many more to follow." His mouth puckered as if he'd just eaten something sour. "Because of your inexcusable inaction, Mr. Fischer, Americans now have expectations of us that we cannot meet. You've placed a burden on Jillian that she thinks she has to carry, and what's worse, Ember and Marco believe she has to carry it, too."

I held up a hand. "No, that's not what—"

"Be quiet!" Elder St. James's order made me freeze.

Reid was shaking. "I... I couldn't... It wasn't right for me to..."

Elder St. James looked at Reid with disgust. "We agreed on your punishment a long time ago. All of you, including Mr. Corsaro, will be sent to different teams to serve under proper leaders. Before you're sent to your new assignment, you, Mr. Fischer, will receive fifty lashes for dereliction of duty."

His words coursed through me like a bolt of lightning.

The worst had happened.

I'd been so wrong.

My team was going to be broken up, and the pieces sent around the country. Reid was going to be whipped because I had declared myself the leader of my team. They were going to strip him to his waist and torture him because of *me*.

"No!" I jumped up and grabbed the front of Elder St. James's shirt. "This isn't his fault!"

He tried to brush me off. "Calm yourself, woman."

"Don't tell me to calm down!" I shoved Elder St. James back and turned on Elder Campbell. "*You*," I spat, jabbing a finger at him. "You said you were sorry for what your son did to Ember. If you were so sorry, you'd keep her in Saint Catherine, with the people who've proven that they'll protect her. You don't give a crap about Ember or the rest of us, do you? You probably just want the whole business swept under the rug so nobody will have to think about how terrible of a father you are!"

My words rang around the meadow.

I pointed at Elder Lloyd, who stepped back. "And you! You're just going to stand there while these guys mutilate two of your own? Is that what leadership is to you? Punishment and judgment? How about standing up for them for once? How about acting like the father you said you'd be to them when your own son died? Did you ever think about *that*?"

He winced.

As quickly as my fury had flared up, it died down. I'd appealed to their sense of justice; now I needed to appeal to their sense of mercy.

"Don't hurt him, please. *Please*. It's not his fault. I—I made them follow me." I didn't care how pathetic I looked or sounded. I pointed to the pillory. "If you want to whip someone, whip me instead. Please. *Please*. Keep my team together. Don't hurt them. I was the one who actually did something wrong. I convinced Reid that I was the best choice. I... I... I listened to civilian music and read novels. They filled my head with ideas that were confusing and exciting and... and then I talked them all into it. I'm the bad influence."

My babbling barely made sense, even to me. I didn't believe what I was saying, but I would've sworn on my honor that I'd walked on the moon if it meant sparing Reid and keeping my team together.

The three elders stared at me. "We...are going to go discuss this," Elder St. James said slowly. "You three stay here."

They hurried off into the woods.

When they'd gone out of earshot again, Reid grasped my shoulders and shook me. "*Why did you do that*?" He sounded so angry, I half expected him to backhand me.

Tears dripped down my face, and I wiped my nose. "I swore to Ember that I wouldn't let them hurt you."

"I will not watch you get my punishment! I stood by for over a *year* while Patrick beat up all of us! Like hell I'm going to stand by while you get the whipping I deserve!"

"You don't deserve it! That's the point! You don't deserve it! I'm your leader and I'm supposed to protect you!"

I collapsed completely, my forehead in the grass. Terror, raw and real, clawed at me. I'd begged for Reid's punishment, but I didn't want to feel the lash tearing away my skin. I didn't want the humiliation and pain. I didn't want any of it. I just wanted to go home. I just wanted to lay on the couch, my head in Benjamin's lap. *Where is Benjamin? Why isn't he here? Is he really that mad?*

Reid's hands fell to his sides, limp. He looked up at the sky, making his tears appear as raindrops on his cheeks. "Oh my God," he groaned. "What's going to happen to us?"

Marco spun around. "Where the hell is Benjamin? Why isn't he here?"

I sobbed harder. "He hates the camp. I told him to stay away from me."

The truth hit me as I said the words: Benjamin wasn't gone because he hated me. He was gone because I'd told him to leave. I'd told him to stay away from me, and he, ever noble, was obeying my wishes. Even if he was still being a "pissy little brat," he probably thought he was helping me by not being here.

Marco kneeled beside me and pulled me up into a hug. "I'll beat him up later," he muttered. "They're not mad at you. I don't think you're going to get punished, at least not a whipping. Be strong."

The three of us kneeled there in the grass, not speaking, not meeting each other's eyes.

When the elders came back some twenty minutes later, we didn't move, though Reid watched them approach with hard apprehension.

Elder St. James pinched the bridge of his nose. "In light of this development, we've altered our judgment. Reid, you're going to assume leadership of your team for a trial period of six months. If you perform well, you'll keep your position. If not, we'll assign you to another team and send a replacement."

Reid nodded once. "And Jill? What about her?"

"Jillian will leave service as of today. Henry Dumont—" I looked up at the mention of Matthew's father's name, "—approached me last week and said his son is willing to marry her. Since Jillian will be coming back to the camp, I see no reason not to go forward with the marriage. I'm performing Mason and Justine's marriage tomorrow, so it won't be any trouble to perform another."

I didn't move. I didn't blink.

Marco's ludicrous prediction that I'd have to marry Matthew was coming true.

Elder St. James kneeled down and stared into my face. "You're going to do it right this time, do you hear me?" His soft voice carried a thousand threats. "No trouble, no problems, not a word that you're anything but a perfect wife. If you don't, we'll reverse our judgment and haul Reid right back here. Have I made myself clear?"

"Yes," I whispered.

Elder St. James tweaked my nose. "We were impressed by the reports of your leadership ability. We knew we could count on you." He got to his feet and nodded at the other two men. "Gentlemen, we're done here."

They left us there.

Marco broke away and ran into the woods. Reid threw his arms around me and hugged me, his body shaking. The cold winter wind blew around us, but we didn't move.

I couldn't let go of him. I was afraid that if I did, I'd sprint toward the gate and leave him to his punishment.

Reid pressed his lips to my ear. "I can make him disappear. I can kill Matthew and nobody will ever know what happened. Just say the word and I'll do it." He kissed my forehead. "Let me help you. Let me spare you this. You've been my sister all this time. Let me be a brother to you now."

I laid my head on his shoulder. "They'll figure out that it was you or me."

He didn't reply.

People began to swarm into the meadow, giving us curious looks as they walked back to their campsites to light fires and cook meals. Children ran around us, laughing and shouting. Mothers and fathers scolded them for this and that. Nobody paid too much attention to the heartbroken superheroes in the middle of the meadow.

Isabel sprinted up to us. "What's wrong? What happened? Jilly, what did they say?"

I looked up at her, but before I could explain, a rough tug on the back of my collar pulled me away from Reid.

I fell at someone's feet, and slowly stared up at Matthew Dumont.

He stared down at me, pure revulsion on his face. "Hello, fiancée."

I swallowed bile. Matthew's extension of friendship had been fake. Of course it had been fake. Matthew Dumont was the most consummate actor I'd ever met, and I'd believed it because I was the stupidest, most naïve woman alive.

"Matthew, I—"

"Shut up." He put his hand down the neckline of my shirt and grabbed my necklace. With one sharp tug the clasp broke, and Matthew dangled the beautiful pendant in the air. "I'll take this, thank you." He tucked the necklace in his pocket. "And you are going on a walk with me while we talk about how this marriage is going to work."

He yanked me off the ground and dragged me in the direction of the creek. I looked back to see Reid and Isabel watching helplessly.

The fox from that morning darted out of the tree line and up to both of them, where it whined and pushed at Reid's legs.

Matthew took me to the edge of the swollen, frothy body of water that flowed through the camp. He stopped on a large, flat rock that jutted out over the water. In the summer, when the water was calmer, kids jumped from the rock into the cool depths.

He shoved the necklace into my hand. "Do it."

I held out the necklace over the water. Time slowed.

I imagined that it represented all my feelings for Benjamin, all my hopes and dreams that we'd one day marry and have children. I closed my eyes and pictured that future, the whispered words of love, the dark-haired and hazel-eyed sons and daughters, the laughter, the joy of watching our life unfold.

I opened my hand and the necklace fell, twisting gracefully in the air, hitting the water without making a noise. The churning creek swept it away in an instant.

"Here's how this is going to go," Matthew said. He pulled me to him. My back was flush against his chest, and his hands gripped my upper arms.

I stared straight ahead while he leaned down to speak into my ear, his hot breath making the hairs on the back of my neck stand up.

When he described in detail how he was going to make me pay tomorrow night for breaking his hand and humiliating him in front of my team, I thought of Reid and Ember, living happily ever after with beautiful children around them. Reid was so gentle with her. He would never hurt her.

When his hands left my arms and traveled beneath my waistband, I thought of Marco and pictured him holding his firstborn child, and the look on his face when the baby grasped his finger. He'd gaze down in wonder at the tiny hand and vow to the child's mother, whoever she was, that he'd always guard their baby from harm. He'd be a loving, protective father.

When Matthew turned me around and kissed me while his hands explored underneath my shirt, I reminded myself that even though Benjamin was not part of my life anymore, I'd promised him I wouldn't try to kill myself.

And finally, when I walked toward the northern edge of the camp as the sun slipped behind the wall, I realized that the elders had never intended to punish Reid.

12

The setting sun was almost below the horizon when I stepped into the woods, the trees partially shielding me from the cold breeze. I'd been assigned to sentinel duty from eighteen hundred to midnight.

The job was simple: walk back and forth over a hundred-yard stretch of wall on the east side of the camp, watching and listening for anything unusual.

I had no intention of going to my post.

I walked with purposeful strides toward Benjamin's assigned area, on the north side. Branches whipped at my face and scratched me, but I barely felt the sting.

The sun slipped out of sight, plunging the dead forest into darkness all at once. I could see fairly easily, but if anyone was following me, they'd get lost.

As I neared the northern wall I broke into a run, shoving aside branches and bushes. I leaped over fallen logs and stumps, caring little whether I stepped in a hole and twisted my ankle. I'd keep running.

A twisted ankle wouldn't compare to the pain of the realization I'd had: I'd been railroaded by the elders. Elder St. James's final comment, that I wouldn't let them down, had slipped down into the cracks and eaten at me for hours. They'd expected me to fight back like the uncontrollable upstart I was.

Almost uncontrollable. I had strings. They were named Ember, Marco, Reid, and—

"Benjamin!"

Benjamin was walking down a narrow beaten track that paralleled the enormous wall that would cage me for the rest of my life. He shuffled down the track with his hands in his pockets, feeling around in the dark for roots or depressions in the ground.

I ran up and threw myself on him, clinging to my boyfriend. I wanted to absorb him into my body, make him a part of me forever. The wind at my back, funneled by the wall, pushed us together. The universe itself wanted us to stay pressed together.

"Jill?" He kissed my lips. "What are you doing here?"

"I'm so sorry," I breathed, leaving a trail of kisses along his jaw. "I'm so, so sorry for yelling at you. Please forgive me." I'd told myself I wouldn't cry, but the tears came all the same. "Why weren't you at the tribunal?"

Benjamin stroked my hair, which had come out of its chignon while I'd run through the woods. "I was angry. I'm sorry. What did the elders decide?"

My relief turned to despair. "They were going to punish Reid, so I asked them to punish me instead." I began to sob. I could barely get the words out. "I have to marry Matthew."

Benjamin gasped. "That's terrible! Don't they know we're courting?"

I paused, my stomach rolling.

After a few seconds, I said, "I told Matthew, but he asked to marry me instead. I... I think they were planning this for weeks."

I remembered the feeling of Matthew's hands on my skin and shivered violently. I squeezed Benjamin tighter, and he combed his fingers through my hair.

Another sob racked my body. "This whole tribunal was a sham. I think that's why it was private but Reuben's was public. They just want to shut me up and make it all go away." My crying slowed and I stepped back. "But... I think one thing could make me handle being married to Matthew."

"What is that?"

I peered at Benjamin through my eyelashes, assessing his blank expression. "I can be a good wife to Matthew if I have one sweet memory of a night with you." I guided Benjamin's hand to my hip. The feeling of his hand on me made my muscles clench. "One night. I can take a whole lifetime of Matthew if I have one night with you."

Benjamin glanced behind him, then at me. "Really?"

I wrapped my arms around him and brushed his earlobe with my lips, inhaling the earthy scent from his neck. "When I'm with Matthew tomorrow night, I'll feel better if I know he's getting sloppy seconds. I want him to smell you on me."

Benjamin wrinkled his nose and he pushed me away. "That's nasty. Sloppy seconds? That's just nasty."

I dropped my head. "Fine. I can't make you sleep with me, so I'll just go to my own watch post. But before I go, can I just ask you one question?"

He crossed his arms. "Make it fast."

I slammed Benjamin into a tree by his throat. "Where's Benjamin, Matthew?"

"Benjamin" gurgled, clawing at my hand.

I released the pressure to allow him just enough breath to speak.

He gasped. "What... you... mean?"

I slammed his head into the tree again. "*Where's Benjamin, Matthew*?"

Benjamin's beautiful face melted away to reveal the shocked, purple visage of my fiancé.

I threw him on the ground, where he tried to scramble to his feet. I stomped on his shin, which broke like a branch under my foot. The sharp snap and tortured scream were music to my ears.

"You broke my leg!"

"Tell me where Benjamin is right now, or that'll be the first of many breaks tonight."

"I don't know where he is!"

He'd said "courting."

Had Benjamin not taken the time to tease me about our terminology and accent differences on our drive to camp, I might never have noticed. And the scent—Benjamin was spicy and sweet, like gingersnaps, while Matthew was earthier.

I kicked Matthew over onto his stomach. He cried out, but I just kneeled on the small of his back and twisted his right arm up and behind him.

"These disgusting hands," I hissed.

Six weeks of terror over the tribunal. Six hours dreading my wedding night. It had all been obliterated in six seconds when I smelled Matthew's scent from Benjamin's neck. Six seconds were all it took for my fears to mutate and take a new, monstrous form that clawed at my insides.

The desire to cause Matthew pain like he'd never known spread through me, guiding my hands.

"I swear I don't know!"

I stroked his thumb. "Remember your little speech today? The one at the creek?" I jerked his thumb back, breaking it.

He howled. I smiled.

"Let's see if I can remember the best parts. I'm going to enjoy causing you more pain than you've ever felt. I'm going to take my time. I'm going to—" I pulled back his index finger until it snapped. "—make you wish you were dead, and I'm not going to give you that." I wrapped my fingers around his middle finger. "When you beg me to stop, nobody's going to come and stop me."

He writhed under me. "Elder St. James told me to pretend to be Mercury!"

I stopped and stared down at the crying man on the ground.

Elder St. James had ordered him to impersonate Benjamin, but why? To what end? And where was Benjamin if he wasn't at his post?

The surrounding forest loomed over me, large and dangerous. He could be anywhere in it. I couldn't be sure he was even in the camp anymore.

I doubted Matthew knew the exact details. He was too unimpor-
tant to be anything but Elder St. James's lackey.

Whatever I did after this would be for my own pleasure, not information. The monstrous rage took shape, urging me to draw out the
experience. It would feel so good.

"Let me go," Matthew moaned.

"No." I grabbed a handful of his hair and leaned down to his ear.
"I'm going to break each hand that touched me today. I'm going to
enjoy your screams. And then I'm going to—"

The forest's stillness was broken by the high keen of a siren. Men
yelled in the distance for all able-bodied adults to muster in the
meadow.

The Westerners were in the camp.

13

I fled toward the meadow, leaving Matthew lying on the ground in the dark. I'd deal with him later.

I sprinted through the woods, and as the trees thinned, I could see men and women rushing around the meadow, calling for their children. Babies cried and clutched their mothers, who looked around wildly for their husbands.

"Jill!" Marco slammed into me. Reid was right behind him. "Where's Ember? Where's Benjamin?"

"I don't know! Is the hunting team still in the woods?"

A massive explosion rocked the meadow, knocking us down. A yellow mushroom of fire and debris blossomed up from the middle of the west forest. Flaming bits of debris rained down on the people in the meadow, eliciting fresh screams of terror.

Just as we'd stood up, a second explosion, closer this time, made us tumble to the ground again.

The forest began to burn, spreading quickly, far more quickly than a normal forest fire. Beneath the smoke was the all-too-familiar stench of gasoline.

The Westerners had never done anything like this before.

A figure clad in dark gray darted into the woods fifteen yards away.

I pointed. "There! Follow me!"

The three of us ran into the woods after the figure. I was the fastest by far, and I quickly caught up to the person, a man in a ski mask. I lunged at him and grabbed his waist, throwing him to the ground, then yanked off his mask.

He was a younger man, maybe in his late teens, and his face was twisted into a scowl. "I'm not telling you anything."

"Bad news for you, pal. I've had a *really* bad day." I punched his nose. It crunched on contact with my fist. He yelped as blood spurted out of his ruined face. "What are you here for?" I shouted. "How many are with you?"

"Let me talk to him." Reid's low growl came from behind us. He strode up to the man and picked him up by his collar, hoisting him into the air with one arm. "Hello, filth. I'm from Coeur d'Alene. Perhaps you've heard of it?"

I leaned against a tree. It wasn't often I saw Reid's darker side. This would be memorable.

The man's eyes widened. "I don't know anything."

A needle-sharp spear of rock burst out of the earth like a dart. Reid caught it without looking. "I don't believe you. I'm going to make this simple. You know what you came here to do. I know all the ways to impale a human being without killing them. Give me the information I want and you'll never have to find out some of those ways."

I snickered. *Go Reid.*

The man eyed the spear. "There are five of us. We came here to get people and set the fire. That's all I know."

I straightened. "*Get* people? What do you mean, 'get' people?"

Reid tossed the man on the ground. "Who did you come to take?"

Marco and I watched in silence as Reid advanced on him.

The man scrambled backwards on his elbows. "I never knew their names, I swear. My job was to set the fires."

Reid's face relaxed. "I believe you."

Before the man could respond, Reid thrust the spear into his heart, killing him instantly.

His eyes glowed white as the ground collapsed on itself, forming a grave into which Reid kicked the bleeding corpse. He covered it as quickly as he'd made it, then turned around and faced me.

There was a beat.

I crossed my arms. "Personally, I would've kept questioning him. He was our only source of information."

Another explosion in the distance jerked us back into the moment. Orange and red flared up between us and the meadow, filling the air with clouds of smoke. The crackling of flames grew louder.

"Time to go," I said, pulling the men with me toward the wall. We ran through the woods, our path illuminated by the omnipresent glow of fire.

The tree line ended abruptly, stopping ten feet from the wall. Reid pointed upwards. "Grab on to me."

His eyes glowed again as Marco and I wrapped our arms around his torso, and the ground rumbled, a loose circle breaking away under our feet. Reid held on to us while we flew twenty feet into the air, above the dense smoke. I clung tightly to him, unused to the sensation of flight.

A quarter mile away, tiny people ran around the meadow, screaming and trying in vain to put out the fires that raged all around them. The forest was on fire in three different places, but two of the fires threatened to merge and become one unstoppable inferno. Here and there the creek glinted in the moonlight, winding through the camp like a silver snake.

"Reid, can you divert the creek toward the fires?" I asked, pointing to where the water came closest to the flames.

"Yeah. Hold on tight."

We sailed through the air toward the meadow and touched down at the edge of the grassy expanse. Marco and I jumped off the piece of rock, but Reid flew back up into the air and disappeared over the trees.

The ground rumbled, followed by an enormous roar of water. The hiss of steam replaced the crackle of flames as Reid carved a new path for the creek, flooding the area. A few tree tops still burned like torches in the night, but the majority of the fire was extinguished.

Beneath the hissing and crackling, I heard a faint rocky, echoing sound, like bricks tumbling together in a large space.

Reid appeared again, silhouetted by the starry sky, and touched down in the middle of the meadow. Men with buckets and wet blankets ran into the woods to put out the rest of the fire. Marco and I joined him in the crowd, patting him on the back.

His eyes flashed with an astonishing fury that made me shiver. He leaned down to my ear. "You need to see something."

"In a minute," I said, spying Elder St. James across the meadow with Mr. Dufresne and other members of the watch team.

I strode up to Elder St. James. He turned to greet me.

I punched him in the jaw.

The watch team stopped talking.

Mr. Dufresne stepped between Elder and me. "What's gotten into you? Explain yourself!"

I threw Mr. Dufresne aside and put my face inches from Elder's. "I spoke with *Benjamin* tonight. He told me what you'd ordered him to do." I narrowed my eyes. "Guess what I did to him."

Elder St. James stepped back, obviously doing some very quick thinking. "Now, Jillian, I know this looks bad."

"Benjamin Corsaro is missing!" I screamed to the crowd. "And this scumbag ordered Matthew Dumont to impersonate him! He's a liar!"

Murmurs ran through the watch team. People began to crowd around us now that the fire was mostly out. Marco and Reid pushed through the throng.

"*What*?" Marco said, disbelief coloring his features. "Uncle, what did you do to Benjamin?"

"Benjamin is fine," Elder said, his hands raised in a placating gesture. "He came to me last night and confessed that he was unhappy as a superhero. He wanted to leave the camp without upsetting you right before the tribunal."

"Bull," I growled. "Benjamin has never hidden his feelings from me. If he hated being a superhero, he would've had the balls to tell me to my face. Now *where is he*?"

"Perhaps he sneaked out of the camp through the hidden tunnel I discovered when I redirected the creek," Reid said, his loud voice rising above the clamor of the crowd.

I looked between Reid, who was white with rage, and my camp's leader. Elder backed away, but the watch team formed a wall to block him in with my team and me.

Elder St. James gulped. "We—we have caverns around here—"

"Don't you *dare* insult my intelligence by suggesting it's a cave. I'd know the difference between caves and manmade work better than anybody. The entrance collapsed when I moved the earth to put out the fire."

"A hidden tunnel?" I said through gritted teeth. A horrible picture was beginning to take form in my mind. "The Westerner we questioned said they came to *get* people! And now Benjamin is missing! Who else is missing? Everyone, form up with your families! *Now!*" Elder St. James moved to go to his hut, but I grabbed him. "You're not going anywhere."

The crowd dispersed in haste to take tally of their families. Reid craned his neck and searched the darkness, no doubt looking for Ember.

"Isabel! Where are you?" My aunt cupped her hands around her mouth and darted from campsite to campsite. "Sweetie! Please!" Her father and sisters joined the search.

"No," Marco gasped. "Not Isabel."

Slimy understanding raced down my spine. "Marco, Reid, look for Isabel."

They raced off, Marco holding up a little orb of light to illuminate the search.

I slowly turned my head and stared at Elder St. James, who wouldn't look at me. "They're not going to find her, are they?"

Elder St. James didn't reply.

"Isabel! *Isabel!*" Marco's shouts crept into hysteria. Adora and Melissa burst into tears. Other families began to call for my cousin.

Elder St. James and I stared at each other for many wordless seconds.

I shook my head in stunned disbelief. "What was it going to be this time? She died in the fire, so there's no body left to find?"

"Jillian...you don't understand. There's so much going on that you could never understand."

"I understand that you threatened Reid to get me to marry Matthew without complaint. I understand that I have seriously threatened whatever little set up you have going on here. I understand that Benjamin and Isabel are gone, and you know where!" My shout echoed around the field. Elder St. James flinched.

I'd tortured Matthew, and had been gearing up to interrogate the Westerner before Reid had stepped in. I could definitely go for a third round with Elder St. James. Where would I start?

Marco's strangled yell made me look up.

Marco had lifted a small, blackened log off of something a few meters into the burned-out expanse where the fire had been.

I smelled what it was before I saw it: corpses.

Black and shriveled, the remains of two unfortunate people smoked on the ground, unrecognizable. No identifying features were left, making it unclear whether the victims had been male or female, or even adults.

Marco sank to his knees, holding his head and sobbing. My aunt clutched her husband and screamed, while he gazed at the bodies, his eyes devoid of emotion. Caroline doubled over and wailed, tears falling freely from her face.

I didn't comfort Marco. Instead, I pushed past the gathering people and bent down to examine the bodies for any clues as to who had died. They were face up, the papery skin rippling away from the grinning skulls in the breeze. I looked at the first body from all sides except one. With extreme care I lifted up the remains—the body was very light—and turned it over.

I immediately saw what I'd been looking for: a small hole at the base of the skull.

I repeated my search on the second one, lifting up the body and spotting the same small hole on the back. I glanced at its feet and my theory was solidified.

I got up and kneeled next to Marco, gently pulling him into a hug. "Stop crying," I whispered into his ear. "That's not Isabel or Benjamin. But we need to go right now. Save your questions for later."

He wiped his eyes and sniffed. "Okay."

I nodded at Reid, who was watching from a distance. He hurried over and helped Marco to his feet, though with difficulty because of Marco's trembling knees.

I gathered the St. James parents around me. "My team and I are going now," I said quietly. "I'm positive that's not Isabel, but I don't think it's safe to go around saying that. Act like she's dead."

My uncle's eyes flashed. "What do you mean?"

"I mean that someone wants you to think Isabel is dead." I broke away from them without another word and grabbed Marco and Reid. "Reid, get us in the air. We're finding Ember and getting the hell out of here."

Reid pulled us close and another large piece of earth rose up underneath us, taking us high into the sky. He pointed toward the canopy spread out below us. "Start thinking Ember's name. She says it's the easiest for her to hear, like we're attuned to our own names."

We soared over the north and eastern forest, where we'd seen the hunting team go that morning. As the trees flew by beneath us, I chanted Ember's name in my mind. *Ember Ember Ember Ember Ember...*

I'm here! I just saw you go by above me!

"I heard that," Reid said, turning us around and descending rapidly. We hopped off and immediately went into defense mode, tense and alert.

Ember crashed through a thicket, thorns and twigs pulling at her uniform. Her face was scratched and bloody, but she was otherwise unharmed.

"I thought you'd never find me," she said, panting. "When the siren sounded, I asked the animals where it was safest to go and they took me over here. The rest of the guys went toward the center, but I know who I can trust in a forest."

Reid gathered her up in his arms and kissed her so fiercely that I blushed. His hands seemed to be everywhere at once, though I didn't sense any sexual intent—it was more like he was reassuring himself that she was truly there.

Ember rested her forehead against his. "Shh, shh, don't think about it. I'm here. I'm fine. Nobody's touched me. The cuts are from the bushes. Benjamin can heal them in an instant." She looked over at Marco and me with an expectant expression. Her smile dimmed when she saw my face. "Where's Benjamin?"

"He's gone." Reid's passionate embrace was still in my mind—how desperately I needed to know that Benjamin was *there*. "So is Isabel. Elder St. James did something to them, and it involves the Westerners."

Ember and I locked eyes. I replayed the day's events for her like a disjointed movie: Reuben's heinous punishment, Reid's near-miss, my coerced engagement to Matthew, his whispered threats in my ear as his sweaty hands slid over my body, his face melting into Benjamin's, and the volcano of my fury unleashing on him. The final memory was of what I'd seen on the back of the burned bodies.

"Oh my God." Her hands fell from Reid's arms. "What are we dealing with?"

"There was a bullet hole on the back of each skull," I explained to Marco and Reid, whose quizzical looks had reminded me that I hadn't told them what had made me rush out of the burned clearing so quickly. "I don't think it was Isabel or Benjamin. I think either the Westerners or Elder killed some poor bastards and wanted us to think it was them. The fact that it was a bullet points to the Westerners, because I've never seen a gun in the camp, nor did I ever hear a gunshot.

"On top of that, Benjamin wears steel-soled boots like the rest of us. If the fire wasn't hot enough to completely destroy the bodies, the steel soles of the boots would've survived, but they weren't there. I think they brought in the bodies and dumped them right before setting the fire. Reid put out the fire earlier than planned."

Marco cursed. "This is big. I don't know what we're looking at, but it's big. I can feel it."

"So what are we going to do?" Reid asked, rolling his neck. "Are we going to go back and interrogate Elder St. James, find out what he knows?"

Marco pounded his fist into his other hand. "I say we beat it out of him. If my sister is hurt or... or..."

My team looked at me for direction.

In a fraction of a second I saw two paths stretched out in front of me.

The first one ended at Chattahoochee. I'd stay here at Matthew's side, his punching bag and broodmare, my freedom given up in exchange for my team's possible safety. I'd grow into middle age, and probably die of disease or injury by my fiftieth birthday.

That is, if I wasn't killed at age twenty-one for punching the elder, torturing Matthew, and generally being unpleasant.

The second path was into the unknown. If I left Chattahoochee with my team in tow, we'd be rogues. We'd cut ourselves off from all resources and support. There were no superheroes in existence that operated completely outside of the auspices of the camps and the elders. The few who dared were killed. If we went rogue, it was only a matter of time before we faced a strike team in combat. That was certain.

There was no question as to which path I was going to choose, but I had to give my team their final warning.

I planted my hands on my hips. "To hell with the elders. I'm going after Benjamin and Isabel. I'll be hunted. If you all go with me, we'll all be hunted. They're all going to come after us."

"I don't give a crap," Marco growled. "I want my sister back. I want blood."

Reid put an arm around Ember's shoulders. "When we said we'd follow you, we meant it. This changes nothing." Ember stared up at

Reid, who looked down at her with the soft gaze of a lover. "I'll protect you," he said softly. "Always."

I stood up straight, my shoulders pulled back. They copied me, waiting for orders.

"That's fine with me. But as of this moment, we're not affiliated with the camps. Elder St. James, and I suspect Elder Campbell and Elder Lloyd, have proved to us that they can't be trusted, nor do they have our best interests at heart. I don't know what's going on or why, but the four of us are going to find out and put a stop to it. We're getting your sister back, Marco."

I peered up at the night sky, where Mercury twinkled brightest among the lights. The sloshing fury in my chest hardened like cooling lava.

"We're not camp heroes anymore, but I believe in right and wrong, and that we have the responsibility as powered people to defend the former and defeat the latter. I believe in the vows I took six months ago. I believe in loyalty to my team, and Benjamin did—does, too. He would never abandon us like a rat in the night."

Marco nodded emphatically. "So we're not going to abandon him. I'm in this to the end."

"Me too," Reid said.

Ember nodded. "To the very end."

"Are we changing our codenames?" Marco asked. "We got our codenames when we were part of the camp system. They're part of our camp identities."

I snorted. "You can be whoever you want now, but I'm going to be Battlecry until the day I die."

Ember whooped. "Heck yeah!"

I clapped her on the shoulder. "I need you to do a scan before we go. Reid, get ready to fly again. We're picking up your brother."

14

Reuben and Peter were encamped at the far side of Chattahoochee, two miles to the east of the main camp. Reid landed the flying earth and we hopped off. We ignored the small group of onlookers.

However, when I saw Samuel Dumont and my sister Allison, who was holding an infant, I caught their attention.

"Matthew is in the forest by the north wall. He'll need crutches for a while." I didn't wait for their response. I found Reuben and Peter's tarp by a small creek. "Hey, Peter!"

Peter sat next to Reuben at the base of a tree. Reuben was laid out on the ground, breathing heavily.

Peter stood and looked at me with curious eyes. "You're Jillian, right?"

The hardened lava in my chest turned back into churning, molten hatred.

I'd kill him. I'd kill everyone like him who didn't defend their teammates from injustice.

I rushed him, slamming him into the tree as I had Matthew, and squeezed his windpipe. He clutched my wrist and I let go suddenly with a yell. My arm hair sizzled. Palm-shaped burns wrapped around my forearm where he'd touched me.

"You're crazy," he gasped, flames igniting in his hands. "I don't know what this is about, but you're going to lose."

This was going to be fun.

I unsheathed the knife on my thigh—the only one I'd brought to camp—and gripped it. "You know exactly what this is about."

Peter shot a bolt of fire at me, then another.

I twisted and ducked around the flames and swiped at his head, which he blocked with a deft motion of his arm.

He aimed a series of jabs toward my face and neck which I countered with my forearm.

A column of flames sent me backwards, but I turned my steps into a hasty spin and kicked him. Peter flew into the creek.

After throwing down my knife, I jumped into the water and held him below the water's surface. I pinned his hands to his neck and used my weight to keep him under. His eyes grew wide as bubbles floated up from his mouth, his air and life leaving him.

He was drowning, just as I'd said Patrick had during my testimony.

"Die," I hissed.

For a brief second, I did not see Peter's pale face below the water, but Patrick's. I was no longer in a freezing creek, murdering Baltimore's superhero leader, but in a living room of a house in which I hadn't lived in six months. I was charging at Patrick, enjoying the naked terror on his face, finally allowing my fear to morph into wrath and fuel me. Weeks later, I'd let that same wrath take over while I delighted in drawing out Patrick's death.

Benjamin had begged me to stop.

Benjamin. Sweet, kind, caring, gentle Benjamin.

Benjamin, who was gone.

I hoisted Peter out of the water.

He dropped onto the bank and coughed, water gushing out of his nose and mouth. I kicked him in the ribs one, two, three times and he dropped, breathing but unconscious.

I walked past my stone-faced teammates. "We're wasting time. Reid, help me get your brother."

If any of them disagreed with my decision to kill Peter, and then to spare him, they didn't show it. I even heard Marco's dark chuckle. He was shaking his head. "You almost killed him. Can you imagine having to explain that to his team?"

"Take a wild guess how much I care."

Reid and I carefully lifted Reuben onto a slab of floating earth. His branding was hideous, bright red and oozing. I could smell the blood from his back.

Reuben's eyelids fluttered. "Gab..rela?"

"Sorry, Rube," Reid said, holding Reuben's hand. "It's just us."

Reuben groaned. "Home."

"We need to take him home to his wife," I said, brushing the hair from his head. "But I have no idea how to get to Baltimore from here. The truck is on the other side of the camp, and none of us can drive."

Reuben opened his eyes and caught my hand in his. "Allies... drove us. Near here."

Ember stood at the head of the slab. "Reuben, I'm going to look into your mind and search for details. I'll guide you into a dream first, though. Is that okay?"

"Yes," he whispered.

Ember rested her fingertips on his face. He sighed in obvious pleasure.

Ember's lips twitched. "Yes... I'm Gabriela. You're at your house. I'm cooking dinner and wearing that white dress you like."

Ember was leading Reuben into a trance-like state to relax his mind so she could sift through his thoughts. She'd once described it as "picking through leaves in fall," and that the trance stopped the wind from blowing the leaves around.

"Oh my, you're in a good mood tonight." Her smile became playful. "Take my hand and take me to our bedroom. Now, close... the door..."

Reuben's breathing slowed and evened out. Ember closed her eyes and exhaled in a long breath. "He's dreaming. I can see his memories now. There's a cluster of houses immediately outside the east wall, near the charity truck entrance. Some of the allies live there. They can drive us back."

"Do you see anything else that might be useful?" I asked.

Ember opened her eyes. "I think we have some friends in Baltimore."

I sheathed my knife. "Then what are we waiting for?"

Reid made another floating disk and guided us above the forest canopy. The metal wall that bordered my childhood home came closer, and then we were over and past it.

I was tempted to take one last look at the place I'd called home for twenty years, but instead I gazed down at Reuben, who was still dreaming of his wife's tender embrace.

I closed my hand around his and stared straight ahead until we landed in the middle of the tiny neighborhood where the non-powered people who served the superheroes, our allies, lived their lives.

15

I rang the doorbell of the nearest house. It was probably between nineteen and twenty hundred, so the occupants would still be awake.

Behind the door, I heard the shuffling of feet, and then it opened to reveal a teenaged girl in frilly green pajamas and slippers.

"You a camp ally?" I was unconcerned with pleasantries. The way I saw it, she worked for me, or had until ten minutes ago. She didn't need to know that we'd defected.

She bit her lip. "Uh, yeah, I guess. My parents are. I'm sixteen, but I can help. You're a superhero, right?"

I pushed my way into the house.

She squeaked but stepped aside to let the five of us inside. The door opened into the living room, which was sparsely furnished, reminding me of the decrepit convent my team and I had lived in until we'd built our new headquarters.

I'd never considered the quality of life the allies had, but if the décor was any indication, it wasn't far up the ladder from the camps.

I looked at her. "Get a first aid kit. Where are your parents?"

"They're out for the night." Her eyes darted toward the door.

I blocked her way. "You're not going anywhere. Get the first aid kit and a computer, if you have one."

She didn't move.

"*Now!*"

She scurried off down the hall.

Reid had lifted Reuben off the floating piece of earth before entering the house, and he'd laid him face-down on the couch with exquisite care.

When the girl rushed back with the things I'd asked for, I grabbed the first aid kit and opened it. "Get a pair of scissors."

She produced a pair of scissors from a drawer and handed them to me.

"Thank you. Get my team some dinner."

I knew I was being abominably rude, but I didn't care. I had no tenderness left in me, and in such times, I'd found that hard orders were more effective than polite requests.

While she bustled in the kitchen, my team hovered around Reuben and me, watching me attend to him.

Ember pulled the back of Reuben's shirt taut, allowing me to snip through the fabric with the dull scissors. Reid inhaled sharply upon seeing his brother's mutilated back, which had only recently stopped bleeding.

Wounds similar to my own scars covered poor Reuben. His scars would be at least as large as mine, if not bigger. He'd received forty lashes for his unsanctioned romance.

"I found some leftovers," the girl said as she exited the kitchen while holding bowls of rice and meat. She placed them on the table and backed away, trembling and not taking her eyes off Reuben's injuries.

"What's your name?" I asked while dabbing at Reuben with antiseptic. My team began to eat.

"Ariel. Ariel Johnson."

I glanced up at her, really taking her in for the first time. She was of only average height, and fair where I was swarthy. But all allies were ultimately from the camps. I was looking at a distant cousin of mine.

"Hello, Ariel Johnson. I'm Jillian Johnson. This is my team. I think we're related."

She bit at her thumbnail. "My dad says his great-grandpa was a superhero."

"And that great-grandpa had a kid with no powers, right?"

"Yeah. We've lived here for a while."

That lined up with what I'd heard. As I understood it, the camp allies were just the unfortunate children of camp people who'd been born without any recognizable power. They were shipped off to ally neighborhoods such as these, and raised by others like them.

"Do you know a boy named Ryan?" Reid asked suddenly.

Ariel shook her head. "Sorry, no. Should I?"

"My youngest brother," Reid murmured. "He was taken to an ally camp when he was four, but I never learned where. He'd be thirteen now."

I unwound a length of bandage and began to wrap it around Reuben's torso, working it under his stomach and back over his injuries several times. Blood seeped through the white gauze, but we'd have to wait until Baltimore to change the bandage.

I shut the first aid kit and flipped open the laptop, and then pulled up the directions between our approximate location and Baltimore, Maryland. It was just under six hundred and fifty miles, about a ten-hour drive.

I turned the laptop toward Ariel. "We need to get to Baltimore. You're going to take us."

Ariel bit her lip. "I can't drive. I only have a learner's permit, and I've never driven that far before."

I narrowed my eyes. "When will your parents be home?"

"Tomorrow. Tonight's their anniversary."

I swore. "Is there anyone around here who can take us?"

Ariel nodded quickly. "Yeah, sort of. My dad buys plane tickets for the camps. He showed me how once."

An airplane? I hadn't even considered flying to Baltimore. I'd never set foot at an airport, much less on an airplane. And didn't airports have tons of security that required IDs, metal detectors, and things like that? We couldn't go to an airport.

"There's too much security at airports. Think of something else."

Ariel typed on the keyboard. "No, no, you don't have to do that. We go to a special government website." She put the laptop down and hurried into an adjacent room.

Though the open door, I could see the blank blue background from the videos the elders sent us. A lectern stood in the corner.

Ariel rushed out with a small notebook in hand. "Just put in some information, and you get these special tickets. You don't have to go through security or anything. They'll kick people off the plane if there aren't enough seats." She navigated to the site. The screen showed an official-looking website with the seal of the Department of Justice.

She entered in a long line of numbers and letters, then paused and glanced up at us. "You guys aren't flagged, right? You're allowed to travel?"

"I doubt we're flagged *yet*, Ariel, but every second we waste here is a second that we could be en route to Baltimore."

She took the hint and went back to entering information. "So what happened to the guy on the couch? Animal attack?"

"He pissed off the wrong people, and those people are going to come after us. If anyone asks you why you bought us tickets, say we threatened your life. We're already in trouble."

"I'm shocked," she muttered, squinting at the screen. "There's a flight that goes from Atlanta to Baltimore. It takes off in three hours. I..." She bit her lip again. "I can drive you to Atlanta. It's only ninety minutes from here."

"Get your keys." For the first time since meeting her I gave Ariel a smile, and she returned it.

I SPENT the entirety of my first flight clutching the arm rests, more sensitive to the changes in altitude and air pressure than anyone else on the plane.

But the *speed*—the speed was unreal. I wanted to feel that acceleration again, but on the ground.

We'd received endless stares from the other passengers as they walked past us in first class to their coach seats, but none dared to speak to us. The pilots poked their heads out of the cockpit before takeoff, no doubt to confirm that they were transporting such important passengers.

At one point during the flight, two of the flight attendants huddled in the galley and debated whether they should offer us free alcoholic beverages. When they correctly guessed that we wouldn't accept them, the discussion turned to what had happened to "that poor man."

As much as I enjoyed the near-supernatural experience of flying, I was relieved when we touched down at Baltimore-Washington International Airport a little before midnight.

Reid helped Reuben through the airport, which was mostly empty because of the late hour. We had no luggage, so we made our way to the entrance.

Ember gleaned Gabriela's phone number from Reuben's mind and dialed it on her phone. "Yes, Mrs. Fischer? Hi. My name is Ember Harris. I work with your brother-in-law Reid." She stopped talking for several seconds. "We're at the airport. Okay, thank you. Hurry." Ember ended the call. "Gabriela's on her way."

While we waited for our ride, I allowed myself a moment's rest on a hard bench. I scanned the airport for threats—armed men, possible supervillains, other superheroes—but found nothing but a janitor and other red-eye travelers.

My mind relaxed a little, so I gazed around the airport, which was my first introduction to the state of Maryland. A large sign on the wall near a baggage cart kiosk displayed a beautiful bird with black and orange plumage, which, the sign explained, was a Baltimore oriole.

I read about the state bird for a few minutes until Reuben moaned in pain and I joined Reid in trying to comfort him. As always, my immediate thought was to call for Benjamin.

Pain gripped my heart. Where was he? What had the elders done?

16

It took half an hour for Gabriela to arrive at the airport, and another half hour to travel back to the Fischer residence, an old brownstone townhouse in a crumbling neighborhood.

Gabriela insisted on helping Reuben inside. Though she'd been quiet through most of the ride, once the door was shut behind us, she gave in to her emotions.

The four of us watched as she laid him on their sagging couch and sobbed over her husband's still form. She touched his lips, his chest, his arms, his hands, pressing kisses into his skin as if she were trying to heal him with the force of her love.

Reuben didn't respond.

Suddenly, she whipped around and glared at us, her bloodshot eyes making her look ghoulish when combined with her ire. "I hate you all."

"I didn't do this to my brother," Reid said, his voice dangerously soft.

Gabriela stood up, her entire body taut. "You watched it happen, didn't you, though?"

I held up a hand to my teammates. "Mrs. Fischer, I understand why you're angry, I really do. But we're not your enemies. The people who did that to your husband are the ones you should hate. We left that world behind when we took Reuben with us."

She narrowed her eyes. "Where's Peter? I can't see that douchebag just letting you take Reuben back here. My husband warned me that he'd probably never be allowed to come back." Her eyes filled with tears, but her glare was icy.

I shrugged. "I nearly drowned him, then I'm pretty sure I broke some of his ribs. I would've killed him, but we needed to go."

Gabriela stared at me, cocking her head to the side. Her face relaxed a little. "Any enemy of Peter St. James is a friend of mine. I'm Gabriela Mendez. Who are you guys?"

"Battlecry, leader of the Saint Catherine, Georgia team. Call me Jillian."

"Firelight, but call me Ember. I'm courting your brother-in-law."

"Marco. Helios."

"And you're Reid," Gabriela finished for Reid.

His curt nod told me that he was still angry that she'd blamed him for Reuben's injuries. I'd devise some way to make peace between them later. Right now I needed to look after my team.

Marco tried and failed to stifle a huge yawn.

"Is there a place where my team can sleep?" I asked. "I'll tell you everything you want to know as soon as that's out of the way."

"You need sleep, too," Reid said. "You've had a horrible day."

"I'll sleep after filling in Gabriela."

"And looking up information on the Westerners, and attending to Reuben, and cleaning your knife, and pacing back and forth like a caged animal for an hour. I know you, Jill."

Aggravation rose in his tone. He was right, though. This was why he was my second-in-command; his common sense provided a necessary counterpoint to my more gung-ho tendencies. "Fine. I'll go to bed right after talking to Gabriela."

"Reid, help me get Reuben up into our room," Gabriela instructed. "Marco, Ember, there's a guest room upstairs on the right. Reid, you can sleep on the couch in the office. Nobody is bunking up with their girlfriend in my house."

Ember and Reid turned bright red.

Gabriela gave me a disgusted little look. "Jillian, you're the leader, right? You can sleep on the floor. Sorry, but I don't have any blankets or pillows for you."

Her tone told me that she didn't hold superhero leaders in high regard. I didn't blame her.

Reid lifted Reuben into his arms and carried him up the stairs. Gabriela rushed to put down old towels on their mattress to soak up the blood. When Reid was satisfied that Reuben was as comfortable as he was going to be, he said his good night and took the blanket and pillow Gabriela offered him.

Gabriela and I were left in her room with Reuben. Gabriela sat next to him on the edge of the bed and held his hand, lifting it and kissing his knuckles every few minutes.

My aching worry for Benjamin crashed down on me and I leaned against the wall and hid my face in my hands. Where was he? Had he been harmed? Would I ever see him again? The uncertainty of his situation gnawed at me.

"Reuben's going to be in agony when he wakes up," Gabriela said. I looked up at her and saw that she was stroking his face. "Do you have any painkillers? Powerful ones?"

"No, but I know people who would." Ember had said we had "friends" in Baltimore. I took that to mean we could trust Reuben's teammates.

She glared at me. "If you mean the allies, there's no way I'm calling them for help. The way I see it, they're part of the system that's responsible for this."

"I meant his teammates. I can call them and never reveal why I need the meds." I pulled out my phone.

She faltered. "He speaks highly of Berenice, and he always said that if I were in trouble and Berenice couldn't help me, I could go to Lark and Topher. I know there's someone named Tiger, too, but he never talks about her."

I didn't know anything about Tiger, either, but I knew and liked Lark, who called herself Valkyrie. She could teleport short distances.

"Topher" might've been Christopher Cannostraci, whose codename was Argentine. Reid had once told me that he could touch any metal and temporarily retain its properties, but still live and move.

But Berenice, my old rival? The pugnacious she-weasel who'd stolen the codename Artemis from me? Either she'd had a personality transplant, or Reuben had seriously bad judgment in friends.

As I ruminated, Reuben moaned in his sleep.

I handed Gabriela my phone. "Call Berenice."

My dislike of Berenice Grantham was not greater than my concern for Reuben's wellbeing.

Gabriela hesitated and dialed a number. I couldn't help but listen in.

"Hi, um, Artemis? This is Gabriela Fischer. Reuben needs help. No! I'm fine, don't worry. But he needs first aid, a lot of it. Painkillers, too. No, Peter isn't with me... I don't know where he is."

Berenice asked her whether or not Gabriela was alone.

Gabriela looked at me, and I shook my head. "No, Battlecry and her team are here. They brought him from the camp."

"Where's their medic?" Berenice demanded. "Why hasn't he helped him?"

Gabriela's eyebrows shot up and she put her hand over the receiver. "You have a medic?" she asked, accusatory.

I massaged my eyelids. "He's not here."

I was too taken aback by Berenice's question to be annoyed by Gabriela's tone. How did Berenice know about Benjamin? My team knew that Benjamin's presence on our team was best left as a quiet fact, lest other superheroes dig too deeply into his past.

However, we all had presence on social media, so her knowledge of Benjamin wasn't exactly suspicious, but it *was* unexpected. How would a superhero like Berenice, who was still in the camp lifestyle and probably not allowed to follow the news or social media, know that a team more than six hundred miles to the south of Baltimore had recently gained a medic?

Gabriela uncovered the phone. "He's not here."

"Give us ten minutes." She hung up.

Gabriela stood. "I'm going to go wait for them by the door. You watch Reuben." She hurried out of the room and down the stairs.

Now that she was gone, I took the chance to take in the bedroom.

Above the bed, next to the Puerto Rican flag, hung a large professional photograph of Reuben and Gabriela on their wedding day. Her shining black hair was swept up into an elegant chignon, and she held onto Reuben, whose grin communicated everything he felt about his wife.

She'd worn a decadent white wedding dress, its large skirt adorned with seed pearls and lace. He'd worn his uniform. The ceremony had not been the traditional superhero hand-binding, but a church affair. The church was nearly identical to the one next door to our headquarters in Saint Catherine.

Bits and pieces of their lives were displayed around the room. The dresser held a framed dollar bill with a small engraved plaque: Gabriela's First Dollar. I understood the name "Gabriela's" to mean the fancy salon she owned. Reuben had told us all about his first meeting with Gabriela there before his trial.

Her parents had died when she was in college, leaving her with a substantial sum of money that she used to open an upscale beauty salon. One night, after hours, a man broke in while she was tidying up and tied her to a chair, then ransacked the place. Before he left he'd decided that Gabriela was too big of a loose end and had aimed his gun at her.

It was pure chance that Reuben was on patrol on that street and saw the broken glass. He killed the criminal with his shadow knife.

Gabriela had offered free beauty treatments for the whole team for the rest of their lives, but Reuben refused. She'd insisted that he at least let her make him dinner, and he was so taken with her determination that he agreed. One dinner led to another, and then they were meeting in secret once a week. Then twice a week. A year went by and Reuben proposed marriage, all the while pretending he was a perfect son of the camps.

They'd nearly killed Reuben for his harmless wife. What would they have done to me for loving Benjamin?

I heard the front door open. Three low voices greeted Gabriela, and then the sound of boots on the stairwell grew louder.

The door swung open.

Berenice, tall, blonde, and ever serious, entered the room with a large medical bag in her hands. Like Reuben and Peter, she wore khaki pants and a snug black thermal shirt with her codename stitched on the breast.

Behind her, Topher hunched his shoulders and bowed his head to fit under the doorway, his brown hair brushing the frame.

Lark peered over Berenice's shoulder and sheathed a telescopic staff. She removed her gloves. The skin of her dark brown hands was scarred and bruised. They all wore masks.

Berenice stared at me. "Battlecry."

"Artemis."

"Where's Imperator?"

"In traction, I hope."

"You beat him up."

"It was fun."

Berenice's lips twitched. She handed the medical bag to Lark, then strode to Reuben's side and kneeled down, taking his hand in hers.

"Hey, Obsidian," she whispered, her voice uncharacteristically kind. "It's me."

To my amazement, Reuben's eyelids cracked open. He cried out.

Lark opened the bag and produced a bottle of liquid painkiller and a hypodermic needle. Both bore the logo of Bell Enterprises.

Lark passed the needle and bottle to Berenice. "Word on the street is that you guys have a medic on staff. Has he examined Obsidian yet?"

I hastily brushed away the tear that spilled over. "No. I need to talk to you guys about why."

Berenice eyed me. "Tears, Battlecry?"

"Shut up. I'm tired." I was hardly going to confess my feelings to the likes of Berenice. She'd probably make fun of me for them.

She didn't reply, instead checking the amount of painkiller he needed on a little chart in the bag. She jabbed the needle into the bottle and removed the required amount, then slid the needle into one of Reuben's veins with expert precision. "There. He won't be in pain when he wakes up."

"Why are you here?" Topher asked in a thick New York accent. "Where's your mask? What's going on?"

"This might be better suited to the kitchen table," Gabriela said. "I want you all to clear out so my husband can sleep in peace."

We trooped out of the bedroom and, after one stricken parting glance, Gabriela shut the door behind us.

All of us settled around the scratched oak table downstairs, though Topher remained standing because he couldn't comfortably fit in his spot.

I rubbed my eyes; my eyelids were heavy. The floor no longer sounded like such an insulting option.

"What's going on, Battlecry?" Berenice demanded. "Where's your freaking medic and why hasn't he healed Obsidian?"

I was too tired to care about her tone. I put my right hand over my heart. "I swear this is all true."

"Good Lord," Lark said. "What happened?"

I launched into the tale of the tribunal and how the elders had dealt with Reuben. Berenice cleared her throat several times when I described his punishments.

When I mentioned the JM-104, Lark leaned forward. "It took away his powers?"

"Yes. Elder St. James said Bell Enterprises makes it for the camps."

She let out a low whistle. "That's heinous."

"You haven't heard the half of it." I explained how the elders coerced me into marrying Matthew. My hand closed around my neck, feeling for the necklace that wasn't there. "And then he gloated about what he'd do to me on our wedding night. Have fun imagining that," I said to Berenice.

Instead of a smirk, she looked offended.

"Matthew Dumont is a psychopath," Lark said, drumming her fingers on the table. "I can tell you some stories from when I lived near his campsite. Marrying you off wasn't the punishment, *he* was. They were trying to put you in your place."

"I feel for you, I really do," Berenice said. "Matthew was always a jackass, and I'm glad you got away. But what does this have to do with your medic not healing Obsidian? He'd better have a good... Battlecry?"

I didn't know what my face looked like, but my expression had stopped her in her tracks.

"What happened?" Her voice was cold.

"Elder St. James ordered Matthew to impersonate Benjamin." When I said his name for the first time, Berenice idly placed her hand over her heart. "As I was questioning him about Benjamin's whereabouts, the Westerners attacked."

Everyone, even Gabriela, stiffened.

"At the end of the night, Benjamin and Isabel St. James were gone, and two bodies that were *not* them were found, conveniently burned beyond recognition. They'd been shot in the head. Reid and I interrogated a Westerner and found out that they were there to 'get' people. Reid found a secret tunnel leading out of the camp. Elder St. James orchestrated this. I can feel it in my bones. We grabbed Reuben and hightailed it out of there when we saw that the bodies had been planted."

"You want us to help you," Topher said. "You're going after them, aren't you?"

Actually, I hadn't considered asking for the Baltimore team's help, but now that he mentioned it, it would be nice to have some more fighters. I had no idea what to expect in the days and weeks to come, but I suspected violence.

"My team won't leave Benjamin and Isabel to whatever fate the Elders dealt them. If you're willing to help, we'll take it."

Berenice raised her hand to her face, hesitated, then took off her mask. Her team did a double take, but said nothing. "Battlecry—"

"Oh, for Heaven's sake, use our real names. We all know who we are."

"Okay... *Jill*, you and I have had our differences. I've never really liked you, but that's fine because you don't really like me. But right now I need you to put aside all that we've ever said and done to each other and answer one question. Whatever you say, I'll believe."

I sat up straight. "Ask it."

"Is your medic Benjamin *Trent*?"

She and I stared at each other for an endless amount of time.

I searched her face for the hidden meaning in her question. She looked the same as ever: light blond hair pulled back into a tight bun, a broad face marked with faint scars, and a tall, muscular body. She was many times stronger than me. If I told the truth, she might challenge me to a fight that I might not win. She could crush my skull like an eggshell.

Then she rolled up her sleeves.

Fresh and faded hand-shaped burns formed a hideous pattern on her skin, signs of Peter's displeasure. I rolled up my sleeve, my own burns now pink and peeling.

Lark copied Berenice and took off her mask, and then Topher did, too.

Lark had changed quite a bit since I'd seen her last; the smooth umber skin of her face was mottled with small burns that I realized, horrified, were probably from Peter's fingertips. Her shiny black hair was pulled into tight braids that were wound into an elaborate bun-like style, but her hairline was odd—part of it had burned away.

Topher's handsome features, which were similar to mine, were marred by a large, shiny burn on his cheek.

"I think we all need to be honest with each other," Berenice said. "The three of us, and Reuben, have kept an ear to the ground about what's been going on in Saint Catherine. We're... We don't... What I'm trying to say is, we're not unsympathetic to you, and we're not going to turn you in.

"But we've dealt with the Trents before. They were based out of Annapolis until recently. I know that one of them is a superfast healer. There can't be two of those in the world. We had a lot of trouble with Benjamin and his creepy dickweed of a brother."

"To be fair, Beau was always the worst by a long shot," Lark pointed out. "He's up there with Matthew Dumont when it comes to being a scumbag. He once had me cornered and started talking about what he's always wanted to do to 'hero girls.' Hitting him in the nuts with my staff felt *so* good." She smiled indulgently.

"The lab," Topher grunted to Lark. "Don't tell me you've forgotten that night."

"Oh, yeah," Lark mumbled. "That's your story, B."

Berenice's face hardened. "We were tipped off that the Trents were going to knock off a chemical lab down by Johns Hopkins. Beau, Benjamin, and Eleanor showed up as planned, and we managed to get them all separated. I cornered Eleanor in a basement room and knocked her unconscious. Benjamin saw me carrying her out."

Berenice lifted up her shirt to reveal her Kevlar vest, pointing at a small dent directly in front of her heart. "He pulled that gun out so fast, I didn't know what had hit me. I woke up hours later in the med bay." She pulled down her shirt. "So is your medic Benjamin Trent or not?"

Was this real? Was this happening? "You...you know Benjamin."

"Yeah, I know Benjamin. I'm beginning to wonder if *you* do."

I flinched.

Berenice chewed on her tongue while she thought. "I'm not so naïve to think that heroes can't become villains and vice versa, but I'm not wasting my time going after someone who tried to kill me, and whose family has caused my team more heartache and pain than any other supervillain family I can name. As far as I'm concerned, he's earned whatever has happened to him."

Her hard stare dared me to disagree.

"Isabel."

"What?"

"Isabel St. James!" I shouted. I banged my fist on the table, making the wood crack. "Marco's little sister! Remember her? Friendly, smart, pretty, can blend in with her surroundings? Any of these ringing a bell, Berenice? She's fifteen years old and our elder did something to her, and now she's gone. Did she earn whatever is happening to her? Should I go upstairs and tell her big brother that?"

Berenice turned pink and pursed her lips. "Don't put words in my mouth—of course I'm not saying that. But do you have an actual *lead*, Jill? Something concrete? The world is a big place."

I sagged in my chair. "No."

All I knew was "west." We were in Baltimore—"west" was basically the rest of the country. And who knew if the Westerners were even based out of the United States? For all I knew, they were from Canada or Mexico.

Lark held up a hand, paused for a minute, and then said, "If you can show me that you have an idea of where they might be, I'll help. But Baltimore is my city, and I won't abandon it without a good reason."

"Oh, come on," Berenice whined. I'd never heard her sound like that. "Don't leave me here."

"Isabel," Lark said, her tone patient but firm.

Berenice sagged as if she'd just been chastised. I couldn't help but be reminded of Ember and me.

"I'm with Lark," Topher said. "I want to see Isabel get safely home. And you know what, I want Benjamin safe, too. It sounds like he's turned his life around." He patted my hand. "I've seen the power of love and how it changes people. No offense, Mrs. Fischer, but Rube was such a jerk before he met you."

Gabriela glowered at Topher. "Did it ever occur to you that he was just unhappy?"

Berenice glared at Lark, then looked at me. "If you can produce a lead, I'll go. For Isabel."

"It's nice to know that you care so much, Berenice."

Marco's tired voice made us all turn in our chairs. Marco, Ember, and Reid stood in the doorway, slouching with exhaustion.

Reid rubbed his face. "We heard Jill yelling and figured we'd have to break up a fight."

"Um, I'm okay," I mumbled. "You can go back to sleep."

The Baltimore three stood up and quickly exchanged introductions.

I looked at Gabriela, who'd been taking it all in for several minutes. "Can I use your computer?"

"My laptop's in the living room. The password is 'obsidian0613.'"

I left the kitchen and logged onto the laptop on the desk, massaging my forehead. There was a growing pressure in the center of my head, a sign that I was going to have a fatigue migraine soon. The brightness from the screen made it flare.

Ember joined me at the desk. "What are you doing?"

"I'm joining all the forums for teams out west. The fans of the western teams are probably more attuned to Super activity out there. I want to see if anyone can tell me about sightings, or weird phenomena, or things like that. Anything we can use to start our search."

"You're exhausted. Go to sleep."

"Give me a few minutes."

"I told you," Reid grumbled.

I hastily joined ten different forums for teams in the major cities, which I figured had the most fans, and thus the greatest chance for a lead. In each forum I started a thread called "Non-superhero Super sightings?"

My threads began with a simple post:

Hi guys! I'm writing a research paper for school about Supers who aren't superheroes. I've heard that there are groups of them out west, but I can't find any good books on them. Has anyone seen or heard about people like this? Message me or reply to the thread. Thanks so much!

I didn't know if there were any books about the Westerners, but if Benjamin—the great lover of all things superhero—had never heard of them, there probably weren't any books to be found. Word of mouth was my best shot.

I logged off the computer and joined the group in the kitchen again. They were eating plates of food Gabriela had fixed for them and talking quietly about Peter.

"He's going to be pissed when he comes back," Berenice said through a mouthful of food, gesturing with her fork.

"Yeah, but that's not exactly a new thing," Lark said calmly. "We'll just act like we didn't see Reuben."

"Oh, come *on*. Jill pounds him and then takes Reuben? Of course he'll come here."

I sat down at the table. "Is Reuben in danger?"

"Yes." All of them answered at once.

I glanced at Gabriela, who was sipping a large glass of wine. "Is his wife in danger?"

Lark tapped her finger on the table. "I couldn't say. Peter has always been rah-rah-rah about protecting civilians, but he has a real short temper, and sometimes people get hurt. I can see him telling himself that Gabriela is a threat, especially if he sees this situation right now as her harboring fugitives."

I swore. "I didn't think of that."

"No, you were thinking about getting Reuben to safety, away from Peter," Berenice said. "I never thanked you for that. I'm very fond of him, and I hate Peter for insisting on the tribunal. We all thought it would be best if Reuben just retired and lived with his wife."

The gentleness of her tone took me off guard.

"Yes, thank you," Gabriela said, extending her hand and curling her fingers around mine. "I didn't give you the warmest welcome. But you and your team brought him home to me, and I'll never be able to repay that."

"Don't you have another teammate?" Reid asked suddenly, looking at Berenice. "Tiger, right? Why isn't she here? Will she pose a threat?"

The three shifted in their seats, clearly uncomfortable. Lark cleared her throat. "Abby, uh, she's at home. She's like our household guard."

"Abby doesn't join us on the streets unless things get really bad," Berenice said.

Reid frowned. "Why? What's her power?"

"She turns into a tiger," Lark said. "And that's the long and short of Abigail Calhoun."

I sensed that there was something going on in the Baltimore team that they were ashamed of. "What do you mean?"

For the first time in my life, I watched Berenice rub her eyes to hide tears. "Abby is just a little different, that's all. She's very nice. She doesn't talk, except the word 'tiger' before she transforms. She spends all her time in her room, and we're okay with that. It's better for her if she doesn't anger Peter."

"What did he do to her?" Ember said, gripping the back of my chair.

Topher's face fell. "She talked a little bit when she arrived to the team. A word here and there. But Peter was convinced she wasn't being respectful enough. So he hot-handed her arm one day to coerce her into talking."

Lark slumped in her chair. "She had a meltdown and transformed. She didn't change back for a week. Ever since that day, she's never said anything other than 'tiger.'"

"We always figured that her problem was simply that she's not really a human in her head. She's a tiger who can't figure out how to live with humans," Berenice said, her green eyes heavy with grief. "Damn, I hate Peter."

I dropped my head onto the table. How many superheroes lived like Abigail and her team, in fear of a leader who'd been taught that he could prey on his subordinates? How many young people endured "hot-handings," or being tossed into walls and choked? When would it stop?

I pushed myself up from the table. "I'm getting some water. You three, go back to your headquarters and wait for Peter to come back. I'll contact you if I get a lead."

The team took a few more minutes to speak with Gabriela and make contingency plans if Peter showed up to her house when they weren't there, while I poured some ice water to wake myself up.

While I sipped and splashed some of it on my face, Topher and Lark went into the living room with Marco and Reid to discuss the Westerner attack. Gabriela went upstairs to check on Reuben, leaving Berenice and Ember with me in the kitchen.

Berenice pulled up her sleeves again and wet a paper towel, pressing the cool water to her burns, not once wincing from the pain I knew she felt. Was she hiding it because I was there?

"Aloe vera helps with burns," I said. "I can go get some from the medical bag upstairs."

"Like I'd use any of the supplies we brought for Reuben. And I know how to deal with a burn. It's a wonder that you do, since you've got that criminal on your team." She glanced at Ember. "Some telepath you are. Jill was actually surprised when I told her about Benjamin's exploits. I'd think it would be a matter of course that you'd listen in on him."

"Benjamin has proven time and time again that he's my friend and brother. I don't invade his privacy," Ember said evenly. "And not that it's any of your business, but I've developed a certain... *distaste* for listening in on people without their permission."

Berenice snorted. "What, are you tired of Jill mooning over her killer boyfriend?"

Ember's eye twitched.

Berenice dropped the wet towel, clutching her head. "Stop! Okay! Okay! I'm sorry! Please, stop!"

Ember merely poured herself a glass of water and watched Berenice hyperventilate on the floor. "Oh, did I make you uncomfortable? My bad. That was just a taste of what Patrick made me listen to day in and day out to intimidate me. Want to see what he imagined when he caught me in his head when he didn't want me there?"

Berenice picked up her towel and threw it away, slamming the lid of the trash can. Her furious expression contained a hint of fear. "No."

"Then stop being a shrew. Maybe Benjamin has a past, but never once has he ever shown the capacity for sadism that Patrick did. Or hell, even Matthew. And not that it makes it totally okay, but you'd just knocked out his sister. If there's one thing I know about Benjamin Trent, it's that it's unwise to threaten people he loves."

"Sadism," I murmured, rolling the word around in my head. "What does that mean?"

Berenice's blank look confirmed that I wasn't the only one who'd never heard of the word.

Ember made a face. "It's when people enjoy causing others pain."

"That sounds like Peter," Berenice said. "I've always gotten the impression that he gets off on the power trip."

Ember rearranged the strap of her knife's sheath, tightening it around her slim thigh. Berenice tore off another paper towel from the roll and continued to dab at her burns.

I watched them, looking between Ember's weapon and Berenice's wounds, putting together something Ember had said. She'd connected Patrick and Matthew's behavior, linking them by their desire to cause pain and suffering. They'd enjoyed it.

Specifically, they'd used threats of sexual violence to terrify and dominate Ember and me. Patrick had attacked Ember when she refused to give in to his demands for information; his attack, while sexual in nature, hadn't been driven by desire. On my end, Matthew *hated* me, and everything he'd said and done after the tribunal had been to drive home how powerless I was.

Powerlessness. It was the true defining attribute of most superheroes.

They were trapped in relationships with leaders who were given complete control over them, leaders who had been told from birth that their word was law, that they could not be disobeyed, that they could use pain and fear to enforce their will. In our thinking, Matthew had been given absolute leadership over me. He'd been no different than Patrick, in that regard.

How many more superheroes had to deal with leaders who thought like Patrick and Matthew? They couldn't all be predators, but the elders had created a perfect environment for sociopaths to grow and thrive unchecked. Were there young, naïve superheroines who believed that they had to submit to their leader's baser whims, just like I'd believed I had to with Matthew?

I leaned against the counter. *Believed.*

I realized that Benjamin's shouted words had taken hold, like so many of his words did. Matthew had no right to hurt me, married or not, just as I had no right to hurt anyone on my team. Patrick had never had a right to hurt us.

Berenice tapped me on the shoulder. "Hey, pay attention."

I jerked back into the moment. "What?"

"We're going now. We'll be by tomorrow. You going to look for leads?"

"Yeah."

Berenice explained how and when to give Reuben more painkiller, then joined her team as they walked out in the night.

Through the closed door I could hear Topher's low voice. "She's not half as bad as you said. I was expecting some fishwife."

"I'm telling you, she's crazy. Back me up, Val."

"Be nice," Lark said softly. "I thought she seemed really, really sad. Truth is, after her brother died, she wasn't the same. I remember..." Lark's voice faded into nothing as they walked down the street.

I sat down at the computer and tried to log on, but my fingers fumbled over the keys.

"You said you'd go to bed after talking to Gabriela," Reid said from the doorway. "Gabriela's gone to bed, and now it's your turn."

I didn't look at him. "I need to be here when the messages come in." Bed could wait. I had to review all the information as it came in. Every second counted.

Ember walked up behind me. I felt her fingertips brush my upper arms.

I sprang out of the chair, a hand on my chest. "Don't," I gasped. "Not without asking. You asked Reuben."

Ember crossed her arms. "You need to go to sleep."

"So you were going to just go into my head and put me down?" I'd begun to shiver. "Why... How can you..."

Hadn't Ember been the one to lecture Berenice about unwanted mind invasions? I understood that sometimes Ember picked up thoughts without trying, but it was another issue if she was going to go into my mind to make me slip into unconsciousness against my will. How could my good friend so easily walk up behind me and... and...

Ember held out her hand to me, her wide eyes apologetic. "Oh. Oh, of course. I'm so sorry. I'll always get your permission first. But please, you need to sleep. You'll get sick if you don't. We need a strong, able leader for the mission ahead. I'll ensure that you have beautiful dreams."

After a moment's hesitation, I took her slim hand in mine.

The world swirled and melted away.

WHEN I WOKE UP, I was bundled in a warm sleeping bag on Gabriela's living room floor, a squishy pillow under my head. The sun streamed in through the windows, high and bright.

I rolled over, trying to cling to the last wispy vestiges of my dream. Benjamin had been there.

The forums!

I bolted out of my makeshift bed and ran to the computer, logging on at record speed. The computer's clock read 11:35, but I couldn't hear anybody moving around in the house. I went to my email, which was clogged with over two hundred notices that people had replied to my posts.

Though I was hungry, thirsty, smelly, and in need of a bathroom, I read each reply. Nearly all of them were various forms of assurances that there were no groups of Supers living out west that weren't superheroes. A few people scolded me for stirring up "those old rumors."

A notification from the Denver team's forums caught my eye.

Unlike the others, the member had sent me a private message. I clicked it open and read member MuirReborn's message.

Hey there,

I just saw your thread. I'm sending this as a message because I don't want tons of people asking questions. Two months ago my roommate and I went on a three-day hike just south of Crazy Woman Creek in Wyoming, off Tipperary Road. We camped out at a lake in the hills. On the first night we were approached by three men in Army surplus-looking clothes. They told us to get off "their" land. When we said we weren't on private land, one of them shot ice at me.

Seriously, ice. It came out of his hand. Joey and I ran for our lives. We

told the Buffalo cops what had happened but they told us that we were
making it up and to stop wasting their time.

Anyway, hope this helps.

I read the paragraph three times before I fully believed what I was
reading.

We were going to Wyoming.

17

"We're going up through Pennsylvania, into the Great Lakes region to Wisconsin, then to South Dakota, and through to Wyoming." As I talked, I traced my finger along the bus trip we'd begin late that night.

I'd spread out an old car map of the United States on Gabriela's kitchen table. My team huddled around me while I explained the plan. Reuben was in a deep sleep upstairs.

They'd returned from the salon an hour after I'd woken up and read the message from MuirReborn. Ember had had her hair bobbed, and once I'd recovered from the shock, I'd been able to admit that she looked great.

What was more, she looked like a civilian, which was essential for my plan once we reached Wyoming. We'd retrace the steps MuirReborn and his roommate had taken, pretending to be civilians to entice the Westerners to come out and confront us.

I placed a different map on the table, a printed map of Wyoming I'd found online. I pointed to a small town east of Buffalo.

"In three days we'll be here, near Tipperary Road. We'll hitch a ride or grab a taxi, whichever is easier, and start our hike here." I dragged my finger to a spot in the road just north of the lake mentioned in the message. "We'll go south, to the lake. That's where the three men approached the two civilians."

Reid reread the copy of the message I'd printed out. "You do realize that this lead is two months old, right?"

"I *know* it's a weak plan, Reid, but it's literally the only one we have."

Reid tapped the Wyoming map, indicating the hills around the lake. "This terrain is similar to my camp in Idaho. In fact, the area itself isn't all that far from where I grew up. I've experienced the types of temperatures we're going to be dealing with. We're going to need *lots* of layered clothes."

"I can help with that," Gabriela said. "But I've been thinking about what your story should be when you meet these people. From what Reuben's told me, they'll probably be trained to spot super-heroes at twenty paces. Looking like a civilian isn't enough." She pointed to Ember's hair. "You're going to need a disarming story. Something that throws them for a loop. Your clothes will have to match that story."

"Like what?" Marco asked. "Maybe, like, we're hunters and our car broke down?"

"We'll need a story that explains why we're there in the dead of winter, with no camping supplies," I said. Gabriela had bought our tickets—I couldn't ask her to buy more for us. "But also a story that makes us totally innocuous."

"Hippies," Gabriela said.

"What?" we all asked.

"Pretend you're hippies, or free spirits, or whatever. I can rustle up some hippie clothes, and you guys can pretend you're on a spirit quest. People go to the butt end of the wilderness all the time for weird stuff like that. You guys can just say you're on a vision quest, looking for a good place to start a commune. Believe me, start talking like that and *nobody* will take you seriously."

"Um, okay," I said, glancing at Reid, who shrugged. "What's a hippie?"

GABRIELA BOUGHT our hippie clothes from the thrift store down the street.

Ember and I wore thick stockings, over which we'd donned long dresses and two skirts. My skirts were far too long, and Ember's were too short, but Gabriela assured us that the inappropriate sizes would be more convincing. We each slipped on several thin, loose shirts, and then two thick sweaters.

Necklaces with odd designs—Gabriela said they were Native American—clinked while we walked, making me miss my J necklace so much I ached to think of it. We traded our combat boots for worn hiking boots.

The multiple layers would keep us warm as well as make it so we didn't have to carry baggage besides beat up backpacks, purchased from the same thrift store from which we'd bought the clothes.

Reid and Marco's clothes were less interesting than Ember's and mine, as men's clothes often are. They wore thick sweaters over old, loose shirts, and battered jeans. They kept their combat boots, which didn't clash as loudly with their outfits as they would with the feminine ones.

Beanies topped all four of our heads. Our backpacks contained scarves, gloves, shawls, basic toiletries, and all the food we could carry.

As we dressed, Gabriela coached us on how to speak "hippie," though I still didn't understand just what a hippie was. I gathered they were some kind of homeless person, possibly in a cult. Benjamin would've known, a fact that for once didn't fill me with sadness, but determination.

When I found him, I'd sit with him and speak about many things, including the "cult" in which I'd grown up. I still didn't accept that we were in a cult, but I no longer felt the prick of anger that I had whenever he'd said so before.

After dinner, I returned to the computer, planning every tiny detail of our trip once we arrived in Buffalo. I checked the projected forecast, the local fauna, the towns, the bodies of water, everything that could affect our time there.

Most of all, I checked the forums, reading the new updates on my threads. There were no other leads.

"We need to leave soon. It's twenty-one hundred. The bus leaves at twenty-three hundred." I fiddled with my watch band. We'd agreed to leave our phones behind because they contained too much identifying information.

We were all in the living room, repacking our backpacks, trying to stuff every possible item in them for our three-day bus trip and the midwinter hiking trip after.

"No, it's nine o'clock, and the bus leaves at eleven o'clock," Gabriela said. "Civilians don't use twenty-four-hour time."

A frantic knock on the door made us freeze.

"It's Berenice!" Ember dashed to open the door.

Berenice hurried inside without a greeting and slammed the door behind her. "Peter's back," she said between pants. "I'm supposed to be on patrol. I don't know for sure that he didn't follow me."

I stood and gripped my knife, which was hidden under a skirt, with a slit I'd designed for easy access. "Has he made any threats against Reuben or Gabriela?"

"Yes, but he thinks they're in Saint Catherine with you guys. Lark told him you'd come and gone. She made it sound like we'd chased you off."

Gabriela gasped, clutching the back of the couch. "What are you going to do? Reuben can't fight right now and I... I... We have to leave. Tonight."

Berenice walked over to Gabriela and took her hand. "The team and I talked last night. We're going to guard your house. If Peter attacks, we'll kill him. Nobody is going to hurt you." She placed her hand over her heart. "You have my word."

I tilted my head to the side. *Huh.* "You're going to fight your leader?"

Berenice glared at me. "Are you saying I'm not allowed—"

"No, I'm saying I'm impressed, and I admire your dedication to

Reuben." I offered my hand to Berenice. "You're alright, Artemis. Even if you stole my codename."

Maybe she was a jerk to me, but Berenice had shown nothing but concern for Reuben, and if there was one thing I valued, it was loyalty. This was a new side to Berenice, and I realized that I hoped to see it again one day. Maybe we'd even be friends.

Berenice stared at my hand, then shook it. She didn't try to break my fingers, but instead gripped it warmly, almost respectfully. "Yeah, I did. You always wanted that name and I figured using it was the best way to screw you over. I guess we both had some growing up to do, huh?" She surveyed my team. "You've got a great crew here."

I grinned. "We have a lead. We're going to Wyoming. Do you still want to come?"

"Had Peter not threatened Reuben and Gabriela, I would. But I'm needed here. I don't know what you guys have got planned..." She paused to look us up and down, smirking. "...but I know you'll pull it off. Like I said, we've all been keeping an eye on the situation in Saint Catherine. I bet there are a lot of leaders that are sleeping less soundly tonight because of you. Atropos was first, and I think Imperator will be next. After that, who knows?"

"It's going to be the elders. They're next."

Berenice chuckled. "Oh, Jill. With you, it's always go big or go home."

She tipped her head toward my team and Gabriela, then slipped out the door.

Two hours later, Gabriela waved goodbye to the four of us as we stepped onto the large bus, unsure if we'd ever see her again.

18

E mber and Marco slept sitting up on a bench in the grimy, dingy bus station. We were deep in Minnesota, two days into our trip west, and we had a three-hour layover between buses.

It was well past two o'clock in the morning. Reid had wandered off to find a vending machine. I stood in front of the large map of the continent, staring at Wyoming and wishing I could teleport.

A thin, weary-eyed woman burst through the glass doors of the small station, followed by a desperate-looking man in overalls and a trucker cap. "Leave me alone, Daryl!"

"Lauren, please! We can work this out!"

"I'm done, Daryl. I'm through. Get out of my life." She saw me watching her. "What are you looking at, you disgusting hippie?"

She stormed outside to argue in semi-privacy, away from the hippie woman who hadn't showered in days. As she screamed at the man, her angry words formed little clouds of breath in the freezing air.

Minutes later, a bus arrived. She flipped him off, then disappeared inside. He stood on the curb and hung his head, then walked away into the darkness.

I turned away and sat down on an empty bench, across the little room from Ember and Marco. Though I was exhausted, I didn't bother trying to sleep. I hadn't slept a full hour since leaving Gabriela's house, and I had a mind to ask Ember to guide me into another beautiful dream.

Reid hurried through the glass doors, two steaming paper cups in his hands and a plastic bag on his arm. "I couldn't find any good vending machines, but there's an all-night convenience store down the street. I got coffee for the two of us and food for everyone."

He handed me a paper cup, and I gave him a grateful smile before I sipped my coffee.

The hot bitterness stirred up a happy memory. I closed my eyes and relived the day I'd met Benjamin, how he'd angled his body toward me on the loveseat in Café Stella, plying me with coffee and pastries.

I associated coffee with him, and all that he entailed: love, affection, gentle caresses, healing, and the hope of a happier life.

"Hey, what's wrong?" Reid asked. "You look down."

I stared at my battered boots. "The last thing I told Benjamin before... well, we argued. I told him to leave. I said I didn't care where he went." Reid set down his cup and put his arms around me while I hid my face in his shirt. "What if that's the last thing I ever got to say to him?"

He gave me a reassuring squeeze. "Don't even think like that. Benjamin loves you, and more importantly, he knows that you love him. We'll find him, and Isabel, and you'll get the chance to apologize. I bet he's already forgotten the argument. I'm sure he just wants to see you." Reid breathed a laugh. "He sure talks about you enough."

"He does?"

"You have no idea. It drives Marco crazy."

"But not you."

Reid let go of me. "I know what it's like to be in love." He gazed lovingly at Ember. "I know what it's like to find the person you want to spend the rest of your life with."

I couldn't help a smile. "You couldn't have done better. And now that we're not part of the camps anymore, you don't have to get permission to marry. You can get married tomorrow, if you want. It would be my honor to bind your hands." I leaned back against the tiled wall. "No more betrothals. Finally. What good were they, anyway?"

I pictured Matthew's face as I'd broken his fingers. An animalistic side of me craved returning to Chattahoochee to finish what I'd started.

"I was betrothed once," Reid murmured, his eyes unfocused. "I liked her."

I sat up. "You were betrothed? When? To who?"

"I was betrothed when I was ten to Stephanie Begay." His voice was soft. "I liked her, and I didn't mind being betrothed."

"What happened?"

"The Westerners happened."

His cup shook so much that coffee sloshed on his hand. He didn't seem to notice.

"They attacked the camp when we were thirteen. I don't know what's been going on in your camp, Jill, but they come to kill people at mine. They got their hands on Stephanie and stabbed her to death." He dropped his head. "I found her body. I was so angry, I hunted down four of the Westerners as they fled and impaled them, just like that kid during the attack a few days ago." Reid looked at me, a fierce glint in his eye. "I've killed more than two dozen Westerners since then."

I chewed the inside of my lip. "Reid, maybe it would be better if *you* lead this mission." I tried to keep the sadness out of my voice. I loved leading, but Reid clearly knew our enemy better. I trusted Reid with my life—stepping aside wouldn't be difficult.

"No."

His firm reply hinted at deeper feelings.

"Why?" I asked, careful to not sound suspicious.

"I don't deserve to lead. I lost that right a long time ago."

"That's rid—"

"It's not," he growled. "You always see the best in us, but I'm not perfect. Stephanie died because I was shirking off on watch that night, giving the Westerners a chance to sneak in. I vowed to be the best superhero I could be after that to make up for it, and where did that get me? I watched Patrick abuse all of you, knowing full well that he was outside of his rights but not wanting to question my leader. And then..."

He covered his eyes with his hand. "And then when I pulled Patrick off of Ember, he actually looked surprised, Jill. He was surprised that I'd defend my teammate against him even as he was trying to rape her." He looked at me. "I do not deserve leadership. You do. You always defended us against him. You always had a backbone. You're the kind of person I want to follow into battle."

A large bus pulled up outside of the bus station just then, its front displaying the destination: Buffalo, WY.

I gave a small smile to Reid and went to wake up Marco and Ember. They yawned and blinked, and we prepared to begin the final leg of our journey.

I settled into my seat next to Marco and tried to sleep, but whenever I drifted off I dreamed of Matthew's skin on mine.

"YOU GUYS TAKE CARE, NOW." The chatty old man in camouflage hunting gear gave us a little wave as we shouldered our backpacks and tightened our scarves and shawls around ourselves.

"We will, Mr. Rose," I said. "Um, *namaste.*" That was a word Gabriela had taught me.

"And thank you for all the local gossip," Marco said, smirking. "That was *fascinating.*"

Ember elbowed him.

Mr. Rose leaned out the window of his truck. "Remember what I said—be careful around here. There's been some funny business in the hills for a while now. A couple years back a man disappeared in the night, left his pregnant wife behind. Of course, she's fine because she ran off with that hotshot sheriff's deputy, but you all need to get inside before sundown."

The man, Mr. Rose, had tried to talk the four of us out of our "vision quest" as he drove us down Tipperary Road. We'd arrived in Buffalo with less than ten dollars, so we couldn't afford a taxi. Hitch-hiking was the only option.

"Be blessed, sir," Reid said.

Mr. Rose shook his head and pulled back onto the road, disappearing over the hill and leaving us at the edge of the vast emptiness of the Wyoming countryside.

The freezing wind whipped my skirts around my legs as I took in the barren expanse ahead of us. Snow dusted the ground in places, crunchy and dry, blowing around like sand. Two miles distant, past Crazy Woman Creek, the tree line began at the foot of the hills.

Nestled somewhere in those hills was the lake for which we were looking, and if we were lucky, the Westerners.

"We'll walk until half an hour before sundown," I said, tightening my thick shawl around my shoulders and tucking the ends of my sleeves into my gloves. "Nobody uses powers unless I say so."

Ember's body trembled with shivers. She'd always been the thinnest of us, and now the wind was cutting through her.

I untied one of my shawls and handed it to her, immediately feeling the effect of the wind. "Let's get moving. It'll keep us warm."

Reid pulled out the map of the area I'd printed out in Gabriela's warm living room and pointed the way toward the lake, struggling to hold the flapping piece of paper still.

We began to walk.

19

I stretched out my aching fingers toward the fire, shivering uncontrollably.

Marco had collected some fallen branches from the nearby forest and ignited a crackling fire, but the heat could not reach my icy core. I huddled in front of the fire and hugged my knees, willing my muscles to still.

We'd considered stopping for the night inside the tree line, which would act as a wind break, but we wanted to be as visible as possible. Every few minutes I considered asking Reid to make a shelter for us, but then reminded myself that no civilian would have the ability to do that.

Reid unwrapped a granola bar and gave it to me. "Eat something. Tomorrow is going to be much harder if you're cold *and* hungry."

I nibbled on the dry granola bar, but it felt like sawdust in my parched mouth. "Thirsty," I mumbled.

Ember pushed a half-empty water bottle toward me. "Here, have the rest of mine."

I shook my head.

The distant whinnying of a horse made me lift my head and peer at one of the far hills. It was so dark, even I struggled to make out distinct shapes at the distance, but I could see that the horse that had whinnied was one of many. An enormous herd of wild horses ambled over a hill about two miles away.

I pointed a shaking finger at the hill. "Ember, can you talk to the horses over there? They might know where humans live around here."

Ember rubbed her forehead and squinted in the direction of the horses. "I... hmm, that's odd. I can't contact them. I guess they're too far away."

I raised an eyebrow. Ember was an extremely powerful telepath. She'd once controlled a dog from across the city, and had later reached out to me from the same distance. Two miles was a small distance for her.

Still, I wasn't in the mood to argue about what she could or couldn't do. I let the subject drop. "We should get to the lake tomorrow."

"What's the plan when we're there?" Reid asked. "How long are we going to wait around for the Westerners? We have supplies for maybe thirty-six hours."

I hugged my knees tighter. "We'll talk about that then."

Eventually the four of us laid down under the blankets we'd brought, clinging to each other for warmth.

A light snow began to fall, stinging our cheeks and lips, and the wind howled in the tops of the trees, mixing with the whinnies of the horses.

REID'S WARNING had been correct—the second day was significantly more difficult to endure than the first.

Though I'd fallen asleep for an hour or two in the night, I'd had no real rest because of the cold. While we stomped out the fire after daybreak, I struggled to keep my eyes open. Every bone and joint in my body ached as though I'd been thrown into a wall—a feeling I knew well—and the sensation in my stomach swung wildly between a hollow ache and mind-consuming hunger.

Around midday, I noticed that though the cold bit at my exposed skin, I was no longer shivering.

I slowly looked around at Reid and Ember and saw that beneath their hippie clothes, they didn't shiver, either. I checked my digital watch, which had a thermometer. It was ten degrees. Marco, however, shivered with such force that I could hear his teeth chatter.

I stumbled many times, my feet fumbling in my too-long skirts as we slipped and tripped up looming hills and down into small valleys with frozen creeks at the bottom. The forest thinned in some places, offering occasional views of the countryside.

The herd of horses remained on the far hill, but I couldn't hear them anymore unless we were downwind of them.

We reached the large lake an hour before sunset.

Marco built another fire on the banks, which we crowded around in silence. As the heat washed over me, I began to shiver again. These shivers weren't like normal trembles, but instead were uncontrollable, violent shaking.

Beneath the fog of cold and hunger, I remembered something I'd learned from a health textbook recently: hypothermia was when a person's core temperature dipped too low. If hypothermia worsened, the sufferer stopped shivering and lost coordination.

"No more hiking. We're not leaving this fire," I said through chattering teeth. "Marco, make it bigger."

Reid clambered to his feet. "I'll help you pick wood that's best for burning."

Marco and Reid retrieved more wood from the tree line and dropped it into the blaze, which flared up. I dropped my head on my knees, drowsy and empty.

We were doomed. Benjamin and Isabel were doomed. We'd freeze to death on the banks of some dumb lake, chasing in vain after a cold trail for people who'd probably been killed days ago.

A lone horse's whinny mixed with the wind, much nearer than normal, possibly under a mile. Ember and Reid sat together, holding each other tight under their blanket. I turned to ask Marco to sit next to me so I could benefit from his natural warmth, but before I could, he slowly stood up.

"There's something moving in the trees."

The rest of us turned our heads and followed where Marco was looking. Sure enough, three shadowy figures approached us. Their general shape and height indicated that they were men.

We all got to our feet. For the first time since yesterday morning, I felt clear-headed. "Everyone, remember the story," I murmured through stiff, bleeding lips. They all made little noises of assent.

The men came into sharper view. They were dressed in dark clothes, perhaps military surplus, and wore black neck gaiters that were pulled up over their noses. Their heavy boots crunched on the gravel lake shore.

Each one wore an M-16 slung on his back. Ember grabbed Reid's hand.

They're Supers, and they want us gone. I don't see Benjamin and Isabel in their surface thoughts.

When they were in talking distance, I worked my face into a gauzy smile and put my hands together as if I were praying. "*Namaste,* brothers."

"You're on our land," the middle one growled. "Leave. Now."

"The earth is our home," I insisted, airy. "We're just poor travelers exploring Mother Earth. My name is Rainbow. These are my spirit siblings, Eagle and his wife, Feather. This is Sunshine," I said, gesturing to Marco. "We're looking for more people like us to begin a community built on—"

"I don't care what you're here for. We said leave." The man on the right took off his glove.

The middle one held up a hand. "Hold it. You're homeless?"

We got 'em. Ember smiled pleasantly at the men. "The earth is our home. But some people might call us homeless, yes. We reject the unnatural idea of property."

The man in the middle pulled down his neck gaiter, revealing a scarred, humorless face. "It's cold out here. How about the four of you come back to our campsite and warm up. We've got food and bedding. I'm sure your... religion will let you eat and sleep in comfort."

I made an awkward bow. "Mother Earth will surely reward your generosity. Eagle, Feather, Sunshine, let's get our things."

They nodded and grabbed our few supplies, shooting glances at me. Ember rubbed her forehead, clearly concentrating deeply.

The middle one is named Bruce. He's the head of the guard. The other two are Charles and Adam. They're going to take us back to their camp for 'sorting,' but I can't get many details. They're worried about something, but... I can't...

She rubbed her forehead again, then looked at me expectantly. We were walking in the woods now, a few paces behind the men. She nudged me and gave me a strange look.

I tapped my temple, the usual sign for her to speak telepathically.

She mouthed something at me. "I am."

Our eyes widened at the same time. Her telepathy had stopped working.

I stifled real fear as the men lead us through the trees. We relied on Ember in situations with unknown variables, and I hadn't planned on going into a Westerner camp without her abilities.

Ahead of us, the muffled sounds of human activity grew more distinct. I heard many voices, all male, all tense and angry. Behind us, not far off, horses continued to whinny.

I saw at once why they'd hidden themselves so well from my senses—the camp was sheltered by the terrain, obscured until we were *in* it. Canvas tents bore woven sticks, twigs, and leaves, disguising them well against the background of the forest.

The only non-tent structure was a metal shipping container that had been retrofitted with a door. A small generator by the shipping container hummed, providing electricity for small lamps.

I counted about two dozen men, but no women or children. Either the camp was non-permanent, military-purposed, or both.

"Get Boone," Bruce told Charles.

Charles ducked into a larger tent on the far side of the camp, then reappeared with an older man who also wore military surplus clothes and an M-16. Unlike the first three, he also had a handgun in a holster at his hip.

Boone wrinkled his nose when he saw my team. "What is this supposed to be?"

"They're homeless," Bruce said. "And barely out of their teens. We offered them food and bedding for the night."

Something in his tone conveyed much more information than what was said, but without Ember's telepathy, I could only guess at his true meaning.

Boone circled us, studying us as one might a car before buying it. "You," he said to Ember. "Are you healthy?"

"Yes. We all are."

"Do any of you have military training? Fighting skills? Anything like that?"

I gasped. "No. We're peaceful people. Fighting is against our beliefs." I pointed to a small bird that was perching on a low branch nearby. "We're like songbirds, harming none, yearning only to bring beauty to the world."

Boone smirked. "That's just fine." He gestured to the shipping container. "My assistants will show you to your lodgings for the night and bring you some food. We'll talk in the morning about how we'll go forward."

Charles and Adam herded us toward the shipping container's wooden door. Once we were inside, Adam turned on a small lantern, and then a space heater that was plugged into a power strip. "We'll get you all some food and bedding in a minute. You're going to stay in here for the night." Charles and Adam left us.

We sat by the space heater, the lantern casting our faces into strange shadows. Adam returned a few minutes later with blankets and thin pillows, while Charles passed out four military-issue MREs. We accepted the items with murmured words of thanks and blessings, and then they shut the door.

A deadbolt locked into place, then another. Finally, I heard a strange whooshing, cracking sound travel around the edge of the doorway.

We'd been sealed in with ice.

"What the hell is going on, Ember?" Marco asked, tearing open his MRE and dumping the little packets on the floor. "Are these the Westerners or a militia or what?"

"I don't know," Ember said, her hands shaking so hard that she couldn't open her MRE. "I... I can't hear anything anymore." She dropped the package and clutched her head. "It's so quiet. God, it's *so* quiet. Is this what it's like to be you guys?"

Reid pulled her close and stroked her short hair. "We'll get to the bottom of this. They probably have someone who can telepathically block people."

"They're going to separate us," Ember said. "I got that much while we were walking here. I have no idea why, but it can't be anything good."

"I didn't see Benjamin or Isabel," Marco said. "We found the Westerners, but not the right ones."

Now that I was finally warm and eating food, my brain was able to work through the events at near-normal speed. "I agree. These aren't the people we want. Tomorrow morning, before dawn, we're going to break out of here. We'll come back at a different time and capture Boone, who's obviously the leader. We'll work out the details about the capture later, though. Right now we'll work on getting out. Marco, do you think you can melt the side of the container?"

"Yeah," he said, running his hand over the thin metal wall. "No problem."

"Then Reid will cause an earthquake. Everyone will fall down, and we'll take advantage of their confusion to get out of here. Once we're clear, we'll fly out."

Reid flexed his fingers. "Can do."

Ember squeezed her head in her hands, grimacing. "There's something here. It's so much worse than Mason's influence on the ants. So much more powerful. If my powers are a fire, then it's a wet blanket. My powers are smothered."

I pushed a pillow toward her. "Let's eat and go to sleep. We're exhausted and not in the best condition to fight. I bet a night's sleep will help you deal with whatever is happening to your telepathy."

We finished our MREs and arranged ourselves around the space heater, pulling the blankets around ourselves. Though the air was warm, the floor was hard and cold as rock, and once again I struggled to sleep. Outside the shipping container, men with unknown plans plotted against us. Benjamin and Isabel were still missing, and for all I knew, we were no closer to finding them.

I listened to my watch beep the passing of each hour.

At zero four, I sat up, listening for noises beyond the walls. I couldn't hear anything except faint snoring and the sounds of the forest.

I shook my team awake. "Get ready," I whispered. "Get your things."

Before Marco could summon his remaining heat reserves, a low rumbling outside the container made us pause. It wasn't Reid's power shifting the earth, but...

"Horses?" I whispered.

The ground shook from the pounding of hundreds, even thousands of hooves, trampling the ground with such ferocity that the container shook. Whinnies and snorts announced the presence of an enormous herd in the camp.

I turned to my teammates. "What the f—"

A bullet tore through the metal, inches from Reid's head.

"Get down!"

We dove to the floor and threw our arms over our heads.

Gunfire lit up the space outside, and then men began to scream for help.

Bullets punched holes in the metal and rained down on us. Shouts of the injured and dying blended together with gunfire, the deafening sound of horses, and crashing trees.

As quickly as they had started, the sounds stopped. I closed my eyes and strained to identify the muffled noises outside.

A man's agonized groan. A gunshot—and no more groaning.

A terrified "No!" before another gunshot silenced the speaker.

Five or six pairs of boots approaching the container, followed by the distinct sound of magazines being loaded into weapons.

A man whispered to the others to leave no survivors.

My muscles coiled, preparing for battle. "Get ready to run. Do not stop for anything. That's an order. Get as far away from here as possible. Marco, I need a flash."

The door crashed open.

A team of armed men flooded in, their weapons drawn.

Marco's light flooded the container and I threw myself at the men. I grabbed the leader's weapon and used it to shove them all to the ground. He grabbed my arm, and we all collapsed into a confused pile.

"Go!" I shouted, still tangled in the mess of limbs and guns. One of the men reached for my hair. I punched him.

My team sprinted out.

Within moments, I'd extricated myself and ran after them. The few seconds I'd spent on the ground with the men meant that I was the last to get to the edge of the camp and into the safety of the trees.

"Get her!" one of the men yelled. I didn't pause to see if anyone was aiming for me.

In my haste, I forgot to lift up my overlong skirts while I ran.

My foot caught one of the hems, and I flew forward into the gravel with a yell, just ten feet from the tree line. I could hear approaching heavy footfalls of a lone shooter, who'd just loaded a magazine into a handgun.

I plunged a hand into the slit in my skirt and grabbed my knife. In a fraction of a second I gauged the distance and direction from the sound alone, then spun around to throw my knife into his neck.

A single gunshot pierced the twilight.

I screamed as my right hand exploded in agony and my knife fell to the ground. He'd shot the knife out of my hand, leaving a gushing, gory hole through my palm.

I cradled my hand to my chest and bowed my head in faux resignation, waiting for him to get close enough for me to attack. I wasn't already dead from a second gunshot, so I expected him to gloat before killing me.

That would prove to be a mistake.

As I expected, the man walked up to me, his boots crunching the gravel. "Any last words, garbage?" His menacing voice was youthful, yet deep.

I glanced up at him to finalize how I'd attack.

His black eyes, visible above his neck gaiter, widened.

I slammed my arm into the side of his knee. He fell with a yell, his gun flying out of his hand with a clatter. I jumped on him and squeezed his windpipe with my left hand, the pain in my right hand all but forgotten.

"Any last words, garbage?" I growled.

Nearby, by the shipping container, five men pulled out their handguns and trained them on me.

Instead of fighting me off, he pulled down his neck gaiter. I let go of his neck with a gasp.

It was Gregory.

20

"Don't shoot! Don't shoot!"

My brother twisted around and held his hands up to the others. They didn't move.

I fell backwards and landed on my injured hand, fiery tendrils racing up my arm. Warm gooeyness seeped from underneath my fingers. I examined my hand and couldn't see through the other side because of the cascade of blood, which poured out of the hole and down my arm, dripping off my sodden clothes onto the gravel.

The stench of horses and gore lingered everywhere. Dead bodies littered the ground, twisted and oozing.

"Get on the ground!" one of the men yelled. All weapons were still trained on me. "Put your hands on your head!"

I looked away from my hand and stared at my brother. "You're dead."

"Get on the ground!"

"Don't shoot! She's my sister!" Gregory tore off his neck gaiter and sloppily wrapped it around the injury. He wiped his eyes with the back of his hand. "It's Jillian!"

The world narrowed to just my brother and me. I hardly felt the pain of my injury as I reached out with my good hand and brushed his stubbly face with the tips of my fingers.

Gregory was alive. Gregory, happy and carefree and sweet, was *alive*. I didn't care how. I didn't care why. I was with my brother again, and everything was going to be okay.

"Gregory..." My bleeding hand fell into my lap. "Where have you been?"

"Long story." He stood up and pulled me to my feet. "*Guys*! For God's sake, lower your weapons! This is my sister!"

I finally focused on the armed men, who slowly lowered their weapons. The pain in my hand flared, causing me to hiss.

Gregory gave me a fearful look and beckoned to one of the men. "Zander, can you cauterize her hand?"

"Where's my team?" I looked back and forth for any sign of the other three, but in the darkened forest, only branches and leaves were visible.

Around us, the rest of the men dispersed and began to collect bodies. One of them, a black-haired man with eyes so light they were visible in the twilight, watched us from a distance.

Zander hurried over to us, his scowl evident above his neck gaiter. "I'm not helping one of *them*."

I scowled. "I'm not a Westerner."

Zander lowered his neck gaiter, and I saw that he wasn't much older than me. "Chick, I'd be more likely to help a Westerner than a—"

Gregory shoved Zander backwards. "I said she's my sister. You'll cauterize her hand or I'm going to—"

"Or what, Johnson?"

"Or you'll have to explain to *me* why you let Jillian bleed to death." The man who'd been watching us strode toward us. He pulled down his neck gaiter, revealing the handsome face of a man in his mid-twenties. His bottom lip was pierced with two close-set rings that I'd recently learned were called 'spider bites'—an odd fashion choice for a warrior.

His icy eyes narrowed at Zander. "Stop the bleeding."

"But she's—"

"That wasn't a request."

Zander glared at me. "Give me your hand. I'd tell you to bite on something, but not showing pain is one of your principles, right?" He sneered when he said "principles."

I held my hand to my chest. "Screw you." I turned to the light-eyed man. "You're the leader of this... this... outfit, aren't you?"

He extended his hand. "Dean Monroe. I really think you should let Zander cauterize your hand."

Instead of shaking his hand, I wrapped the neck gaiter tighter around my wound. "And I think you should learn basic tactics, dumbass. What kind of idiot runs into a building without knowing who's in there?"

Dean raised an eyebrow.

"And you know what, Monroe? I'm in the middle of looking for my *own* medic, and your team's interference has just made that process even more difficult than it already is. So take your faux concern and shove it." I turned back to Zander. "My medic, by the way, is a former supervillain who tried to kill superheroes, and he's a better person than you are. Go to hell."

"You'll bleed out before you find your medic," Dean said. "Do you have a way to stop the bleeding?"

"As a matter of fact, I do." Marco could direct a thin beam of heat into my hand, effectively cauterizing the severed veins. It would be agonizing, but I wouldn't die. "If you'll excuse me, I need to find my team." I'd get them, circle back for Gregory, and then get away from Dean Monroe and his soldiers.

Resisting a powerful urge to flip him off, I stomped away toward the tree line, stopping only to grab my backpack. Beneath my ire, a steady drumbeat pounded: *Gregory is alive, Gregory is alive, Gregory is alive, Gregory is alive.* The thought should've comforted me, inspired me, thrilled me...something.

However, the shock had already worn off, and only dull aggravation remained. Benjamin and Isabel's deaths had been faked; it followed that Gregory's had been, too. What about all the other people who I'd long thought deceased?

"Jillian! Wait up!"

Dean's voice already irked me. I shoved a tree branch aside and kept walking. "Go back to your gang, or whatever you call yourselves." I paused and scanned the trees for any sign of my team.

He caught up with me. "I need to talk to you."

I faced him, hoping he'd shrivel up and die under the intensity of my death glare. "I'm getting my team and leaving. And I'm taking my brother with me."

"You're going to pass out from blood loss before you find them, and Gregory won't go with you." He was slightly breathy from chasing me. "Stay with us and we'll take you back to our medic. Our real medic," he said when I began to argue. "We have a doctor who can help your hand. Zander's heat ray is just for emergencies."

I wrenched open my backpack so hard the zipper broke. "You know what? I'd rather bleed out then go anywhere with you." I grabbed a little pink pouch and pulled out a tampon, then pushed out the cotton. "I can handle a damn bullet wound." I plugged the bullet hole and rewrapped it. "Say something. I dare you."

Dean held up his hands and backed away. "Not saying a thing. But I have to say that Gregory won't go with you. He's one of us."

I crossed my arms. "And what, exactly, are you? Guerrilla fighters? Rogue soldiers? Idiots running around in the woods and almost murdering innocent people? Yeah, it's definitely the third one, because I heard you tell your men to leave no survivors. You *were* going to murder us."

Dean took a deep breath. "We're the Sentinels. Well, some of them. I'll explain everything later when we're back at our camp. Everything, I promise. We received bad information about the occupants of the shipping container, and I swear I'll figure out what went wrong. If you come back with us, we'll get everything sorted out and you can talk to Gregory, see our doc, all that."

I narrowed my eyes. "My team should've doubled back to look for me by now. Where are they?"

Dean rubbed the back of his head. "They're probably with the other half of my team. They ran off in that direction."

My chest constricted. "I'll go back to your camp if my team is alive. If your men killed them, I will scalp you and make your team watch. That's a promise. I tortured and fought my way out of Chattahoochee, and right now I'm in the mood to do it again. Try me, Monroe."

He gave me a dashing grin. "Gregory wasn't lying about you. I've wanted to meet you for a while."

"I... What?" I scrambled for a response. "Why?"

"Because you're Battlecry, the woman who pissed off everyone. We've heard about what you did in Saint Catherine."

"You mean how I beat my leader nearly to death?"

"Something like that."

"Dean! We're done!" Another man's voice called from the clearing.

Dean inclined his head toward them. "We need to bury the corpses, and then we can go."

"Take me to my team first."

Dean sighed, called for his men to wait, and then beckoned for me to follow him. We walked farther into the woods.

After a few minutes, the sound of horses reached my ears, and then male and female voices. One of them was achingly familiar.

I broke into a run. "Ember!"

"Jill?"

I shoved two people aside and halted at the edge of a small clearing edged with horses.

Reid kneeled with his hands on his head. Two men stood behind him with M-16s trained at the back of his skull.

Ember was sitting next to an unconscious Marco, whose head was bleeding. She dabbed at his wound with her sleeve. Behind her, another man stood with an M-16. His bored expression communicated just how much of a threat he thought she was.

"Lower your weapons!" Dean called from behind me.

The men obeyed, and I ran to Reid to offer him a hand as he stood up. He glared at the men who'd been guarding him.

I fell to my knees next to Marco. "Are you guys okay?" His even breaths were comforting, though I didn't like the look of the gash on his scalp. He'd need stitches.

Ember shot an icy look at the men behind Reid. "I couldn't hear the group. We were in the woods and then they were on top of us. Marco got into a tussle with that guy," she said, jabbing her thumb at one of the guards, "and he cold-cocked him. We were given the choice of surrender or a bullet to the head. We'd just surrendered when we heard the gunshot back at the clearing. When you didn't join us, we thought they'd shot you."

I showed her my hand. "They did. Actually, my brother did. *That* was a pleasant surprise."

Ember frowned. "Mason?"

"Gregory."

Ember took a step back. "How much blood did you lose?"

I sighed. "Benjamin and Isabel are alive. Gregory's alive. From this moment on, let's assume that every damned person supposedly killed by the Westerners is alive."

"Except all the people killed at my camp," Reid said, his voice hard.

Before I could respond, Dean wandered over, having finished speaking with other men. "Jillian, we need to get you and your teammate to our medical tent." He nodded toward a beautiful chestnut-brown horse. "Have you ever ridden one?"

My team and I exchanged confused glances. "No. Don't you have trucks or something?"

"Horses are faster and can go to the places Westerners tend to hide." He beckoned two men over. "John Carl and Bobby will put your teammate on a stretcher, though, and take him to the truck nearby. He's going to be fine. But if you won't let Zander cauterize your hand, we need to get you back to camp as quickly as possible."

My hand throbbed, and already my arm felt cooler than it

should've been. I wasn't dizzy yet, but soon I'd begin to feel the effects of blood loss.

Still, I hated to be separated from my team again, especially when we were in the company of weird, unknown people. Though my brother was among them, I didn't know who they were or what they did.

"I'll go with you," I said. "But Ember is coming, too. Reid, guard Marco."

"That's fine. Ember, you'll ride pillion with Graham, my acting SIC. Jillian, you'll be with me."

As Dean went to get the horses, my team huddled around me.

"Who are these people?" Ember hissed. "What is going on?"

I massaged my temples. "I don't know. All I know is that they hate Westerners, and at least some of them have powers."

Reid's eyebrows flew up. "They hate Westerners?"

"Yeah. I'm not sure why, though."

Reid thought for a minute. "I'd say that any enemy of the Westerners is a friend of ours. Maybe we just all got off on the wrong foot."

Ember let out a little gasp. "That was fast. These people are violent. I don't *want* to be friends with them."

A headache was beginning to blossom in the center of my forehead. "We're violent, too. But that's not the point. Back at their camp we'll figure out what's going on and then make a decision. Nobody antagonize them, okay?"

"Fine," Ember muttered.

Reid was watching John Carl and Bobby approach with a canvas stretcher, his expression turning thoughtful. He let go of Ember's hand and walked toward them. I heard him offer his assistance.

Ember balked.

"Let's go." I pulled Ember toward the horses. A pleasant-looking brown-haired man standing near a black horse introduced himself as Graham and politely explained to Ember how to ride behind him. He helped her onto the horse's saddle.

Dean swung himself up onto his chocolate-colored horse and

offered me his hand. "Since you're injured, you sit in front of me so I'll hold onto you. Less risk of falling that way."

Rolling my eyes, I accepted his aid and jumped up onto the horse in front of him. I disliked the experience immediately, from the feeling of the horse's spine under me to the disgusting smell of the animal. Everything about this day was terrible, and I wanted to go home.

Dean drew me to his chest. "Christiana!" he yelled over his shoulder. "We're taking two!"

"No problem, Dean," a woman's voice called from somewhere unseen.

Graham and Ember trotted up to us while we walked through the trees.

"Gregory's told us a lot about you," Graham said, his neck gaiter puffing a little with each word. "And we've heard a little about what's happened in Saint Catherine. You're Battlecry, right?"

Dean pulled up his neck gaiter. "Yep, this is the one we've been hearing about. What were the chances that it was you in the container?"

He lightly kicked the horse with his heels, and the horse trotted a little quicker through the trees, toward the open field in the distance. I was surprised to realize that the pounding of the hooves wasn't unpleasant now that I'd gotten used to it.

When we exited the tree line, the horses broke into a gallop and I almost smiled.

It was as if the veil of anger, shock, and pain that clouded my mind was suddenly removed. The freezing morning air made my eyes water as we raced toward the east, where the sun peeked over the horizon, spreading rays of pink and orange across the clear sky. The horses' hooves echoed around the hillsides, earthy and solid.

I closed my eyes against the wind and let myself enjoy the speed which, while less than that of the airplane's, was incredible. Though I could hear the steady pounding of the horses' hooves against the hardened earth, the smooth motion of the horse made it seem as though we were flying.

Pure power coursed through me. I sat up as much as I could. Dean held me tighter against his warm chest.

We traveled a few miles to the east, then turned south, over a hillside that was unusually green and lush for the season. A campsite was nestled between two hills, filled with large tents made of thick canvas, perhaps thirty in all. A frozen stream wound its way through the camp. More men, and a few women, attended to early morning chores.

Dean slowed the horse to a walk at the edge of camp, jumped off, and carefully lowered me. My thighs ached.

Next to us, Graham helped Ember down. He gave her a genuine smile of appreciation when she took his hand, and I thought I saw spots of pink bloom in her cheeks.

A large growl from my stomach reminded me of the gnawing hunger there. "Graham, please bring Ember to the mess tent, or wherever it is you eat." As they walked by me, I put a hand on Ember's shoulder. "I'll join you as soon as I've seen the doctor."

She nodded and left with Graham, who asked if she liked pancakes. She brightened, and they were still chatting as they disappeared into a large tent.

I was left alone with Dean, and my mood plummeted. "No more delays, Monroe. Where's the doctor?"

Dean pointed down the crude path beaten by boots and trucks. "Just over there." We walked toward a white tent in the distance that had a large red cross painted on the side. "You're going to be fine. I promise."

"Yeah, right, okay." I doubted I'd ever be truly fine again—there was a literal hole in my hand—but maybe the doctor had painkiller.

Dean grinned crookedly at me. "This has been such a wild couple of days. You and Gregory aren't even the first shocking sibling reunion, though I have to say yours was the more exciting. I thought you two were going to kill each other, if we didn't kill you first."

"I'm deeply moved by your concern."

Dean just laughed. "We're here. Oh, I hope you don't mind some coughing and sneezing. The flu is going around the camp." He stepped through the flap of the tent. "Hey, doc! Got a bullet wound for you."

"How many times do I have to tell you? I'm not a doctor."

I shoved Dean aside so hard he fell into a muddy puddle.

Their "doctor" was Benjamin.

BENJAMIN LOCKED EYES WITH ME, then dashed to my side and touched my face. Warm, tingling energy washed through my body, and the pain in my hand dissipated. I felt the plug of cotton pop out of my hand, and when I unwound the neck gaiter I was met with a smooth, uninjured palm.

I wiggled my fingers and smiled. "Good as new, like always."

"I shouldn't have had to heal you." He glowered at Dean. "Did any more of my team get bullet wounds in your care? Should I expect to see brain tissue today?"

"As a matter of fact, yes," Dean said evenly. "One of my men bashed the short one's head in when he tried to fight back. You'll want to take a look at that when he gets here."

"Marco? You hurt Marco?" Benjamin's fists clenched. "And Reid and Ember? Did you maim them, too?"

"They're fine," I said, putting a hand on Benjamin's shoulder. "Don't get upset."

"Yeah, don't get upset, doc," Dean said. He winked at me and ducked out of the flap, then stuck his head back in. "Hey, Jillian, since I know who you are and that you're not a threat, I'll give you the big speech later, after everyone gets back. Bring your team."

I nodded once, and he left.

Benjamin gathered me into a tight embrace, his whole body shuddering. "You're here," he whispered, breathing in deeply, perhaps inhaling my scent as I often did his. "Did they capture you, too? What happened at the tribunal?"

Before I could answer, he kissed me so hungrily that the words faded from my mouth. I squeezed his firm waist, and he combed his fingers through my hair, pulling me even tighter against him.

We broke for air, and he began to pepper my face with little kisses, his desperation coming through. "Oh *God*, I was so worried. I thought they were going to do something horrible to you. I thought I'd never see you again." He took a shaking breath. "Did they hurt you? Did Dean hurt you? If he did, I'll k—"

I cupped Benjamin's cheek and kissed him again, slowly and sweetly. His breathing slowed.

I guided his hand to my heart. "This heart is still beating because I wouldn't have dreamed of dying until I knew you were safe."

"Yeah, doc! Get some!"

Several wolf whistles came from the far end of the tent, where people I hadn't noticed were lying on narrow cots, wrapped in blankets and surrounded by crumpled tissues.

"My patients," he muttered. "Idiots, all of them."

"Is there somewhere we can talk?" I glared at the men who'd whistled. They waggled their eyebrows at me. "Somewhere private?"

"My tent." He looked at the men on the cots. "Don't get out of bed."

Ignoring their indignant replies, Benjamin led me out of the medical tent into the watery morning light. The freezing wind cut through me far more than usual, since my clothes were sodden with blood and horse sweat.

I shivered, and Benjamin pulled me closer to him. "We'll get you warmed up soon." He hadn't stopped touching me since he'd healed me.

His tent was a small canvas affair, big enough for only two cots and a bag. He held the flap back for me and I ducked into it, then gasped.

"Eleanor!"

Eleanor Trent sat on the edge of one of the cots, yawning and pulling on boots. She wore the basic uniform of the Sentinels: dark gray winter gear, combat boots, gloves, and a black neck gaiter.

How many other missing or "dead" people would I meet today?

She gave me a curt nod. "Jillian."

Benjamin sat down across from her on the other cot and gestured for me to sit down. When I had, he threw a thick wool blanket over my shoulders. "El, can you go to the supply tent and get some women's clothes for Jillian, please? Actually, can you get some clothes for the whole team? Two men, two women. They'll be here soon."

Eleanor pulled her hair back in a messy bun. "No problem. But I can't chat after that. Dean wants to talk to me right after everyone gets back."

"He'll be giving us 'the big speech' then," I said, making air quotes around Dean's term.

Eleanor frowned. "He doesn't even know you."

If it were anybody but Eleanor speaking to me, I would've said she sounded a tad hostile. "Apparently my reputation precedes me. I'm the woman who pissed everyone off, remember?"

"Got that right," Eleanor grumbled. "After hearing about the hurricane fiasco and all that business, he did mention that he wanted to meet you."

Benjamin's mouth twisted as if he'd smelled manure. "Of course he did."

Eleanor's jaw hardened. "Get over your issues. Your girlfriend is back, so unclench, will you?"

She shoved the tent flap aside and left.

Benjamin put his arm around my shoulder. "You're really okay? How did you find the Westerners? What happened after I was taken?" His eyes searched my face.

"Back up. You tell me what happened to you, and then I'll tell you my version of events."

Benjamin ran a hand through his hair and hesitated. "After I went to my watch post, I heard someone in the woods nearby. I went to investigate. The last thing I remember was a sharp pain on my neck." He brushed his fingers over a patch of skin near his ear. "I woke up in the back of a van across from someone, a girl, I think. We were zip tied, gagged, and blindfolded. I don't know how long we were in the van, but I'd say about a day. At some point they stopped and took the girl." He held his face in his hands. "I remember her screaming in the gag when they took her. I wish I knew who it was."

"It was Isabel St. James." I put my arm around him.

His face fell. "Marco's little sister? *Damn* them."

"What happened after that?"

He looked away from me. "We drove for a few more hours and the two guys up front stopped and got out for a long time. I took advantage of their absence and got out of the zip tie, then ran as far and fast as I could. I bumped into the Sentinels two days ago, and I've been here ever since."

"You got out of a zip tie? Wow." That wasn't impossible, even for someone of average strength, but I wouldn't have expected Benjamin to know a trick like that.

"Yeah. I don't like to talk about it, but I've picked up a skill or two over the years. It comes with being a Trent."

"What other skills do you know? Have you ever—"

"What happened at the tribunal?" He took my hands in his. "What did they do to you? I've been out of my mind thinking of all the possibilities."

I opened my mouth to tell him the full story, but stopped. Ugly memories of the tribunal washed over me. Could it only have been four days ago? I didn't know whether to tell him about Reuben and segue into the conversation I had with Berenice, or go right into my judgment and how badly they'd cornered me.

And what would I tell him about Matthew and what he'd done to me at the edge of the creek? Would Benjamin understand why I hadn't fought back? Why even though I had super strength, I'd let him touch me?

You're a superhero. The only person stopping you is you.

Benjamin's angry words before the tribunal came back to me, and a cold, slimy feeling twisted in my stomach: shame. I'd let Matthew threaten me. I'd let Matthew molest me. I'd let Matthew kiss me and grope me and make me wish I were dead. I'd let him do all of it because I'd been too loyal to the elders to tell him no.

Even while we were still deep in the teachings, Ember had fought back against Patrick. She'd fought tooth and nail.

I'd stood still.

The shame deepened when I remembered that I'd thrown away my beautiful necklace. I had super strength; I could've said no and thrown Matthew into the creek, instead. Why hadn't I? Because I'd been scared for Reid? Reid was a superhero, too. We all could've fought back. What stopped us?

I couldn't remember. All I could remember was Matthew's hands on my body, and the rage that drove me to cause him as much pain as I could. To drown Peter and relish his struggles for air.

I'd let myself be a victim. What had happened was, fundamentally, my own doing.

I was never going to be a victim again.

I shrugged. "The tribunal didn't go well. They were going to remove me from service and make Reid the leader, but before anything happened the Westerners attacked, and we decided to go after you."

I didn't see a reason to give him the dirty details. He'd just get enraged at me again for not fighting back.

Benjamin looked relieved. "That's it? No punishments?"

I snickered. "Well, Matthew didn't do so well."

"What happened?"

"I caught him impersonating you. When he wouldn't tell me why, I broke his fingers one by one to persuade him to part with the information." I held up my hand and wiggled my fingers. "Oh, and I broke his leg."

Benjamin didn't laugh like I thought he would. Instead, he looked almost troubled. "You tortured him."

"Who cares? It was Matthew. He deserved everything he got."

"So that's two people," Benjamin murmured.

"What do you mean, two people?"

"Two people on which you've deliberately inflicted pain to get revenge. Patrick was the first. I watched you do it."

Irritation flickered in my chest. "Yes, two people. Two *awful* people. Don't worry about it."

Benjamin squeezed my hand. "I just don't want to see you lose yourself to violence. I know that world, Jillian. I know how easy it is to write off an atrocity. It starts with telling yourself that awful people deserve it, and then suddenly you're doing things you said you'd never do."

"Like shooting superheroes?"

The words came out before I could stop them.

There was a pause. Benjamin's face smoothed over, and he let go of my hands, breaking off physical contact with me for the first time since we'd been reunited. "You've been to Baltimore."

"Yeah. We took Reid's brother Reuben there after the tribunal to tend to Reuben's injuries. We met the whole team. Berenice had an interesting story about the Trents. You know her as Artemis."

He blinked quickly, then said, "What was wrong with Reuben?"

"He was hurt. Why are you avoiding the subject?"

Benjamin glared at me. "You've already decided that I'm guilty, haven't you?"

"Guilty of what? I just want to know what you haven't told me about your past."

"You knew before I joined the team that I'm a Trent. I've committed crimes. This isn't new information." Color was rising in his cheeks.

"You never told me that you've had multiple fights with the Baltimore team." I stood up, and he did too. "You never told me that you tried to kill one of us, and yes, that's an important detail. Berenice didn't want to even help us for a while because she still has the dent in her armor from your bullet."

"I don't have to tell you everything," Benjamin growled. "What happened that night at the lab was need-to-know, and you didn't need to know. It hasn't stopped me from serving on your team."

"I need to know if there are superheroes out there that might be carrying a grudge against you. You lied to me, Benjamin. I asked you that night in your bedroom if your run-ins with the DC team and the New York City team were your only altercations, and you said—"

"Why would I have told you the full extent of my rap sheet? Until recently you believed that anybody who...who jaywalks deserves to be lynched. Or have their leg and fingers broken." He crossed his arms. "If pretending to be me earns torture, God knows what you would've done to me before you got your head screwed on straight."

"My head *screwed on straight*?" I shouted. "So there it is again. I'm too uneducated and brainwashed—"

"That is not what I said! Don't put words in my mouth!"

"That *is* what you said! That's what you always say! You said that before the tribunal! And six months ago you said that you'd never met the Baltimore team!"

"I don't have time for this," he spat, storming past me. "I have patients to take care of."

I let out a derisive laugh. "Which ones? The ones you can heal in an instant, or the ones you can't do anything for?"

He froze, his hand on the tent flap. He turned his head partially as if to speak to me, but then he ducked out of the tent.

I was fuming, yet too tired and cold to go after him. I sat down on his cot and pulled the blanket around me again, replaying what had just happened. Something had gone wrong in the last five minutes, but what? The argument had started when I'd brought up Baltimore. Clearly it was a sore spot, though I couldn't begin to guess why. Berenice had been the target, not him.

Eleanor poked her head in the tent. "Is the battle over?" she deadpanned.

I wrinkled my nose. "You heard that?"

"I'm pretty sure people in Montana heard that." She handed me a bundle of clothes, then sat down on the cot opposite me. "But don't worry about it. Tempers are typically pretty high in the days before and after raids, so yelling isn't uncommon. I don't know what you're mad at him about, but give him a break. He doesn't need you harping. He's dealing with a lot right now."

"Like what?" I muttered, peeling off my bloody clothes.

"Well, for one thing, he killed two people the other day. He's been beating himself up for it ever since."

I gasped. "He killed people? When? Why?"

Eleanor's shoulders slumped. "The men in the van. They were at the other Westerner camp near here. I think Benny was scared for his life, and he just attacked when he got the chance. Dean and the guys raided the camp right after. They found Benjamin with the gun in his hand, standing over the two bodies. Dean pointed his weapon at Benny and told him to get on the ground. Benny, being Benny, told Dean to go screw himself. Dean was about to open fire when Graham recognized that Benny was wearing a superhero uniform and suggested that maybe he wasn't a Westerner."

"That is *not* the story he told me. He never mentioned killing anyone."

"He was probably embarrassed. He likes to pretend that he's as pure as the driven snow. Stuff like that probably reminds him that deep down, he's not your Mercury." Eleanor tilted her head toward me with a hard smile. "He's Benjamin Trent, and no amount of playing superhero will ever change that." Her tone had taken on a mocking edge.

This wasn't the Eleanor I knew. In fact, nothing about this woman matched my memory of the sunny, sweet woman for whom I'd developed a slight fondness.

When would the surprises stop?

All my questions about where Eleanor had been these last few months vanished. I wanted to get out of her presence, unwilling to deal with possibly more deception.

I quickly pulled on the clothes she'd given me, finally warm and dry in thermal undergarments, Army surplus pants, and a black fleece. I missed my steel soled boots, but my "hippie" boots worked well enough, especially with my new wool socks.

I made my excuses to Eleanor and left the tent.

The sun was fully up, and the camp was awake and bustling. People walked with purpose from tent to tent, carrying weapons, paperwork, large boxes, and various other items. Men leaned over the outdoor shaving area, which was a flat board laid across two fifty-five gallon drums, and a dingy mirror propped up at ninety degrees. A large tent's flap opened, and I smelled the enticing aroma of pancakes and sausage. The whole scene reminded me of a military installation, but happier.

While I took in the sights, the ground began to shake, and the distant sound of horses' hooves grew louder each second. Hundreds of horses crowned the hill to the north, most without riders. The lead horse, a shimmering black-coated beauty, was ridden by a woman whose strawberry-blonde hair shone in the sunlight as it streamed behind her.

As I watched, the horses with riders broke away from the rest of the herd and trotted to the edge of camp. The other horses continued to gallop over the hill and out of sight.

The woman dismounted first. Her horse had no saddle, but its mane contained several tiny braids and beads. I caught a glimpse of her profile as horses walked around her and my suspicions were confirmed—my cousin Christiana was alive.

I hadn't seen her in more than ten years, and back then she'd been a shaking, spacy, psychotic mess that complained of hearing voices. Now she was vibrant and thriving; she laughed and spoke with a few men that stood around her and teased her gently about her messy, windblown hair.

I couldn't find Gregory, but I recognized a few of the riders as men who'd stormed the shipping container. There was another rumble, mechanical rather than equine, and a military truck rolled up, bumping and tossing on the uneven ground. I recalled from childhood training that the truck was called an LMTV, but I had no idea where the Sentinels had purchased it.

The LMTV came to a stop on the top of the far hill and people began to jump out the back. Two of them unloaded Marco's stretcher.

I ran toward them, relieved to see that he was finally awake.

As I approached, he rolled his head to the side and gave me a weak smile. "You're okay."

I smiled for some reason. "I was shot. Right through the hand."

"Your hand looks fine to me." He sat up with a small groan. "Guys, let me down."

John Carl and Bobby lowered the stretcher, and I helped Marco to his feet. "Benjamin healed my hand. He's here. But that's not the wild part of the story. Ask me who shot me."

"Um, okay. Who shot you?"

I looked Marco square in the eye. "Gregory."

Marco stared at me without blinking for several seconds. "Jill, that's a sick joke."

"Marco, Gregory shot me in the hand this morning."

"Stop saying that!" His voice higher than normal. "Greg's... Greg's dead."

"He's alive, like my cousin Christiana over there. Benjamin's in the medical tent. The elders said they were dead, but they're alive."

"Gregory's dead!"

"No, I'm not."

My brother's deep voice, so unlike my memories of him, came from a nearby tent, where he was watching us. Gregory walked toward us, twisting his neck gaiter in his hands.

Marco stumbled backwards into a horse. "What... what is... what's going on? Jill, I don't understand." His eyes darted back and forth between Gregory and me. "Tell me what's going on."

Gregory walked up to Marco, who was now several inches shorter than him. "Marco, I never died. I was taken by the Westerners. I'm really here. I'm okay." He stared down at our dumbstruck cousin. "I thought I'd never see you again, too."

Marco shoved Gregory away. "What is going on? First Gregory is alive, and then Benjamin just shows up? Where's Isabel? Are there more people that I don't know about?"

Gregory's eyes were heavy with grief. "You have no idea."

21

M y team, sans Benjamin, sat around a collapsible table in a large tent. Benjamin had already received the briefing, as he'd snippily informed me when I'd told him to report to the command tent ten minutes earlier.

Dean stood at the end of the table, while Graham, Eleanor, and a tall man named Ken sat opposite us. Dean unfolded a map of the western US and smoothed it out on the table. The western states were covered in several dozen tiny red dots and a handful of blue dots.

He looked at me. "Before giving this brief, I always ask the newcomers what they think they know about the situation. I've never heard the same answer twice."

I leaned back in my chair. "A week ago I would've told you that the Westerners are people who think they're better than everyone, and they kill the people in the camps because we serve the public, which they find personally offensive."

"And something happened within the last week to make you change your mind."

"There was an attack on Chattahoochee while we were there for a tribunal. Benjamin was taken, along with Marco's sister Isabel. We questioned one of the Westerners and he said they were there to 'get' people. We deduced that bodies had been planted in a fire to make it look like Benjamin and Isabel had been killed."

"Planted bodies?" Dean repeated. "That's new."

"Could be they're getting scared of being found out," Ken said. "This gravy train can only go on for so long. A few bodies would lend credence to their charade."

"There are lots of bodies back at my camp," Reid said, his voice hard. "That wasn't a charade."

Dean nodded, thoughtful. "You're from the Idaho camp, aren't you?"

"Yeah."

"We'll get to that soon enough."

"Anyway," I said, getting back to the story. "We got a lead that took us out here. We tricked the Westerners into taking us to their camp, but once we saw that Benjamin and Isabel weren't there, we planned to break out. Then you showed up."

"And all these people who I thought were dead are actually alive," Marco said, his fists clenched so hard that they were turning white. "And I want answers. I want to know why Gregory shot Jill. I want to know why I saw Hank Theodorakis shaving his face this morning. I want to know why all these people are here but Isabel *isn't!*" He slammed his fists on the table. "What is going on?"

Dean sat down and folded his hands on the table. "Money," he said simply. "This is all about money."

He pulled the map toward him and pointed to a dozen different spots in the west, all marked with small blue dots. "Each of these blue dots either were or are known Westerner compounds. We've attacked six of them and rescued as many captives as we could, but there are still six remaining."

He pointed to a remote location near the Canadian border. "The one here, in Idaho, has about one hundred people." He pointed to another remote area. "This one here, in Montana, is the command center, so to speak. It's where the leaders and their families live. Our intelligence is that two hundred people live there."

"And that's where the people are taken?" I guessed. "To the compounds?"

"Yes. The Westerners have struggled to keep up their populations for a long time, just like you guys. Over the last thirty years, they've resorted to dealing with their devil, the camps, to bring in new people. They buy women for childbearing and men for labor. Or, I should say, they buy girls for childbearing and boys for labor. They seem to prefer them young, probably because they're easier to control but still useful."

His words sounded rehearsed. How often had he given "the big speech?"

"Childbearing," Marco said, horrified. "Oh my God. Isabel is—"

"We're going to rescue your sister," Dean said. "We know where she is. The doc's description of the journey pointed to her being dropped off at this sorting station here." He pointed to a red dot in Montana. "They only stop there if the captive is headed for the leaders' compound."

"Sorting station," Ember said, her voice distant. "Sorting... I remember that the Westerners were going to 'sort' us. What's that mean?"

"It's where they decide who to give you to," Ken said flatly. "The compounds put in requests and the sorting stations try to meet them."

My team made noises of disgust.

"This is what you do, isn't it?" I asked. "You rescue the people the camps sell."

Dean nodded. "I'm the son of Lisette Monroe. My mother was sold more than twenty-five years ago by your camp. I escaped when I was a teenager with some others, and we founded the group that became the Sentinels. We call ourselves that because we're always watching the Westerners, looking for people who need help."

Lisette Monroe had been a friend of my mother's. In a different life, Dean might've been a camp boy. Maybe even a superhero, if his power allowed it. What *was* his power? I envisioned him in one of my team's tunics, a knife in his hand, and enjoyed the image.

I drummed my fingers on the table. "That doesn't answer the main question, though. Why are the elders selling people in the first place? Why would they deal with *our* devils?"

Ken pulled the flaps on the tent closed, casting us into the dim light of the lanterns. Dean reached into his pocket and pulled out a little box, no more than two inches long, an inch wide, and an inch deep.

He opened it and removed a small item from the case, then put it on the table. "Do you know what this is?"

"That's JM-104." I recognized the tiny vial, which was even smaller than the one Elder St. James had used on Reuben.

"You call it JM-104. I call it the heart of the slave trade you never knew about."

DEAN PUT the vial of JM-104 back into its little box. "We've had to question a lot of people to get this information. I can assure you that it's true. Did you ever wonder where we all came from?"

"You mean the Supers?" I asked. "Sure, but nobody knows, right? I think the science is that we're an elegant quirk of nature, like your blue eyes."

Eleanor scowled at me, but Dean breathed a laugh.

"I'm flattered, but that's not quite right. We were made by Bell Enterprises, though not on purpose. BE works very hard to keep that secret. What's not a secret is that before they were an international chemicals and pharmaceuticals manufacturer, they were Bell and Sons. They made miracle elixirs and snake oil back in the days when nobody had to put the ingredients of that kind of stuff on the label. One of their products got popular. Really popular. It was called Dr. Bell's Energizing Concentrate, and it was basically the late 19th century version of an energy drink."

"The slogan," Eleanor said, humorless. "Tell them the slogan."

"'It makes you stronger.' But the product was pulled off the shelves after a few years and never produced again. The Bells never officially explained why, but our... associates have recovered documents that explain exactly why. A highly specific demographic, one tenth of a percent of pregnant women who drank it, reported that their children weren't normal. They had *abilities*."

My teammates gasped.

"They were Supers," I said, breathless.

The timeline, if I was guessing correctly, lined up with what I knew about the first superhero, my great-great-grandmother Christina St. James. She'd gone public with her powers during the First World War to rescue her son from a German prison camp.

"Yeah. And the Bells knew they'd created them. And that's where things get dark."

I leaned toward him. "Tell me."

"The Bells have worked for years to make sure that our people are taken care of, so to speak. The Bell family lobbies for us in Congress, pays for the Super hospital in Virginia, and contracts with every team to provide their medical supplies. I think they feel bad." He smirked. "Their business rivals, Howard Chemical Engineering, on the other hand, were able to create an antidote for our condition sometime in the late 60s. They called it JM-104. Don't ask me what it stands for, because none of us have been able to find out."

"Oh my God," Ember whispered. "We don't need an antidote. There's nothing wrong with us."

"Get to the point," Marco growled. "My sister. Why did they take my sister?"

"I'm getting there. You have to understand the background to understand the current situation. The Bells realized that the Howard antidote would certainly be used against our will at some point, so they straight up stole it. They stole the formula and every known supply of the stuff and told the elders they planned to destroy it. The elders said no."

"Because they had a method to control us," I said, cottoning on.

"Bingo. The Bells had given them the single most useful tool to control the superheroes ever made. But the Bells didn't want it used like that, so they destroyed the formula and told the elders that since the supply was limited, they'd have to pay for it."

Eleanor cut in. "When the Howards started hiring every supervillain in existence to find the stupid stuff, the Bells demanded even more money to defray the costs of the damage. Bombs, break-ins, assassinations... it all gets quite expensive, you see."

"You said this is all about money. Let me figure this out." I held up my hand while I thought.

Money was the one resource that was always scarcest in the camps. I'd been told all my life that we were so poor because we couldn't have jobs. That was certainly true, to an extent. But why couldn't we have jobs? To keep us under the thumbs of the elder, away from anything that could expand our minds. But without jobs, or any other regular income, how would the elders even begin to pay the Bells for storing JM-104?

In the absence of traditional employment, they'd have to sell some*thing* to earn money.

I could think of just one ultra-valuable commodity in the camps.

I swallowed down the bubbling hatred that had just burst back into life. "The elders are selling people for money. Money to buy JM-104 and keep us in line."

"That's... really hard to believe," Reid said slowly. "That this is all a multi-generational conspiracy to control us. We'd never even heard of JM-104 until last week. And it doesn't explain why my camp actually has casualties."

Dean let out a long breath. "That's what I thought, too, when I first heard it. I believed for years that my mom had been snatched by the Westerners simply because their numbers are low and they needed women. But then someone pointed out to me that children of elders never get taken."

He let that sink in.

"And did you ever notice that the missing people are always in their teens? And that none of them are ever on the superhero track? That seems odd, doesn't it? You'd think that eventually somebody would break that mold, but no. It's almost like they're being chosen beforehand," he said acidly. He looked at Reid. "There's one camp that refuses to sell. Guess which one."

Reid made a little choking noise. "Why doesn't Elder Lloyd do something? They killed my fiancée. She was *thirteen*."

Ember patted his hand.

The sarcasm in Dean's eyes softened. "Your camp is too small to stand up against the other five. St. James, Campbell, McClintock, Wiśniewski, and Calhoun have been browbeating Lloyd for years, but he won't budge. They've made it clear that if he rocks the boat, his camp will be destroyed. So, kids in other camps continue to disappear in the middle of the night, and Lloyd can do nothing while his kids die. I can honestly say he's the only elder I don't completely hate."

I couldn't deny the truth now. It all made too much sense. There were other odd circumstances about the disappearances, now that I thought about it. Both Isabel and Gregory had been too young to be on watch when they were taken, and I was certain that if I asked Christiana, she'd tell me that she was on watch, too. Benjamin had been on watch.

Wait a second. "I believe you, but what about Benjamin? He's an active superhero."

Eleanor glared at me, but Dean gave me a look that bordered on pity. "You mean, why would the elders want to sell the young, healthy guy who can *heal* people? The supposedly no-name, no-family guy who is untrained in combat and would be ridiculously easy to overpower and transport? You couldn't have brought a better target into the camp if you'd tried. I bet St. James pissed himself with joy when he found out that he could tell the Westerners that he could sell them a healer. He probably got thousands for him."

"He's not so weak," I shot back. "Or did you forget how you found him?" My eyes flickered to Eleanor.

"Oh yeah. Standing over those two guys, covered in blood and pissed off as hell. I still can't believe that he had the stomach to do that."

My team gasped in unison, and I remembered that they hadn't heard the sordid tale.

"He's a Trent," I said. "He's done a lot of things."

"That's right, you guys used to wear black hats. We'd all be up a creek without you, El. And the doc *is* useful." Dean gave Eleanor a rakish smile and winked at her, causing her to turn vermillion.

Dean's appreciative tone clashed with my internal turmoil. His description of his first encounter with Benjamin reinforced the fact that Benjamin had lied to me about how he'd escaped from the Westerners.

On top of that, my assertion that he'd "done a lot of things" was certainly true, but I didn't know the details. But now that I understood why Benjamin and Beau had been robbing the Bell Enterprises Industrial Complex—and possibly the chemical lab in Baltimore—I wondered how much Benjamin knew about JM-104.

Had he ever been involved in a plot to recover the substance that could take away our powers?

"Excuse me," I said, standing up from the table. "I need some air."

22

"K nock knock," I said, standing outside the tent Benjamin and Eleanor shared.

"Come in," Benjamin's weary voice answered.

I stepped inside and saw him stretched out on his cot, his scratchy wool blanket draped over him. He didn't smile when he saw me, though it might have been because he was exhausted. Deep blue shadows underlined his eyes.

I sat down on Eleanor's cot. "Sleeping in mid-morning? What hours are you working?"

He yawned. "I've been working all hours since I got here. Nobody here has any medical education whatsoever. I convinced Christiana to take a break from her horses to keep an eye on the flu patients. She's already had it, so I don't think she'll get it again this season." He rubbed his eyes. "What's up?"

"I just spoke with Dean. He got us caught up on, well, everything."

Benjamin propped himself up on his arm. "I wasn't surprised when I found out that the elders orchestrated all of this. I never liked them."

"It was a shock to *me*. But what wasn't a shock was the part about supervillains being hired to find the JM-104."

Benjamin sat up. "What about it?" Anger flashed in his eyes. "You think I'm hiding something from you?"

"Excuse me, I *know* you're hiding something from me. I came to ask if you knew anything about JM-104, but if you're going to be a brat, then I'll just leave."

"A brat? You're the one who's walking around assuming the worst about me because of what Artemis—"

"Was she lying, then? Did Berenice look me in the eye and lie about who shot her and why? Because she had no reason to lie, whereas—"

"Oh, get out. Just leave me to get five minutes of peace without having to deal with *you* and the stupid network of superheroes. God, none of you can ever lie to each other, can you? You're all as righteous as the dawn. It's just *integrity* and *honesty* and the usual crap which, from what I've seen, none of you actually believe in."

A heavy silence followed his words. We'd argued before, but he'd never used that tone with me.

"I believe integrity and honesty are important in a relationship," I said, struggling to keep my voice even. "And if you think that's 'crap,' Benjamin—"

"I think everything you believe about being a hero is crap! How can you not? All those principles and traits were fed to you by the same people who shot me in the neck and sold me like chattel! How can you honestly sit there and tell me that any of it is real? Wake *up!*"

I stood up and strode out of the tent without a word.

Patrick had said the same thing to me once, right before killing nearly two hundred people and gloating about trying to rape Ember. He'd declared that none of our teachings were real, ergo, morality didn't exist because we'd been taught morality, too.

I'd always based my morality on what I'd learned from the elders. The principles did exist. The traits did exist. Modeling them was the basis of being a hero.

At least, I thought it was.

I pressed the heels of my hands into my temples. I was so confused. Benjamin wasn't evil, so I didn't believe that he'd arrived at the same conclusion Patrick had. He wasn't about to make it rain heli-copters and try to rape Ember, or anyone else. But he was mocking my deeply-held beliefs *again*. He'd done this before, and it pissed me off every time. He made me feel inadequate and stupid, as if not understanding something he was saying was a crime.

Fatigue settled on me, but I realized that I'd never been assigned a tent, nor did any of my team have a place to rest. Some leader I was.

Dean and Graham were just leaving the leader's tent when I walked up to them. "Dean, can I talk to you?"

His face lit up. "Sure, what's going on?"

"My team needs places to sleep. Who's in charge of that?"

Dean checked his watch. "Actually, we're breaking down the camp in two hours and going back to the main location in Colorado, about six hours south of here. If you want to sleep until then, feel free to use my tent. Reid and Ember mentioned speaking with Christiana about the telepathic block. Marco went to look for Gregory."

"What does Christiana know about the block on Ember's telepathy?"

"I'm guessing a lot, since she's the one causing it." Dean glanced over his shoulder. "Hey, wanna get breakfast with me? They'll stop serving in half an hour."

"Sure." I was hungry, and I didn't want to sleep if my whole team was going to be awake.

I followed him into the steamy mess tent, and was pleased to see that only a handful of people were eating. Dean and I would get a chance to talk without being overheard.

We grabbed plates and piled small pancakes and sausage patties on them, then filled foam cups with orange juice. I sat down opposite him at a corner table.

Dean offered me his hand. "We never really got properly intro-duced. Like I said earlier, I'm Dean Monroe. I really am sorry about the way we met."

I shook his hand. "Jillian Johnson. I'm sorry for calling you a dumbass."

He began to cut up his pancakes. "Consider it forgotten. Actually, when you started ranting at me even though you were injured and surrounded by shooters, it impressed me."

I looked from my plate, startled.

He continued, "I've heard about you for years. After we rescued Gregory and explained what had happened and why, he wouldn't stop insisting that we had to go to Georgia and get you. He was convinced that St. James disliked you and was going to sell you next. We had one hell of a time explaining to him that future superheroes don't get sold."

"He wasn't wrong about Elder," I mumbled. "He made sure I got my ass handed to me at the tribunal."

"That couldn't have been pretty. I bet they made an example out of you."

I nodded, too glum to answer. Benjamin's angry face floated in front of my eyes. I took a bite of my pancake, but the sweet syrup only reminded me of him more. He loved sweet things.

"That's the third time you've sighed," Dean said. "You thinking about the JM-104?"

"No." I stirred my pancake pieces around my plate with my fork. "Just dumb relationship stuff."

Dean stopped eating. "Relationship? With who?"

"Benjamin," I muttered.

Dean cracked up. "You're with the doc? I did *not* see that coming." He drained his orange juice. "So, what's the problem?"

"I don't want to talk about it. And I'm not hungry anymore." I pushed my plate away.

Dean leaned toward me. "I know it's been a rough day for you, with the injury and your brother and everything. If you want to talk, though, I'm here to listen. Gregory is one of my best fighters, and he's told me a lot about you. I feel like I kinda know you already, strange as that sounds."

I looked up at him, surprised by the kind offer. Dean didn't look like the kind of guy who'd be the sensitive, caring type. His lip piercings hinted at an edgier side, and his bright blue eyes lent his features an intensity that few men possessed without anger to fuel it.

But here he was, offering me a chance to vent. I didn't feel like complaining about my stupid relationship problems with anyone on my team, who would be naturally biased toward one of us.

I put down my fork. "Benjamin and I had two fights today."

"Two? Since you got here this morning? That's gotta be some kind of record."

"Yeah." I dropped my head. "And a third right before he was taken. We always end up yelling at each other these days."

"What were the fights about?"

"The one before the tribunal was about..." I trailed off, not sure if I was comfortable divulging to Dean the real cause of our first fight. "...well, he kept saying that my team grew up in a cult."

"You did. You were very much in a cult. I've spent the last ten years deprogramming camp people, including your brother."

"We're a cult?"

Hearing the words from Dean wasn't like hearing them from Benjamin. Dean was so matter-of-fact that it was like a doctor's diagnosis instead of an accusation.

"Yes. So if the first fight was about that, then... well, he's right."

"It wasn't just that. I hate the way he talks about us, though, like we're... we're..."

"Inferior?"

"Yes," I gasped. "How did—"

"You're not the first person to have this problem. We're going back to our main settlement, where there are a lot of people who've never lived in the camps. I see arguments between freed slaves from the cult and the others all the time. People don't understand what it's like to be in a cult and how hard it is to get out. I bet, right now, you believe something weird the cult taught you that you don't even consciously realize you believe."

I remembered his words about marriage and consent. "Benjamin pointed out something like that. I didn't realize that other people believed something else. It never crossed my mind."

"Get ready for a whole lot of that. You're in for a psychologically uncomfortable ride. Although, since you're the first female leader in so long, I assume you're familiar with cognitive dissonance. That's when you believe two opposite things at once, like that women can't be leaders *but* also that you're a perfectly capable leader."

I exhaled heavily. "The other fights weren't about that, though. He used to be a supervillain. I found out in Baltimore that he'd shot a superhero, but he gets really angry whenever I bring up his past. Like, I just want him to be honest with me, you know? I don't think he's ever murdered babies or anything, but I want to know who I'm dating."

Dean thought about that. "I don't know what to tell you other than relationships are built on honesty and trust. If you can't trust him, can you really be with him?"

I was still digesting that when Ken yelled from outside the tent, "Dean! The trucks are here!"

Dean frowned. "They're early." He picked up his plate. "On the road, why don't you join me and Graham in our jeep? It would be nice to have some other company for once. I'll ask Eleanor to sit with Christiana."

I couldn't help but smile. "I'd be happy to."

I left the tent and helped the Sentinels break down their camp, rolling up tents and poles, loading them onto yet more LMTVs.

An hour later, after the last cot had been tucked into the last truck, I found my four teammates and discussed seating arrangements.

"We're okay riding with Christiana and Eleanor," Ember said. "Christiana is really nice, and she thinks that with some practice she can remove the block on my telepathy. And I'm sure Eleanor will warm up soon. I think she's just upset about what happened to Benjamin." She craned her neck to look at Eleanor, who was standing against a jeep, scowling at Dean and Graham. "Well, I hope she warms up soon."

"Just ask for her opinion about the Monty Hall problem," Benjamin said. "Not only will she start talking, she'll think you're a brilliant conversationalist."

"I'm sorry, but I already told Ken we're riding with him," Reid said. "He wants to talk about my past experiences with the Westerners."

Ember wrinkled her nose. "I don't see how I'd be a useful addition to that conversation. And why can't you talk to him about that later? I already told Christiana and Eleanor we'd ride with them."

"I don't see how I'd be useful in *that* conversation."

"How about you both come to the obvious conclusion and ride separately," I said. *Good grief.*

Ember and Reid exchanged unhappy expressions, but nodded.

I turned to Marco. "Where are you riding?"

"With Gregory. He and the guys are taking the cattle car."

"Lucky you," I teased as I eyeballed the cramped, smelly truck they used for transporting the bulk of the Sentinels. I turned to Benjamin, whose crossed arms implied how he felt about being in my presence. "I don't care who you ride with."

"And where are you going to ride?" he asked, his voice flat.

I gave my most nonchalant shrug. "With Dean. He asked me to ride with him."

Benjamin stood up a little straighter. "He did? When? Why?"

"He said my company was desirable while we were eating breakfast together."

I enjoyed the shock on Benjamin's face.

Marco and Reid gave me confused looks, but Ember glared at me.

His shock morphed into petulance. "What else did he say? I'd love to hear what Spider Bites has to say about your company."

"What do you care? You wanted five minutes of peace without having to *deal* with me, right? And the stupid network of superheroes?" I gestured around to the other three. "Well, thanks to 'Spider Bites,' you won't have to *deal* with me for six hours. As for the superheroes and our stupid network, you know where we're all riding. Pick one of the other trucks, if you care so much."

Benjamin looked as though he were about to say something, but without a word he turned and walked away in the direction of Ken's jeep.

Marco shot me a dark look. "What's your problem?"

I waved him away. He stormed off toward the cattle car.

Ember and Reid gave me looks of clear disapproval. "I don't know what just happened, but it wasn't nice of you, Jill," Ember said. "Obviously you two had a falling out, and you just dragged us all into it. That kind of thing should stay private."

"Save it," I snapped. "I'll see you all in Colorado."

As they walked away, I saw a small bird a few feet from me, standing on the top rack of a jeep. It cocked its head to the side as if studying me.

I put my hands on my hips. "What do you want? You mad at me, too?"

It looked at me for another second, then flew away in a rapid fluttering of wings and squeaks. I shook my head. *You're going crazy, Jill.*

I left them and climbed into the passenger seat of the lead jeep. Graham sat in the back next to a small safe, which I assumed contained the JM-104.

Dean was at the wheel. "Buckle up," he said, grinning crookedly. "We've got a long ride ahead of us. Rest if you need—you look like you haven't slept in a week."

"I might just." I sighed, relieved to not have to deal with my team for so long. Beneath the relief lurked concern for Benjamin, whom I hoped had found a comfortable place to spend the drive.

As the convoy rumbled to life, I stared out the window into the distance, a heavy dread seeping into my core. Though we were in the wilderness, the specter of the camps still prowled around the edges of my mind.

They were watching. They were waiting. As soon as I blinked, they'd take aim.

I could not afford to rest.

DEAN ENTERTAINED me with tales of how various members of the Sentinels had come to join the group. Gregory, like most of them, had been rescued during a raid on a compound. He'd been with the Sentinels for three years.

As I listened to Dean tell me about my brother's skill in battle, I felt as though I were listening to stories about a stranger, and not the boy I remembered. I couldn't get the memory of Gregory's hate-filled eyes out of my head, nor the memory of the sound of him loading the gun with which he'd intended to kill me.

I caught a glimpse of Eleanor in the jeep's rearview mirror. She and Ember were deep in conversation while Christiana drove, looking in her own jeep's rearview mirror every few seconds and nodding along. All three of them were smiling, and I took a moment to marvel at Ember's natural ability to ingratiate herself with people.

Eleanor looked as I remembered her from long-ago summer days in Saint Catherine: sunny, amiable, and happy. Ember said something and Eleanor threw her head back and laughed, falling against her seat.

I turned to Dean. "Where'd you find Eleanor? I hope she wasn't taken by the Westerners."

"Now there's a story," Graham said, leaning forward with his elbows on the sides of the front seats.

"Eleanor is our financier," Dean said, looking at the rearview mirror and smiling with affection. "You might find it hard to believe, but until a few years ago, the Sentinels were a fly-by-night operation with few guns, fewer bullets, and no hope of ever truly hurting the Westerners."

Dean's expression turned distant, as if he were recalling a fond memory. "We were in Las Vegas, and I was following a lead on the strip. Halfway through, I figured out that I was the one being followed, so I hid in a casino. That's when I saw Eleanor for the first time. Her hair was up, and she was wearing this glittery red dress cut down to—well, er, anyway, she was killing it at the roulette table."

I could picture the scene. "She must be lethal at casinos." I was able to appreciate what a woman of her intelligence and power could do at games that combined skill and chance. Benjamin had taught me how to play poker in October and explained that while he loved the game, he refused to play with Eleanor, who never lost, or Beau, who cheated.

"She is," Dean agreed. "We made eye contact, and I kid you not, she collected her winnings and walked right up to me and said, 'You're my best chance of being free. I'm going with you.'"

I elbowed Dean. "Tell me you asked for her name at some point in the evening. Or were you too dazzled by her cleavage to ask for that minor detail?"

Dean cleared his throat. "After I'd recovered from the shock, we got to talking and she explained that she was a Super, who her family was, and that she wanted a new life. One thing led to another, and within a few months we'd earned enough money in the casinos to buy everything we own. We were even able to found a permanent settlement, which is where we're going now. It's filled with people who owe her their lives. Well, with one exception. Christiana was an interesting case. She actually found us."

"How?"

"She calls herself a horse telepath, but her power is so beyond that, it's ridiculous. She's essentially the worldwide queen of horses. Whenever she's around them, she becomes the alpha, for lack of a better word. She can speak to them, command them, lead them, anything at all. She says that when she was a kid in the camps, she'd hear horses from nearby farms, but nobody realized what was going on. After she was sold out here, where there are wild horses, she discovered the extent of her powers and used the horses to break out. We ran into her a few years after we escaped."

"She'd live with the horses if she could," Graham added from the backseat. "Sometimes I feel as though the Sentinels are a side gig for her."

"But she can also block Ember's telepathy?"

Dean sighed. "Yeah, that's the downside to having Christiana around. From what I've noticed, people who are telepathic toward one animal can block other psychic talents. There's a few people back at the main settlement who can cast illusions and the like. They hate it when Christiana is around."

Ember had described Christiana's influence as a "wet blanket." Considering how powerful Ember herself was, Christiana must've been a force of untold potency.

"It's a shame about Ember's telepathy, though," Graham said. "We could use it to find the remaining JM-104. We could have her listen in on leads. She could question people."

I grimaced at Graham. "Find it? Why do you want to find it? I don't want to get near it."

"To destroy it," Dean said. "It's the ultimate reason any of this is happening. Take away the JM-104, and the whole trade collapses. Our intelligence is that there's only twelve or so ounces left, but none of us have any idea where it might be. Bell is keeping that secret. It's probably not even written down."

"Do you think Ember would be willing to travel for the search?" Graham asked, rubbing his chin. "Man, she'd be useful. Dean, think of the possibilities."

"Maybe," I said. "Though I know where it is at Chattahoochee."

Isabel had told me that she'd seen Elder St. James hide it in his hut. If there was any more besides the vial he'd used on Reuben, it would be there.

Graham whipped around. "Where? You have a lead?"

"It doesn't matter, because nobody's going there," Dean said, annoyed. "We've talked about this. It's too risky."

Graham glared at the back of Dean's head but dropped the subject.

THE TRUCKS ROLLED through the mountains all afternoon. When the sun was low and light snow had begun to fall, the convoy turned down an unpaved track similar to the one that lead to Chattahoochee camp.

We bounced and jolted for twenty minutes, then the road evened out. Modest, simple homes lined it, tucked in the tall conifers of the Rockies. Children in warm clothes waved at us as we drove by.

"Get ready to unload," Dean said. "We're here."

The road widened and ended in a clearing, which was surrounded by plain, unmarked buildings. Women, children, and a few older men hurried out from houses and the plain buildings, calling to people in the convoy. The cattle car opened, and the twenty occupants jumped out and ran to meet their friends and family.

Gregory hurried to embrace an older couple. I was too shocked to be sad.

Dean put his hand on my shoulder. "This is the main settlement. We call it Liberty."

I gazed around the area, trying to figure out what was missing from the little town.

"It's so unprotected," I said after a few seconds. "Aren't you worried the Westerners will retaliate?"

"No. We don't leave survivors, so nobody follows us. We chose this location because it's nowhere near any of the Westerner settlements. The mountains and trees provide natural cover, and we're so far from civilian towns that nobody will ever accidentally drive here."

"Not even a wall?"

Dean gave my shoulder a playful punch. "Go tell the ex-slaves that you want to wall them in, and then come back and tell me their response." He looked down at his watch. "I've got to go talk to some of the guys. Christiana will help your team get situated while I'm doing that, and then I'd love it if you came to the after-action review."

His blue eyes shone with eagerness.

For a moment I saw Benjamin's face in my mind, the same eagerness in his eyes as he sat across from me on a loveseat at Café Stella and asked me questions about my team. He'd always admired superheroes and longed to touch our world.

Except he had touched our world, many times over, when he'd engaged the Baltimore team in battle.

Ice filled my stomach as I realized that Benjamin hadn't been questioning me about the team out of pure interest when we'd talked in the café last year. He'd been conducting reconnaissance on possible enemies, learning who the team leader was, what our powers were, and our combat statistics.

"I'll be there," I said, searching for a private spot in the trees.

Dean smiled at me before waving down Ken and walking away.

I dashed behind the tree line and took gulping breaths to stop the pain that gripped my heart, but to no avail.

After a few minutes, I found Christiana and asked her to show my team and me our new quarters.

Our house was snug and warm, with two bedrooms, a living area, and a kitchen that had a small supply of shelf-stable food. Two couches faced the small fireplace in the living room, and a coat rack stood next to the door. Our bedrooms contained narrow beds with brightly-patterned homemade quilts on them, donated by the residents of Liberty.

Though the house contained little in the way of decoration, the scratched kitchen table bore a vase of fresh flowers, blooms of vibrant yellow and white that filled the room with pungent fragrance. Where had those come from?

Ember and I shared one room, while the men were crammed in the other. If anyone disliked the arrangements, they hadn't said anything, though I had to admit that my team hadn't said much of anything to me since leaving Wyoming.

Reid and Ember, though civil, gave me furtive glances now and then, while Marco was openly hostile.

Benjamin was ignoring me completely. As soon as we'd been assigned our cabin, he'd disappeared into the infirmary, a white building with a red cross painted over the door.

But that was fine. There were other people who wanted to talk to me.

23

S now swirled around me as I plodded from my team's small house, one of many reserved for newcomers to Liberty, to the large building at the far end of the clearing.

Liberty... the place where liberated people lived. While I walked toward the main building I had to admit that it wasn't so much a town as a haphazard collection of structures.

There were perhaps three dozen total buildings lining the main road, which was also the only road. Most of them were houses, with warm yellow glows lighting their front windows as the inhabitants ate dinner and prepared for bed.

Others, all unmarked, contained hints of their true purposes: one smelled strongly of gun oil and metal, and next to the door stood a clearing barrel—an armory.

Another building had a well-used playground in the back, indicating a school.

A third was the infirmary, where Benjamin had gone.

The fourth, a long and low building next to my destination, hummed from within. There was some kind of electrical equipment running, though I couldn't say what. As I passed, I thought I smelled flowers and other types of vegetation, suggesting a greenhouse or nursery.

The smell of the possible greenhouse attuned my attention to the other odd bits of plant life in Liberty. Though it was midwinter, the surrounding flora was surprisingly lush. The evergreens exploded with life, their emerald needles plump and shining amid the snow that coated their branches.

Each house had a small flower garden in front of it, and underneath the snow I could see hints of purple and pink.

I paused at one garden and brushed snow off a tulip, which had only begun to wilt. Wasn't it four or five months too early for tulips? What kind of fertilizer were they using here?

I reached the main building and opened the door. The gush of warm air was a welcome feeling. The large room inside reminded me of the social hall at the church next to my team's headquarters in Saint Catherine. However, instead of scratched linoleum, this room was carpeted. Twenty Sentinels milled around and chatted quietly. Most of them were young men, some of whom couldn't have been older than seventeen or eighteen.

In the corner Eleanor conversed in hushed tones with Christiana. Eleanor glanced up at me when I entered and gave me a look of deepest loathing.

I didn't care. I didn't really know Eleanor, anyway.

Gregory stood in the corner, leaning against the wall and watching everyone with an unreadable expression.

I walked up to him and he looked away, his face turning red. I reached out to touch his arm, but he flinched.

"We can talk later," I said, turning to go find my own patch of wall to brood against.

"No, wait. I'm just... I'm just still dealing with what happened. It's only been fourteen hours."

Had it just been this morning? I felt like I'd known the Sentinels forever. "Please forgive yourself. Don't beat yourself up."

"You're my sister. I have the best damned eyesight of the entire human race, yet I didn't recognize you when you were running away. So yeah, I'm going to beat myself up."

"It was a good shot, though." I gave him a little smile even though I felt no happiness. "Right through the hand. One in a million shot, right there."

"Oh, please, not if you're me. That was easy." He turned his eyes toward me, and for a fraction of a second I saw a killer who'd taken the time to call me garbage before he'd intended to execute me.

I stared at my brother, the man I'd once considered my best friend. He and I had been inseparable. When I'd climbed over the rail of the bridge, I'd chosen to picture him in my final moments.

But now that the impossible had happened, and he was alive and well, I felt nothing. The name was the same, but the person was off. My Gregory giggled while playing tag. My Gregory hung upside down from trees and blew raspberries at the trainees while they tried to ignore him. My Gregory cried when his pet tent moth died.

This Gregory? This Gregory wore camouflage pants and combat boots. This Gregory shot to wound and torment. This Gregory's eyes were laden with sorrow, and the hatred that was born from it.

"What happened to you, Gregory?" I was afraid to reach out to him.

His flinty eyes narrowed. "Didn't Dean fill you in? Elder sold me to the Westerners to be their slave. I'll let you imagine the dirty details, but I'll give you a hint: think of the most horrible thing you can, then triple it. That was my life for a year."

"Then the Sentinels rescued you?"

His face softened. "Yeah. Then the Sentinels rescued me. They taught me what it means to be a real hero." His eyes tightened again. "You have no idea what that word means, do you?"

A small flame burst to life in my chest.

"I know what it means," I said, my voice dangerously soft. "Don't you dare imply that my teammates are anything other than heroes."

He rolled his eyes. "Your team grew up in the cult. What the hell would they know about heroism?"

I took a step toward him. "Those four are some of the bravest, best superheroes who have ever served the American people, and I will not let anyone, even *you*, say otherwise to *me*."

I didn't know what I'd do to him if he kept talking, but my fingers ached to hit something. He was the nearest target. Simple enough.

Gregory blinked rapidly. "All right, fine. Sorry. God, relax." After one last disgusted look, he walked away, heading toward another group of young men.

I leaned against the wall where he'd been leaning and watched everyone, silent and seething.

A few minutes later, Dean and Graham pushed through the doors. The quiet hum of voices dwindled to nothing and everyone made their way to the middle of the room, forming a half circle around Dean.

He held up a piece of paper. "Before everything, I want you all to know that Andrew's team just raided a compound in North Dakota. Sixteen bodies and intelligence about the compounds!"

The group cheered.

I clapped, unable to summon enthusiasm.

Dean waited for everyone to settle down, then continued, "That's the good news. The bad news is that we're going to move out in forty-eight hours to raid a sorting station in Wyoming again. However, unlike last time, we're going to have some new faces. Sentinels, meet Battlecry, or as she lets me call her, Jillian. I think we've all heard about her." He pulled me by the elbow into the middle of the circle.

Laughter ran through the group. Some of them nodded and smiled encouragingly, but most just scowled.

Dean beamed. "The famous heroes of Saint Catherine, Georgia joined our team today."

I did a double take. "I never agreed to that. I need to talk about it with my team."

After the momentary surprise, anger flickered again. Who the hell did Dean think he was, *telling* me that I was on his team?

"Come on! Fight with us!"

"You're a Sentinel now!"

"The Johnson siblings! Woo!"

"Screw the principles!"

Sentinels yelled at me, some of them explicitly urging me to abandon my vows and declare myself one of them. Their excitement extinguished some of my anger, but I did not share it.

I bit my lip. "All right, all right." I gestured for them to calm down. "I want this to be very clear," I said, raising my voice. "I am my team's leader, but right now I speak only for myself. My team and I aren't affiliated with the camps anymore—" I waited for the booing to stop, then continued, "—so our status as superheroes is in question. It's very possible that we'll be hunted for abandoning the camps."

"Then we'll kill 'em!" someone yelled from the back.

The room erupted into cheering that was simultaneously jubilant and terrifying.

When they'd stopped, I said, "Until we figure out what we're going to do next, I will aid you as a Sentinel. However, I will not pledge my team's allegiance. They have to make that decision for themselves. I don't want to hear that anyone is pressuring them or expecting something from them. Can everyone agree to that?"

The Sentinels nodded and murmured among themselves.

I turned to Dean. "Happy?"

Dean inclined his head. "Very."

I gave him a cold smile. "Oh, by the way, I'm your new second-in-command."

The resultant *ooh*ing of the Sentinels seemed to carry a challenge to Dean.

Dean laughed. "What? No, you're not. Ken, Andrew, and Graham are my executive officers."

"Buddy, I did not risk my life to take over my team, torture and fight my way out of the camps, and then come all the way across the country to stand here and have some pretty boy *tell* me that I'm going to join his team, and then not get to call some of the shots. If you've got a problem with that, I'll show you what I did to the last leader of mine who overstepped his boundaries."

Dean's crooked grin made my stomach flutter. "I think I can find a place for you in the chain. Tomorrow morning, report back here and we'll go over the preliminary plans for the next raid."

I stepped to the edge of the group, where a few men moved aside and patted me on the shoulder. "I believe you were telling us about how we're going to save people?"

The group cheered again. Dean began his briefing. Every few minutes, he'd glance at me with a little smile.

Sometimes I smiled back.

I SHUT the door to my new house a little too loudly.

Though I was sure in my decision to have joined the Sentinels an hour earlier, my hands trembled as I walked into the living room. I hadn't taken my multivitamin in several days and I was sleep-deprived—surely that was the source of my muscle tremors. I just needed to eat and sleep, and then I'd be fine.

That was probably also why I was unable to summon happiness at being a Sentinel, or speaking with my brother. Or anything.

"We need to talk," I said to the empty living room. My team would hear me.

Ember wandered out of the kitchen. "How was the meeting?"

"That's what we need to talk about."

Reid and Marco exited their bedroom. Reid's expression was politely curious, but I could tell from Marco's squint that he was still angry at me for... what? I couldn't even remember, nor did I care.

I took a deep breath. "Bottom line: we've been invited to join the Sentinels. I took the invitation, but said you all would decide on your own."

"So... are you not on our team anymore?" Marco asked. "You're a Sentinel now?"

"No, I'm still on the team."

Marco looked confused. "You're a superhero *and* a Sentinel? At the same time?"

"I'm..." I faltered. What the hell was I now? I gave my head a little shake and changed direction. "As long as we're here, I want to be useful. I want to make the Westerners pay for what they've done to us."

"Yeah, about that," Ember said. "How long are we staying here? The way I see it, we found Benjamin, so our next job is finding Isabel, then going home."

"And the minor detail of Gregory being here doesn't matter to you," Marco said, throwing her a look of disbelief.

"No, that's not what I'm saying," Ember said. "But we're not Sentinels." She gave me a significant look. "We're superheroes."

"I'm in," Reid said.

Ember's eyebrows shot up. "What? Just like that? Shouldn't we talk about this?"

Reid waved her off. "Why? The Westerners have decimated my camp for years. Now I have a chance to serve with a group that's actually doing something about them. I'm able to help the Sentinels, so I have a responsibility to do so."

"No, you have a responsibility to Saint Catherine," Ember hissed. "We need to work out a way to get back home. I don't see what's complicated about this."

"We're out of the camps," Reid replied, his voice cold. "Saint Catherine was our camp assignment. And they have a police force. The captives have nobody but the Sentinels."

"So you're just going to drop everything and join a *militia*? Because of your sense of responsibility? What about your responsibility to your team? To me?"

"He doesn't have a responsibility to you," I cut in. "No more than I do to Benjamin."

Ember whirled around and glared at me. "Stop dragging us into your personal problems, Jill."

"And speaking of Benjamin, when are you going to stop being a jerk to him?" Marco asked. "He's not here right now because he doesn't want to see your face. I can't say I blame him. You've been a butthead since the tribunal."

Heat flooded my cheeks. "Did it ever occur to you that maybe

Benjamin isn't blameless here? I'll stop being a jerk to him when he decides to strap on a pair and tell me the truth about his past."

"He did! He told you he was a criminal and now he's not. He doesn't have to tell the details."

"Yes, he does!"

"Stop arguing, both of you," Ember growled. "You're acting like children."

I turned on her. "Oh, the woman who got mad because Reid didn't ask her for *permission* to avenge his camp is telling me I'm acting like a baby. That's rich."

Ember's nostrils flared. "Marco's right. You have been a jerk since the tribunal. Stop acting like a toddler and just tell us what's on your mind."

"The elders have been selling people into slavery, and you're asking me why I'm angry? How stupid *are* you?"

"Don't talk like that to her!" Marco yelled. "Patrick talked like that to us and you killed him because of it!"

"I killed Patrick because... I didn't kill Patrick, Benjamin's mother did," I shot back. "And I'll talk like that to anyone who actually has to wonder why I'm angry. I just found out that the elders are selling people into slavery. My brother is alive and doesn't want to talk to me. Benjamin lied to me. I can still feel Matthew's slimy hands in my pants when I fall asleep. Any one of those reasons is enough to be pissed off!"

"We're all angry about what the elders did," Marco said through gritted teeth. "Gregory is upset that he shot you. Benjamin doesn't have to tell you everything. And *God*, get over Matthew, already. You got your revenge on him." He snorted. "Is *this* what this is about? He felt you up so now you're pissed off all the time? Grow up."

Ember and Reid gasped.

"Shut up, Marco." My low voice was shaking from the effort of holding myself back. The monstrous rage that had driven me to torture Matthew and kill Peter took solid form again.

I clenched my fist, calculating where Marco was weakest. I settled on his throat; he wouldn't be able to speak for a week. Punching him would feel so good.

Marco took a step toward me. "Why? Am I saying something you don't like? Does the truth hurt?" He shook his head. "No wonder Benjamin doesn't want to talk to you. The second someone says or does something you disapprove of, you turn into a psycho."

"*Shut up!*" I screamed at him, tears flowing down my face. "Just *shut up!*"

"*No!* You're a terrible person, a terrible leader, and a terrible friend! I... I wish Reid *had* taken over the team and you'd stayed with Matthew! We'd all be happier!"

"Marco! Apologize!" Reid's thunderous shout reverberated in my chest.

"How can you *say* that?" I screamed at Marco. "You know what he's like!"

"I know that you have super strength and could kill him with your thumb! Stop acting like he was a threat!"

"If I fought back, they would've whipped Reid nearly to death! I couldn't do anything!"

Even as I said it, the truth of Marco's words sliced me. I had been able to do something, but I'd chosen not to. I could've grabbed my team and ran, but instead I'd submitted to Matthew.

I agreed with Benjamin's claim that Matthew never had any right to touch me without my permission. I understood now that I had grown up in a cult. All the things that I'd believed so firmly, the code of conduct that had made up my life, were false. That's what Patrick and Benjamin had been trying to tell me.

The words hit me like one of Patrick's psychic shoves: none of it was real.

Marco was yelling something at me. "—and you *could've* fought back! I don't want to put up with your emotional problems that you brought on yourself!"

"Marco, stop talking, *now!*" Ember shouted. "You have no idea what you're saying!"

"No, I won't stop talking! Jill is acting like she's some kind of victim! The people the Sentinels rescue are the real victims! I don't want to put up with her crap. Did you know Gregory was beaten every day while he was a slave? Matthew didn't even hurt her! It wasn't like you and Patrick!"

Ember buried her face in Reid's chest.

"Marco, please stop talking," I whispered.

None of it was real.

I'd let myself be a victim all my life even though none of it was real.

I'd dedicated myself to a system that wasn't real.

I'd let Matthew grope and molest me to protect Reid from authority that wasn't real.

Everything—*everything*—the elders taught was crafted for the sole purpose of molding people they could control and corrupt. Nothing about my upbringing was safe to believe. I'd believed their teachings about leadership and let myself be a victim of Patrick. I'd believed their teachings about consent and let myself be a victim of Matthew. I'd believed their teachings about the Westerner attacks. I'd believed their teachings about the dangers of leaving the authority umbrella. I'd believed their teachings about education, and beauty, and deprivation, and a million other things.

All of these beliefs had harmed me in some way.

And all teachings traced back to the twenty-nine principles.

There in the living room, with my team yelling at each other, I closed my eyes and let go of the principles, the core of superheroism, imagining the foundation of my very being as nothing more than leaves in the fall wind, blown away forever.

I expected lightness to replace the crumbling brick of the principles that had held me back, but the emptiness in my chest was not quite what I'd hoped for.

Marco, Ember, and Reid were still arguing, the anger and pain pouring out like pus from a rotting wound. I held my head, straining for the peace that had seemed so close... just out of my grasp. Where was it? Why didn't I feel better?

Marco balled his fists. "Everyone keeps telling me to be quiet, but I'm tired of being quiet!"

"I think everyone should be quiet and let our neighbors sleep."

The shouting ceased.

I looked up to see Benjamin was standing in the doorway, taking in the pathetic scene in the living area: my blank face, Marco's fists, Ember clinging to Reid. Benjamin looked somehow even more exhausted than he had that morning in his tent.

"How much of that did you hear?" I asked dully.

"Enough to know that this isn't a conversation to have after the day we've had." He turned to Marco. "Why are they telling you to be quiet?"

Marco relaxed and crossed his arms. "I pointed out that Jill is being a jerk to everyone because of what Matthew did to her. She needs to freaking get over it and act like a leader."

Benjamin paused, then looked at me with an odd expression, as if he didn't understand what he'd just heard. "What?"

Emotion rushed into the cavity the principles had left behind. I did *not* want Benjamin to know about Matthew, and how I'd let myself be a victim. "We all need to take a break and go to bed. I'm going to my room now. This discussion is over."

Benjamin's face softened and he held out his hand to me. "I'd like to go for a walk with you, if you don't mind."

I shoved his arm aside. Before I entered my room, I turned around. "I'm a Sentinel now," I said to him. "You're invited to join them, too."

I expected him to make a face, but he just looked at his feet.

"Jill's right," Ember said. "We all need to go to bed. I'll see you guys in the morning." She broke away from Reid and walked past me to our bedroom. Reid disappeared into the men's room.

Benjamin's confusion had turned into a hard stare directed at Marco. I shut my door with a loud bang, not caring what Benjamin's problem was.

While I took off my clothes, I heard the front door open and shut, and then low male voices, tense and sharp. Marco and Benjamin were arguing behind the house.

I put my pillow over my head, aching for sleep. "Ember?"

"What?"

"Can you put me in one of those dreams?"

There was a long pause. "My telepathy doesn't work, remember?"

"Oh."

We laid in the dark for a few minutes.

"Jill?"

"Yeah?"

"Marco's wrong."

"What do you mean?"

"I mean... I mean I know how you feel, and if you ever want to talk about it, I'm here to listen."

"Thank you."

There was another silence.

"Ember?"

"Mmm."

"I'm sorry for being a jerk earlier." Maybe the principles didn't exist, but I still felt bad for calling her stupid.

"I forgive you."

After a while her breathing slowed and I was left awake in the dark, curled up into the fetal position and shivering. Marco's furious accusations, Benjamin's gentle face, and Matthew's whispered words and creeping hands swirled in my mind.

Beneath it all simmered five words: *None of it is real.*

I had to destroy everything I thought I knew. No more principles. No more traits. No more virtues and heroics and... and... *purpose.*

No, that wasn't right.

I was a Sentinel now. In a very short amount of time I'd be saving people with them—my heart swelled at the thought—and I'd be fulfilling a new purpose. A better purpose. A purer purpose. No lies. No ridiculous hoops and rules. Just serving others and being part of a team.

That sounds a lot like being a superhero, actually.

I smiled a little. Maybe the transition wouldn't be so hard after all. I had two days to adjust. I'd done more in less time. I'd gone from being on the run to being the leader of my team. I'd commanded a rescue effort and saved people in the hurricane shelter. I'd figured out a plan to rescue Benjamin and Isabel.

I'd left the camps behind only days before, but I'd still clung to my identity as a superhero with all ten fingers. I'd let that identity guide me, push me, pull me, and lead me in my mission to find Benjamin and Isabel. I'd found Benjamin, but Isabel was still in danger—and superheroes did not fight the Westerners. Sentinels did.

I was a Sentinel now. But what did that ultimately mean?

The answer came immediately: it meant I had two days to burn the woman called Battlecry to the ground and leave no trace that she had ever lived.

I set my watch's alarm for forty-eight hours.

24

The next morning found me chopping wood in the backyard.

I'd crawled out of bed at dawn, the sounds of Liberty waking up in the background, and gasped when my feet had touched the cold hardwood floor.

Intent on building a fire in the living room, I'd pulled on my warm Sentinel clothes and grabbed the ax leaning behind the water heater in the kitchen. Twenty minutes later, I'd chopped a small stack of firewood.

With each thud of the ax, Dean's pseudo-command for me to join his militia pounded itself deeper into my brain. For all my rejection of the principles, I just wasn't comfortable serving with *him*. The guy was such a cocky bastard, and cocky bastards were bad leaders.

At least... that's what I'd always thought. *Superheroes* were supposed to be sober, circumspect, and humble. Superhero leaders, even more so. As a superhero leader, I was supposed to rise early and chop wood so my team could eat breakfast in a warm house.

I lowered my ax. If I was making a decision based on what a superhero was supposed to do... was this yet more brainwashing?

Well, no. Of course not. I was being a decent human being.

Building a fire was a common courtesy—a courtesy based on reverence for my team, and general human kindness.

You mean the fourth and seventh principles, hero. Gregory's mental voice whipped at me.

I gave my head a little shake. "Focus," I whispered to myself.

Gregory's sneering mockery was quick to reply. *The tenth principle: attentiveness. I will focus on the tasks assigned to me. Just like a good little minion.*

"The house is cold, kid," I said aloud. "And I was the first to get up. Take off the floaties, it's not that deep."

I could somehow feel my little brother's mental self walk away and sulk.

I checked my watch. As much as I hated to admit it, I *had* made the decision to chop wood based on the principles. I had only thirty-six more hours to get my act together. No more superhero bullcrap. No more principles. No more "I'm a superhero, therefore."

Thirty-six hours to undo twenty years. *Good luck to me.*

The whish-bang of the back door alerted me that I was about to have company. I hoped it was Ember.

"Morning," Marco grunted.

I didn't turn around. "What do you want?" The thud of the ax echoed around the backyard.

"I came to apologize."

I stopped mid-swing and turned around. "For what?"

He wouldn't meet my eyes. "For what I said about Matthew hurting you. I was angry, and that was the cruelest thing I could think of."

"You believe it, though. Or else you wouldn't have said it. Because it can't hurt if it's not true, right?"

He fiddled with the hem of his shirt. "Well, I mean... he didn't try to rape you, like Patrick did with Ember. All he did was touch you, and then you tortured him. It's over now. I really think you should just move on. You're so mad now, all the time. I can see it in how you hold yourself and how you look at people. You've got this rage inside."

His apology, such as it was, didn't soothe the emptiness in my chest. "I *am* angry. But it's not about Matthew. Well, maybe Matthew. It's all those things I mentioned last night."

Marco's large eyes finally found my face. "Be angry, then, but don't be angry at us, Jill. We haven't done anything to you. Take out your anger on people who deserve it, like the Westerners. Talk to Benjamin. He was upset that I was being mean to you last night." He let out a long breath. "Really upset. He can get intense when he wants to."

Before I could ask for details, Reid bounded out the door and down the back steps, pulling on his Sentinel gear. "Hey, Jill, I want to go talk to Dean about joining. Maybe I can help with information about the past attacks in Idaho."

"Sure. Are Ember and Benjamin coming?"

He grimaced. "No. Ember won't have anything to do with them and Benjamin said, and I quote, 'I heal people, not butcher them.' He's at the little medical building now, taking care of the flu patients."

"That sounds like Benjamin," I muttered. I picked up several logs; Marco and Reid retrieved the rest. "Marco, are you coming?"

"Yeah. Believe me, I'm going to be there when they kill the people who have my sister."

"Then let's go. Reid, what's Ember going to do today?"

"Work with Christiana about getting past the telepathic block, I think."

I put the ax back in the corner behind the water heater. As we trooped through the living room, Ember's furious eyes followed Reid. He didn't say anything.

I'd just shut the front door when a distant man's shout caught my attention. A second later, the unmistakable crashing of brush followed.

Damn it. Save someone or help Dean?

As if there was ever any question.

"Go ahead," I said quickly. "I'll catch up."

I sprinted into the woods, rushing past the infirmary.

"Jillian!"

I stopped, steeled myself, then turned around. "Yes?"

Benjamin was on the back porch of the infirmary, eating a roll covered in jam. "What's the hurry?"

"I heard something in the forest. Someone's probably hurt."

Benjamin wolfed down the rest of his breakfast and dusted off his hands. "Sounds like a job for a medic."

Oh boy. But he was right.

A heavy silence hung between us as we slogged through the snow. Fortunately, the uneven, snow-covered terrain demanded our full attention, and we were more concentrated on not breaking our ankles than talking about the night before.

After ten minutes, we were well out of eyeshot and earshot of Liberty. I turned around, my permanent, dull irritation melting away as I took in our surroundings: trees, snow, more trees, bushes, and trees. Who would come out here?

"Hello?" I called. "Does someone need help?"

Benjamin cupped his hands around his mouth. "Make some noise!"

A whisper of noise, vaguely feminine in nature, made me hold up my hand to Benjamin. "Stop shouting."

No... not feminine. Twittery and pleasant, but animal. A bird was chirping loudly in the distance. Perhaps the man had disturbed it? I beckoned for Benjamin to follow me down a steep incline, toward the sound.

A low, male groan came from beneath a mess of logs and snow, and a familiar scent met my nose.

"Graham!" I rushed over to the splintery, icy pile.

Before he could answer, I hoisted the log off of Graham. Cuts and scrapes, and one large gash, lined his face, and he couldn't focus his eyes. "Wha...wha happened, Amy?"

"Sorry, Graham," I murmured, smiling as gently as I could. "There's nobody named Amy here." I helped him sit up while Benjamin touched his face. The injuries faded, and Graham's eyes slowly unglazed.

Benjamin kneeled down casually. "What were you doing out here, so far from Liberty?"

He groaned and shook his head. "Security sweep. I've always gotten on Dean's case about not having any real protection around this place. I'm kind of hung up on it, I know, but we're so—"

"—unprotected," I finished for him, nodding. "Yeah, I spoke to him last night about it, too. We should start a club." I helped him to his feet. "Who's Amy, by the way?"

He paused, his face betraying perfectly equal amounts of hurt and shock. "How do you know that name?"

"You called Jillian 'Amy,'" Benjamin said. "Who is that?"

Graham visibly fought tears. "Amy is my little sister. She's still with the Westerners." He cleared his throat. "She looks a little like you."

Benjamin and I exchanged a sad glance, then helped him out of the gorge. Above us, a pretty little songbird sang a simple tune. Graham scowled at it. "Don't tell anyone, but I wasn't paying attention where I was walking because I was having a Daniel Boone moment and trying out my bird calls."

Benjamin and I laughed until Graham barked at us to shut up.

At the infirmary, Graham hurried ahead of us to the main building. I was about to follow him when Benjamin caught my sleeve. "Hey."

I tried to keep my face expressionless. "What?"

"Did Marco apologize to you?"

"Yes."

The heavy, awkward silence from before descended on us. Finally, Benjamin said, "Well, good. What are you doing now?"

"I'm going to speak to Dean about how we're going to rescue Isabel, and don't you *dare* sniff at me for it, or I'll tell Marco that you objected—"

"No. I'm not going to stop you from saving Isabel," Benjamin said, surprised. "Why would I—"

"Because you've been arguing with me about every other thing I do, so why not this?"

Pain flitted across his face and he stepped closer, his lovely, spicy scent riffling my nose. "I don't know what you think you know about me, but I want Isabel safe. I want them all safe. I want you safe." His voice was rich with emotion. "I'm still your Benjamin."

"Jill! Hurry up!" Marco called from across the street. "We're waiting for you!"

Benjamin and I stood in the snow for a second more, and then I turned and stalked away.

My Benjamin—the term didn't have as much cache now, since I had no idea who Benjamin really was.

DEAN, Graham, and Ken were sitting around a table and studying a terrain map of Wyoming when we entered the main building, which I'd deduced was the tactical center of the Sentinels. Next to the map was a small 3D model of a walled compound.

Dean looked up and grinned when he saw me. "Hey, it's my new SIC. You two are Marco and Reid, right?"

"I think we got off to a bad start yesterday," Reid said, extending his hand. "Let's start again. I'm Reid Fischer, from the Coeur d'Alene camp in Idaho. I'd like to offer my assistance to your cause."

"I want to rescue my sister," Marco said flatly. "When are we raiding the camp that has her?"

"Soon, I promise." Dean beckoned us to join him around the map. "We're planning a raid now on a sorting station in the northwest part of Wyoming, near where we found you guys. We found the doc at a third one near the Montana border."

"What do you need us to do?" I asked.

"We've been discussing your role in the raids. Most of the Sentinels have superpowers, but none of us are trained to your level when it comes to close quarters combat. On the other hand, you don't have any firearms training, do you?"

"No," I admitted. "We worked with tranquilizer guns recently, but I've never fired a proper firearm in my life, nor has anyone on my team, to my knowledge."

"Except the doc," Dean pointed out, tapping his chin. "But when I asked him if he wanted to be our combat medic, he told me to shove my weapon in a wildly inappropriate holster."

"Why does he hate you so much?" Marco asked. "You've known each other for three days."

"He didn't care for our introduction. I thought he was a Westerner and was about to shoot him, but Graham did point out that he was wearing a superhero uniform. He wasn't exactly warm after that, but when I pointed out that his victims had been shot between the eyes and how unusual it was for a superhero to be a crack shot, he got angry. Now that I know he's a Trent, I'm not surprised. You're a super-hero—you know what they're like."

"What do you mean?" I asked, leaning toward Dean. "I really don't."

"They've killed a lot of people to get to the JM-104. The only reason I haven't evicted Benjy from the camp is because Eleanor vouched for him, and I trust her completely."

I wanted to talk to him about Eleanor, Benjamin, and all the Trents, but Graham cleared his throat. "We were talking about the raid."

Dean looked sheepish. "Oh, right. You three are going to be a special tactical unit that works alongside the rest of the Sentinels, but in a separate capacity. Jillian, you'll be the leader, of course, and during missions your team reports to you, and only you. You know your team's capabilities better than I do. However, I'd like it if you all started firearms training today. If you perform well, I'll see that you're issued weapons for the mission."

I tried to hide my surprise, but my excitement still came through. "Really? A firearm?"

"Yeah," he said, amused. "Westerners have superpowers, too. It's best if you don't get too close to them. In fact... tell you what—I'll set up a class where you can teach the guys some basic hand-to-hand later, like a training swap. I know two days isn't a lot of time, but I want to get the guys trained as fast as possible."

"Can I go to the range with Gregory?" Marco asked, his hard exterior melting away at the prospect of spending time with my brother. "He's your best sniper, right?"

"Sure is. I'll arrange that right after we're done."

"I'd like to talk about how my powers can best be used during raids," Reid said to Ken. "We never got around to that during the ride here."

Ken nodded and gestured for Reid to sit down across from him.

Dean wrapped up the meeting and Reid sat down with Ken, and they were quickly absorbed in conversation about various terrains, tactics, and past fights with the Westerners. Marco hurried off to find Gregory.

While Dean collected papers and maps, Graham beckoned me to join him in the corner. "I'll make this quick," he said, his voice hushed. "I'm going to approach Dean about sneaking into Chatta-hoochee to get the JM-104. If he says yes, will you join us?"

I glanced at Dean. He was reviewing a piece of paper with a thoughtful look. "No. I don't want to go back."

"But you'll tell us where it is, right? We could get in and out in under an hour. Nobody would have to get hurt."

"Graham, I understand that you want to see the end of this, but Dean said no. If he's the Sentinel commander, then his word is final, and I respect that. Besides, if we were caught, God only knows what would happen. They're willing to kill to keep their grip on power."

On top of that, I wasn't even sure if the JM-104 was still in the camp.

Graham frowned but nodded. "Fine." His eyes softened. "On a different note... do you think I have a chance with Ember?"

I couldn't help a surprised laugh. "Oh, gosh, Graham. I'm sorry, but no. She's with Reid, and he's so wound up over the Westerners these days that it would be foolish to start hitting on his girlfriend. Try someone else, for your own safety."

Graham shot Reid an annoyed stare over my shoulder, then looked back at me. "Protective type, huh?"

"You have no idea."

Graham appeared to think for a moment. "How are you and

Benjamin doing? I heard that there's been some adjustment pains since coming here."

My face twisted into a scowl. "Does everyone know about our fights?"

"Um... yeah."

"We're okay," I muttered. "If you hear any Sentinels gossiping about us, tell them we're fine and to mind their own business."

"That's not true, though, is it?"

"Like you said, we're adjusting," I insisted, embarrassed that an almost-stranger knew so much about my personal affairs.

"Don't let him treat you badly. You deserve someone better than that." He checked his watch and startled. "Crap, I gotta go. See you later." He gave me a small smile and hurried out of the building.

I hung back, waiting for Dean to finish. He joined me at the door and we walked outside, where it had begun to snow.

My irritation melted away and I pointed ahead as we walked. "I'm going to the armory," I said, trying not to sound like an excited child. "I've never shot a gun before and I'd like to start target practice right away."

"I don't think you'll have much difficulty. Your super strength will minimize the recoil, and your senses and reflexes will certainly help your aim. I can't wait to see the guys' faces when you can outshoot them. You'll be dropping Westerners like a pro by next week."

I began to walk backwards so I could face him. "How about by tomorrow? I bet I'll bag more than you do."

Dean threw his head back and laughed. "You're the cockiest woman I've ever met. But I guess if I'd done what you did and lived to tell about it, I'd be cocky, too."

"Would be? You *are* cocky. Telling me I was your newest Sentinel in front of your whole damn team? I had half a mind to punch you for that."

He snickered. "I was disappointed that you didn't. Like I said, we've heard a little bit about what's going on in Saint Catherine. Between the reports of Battlecry's insurrection and what Gregory has told me, I was expecting more of a firebrand. You're cocky, but not nearly as exciting as I'd hoped."

I stopped in my tracks and pointed at him. "Tomorrow, I'm going to kill more Westerners than you, and I'm going to shoot them all. No knives, no superhero stuff. Bullets."

Dean stopped walking. "Care to place a wager on that?"

"Sure. What's the bet?"

"That I'll kill more Westerners than you do. Loser has to do something embarrassing. Winner's choice, of course."

"That's fine. Get ready to taste humiliation," I said, smooth as silk. "What can I make you do in front of your whole team? I'll have to think on that."

"I already know what I'll make you do." An unnamed emotion stirred beneath the humor in his eyes.

We arrived in front of the little school just as the door opened. A dozen children of all ages ran out.

Two of them, tiny girls in large winter coats, squealed with delight and ran across the road. They ran up to him and tugged on his sleeves. "Dean! Dean! Make flowers for us!"

"Easy, easy," he said, laughing. "Do you have any seeds for me?"

The smaller of the girls dug in her pocket and produced a small seed. "I saved this from last time."

Dean held out his gloved hand and accepted the seed. He kneeled down and brushed away the snow from a small patch of earth, then pressed the seed firmly into the ground.

"What are you doing?" I asked.

Instead of answering, he pulled off his glove and held his hand to the ground for a second, then stood up. "Watch," he whispered.

The girls were staring fixedly at the spot of earth.

It was like a time lapse video: a small shoot popped out of the earth, growing and expanding before my eyes. The shoot thickened and stiffened into a stalk bearing thick, waxy green leaves. The stalk divided again and again, forming a lush bush dotted with yellow-tipped round bulbs. Finally, after only ten seconds, the tips opened and exploded into plump yellow roses, more beautiful than any I'd ever seen.

The girls squealed again.

Dean snapped two roses from the bush and handed one to each girl. "Go tell your friends that they can come get some flowers. Hurry, though. The bush will be dead by tomorrow in this weather." Clutching the roses in their hands, they dashed across the road and called to their playmates at recess.

Dean snapped off the largest rose and handed it to me. "Before the smaller ladies come and pick it clean."

I hesitated, then accepted the rose, inhaling its fragrance. "I love roses," I murmured. "They're my favorite scent."

"I've always preferred wood smoke, myself. But I can see the appeal in roses."

I put the rose to my nose again. "You have a gift, Dean," I said, my voice as soft as the rose's petals. "I think your true value isn't to be found on the battlefield. You're like Benjamin that way. Together, you two could change the world."

His smile faded, and his face took on a vacant, far-away look. "I was a field slave, back before I escaped. I hid the extent of my powers and pretended that I could run out of juice. If they'd known that I could produce crops over and over without stopping, they would've worked me to death. Or at least had an armed guard on me at all times. That's what Benjamin would've had to look forward to, if he hadn't killed his captors." He was silent for several seconds, lost in thought. "I'm glad he's safe."

He looked at me. I had to avert my eyes from his piercing gaze.

I twiddled my rose. "How did you escape?"

"My mom broke her ankle one day, when I was fifteen. My father, our owner, decided she was too much of a burden, so he shot her. That night, Ken, Andrew, and I made a run for it, simple as that. Ken can turn into a wolf, so he could smell and hear if they were following us. I covered our tracks with growth, and of course made food while we were in the wild. We were all fifteen, desperate, and terrified. I've never forgotten that feeling. I saw a little bit of it in your team when we met you."

I sniffed the rose again. "Yeah, we were. We'd gone to so much trouble to find Benjamin and Isabel, and we wound up nearly freezing to death, then in the custody of the wrong Westerners. Then suddenly there was shooting and horses and death. And then my brother." My voice broke. "He hates me."

Dean put his hands on my shoulders. "No, he doesn't. Gregory is adjusting as much as you are. A lot of the guys have trouble seeing the camps as anything but evil, and superheroes, to them, represent the camps. Gregory has a lot of hatred and bitterness he needs to work through. He's trying to reconcile the sister he loves to the ideology he hates. Give him time. He really was beside himself when he found out that he'd shot his beloved sister. All of us have heard the most amazing tales about you. I decided years ago that if half of them were true, you were the kind of woman I wanted to meet."

"Really? What did he say?" I looked into his eyes, then away, unable to stand the intensity.

"That you hate rules, always had a chip on your shoulder, and couldn't be told what to do."

"I was hauled before the tribunal for those qualities," I mumbled. "As punishment, they threatened to whip Reid if I didn't marry this really awful guy."

A flash of anger crossed Dean's face. "Tell me you grabbed your team and ran off right then."

"Not exactly." My words were barely audible. "I didn't realize I could until after Matthew had taken some liberties with me. I'm having some trouble dealing with it. Don't tell anyone, okay?"

Why was I able to tell Dean this, but not Benjamin? The words flowed out of the emptiness inside me. Unlike many other anguished confessions, I didn't yearn to take them back. Telling someone relieved my pain a little, but not enough to erase the fact that I'd brought it on myself.

To my shock, Dean wrapped his arms around me. "I won't. Please tell me you don't blame yourself."

"Well, yeah," I said into his shoulder, still shocked by the gesture. "I have super strength, but I didn't do anything to stop him."

"They were threatening Reid," he said gently.

"Who also could've left whenever he wanted."

"You guys didn't know that. Part of being in a cult is psychological control. I've dealt with so many people who blamed themselves for things that happened to them while they were in the camps. You are not responsible for what happened." He rubbed my back.

"But Marco said—"

"Marco grew up in the cult, too. He probably still believes something really weird." He let out a little derisive snort. "Camp men are... well, they might not admit it, but a lot of them think they're inherently superior, that their word is always law. They'll tell you to your face that they love you and respect you, but just last week I had to counsel a married couple who came to blows because the Mrs. turned down the Mr. for sex. He thought he was entitled to it."

I pushed away from Dean. "That's what Benjamin and I argued about before the tribunal."

Dean's face fell. "You're married to the doc? He never mentioned that."

"No... no, we're not married." Though I loved Benjamin, I could no longer find joy in the idea of binding my hand to his, like I had in the past. "He wouldn't sleep with me because I believed if we were married, I couldn't say no to him." I buried the urge to assure Dean that I wasn't in the habit of seducing men.

Dean turned to stare over his shoulder at the infirmary, then sighed and turned back to me. "He's ethical, I'll give him that. Maybe I should have mercy on him and stop calling him 'Doc.' I only do it because it pisses him off."

"He's still not telling me the truth about his past, so piss him off all you want."

Dean grinned. "I'm glad we had this talk." He looked at the infirmary again. "Although, I think you should talk to the doc about what you told me, if you haven't already. If something like that happened to my girlfriend, I'd want to know."

"That's never going to happen. I don't want him to know."

"Why not?"

My shoulders slumped. "Benjamin has always thrown the cult in my face and acted like I could just waltz out of it whenever I wanted. I... I can't stand that he's right. He was so angry that I was going to accept the judgment of the elders. What would he think of me if he knew that I'd let Matthew stick his hand down my pants?"

"If he's anything like me, he'll want to make sure you're okay, then he'll want to kill Matthew."

"And that's the other thing." My voice grew louder. "Why should I tell him about one of my worst experiences when he won't tell me about the crimes he committed? I'm not going to call the cops on him, I just want him to be honest."

Dean shrugged. "I don't know what to tell you there. But I do still think you should tell him about Matthew." The snow began to fall harder, swirling thickly around us. Dean pointed ahead of us to the armory. "Let's get inside and get you a weapon."

I tucked the rose into my braid, and we hurried to the armory.

The inside of the armory was warm and smelled strongly of steel, lubricant, polish, and lead. Cages of weapons lined the walls and center of the cement room, each one padlocked shut. Metal cabinets flanked the front door—I assumed they contained ammunition. I pulled off my gloves, aching to hold one of the many firearms displayed around me.

I walked around the armory and examined the collection, taking in the sight of so much raw power. Dean followed me around, tender amusement written on his face as I admired each weapon.

While I walked past an ammunition cabinet, a metallic clatter near my feet made me look down. Several stray bullets were littered around one of the cages.

"That's weird," Dean said. "The guys know better than to leave live ammunition laying around like that."

He kneeled to pick up the bullets, and I joined him, reaching into the dusty space underneath the cage to grab the last few bullets.

I felt a pinprick on my hand and hastily removed it. A black spider the size of a dime scuttled out of the shadows, and I smashed it with the heel of my hand.

"Ugh, it bit me." I squinted at the side of my hand, then shook it. I looked up and saw Dean's surprised face—then cracked up.

"What's so funny?"

I pointed to his lip piercings. "Now we've both got spider bites."

"Yeah, but mine look cooler."

"They do. I'll give you that. I really like them."

He gave me the goofiest smile I'd ever seen, which only made me laugh harder.

When we'd finished putting the bullets in their box, I stood up and put the box in the cabinet. After locking it again, Dean led me to a smaller cage in the corner. "Your gun's in here."

I peered through the holes of the cage. "Which one's mine?"

Dean pulled out a key on a string from around his neck. "I'm starting you off with a handgun. Small, easy to use. I think you'll enjoy the similarities to your knives, since you're used to a smaller weapon." He removed a pistol and placed it in my hands. "An M9. Military issue and very dependable. Semiautomatic, nine-millimeter rounds."

I held the sleek black handgun up to the light, enjoying the weight of it. "I once stopped a hostage taker. He had one of these. Held it to his wife's head."

"Did you kill him?"

"No. I should've, though. But I didn't want to make waves. Patrick was still alive."

"Patrick?"

"My old leader."

"Ah, the much-despised Atropos." Dean handed me a thigh holster. "Try this on for size."

I strapped it on. "I almost killed another leader after the tribunal. But when I was drowning him, I saw Patrick's face. My team has accused me of harboring anger, and I think it's at Patrick. I have a lot to be angry about, but I feel like Patrick is the root."

Dean studied me, tutting for a second while he thought. "I want you to take that anger and let it drive you when you're fighting the Westerners. During the 'pretty boy' speech last night you mentioned torturing someone, right? I assume that was Matthew. Did the anger drive you then?"

"Oh, yeah. *God*, yeah."

"Good. Let that take root. Nurture it. Take every shred of hatred for Matthew, Patrick, and everyone in the cult who has ever hurt you and make it your fuel. Their victim will become their executioner. That's what I told Gregory and all the others."

I ran my fingers over the pistol and tried to visualize executing my enemies. It was an enjoyable picture, but odd. A question popped into my head.

"Why don't you guys use your powers? Why don't the Westerners use their powers?"

Dean leaned against the cage. "You just revealed more of your cult brain. Powers are rarely reliably useful in combat, and it can take years to become a proficient hand-to-hand fighter. No offense intended, but superhero-style fighting, with fists instead of guns, is flashy, but stupid. No offense. Even the Westerners don't normally use their powers as their first weapon. Guns make everyone equal. Besides, very few powers have the range of a handgun. Almost none have the range of, say, an M-16."

"Oh."

Like an aftershock from the mental earthquake of the night before, my brain shook as another pillar of belief collapsed into dust.

I'd never considered that my style of fighting was a problem. I was so *good* at superhero-style fighting... but then again, why did we all wear bulletproof vests?

I let myself imagine me holding a firearm again, and this time it didn't feel odd. I was going to be so much more badass now.

The emptiness in my chest began to fill. I lovingly brushed my fingers over the M9 in its holster, then realized that my index finger was stiff.

I glanced down. "Oh, crap." My finger was swollen from the

spider's venom. I unstrapped the holster with the gun still inside and handed it to Dean. "I gotta go see Benjamin."

"Good idea. And while you're there, talk to him about Matthew. Afterwards, come see me, and I'll get you started on shooting practice. You're going to need a lot of it if you're going to win that bet. Which you won't, by the way."

"Prepare to eat humble pie, Monroe," I said over my shoulder as I walked out of the armory.

He was still snickering as I closed the door behind me and walked to the medical building, sucking on my finger.

I pushed open the medical building's door. The entrance opened into a short hallway that led to a large back room containing half a dozen hospital beds and an examination table. On the right of the hallway, a door opened to a bedroom with two twin beds. On the left, there was another room, probably a bathroom. Though sterile, I had to admit that it was a very nice set-up.

I walked into the back room, where I was greeted by the sharp smell of blood. Benjamin was tending to a little boy who'd had an exciting time on the playground, if the bloodstain on his collar was any indication.

Of course, with Benjamin attending to him, his wound was gone, and he was chattering away with a friend while Benjamin washed up at the sink.

Benjamin looked up as I walked in and turned to the boys, who were sitting on a table and swinging their legs. "Jonah, Alden, you can go back to class now."

They hopped off the table and ran past me. "Bye, Doc!"

Benjamin shook his head. "Doc," he muttered.

I squeezed my finger, which was starting to throb. "Do you have anything for spider bites?"

Benjamin made a little noise of disgust and turned around, his hand on his hip. "Yeah, take them out and let them close up so you don't look like a washed-up reject from an emo band. Why are you here, Jill?"

I held up my hand, which had swelled even more in the last few minutes. "An actual spider bite, smartass. But I think I'm just going to go home and see what happens."

"No, don't!" He turned red and began to fish around in a drawer. "I'm sorry. I have some antihistamines in here." He popped two pink pills out of a foil blister pack. "Do you know what kind of spider bit you? Are you breathing normally? Does your hand hurt?"

He handed me the pills and a small paper cup full of water.

I swallowed the pills. "No and yes. And my hand doesn't hurt. It just feels kinda weird."

"The pills will help with the swelling, but if you start having muscle pain or anything serious, come back. You might need some antivenin."

Benjamin squeezed an ice pack to activate it, then gently placed it on my swollen finger and held it there. The warmth of his hand clashed pleasantly with the coolness of the ice pack.

He looked up at me, his eyes apologetic. "I'm sorry for being rude just now."

I curled my fingers around his. "I forgive you," I said quietly.

"We didn't really get a chance to reunite properly, did we?" Benjamin said before he kissed my knuckles. "We should try again."

I looked up into his shining hazel eyes. The shadows underneath them had only deepened since the previous day. I hoped he didn't have nightmares of his ordeal with the Westerners like I had nightmares of Matthew.

Instead of asking him, though, I grazed his cheekbone with my fingers. "I'm so happy you're safe. I almost lost my mind when I found out that you were gone."

The whirlwind of the tribunal's aftermath came back to me, carrying with it the pain and fear I'd felt. Dean was right; Benjamin would want to know about those memories.

He'd care, because he always cared. That was one of the reasons why I loved him.

I continued to stroke his cheek with my good hand and he lovingly caught my hand in his. "I... I want to talk to you about something. Something important."

Our reunion had gone wrong when the discussion had turned to the tribunal. This time I'd be honest even if it killed me.

"What is it?" He gazed at me, concern evident in every corner of his face.

I squeezed his fingers, searching for the words to describe what Matthew had done to me and how I still felt about the events of that terrible day. "The tribunal didn't go well," I began after a shaky breath. I pulled my hand away from his and nervously stroked my braid, waves of wretched memories crashing over me. "They made Ember stay away, probably because she could hear what they had planned, and then... I mean, they said Reid had to—"

My nervous fiddling caused the rose to fall out of my braid.

He picked it up, staring at it quizzically. I held out my hand to take it back, but he kept staring at it.

"Where'd you get a rose around here? It's Jan..." He looked up at me, his eyes darkening. "Did *Dean* give this to you?"

I was startled by the venom in his question. "Y-yes, but—"

He shoved the rose back in my hand. "You were saying?" All warmth was gone.

I scrambled to find my words. "I... I was talking to him just now and he thought I should talk to you about..."

Benjamin rolled his eyes. "Oh, I have to hear this."

A lump formed in my throat.

I shoved the rose into my pocket. "You know what? Never mind. Thanks for the pills, *Doc.*"

Benjamin glared at me. "Now you're doing that, too?"

I crossed my arms. "I'll stop right here and now if you tell me exactly what happened at the chemical lab with Artemis. Go ahead. I'm listening."

Benjamin turned red but said nothing.

I snorted. "Yeah, that's what I thought. If you feel like talking, I'll be at the range learning how to shoot. I'd ask you to teach me, seeing as how you can hit hearts and between the eyes with no problems, but I don't really want to take lessons from a liar."

He swallowed. "You're learning how to shoot now?"

"Yeah. I'm a Sentinel, remember?"

"You're going to kill people?"

"Uh, *yeah*. Hence the gun."

"And you have no problem just showing up to a camp and mowing everyone down?"

"Not really." I shrugged. "I have a bet going with Dean. The person who kills the most Westerners tomorrow gets to make the other one do something embarrassing."

Benjamin's mouth fell open. "You're making a game out of ending people's lives?"

I raised an eyebrow. "They're Westerners. Who cares?"

"*I* do! I care that you're so flippant about torturing people who make you mad and killing people you don't like! They may be Westerners, but you'll never forget the look in their eyes as you kill them! You can't pretend your decisions don't have moral consequences, Jillian!"

There was a long pause.

"Wow. You really are Bleeding Heart Benjamin."

I turned and opened the door, catching a glimpse of his devastated face in the mirror on a medicine cabinet.

I stepped out into the snow and strode toward the range behind the main building.

Whenever guilt pricked at me, I pictured Patrick and Matthew, and soon I was too angry to care about anything other than revenge.

25

The rules were simple: always keep our weapons pointed in a safe direction. Keep our fingers off the triggers until we wanted to shoot. Don't load our weapons until we're on the firing line and the range is "hot." The shooting must stop when someone yells "cease fire." Wear ear and eye protection.

Judd, a rugged, surly Sentinel no older than my brother all but snarled as he told my team and me the rules and presented us with our weapons. Marco and Reid accepted their handguns and walked to the far end of the range, where a bored Gregory greeted them and began to demonstrate a proper shooting stance.

Judd handed me a tiny handgun better suited to a child. There was a malevolent gleam in his eyes.

I refused to pick it up. "What the hell is that?"

"It's your weapon, hero."

Nearby, three Sentinels stifled their laughter. Beyond them, Eleanor watched us, her forehead wrinkled slightly.

"No, my weapon is a standard-issue nine mil. Dean assigned it to me less than an hour ago."

He crossed his arms. "And why would he give you that? You can't hurt anyone with this gun. If you want, I can paint it pink."

The other three Sentinels didn't bother to hide their laughter anymore.

The monstrous rage that had driven me to torture and kill returned. My fingers trembled while I slid the gun toward Judd. "Get my weapon or explain to your commander why you're disobeying him."

Judd raised an eyebrow but didn't move. "Have you ever shot a gun before, chick?"

My face, I was sure, was white. Judd had not given lip to Marco or Reid. He hadn't offered them the ridiculously tiny gun.

I leaned in close to him. "Have you ever felt your bones snap one by one while you're lying on the forest floor with a broken leg? Your internal organs turn to mush as I punch them?" I dropped my voice to a whisper. "Would you like to feel your lungs fill with water as I hold you beneath the surface and watch the light leave your eyes?"

Eleanor strode toward us. "Judd, give her the gun she was assigned, then leave."

"But—"

"I bought them, so these are my guns. Clearly you aren't mature enough for this job." Eleanor gave him an expectant stare, and he pouted.

"Fine," he spat, pulling my assigned weapon from a box beneath his table. "Try not to shoot your eye out. Or do. I don't care." He shoved the gun and holster into my hands and stormed out of the range.

After he'd left, Eleanor spun around and gaped at me. "Woman, get a grip. Judd's a dick, but there was no reason to attack him."

"What are you talking about?" I strapped my holster back onto my leg. "I was never going to attack him, just make him think I was."

"The probability of you attacking him was rapidly approaching. That would've set off so many possibilities, there wasn't much I could do." She narrowed her eyes. "Listen to me. People here don't like you. I can't imagine why. Since I can't make people like you, you have to start trying to make friends. Be less *you*, more the girl you pretended to be when we met."

My mouth fell open. "I may have pretended to be a civilian, but I didn't... I didn't..."

Was *this* why Eleanor was unhappy with me? She thought I'd lied to her about what I was like? That was ridiculous, and though I was reeling from my fight with Benjamin and the incident with Judd, I was determined to smooth things over with Eleanor, with whom I had no argument.

Before I could ask her to step outside, so we could speak in private, the door opened with a cold blast of air and Benjamin walked in.

I couldn't help a small smile, though his pained expression made me swallow a new lump in my throat.

He looked at me for a fraction of a second, and then to Eleanor. "Can I talk to you?"

Eleanor's face softened. "What's wrong?"

Benjamin's eyes flickered to me again. "I just need to talk to you."

Eleanor nodded and hurried out with him, leaving me alone at the range with a weapon in my hands and no idea what had just happened.

MARCO, Reid, and I kicked the snow off our boots and walked into our house, which was warm and cheery from the fire Ember had built. After eight hours at the range, our hands ached and our ears rang, but we were happy. I was a natural, as I'd predicted. Marco and Reid, on the other hand, were going to just use their powers tomorrow.

Ember sat on the old couch in front of the fire. Eleanor was sitting next to her, her eyes red-rimmed and damp.

"Hello," I said stiffly.

Reid and Ember exchanged furious looks. Ember jumped up and stormed into her room. Reid watched her leave with a hard stare, then disappeared into the kitchen.

Eleanor stood, her eyes almost sparking with fury.

"What's up, Eleanor?" I asked coolly.

"Bleeding Heart Benjamin. You *cow*."

"Oh boy," I grumbled, shrugging out of my coat. "This is going to be fun."

"How dare you treat him like that after—"

I whirled around. "Who the hell are you to tell me how to speak to Benjamin?"

"I'm his *sister*!"

"No, you're the woman who disappeared on us and left him heartbroken and scared. That was nice, by the way. Thanks for assuring us that you hadn't been murdered or kidnapped or anything. And you say I'm the one who lied? Get real."

"I was with the Sentinels. It's not like I could've told you."

"You know, actually, you could have. You could have told us about the slavery and the lies. You could've let me know my brother was alive."

"Let me give you a little insight into me: I don't do anything if the odds aren't in my favor. My one goal in Saint Catherine was to get my brother to join me, not convince a brainwashed superheroine that she's being brainwashed. At that time, there was a good chance of getting him. But every damn day it dwindled, and I couldn't figure out why. And then I met *you*, and I realized why."

I lazily crossed my arms. "My southern charm?"

She made a face. "*Feelings*. The one thing I can't control. I realized it the second I saw you in the park. You were so obviously Gregory's sister. I saw you and realized my superhero-obsessed brother was besotted with pure poison. Everything made sense."

"Aren't you a peach. Poison, Eleanor? Really?"

"You're all poison! My brother got sucked into this Westerner slavery crap because he met

you! He could've been here with me, safe and sound the whole time while he got to be the soldier nurse he's always wanted to be, but instead he got involved with *you,* and look where that landed him. They could've killed him! Do you know how much danger you put him in? Do you know what they do to their slaves?"

Her pale face was slowly becoming splotchy and red. Goodness, it was easy to yank this woman's chain—and I was in the mood to yank chains. I quirked my eyebrow. "Are we poison because of the cult, or are we poison because Artemis kicked your ass in Baltimore that one time?"

Ember appeared in the doorway, her face carefully neutral. "Jill, I need you in our room. Eleanor, I'll see you tomorrow."

We both ignored her.

"I hate you," Eleanor spat.

"If you hate me so much, why did you rearrange heaven and earth to get your brother and me together? You literally locked us in a room."

She squeezed her eyes shut in frustration. "There was such a high chance that he'd be turned off by you telling him about the cult. *Such* a high chance. But stupid me, I couldn't see how much he liked you. He liked you, and I couldn't calculate the effect his feelings would have on the outcome." She opened her eyes. "I could feel my chances of success plummet the second I locked you in there."

"And then you just dipped out because you'd failed? Nice."

"I waited for the rare window of opportunity I needed to leave without anyone following me. Patrick's attack gave me that."

So, it was Eleanor's personality that had been the façade.

I was surprised by how much the revelation wounded me; I'd spent months worrying about her, hoping she was safe. Now here she was, yelling at me for merely existing.

Still, she was nearly thirty years old—something about her behavior was a bit over the top. She knew as well as anybody else that I hadn't wanted Benjamin to be sold into slavery and acting like I had was unfair. The mere memory of discovering that Benjamin was gone was enough to take my breath away for a second.

I had just one more question for her.

"Is anything I think I know about you true? The ex-boyfriend who you dumped for not knowing anything about kids in China? The one that you thought was too stupid for you Trents? Is he real?"

Curiously, she seemed taken aback. "That... how did... Dean and I had an argument before I came here, okay? But he's not my boyfriend," she said quickly. "I just added some extra details about the situation that my brother would believe and sympathize with. He's protective, and like *you*, he needs to feel superior. I wasn't lying for lying's sake. I needed a good story."

She sounded a bit defensive, even embarrassed.

"Well, I'm glad we've had this little chat," I said, kicking off my boots. "Thank you for illuminating just how much the Trent siblings have misrepresented themselves."

She wrinkled her nose. "What do you mean?"

"Ask Benjamin." I turned to go to my bedroom.

"We're not done here!"

I whirled around. "Oh, yes, we are. Don't let the door hit you on your way out."

I hurried down the hall and slammed my bedroom door behind me, collapsing on the bed and staring up at the cracked ceiling. I let out a long breath. "What did you need, Em?"

"I needed you to back out of that fight before Eleanor hauled off and decked you."

"...Fair enough."

Ember sat on the edge of her bed. "She's not actually *that* angry at you, you know."

I scoffed. "Could've fooled me. The way she tells it, everything she's ever done was a calculated effort to keep me away from Benjamin. I can't believe I spent so long worrying about her."

Ember shook her head. "At least some of that was lies. She was scared for her brother. I think you know the feeling?"

I turned on my side and faced Ember. "I might." Some of my irritation melted away, and I plucked the rose out of my pocket and tossed it to Ember. "Here, you can have this. Sorry that it's all squished, but it still smells nice."

"Where the hell did you get a rose from?"

"Dean can grow plants in an instant. This was from a bush he grew in ten seconds today."

Ember gazed down at the rose. "Oh. I see."

"Whatever. The raid's tomorrow night. I need to get some sleep."

Ember placed the rose on her bedside table. "I know you're hurting, and like I said, if you need to talk to me, I'm here to listen. Your anger is going to burn you if you don't suffocate it."

"What about you and Reid?" I could hear little sounds coming from the kitchen. "I saw that look you gave him. You could've withered the rose bush with it."

Ember shoved the rose into her bedside drawer and slammed it shut. "He's being a jackass. Every time I try to talk to him about this new attitude of his, he blows me off. I don't understand where it came from. He was never like this before, not in the whole time I've known him."

I rolled onto my back. "Tell him that you've got options. Graham pulled me aside today and asked if he had a chance with you."

"He's cute, but I'm not interested. How old is he, thirty? Besides, I *am* with Reid. This is just a rough spot."

We chatted for a few minutes more until we both rolled over and laid in the dark in silence.

"Hey, Jill?"

"What?"

"Think about what I said, okay?"

"Don't worry," I assured her. "I talked to Dean about the anger. He said I'll be okay soon enough."

Ember drifted off, but I stared at the wall, my eyelids determined to stay open. There was too much to think about before I fell asleep.

My first full day of being a Sentinel was drawing to a close, but I didn't feel like I'd achieved anything. Sure, I'd been issued a weapon and had proved a natural sharpshooter, but... so what? The Sentinels hated me.

I shifted uncomfortably. Why did I even care whether they liked me? My life wasn't a popularity contest, and goodness knows I'd had detractors all my life. Yet, my altercation with Judd had left me grasping and cold, as if I were trying to cover myself with a too-small blanket.

What was I doing? Who was I doing this for?

"For Isabel," I whispered.

"Hmm?" Ember murmured. "Wha zat?"

"Nothing," I said. "Sweet dreams, Em."

For Isabel. I was a Sentinel now. Saving Isabel was my purpose. If for nothing else, I'd keep going for her.

26

"Right arm up like this," I said, demonstrating the correct position. "Left arm back here. Then strike." I punched the foam dummy's neck; had it been a real person, they wouldn't have been able to breathe for a few seconds. "The idea is to incapacitate your opponent with as little effort as possible."

"Well, duh," one of the Sentinels said. "That's why we have guns."

Some of the other Sentinels sniggered and nodded.

My team and I were in the main building, called there by Dean to demonstrate basic martial arts moves to any interested Sentinels. Several, including my brother, had shown up.

At first, I'd been hopeful that their presence meant that we'd finally bridge the gulf between our teams, but so far none of them had asked questions or shown any particular interest in what I was teaching.

I dropped my arms. "What's your name?" I asked the Sentinel who'd just spoken.

"Antonio Grantham." He glanced at Gregory, who gave a little shrug. "What about it?"

"Grantham, huh? This might come as a shock, Tony, but you're related to a superhero named Artemis. Try not to kill yourself out of shame." The Sentinels tittered. "How would you kill her, if you were so inclined?"

"I'd shoot her." He sounded confused.

"The doc tried that once. Artemis is still alive. The only reason the doc's alive, too, is because he can run faster than a train. Unless you can run as fast as that, what are you going to do when Artemis jumps up and bends your little gun like it's made of tin foil?"

"I'll, uh, pull out another gun?"

Gregory patted him on the shoulder, but other Sentinels were shooting him doubtful, unimpressed expressions.

"I hope your will is updated." I turned to the other Sentinels.

"Let's be real, though," a red-haired Sentinel said. "We're not going to fight Artemis. What's wrong with our guns?"

"What's your name?" I asked.

"Ned Cohen."

"Ned's raised a good point," I said, looking around at the handful of men. "You probably will never fight a superhero. But some of you have already been in a situation when the person you were shooting at wasn't a Westerner." I held up my hand, purposely not looking at my brother. "What if the circumstances had been different and one of you'd simply killed me?" I lowered my voice. "Or Ember?"

Reid wasn't the only one whose face became grim.

"It might not have been superheroes in there. It could have easily been your brothers, sisters, cousins, or any other captured children from the camps. My point is, there is strategic value in knowing how to fight someone without killing them. Any of the men at the sorting station that day could've had information on the compounds, but we'll never know because none of you can capture, just kill. That makes you weak."

I caught Marco's eye and he gave me a curt nod. I grabbed his arm and threw him to the ground, pinning him in such a way that he couldn't escape.

The Sentinels gaped—the whole move had taken less than a second.

I let go of Marco and brushed off my hands. "I get that you guys don't have any respect for superheroes, but anyone with two brain cells to rub together can see the value in knowing how to use your body as a weapon. Guns run out of ammo."

A young man with skin slightly darker than Marco's stepped forward. He gave me a nervous smile, the first Sentinel that morning to do so. "Can you show me what to do when someone in front of me points a gun at me?" There was no sarcasm or disdain in his question.

"I'd be honored. What's your name?"

"Gabe. Mom said that when she was at Oconee, her last name was Spivak."

A rare feeling spread through me: happiness. "I know several Spivaks. Lark Spivak serves in Baltimore with Artemis under the codename Valkyrie. She's incredibly sweet and very brave. She'd want to meet you." I handed him the orange plastic handgun we used for demonstrations. "Point this at my head. I'll show you the block quickly, then slowly. Then we'll go through it move by move."

Gabe nodded and pointed the orange gun at my forehead.

Muscle memory took over. I pushed his hands up, pantomimed kicking him in the groin, then shoved the gun into his solar plexus. He let go of the weapon and I drew back, pointing it at him.

He coughed, clutching his stomach, but grinned at me. "That was fast."

"All battles are fast. Every altercation between you and criminals... I mean, you and Westerners, is a battle. Here, point it at me again and I'll show you what I did in slow motion."

The other Sentinels crowded around us, finally quiet and straight-faced. I demonstrated the simple block a few times, then told them to pair up and try with their partners.

Gregory and Antonio went to a corner, though instead of practicing Antonio sulked while Gregory stared angrily at me. Because there was an uneven number of Sentinels, Marco paired with Gabe. They chatted about the Spivak family while they practiced.

Reid and I moved to the corner of the room. He tossed the gun to the ground. "You know what I haven't had in a while? A good sparring session."

"Got a lot of tension?" I asked, cracking my neck. "Because I do."

"Yeah," he muttered. "First on the floor loses?"

"You're on. I promise not to go, you know, full Battlecry on you."

We fell into our stances, and then without warning he threw a punch. I ducked and swiped for his chin, just slightly slower than I would a real opponent, and we fell into the comforting pastime.

After a minute of fighting, I grabbed his arm and spun him to the floor.

Applause lit up the room. I looked up, my mouth open. Most of the Sentinels had stopped practicing to watch us, and a few of them were even smiling. I blinked, then helped Reid up.

He gave me a good-natured wince and rubbed his shoulder. "Three out of five?"

"We're supposed to be teaching them," I whispered.

"They're starting to like us," he whispered back. "Competence is hard to disrespect."

I held up my hands to calm the applause, then turned to Reid. "Do you think they're ready to learn that move?" I said loudly.

Reid smirked, catching on. "I think so."

"What move?" a Sentinel asked. "Teach us!"

"Yeah, show us what it is!"

I put my hands on my hips and held my head up. "Now, I know none of you would ever deserve a punch to the face, seeing as you're all sweet as pie," I began, giving a significant look at Judd.

The Sentinels howled with laughter, some of them playfully punching him on the back and shoulders.

"But should you find yourself in that common fighting situation, you should know how to defend yourself."

As I spoke, the door opened, and Eleanor slipped inside and sidled along the back wall, watching us with a blank expression.

"Reid and I will show you some of the various methods of fending off a frontal attack, depending on the type of punch your enemy uses."

Reid and I slid back into our first positions and breathed for a few seconds. I met his eyes and counted down to the hit. "Three... two... one..."

His fist flew toward me.

My left ankle wobbled, suddenly unable to bear my weight.

Reid's fist, and the full power of his arm, collided with my face.

I cried out and fell to my knees, hot blood gushing out of my crunched nose. My eyes watered nonstop as pain crept into all corners of my cheeks. The Sentinels were silent, too stunned to react.

"Oh my God," Reid gasped, kneeling next to me. "What happened? Why didn't you block it?"

I waved him away and struggled to my feet. My ankle throbbed, weak from its momentary hyperextension. Holding a hand up to my nose, I tried to smile, but the tears coming from my eyes certainly dampened the effect. "That's, uh, that was how not to block a punch," I said lamely.

The Sentinels had recovered, and a few laughed silently.

Gabe handed me a towel and I accepted it, dabbing at my face. He glared at his laughing comrades. "You should go see the doc."

I instructed Reid and Marco to keep demonstrating to the guys, then limped toward the door.

Eleanor held it open for me. "That was unfortunate." She slammed the door behind me.

I stared at the door, still hardly able to believe that she was the same woman I'd met last summer. After a minute, I began to make a slow path down the main road, little drips of blood falling from my chin onto my clothes.

Though I was in pain, I couldn't help but feel a spark of hope. I'd won some kind of regard with a few of the Sentinels, and though my lesson had ended poorly, I'd accomplished something.

I limped down the road, taking in the quiet daytime activities of the snowy town. As I passed Dean's house, I heard the sweet, tinny sound of a harmonica. Through the thin white curtains of the front window I could see him perched on the arm of his couch, playing the small instrument.

I closed my eyes and let the simple tune carry me up and away, to years before when life had been simple, and Gregory had loved me. The harmonica's tune was similar to one I'd sung for my brother when he was small and afraid of the monsters he believed lived in the forest.

I'd once held him in my arms and comforted him by promising that I'd fight off every monster. He'd hugged me and said—

"Hey, Antonio! Wait up!"

Gregory rushed out of the main building and chased after Antonio, who was halfway to the range. When he caught up, they fist-bumped. Antonio glanced my way, then muttered something inaudible to Gregory, who looked at me briefly.

Gregory said something in return, and they both broke into loud laughter. Antonio mimed punching Gregory in the nose. Gregory laughed harder.

Something in my heart crumbled and blew away.

I continued down the road.

I stopped in front of the medical building and stared at the door. I didn't want to see Benjamin just yet. Though I knew I was being immature, I turned and wandered toward the school building. It was Saturday, so it would be mercifully empty. I turned the doorknob and walked into the cold, dark wooden room.

Instead of desks, the room contained a dozen long tables with mismatched plastic chairs crowded around them. Old books on various subjects lined the crude wooden bookshelves. An ancient upright piano sat in the corner, its yellowed keys displayed forever because of its lack of key cover. Though drafty, the cozy room was deeply comforting, like a hug from a long-lost friend.

My fingers grazed the piano keys, plunking notes at random. They needed to tune it.

I perused the bookshelf, pulling out random volumes. I sat down with books on astronomy, herbal remedies, and the intriguingly-named *Language of Flowers*. I couldn't deduce what kind of curriculum the students learned here—none of the books were proper textbooks, nor were there any volumes on history that I could see. The map on the wall behind the teacher's desk showed the USSR, which I was certain didn't exist anymore.

I was probably better educated than some people in Liberty. I'd never considered myself better educated than any non-superhero in my life.

I sat down and flipped through the astronomy book, enjoying the grainy black-and-white photos of constellations, nebulas, and satellites. I already knew the information, so I quickly turned my attention to *Language of Flowers*. Apparently, flowers and plants bore traditional meanings. People used to send coded messages to each other in bouquets to avoid prying eyes.

I flipped through the book with interest, reading about flowers familiar to me like irises, oleander, evening primroses, marigolds, and lotuses. Others, such as lily of the valley, linden tree, coltsfoot, wormwood, and belvedere were new, but no less fascinating.

Finally, I flipped open the book on herbal remedies, smiling a little as I realized that the books were in the school because of Dean's value of plants. I browsed the book for a few minutes, memorizing the uses of common kitchen herbs in case I ever needed the information.

One of parsley's many uses was the healing of bruises. Oregano had antiviral properties. Peppermint tea could relieve menstrual cramps.

I read page after page of the herbal book, fascinated by the wide range of uses of plants I could find on Reid's spice rack.

Blood dripped off my chin onto the page about tansy.

I jumped up, ashamed that I'd left permanent, macabre stains on one of the few books the students had. I put the books back onto the shelf and wiped at my nose a little, then left the school house.

Maybe Benjamin and I weren't getting along, but my stubbornness had just damaged someone else's property. I needed to get healed. My ankle felt swollen, too. I limped up the steps to the medical building, took a deep breath, then turned the knob.

Though it was about midday, the medical building's interior was shaded and watery, like an old photograph. Benjamin was alone, for once not attending to flu patients, who probably preferred their own beds.

He looked up from a thick book he was reading on one of the patient beds. Concern colored his features. "Good God, what happened to you?"

"An accident during sparring. My ankle gave out and I couldn't block Reid's punch."

Benjamin crossed the distance between us and touched my cheek. I sighed from the instant relief, as well as the warmth of his fingertips. After an awkward moment, I turned to go. I doubted he wanted me around. "I'll leave you to your reading."

He reached out and grabbed my hand. "Please don't." Moving quickly, he pulled a washcloth from a shelf and turned on the tap, steaming water soon rising from the sink. "I hate the sight of your blood," he said quietly without looking up. "It always reminds me of that night in the warehouse."

Instead of handing me the hot, soaking washcloth, he began to dab at my face himself. I sat down on an examination table and let him.

"I don't think I've ever been so shocked in my life," I said, smiling despite myself.

"That makes two of us. That was the worst night of my life, and that's saying something."

"As awful as it was... it was important for us to know the truth about each other." His eyes met mine for a fraction of a second, then he looked away. "I do wish my throat hadn't been slit, though. That was rough." I chuckled at the onslaught of memories, one of them surprisingly funny, in a dark kind of way. "Did I ever tell you that I was actually happy that I was going to die like my grandma?"

"No," Benjamin murmured through stiff lips. "You've never told me that."

I sighed. "Yeah, I was pretty messed up back then. That's why I didn't want you to call an ambulance. I wanted to die with some kind of honor like she did. When you healed me, I decided to jump off the bridge because I didn't think I had any other option besides going home and telling Patrick."

Benjamin wiped away the blood from my chin. "Would you have told him you were friends with a supervillain?"

"No. I would've had to explain the blood on my uniform, though. It would've come out that I'd fought you, and that you got away. No matter what, I would've been punished for some kind of failure. Jumping off the bridge looked like a better option for a while."

Benjamin stopped cleaning the blood. "Why didn't you?"

"I was a superhero," I said simply. "I'd taken vows to protect the city, and I had responsibilities."

Benjamin set the washcloth on a little metal table and caressed my cheek with such tenderness that I shivered. My days of late had been pockmarked with hits, punches, and slaps—but precious few gentle touches.

I bowed my head toward his, and then he was kissing me, his thumb gently massaging my cheek.

I broke away for air. "I'm sorry for calling you that horrible name," I whispered. "Please forgive me."

"Yes," he breathed, and then he kissed me again. After a few seconds, he pulled away and gazed into my eyes. "You *are* a super-hero. Present tense. Never forget that. You decide what that means, not the elders."

His intensity kindled a small flame in my chest, and I took his hand in mine.

He squeezed my fingers. "Your vows kept you going when you were on the bridge. Let them keep you going now. You have to stay alive." He swallowed. "You have to, if only just for me."

I pulled Benjamin so he was standing between my knees. His nearness stirred old desires and passions to the surface, and I drew him into yet another fiery kiss. I imagined that we were in the sick bay of our home in Saint Catherine, that the tribunal had never happened, that I'd never felt Matthew's sweaty hands on my skin. The memory of Matthew pulsed in my brain like a bruise, pulling me out of the moment. I rested my forehead against Benjamin's as he caught his breath.

"I'm sorry," I said, my chest heaving.

"For what?"

"For everything."

He tilted my chin up. "You're taking the blame for something you shouldn't. I know you. You want to carry the world on your shoulders. Whatever it is you think you have to apologize for, you need to let it go, sweetheart."

How could I "let it go" when I wasn't even certain what "it" was? Benjamin was right—it was as though the weight of the world was on my shoulders. I'd felt it when I'd passed the memorial to the family that had drowned in Saint Catherine. I felt it when my team fought and argued. It crushed me when I recalled how I'd let Matthew assault me.

I felt responsible for all those things, though in different ways, and though I knew intellectually that I shouldn't. Perhaps I could alleviate my guilt by taking responsibility for the *right* things in the future. Responsibility was a fuel to me, keeping me alive when little else would. What was I responsible for now?

My mind drifted back to the school building, in which I'd seen no history books. I had knowledge the citizens of Liberty did not, therefore I had power they did not have. The underlying belief of all superheroes was that our powers gave us the responsibility to protect and serve.

How could I protect and serve the people of Liberty with this type of power?

It occurred to me that in all his explanations of the Sentinels and Liberty, Dean had never once mentioned the federal government. Slavery was illegal, and even though the Westerners would deny it, they were under federal jurisdiction.

Could it be that Dean and the other leaders simply didn't know they could turn to the law for help?

Benjamin had moved away from me to rinse out the bloody washcloth in the sink. "Benjamin?"

"Yes?" He glanced at me, smiling lightly.

"How do I contact the FBI?"

Benjamin froze, then spun around, open shock and fury written on every line in his face. "Why?"

We stared at each other for several tense seconds.

I hopped off the table. "Is there something you want to share with me?"

Benjamin's face flushed deep red. "You... *why do you want to contact the feds*?"

I flinched back from his shout. All I could do was stare at his scared, angry face. "You really think I'm going to turn you in, don't you?" Benjamin's fists clenched, and my eyes flickered down toward them, then back up. "Why don't you trust me?"

He took a step forward. "Why don't you trust *me*?"

I took a step back. "Because for once, I'm not the one making fists."

I turned and strode out of the room.

"No, Jillian, wait! Please!" There was a breeze, and then he grabbed the back of my arm, just beneath my shoulder.

"*Don't touch me!*" I shoved him away from me into a wall. I massaged my arm where he'd grabbed it. "Don't *ever* grab me like that again, do you hear me?" My teeth chattered as clammy sensations oozed through my veins, snaking into each corner of my body. "Or I'll make you as sorry as I made Matthew."

Benjamin's shock morphed into worry. "I'm sorry, I won't do that again," he said quickly. "But... but I thought you tortured Matthew because he pretended to be me."

My heart rate increased. "Yes, that's true." I stumbled backwards toward the door now. "I have to go now."

Benjamin held out a hand. "Is there something you're not telling me?"

"Oh, you're one to talk," I spat.

I wrenched open the door and dashed down the steps into the deep snow drifts. I walked as quickly as I could to our little house. As I approached, furious shouts from within grated against my ears.

"I am not staying one second in this stupid town longer than I have to!" Ember's voice was louder than I'd ever heard her before.

"What are you going to do, go back to Saint Catherine by yourself?" Reid's thunderous shouted reply reminded me of Patrick so much that my heart rate increased.

"If I have to, yes! That's our home, not this hole!"

"Don't call it that! These are good people!"

"Saint Catherine has good people and you promised to protect them!"

"The Sentinels need me! Why don't you *get* that?"

"The Sentinels are nothing more than an armed gang, Reid! They don't get a pass for murder just because the Westerners are horrible!"

"Nobody else is stopping them!"

"*That doesn't make murder okay!*"

"It's not—"

"*Yes, it is!*" I'd never heard Ember sound like that. "You do not have the right to pick up a gun and shoot anyone you want to just because you don't like them! Dean is a murderer! They're *all* murderers!"

"It's not that simple!"

"Then why don't I just shoot you? Because God knows I don't like you right now!"

There was a long silence. Finally, Reid said, "You're too upset for this. We'll talk later."

She snorted. "Let me translate that. 'Shut up, hysterical woman. You're saying words I don't like and it's making me uncomfortable.'"

"Ember..."

"We swore to defend the laws, *Tank*. The laws are there so people don't resort to freaking mob justice. How are the Sentinels any different from any other lynch mob?"

"Sweetie, the Westerners *are* horrible." Reid's fire had died down. "If you'd grown up in my camp—"

"I grew up with Patrick Campbell. Don't you dare lecture me on your hard childhood."

"Well, there you go," he shot back. "Jill killed him."

My stomach clenched.

"As a last resort, dumbass! Or were you not there for that whole sick drama? She gave him multiple chances to surrender. He went crazy and tried to kill everyone, so she put him down like the dog he was."

"Oh, so now we're calling each other names? How mature."

Ember's cold laugh chilled me to the core. "Mature, Reid? You want to talk about maturity? Okay. 'Hi, I'm Reid Fischer. I didn't want Benjamin to join the team because he was an evil, heartless *criminal*, but I don't see any problem joining an unauthorized private militia and committing federal crimes. But I'm not a huge hypocrite because I don't *feel* like a criminal.'"

I heard Reid's heavy footsteps as he walked to another part of the house, then the sound of a door slamming.

I collapsed on the front steps. As much as Benjamin claimed I bore undue guilt, I had been the one to rope Reid into joining the Sentinels. I could very easily be the one at whom Ember would yell at next, and she was one of the few people I loved who wasn't semi-permanently angry at me for something.

I hugged my knees and tried to tune out the unhappiness in the air by thinking about what I'd say to the FBI when I talked to them.

So, I would like you to go after every superhero camp in America and arrest their entire leadership structure because I said so.

Yeah, like that would work. The feds and the camps had been friends for generations. They'd demand proof.

A secret network of antisocial superhumans has been trafficking children from the camps since the Ford administration. Another secret network of superhumans has been rescuing them.

That sounded like the plot of one of the Danger novels. I'd be laughed out of the FBI building.

My father basically sold me to a predator because I dared to stand up to Patrick, another predator. Right after that, I found out my boyfriend had been sold by my elder to evil people who live in whacked-out compounds in the wilderness. The evil people are being hunted by a militia made up entirely of angry men who hate superheroes even though we're victims, too. On top of it all, for some reason everyone is mad at me.

That sounded like a letter I might read in the advice column of the Saint Catherine Times-Mirror.

I need help and there's nobody else to turn to.

That was too honest.

While I huddled on the steps, I watched people as they walked up and down the road, attending to various tasks. Few of them were alone—children walked in loud, giggly groups, while women walked in twos and threes, speaking quietly amongst themselves. Sentinels hurried along in packs, their deep voices low rumbles in the distance.

Only one person, Eleanor, was by herself. She walked out of the main building and headed toward Dean's house. As I watched, she headed partially up his steps, then seemed to chicken out and decide against whatever action she was going to take. She gave her head a little shake and turned around to walk away. She looked up and saw me on the steps.

All the snow on the front of my house's sloped roof fell on me, crushing me in pounds of wet, freezing ice.

As I lay underneath the suffocating snow, my face pressed into the earth, I heard the faint, muffled sounds of laughter. With a groan, I pushed myself up, shrugging off the snow. I was already shivering uncontrollably. Melting snow leaked down my collar and thermal underwear, and it was already soaking through my socks.

Nobody had bothered to help me get out from the snow. Had a normal person been under there, they might have suffocated, or froze, without someone digging them out.

Hugging myself, I began to walk up my steps, intent on nothing more than a long, steaming bath.

"Today is not your lucky day, is it?" Eleanor's bored voice made me whip around. She was standing a few feet away—just out of striking distance—and a tiny smile played around her lips.

Horrible realization hit me, stronger and colder than the snow: Eleanor had caused my ankle to fail, resulting in a broken nose, and she'd just tried to crush me with snow.

I began to shake violently. "You're psychotic."

Her smile vanished. "I'm protecting my brother."

"I haven't done anything to him!"

My scream echoed around the road, making passersby stop and stare. Behind her, the door of the medical building opened, and Benjamin poked his head out.

"You're the reason he's so miserable all the time!" Eleanor's face had turned splotchy again.

"You don't know anything about our relationship!" Little sparkles floated in my vision. I hoped she could feel how much I wanted to hurt her.

"He told me everything! Every horrible thing you said to him, every time you let him down! You're a terrible girlfriend!"

"El, stop!" Benjamin had dashed over to us. He pushed Eleanor away from me. "Shut the hell up."

Eleanor bared her teeth at me. "You *are* poison. All of you are, but you're the worst."

"Go!" Benjamin yelled. He shoved Eleanor backwards. "You're embarrassing me."

"I'm helping you," Eleanor hissed, but she marched away toward her house.

Benjamin spun around. "What was that about?"

"Did you ask her to hurt me?" I backed into the front door, as far away from Benjamin as I could get.

"What? No! Why would you think that?"

"Because you told her everything, and then I started having accidents." I groped around for the doorknob, but it was locked, just as another knob had been in the John Mosby library many months before.

Unlike last time, though, I wasn't afraid to break the lock. I gave the knob a quick turn and forced the door open. I stumbled backwards into the house.

Benjamin blurred to the door before I could shut it and stuck his hand on the frame. "Jillian, listen to me. I *swear* I never asked her to cause you accidents." A furious gleam appeared in his eyes. "She's never going to hurt you again. You don't have to be afraid of... of my family," he finished, his fury suddenly gone, replaced by immense sorrow. "We're not going to hurt you." He held out his hands as an invitation for an embrace. "Please, sweetheart. Please believe me. Please come here. I can make this right."

I turned around and ran to the bathroom, shutting the door behind me and locking it, then sliding down.

I sat on the floor and hugged my knees for two hours, crying my eyes out.

Would I ever be happy again? Did I have any friends anywhere?

"Hey, look who finally decided to let us use the bathroom," Marco said as I joined him, Ember, and Reid around the kitchen table for an early dinner.

Reid wordlessly served me fresh corn and green beans from the greenhouse, a roll, and a small piece of herb-baked chicken.

Ember wrinkled her nose at the meat.

"We need protein," Reid said in a hard voice.

"I didn't say anything," Ember snapped.

"Yeah, but you were thinking it, weren't you?"

"Oh, so *you're* the telepath? Can you hear what I'm thinking now?"

I hid my face in my hands. "Please don't do this here. It's been a long day for all of us."

"Is that why you shouted at Eleanor in the middle of the street?" Marco asked.

I uncovered my face and took a calming breath. "I shouted at Eleanor because she was using her powers to hurt me."

Marco snorted. "And shouting like a kid was the best way to handle that situation?"

I slammed my fork onto the table. "Well, see, you shouted at me for not sticking up for myself when Matthew sexually assaulted me, so I decided to actually stick up for myself when Eleanor started attacking me for no reason. Did I not meet your impossible standards this time, Marco? My apologies."

Marco's mouth fell open, and even Ember and Reid watched us, all quarrels forgotten.

Marco gave his head a little shake. "He didn't sexually assault you. Stop being dramatic."

The thin fork bent in my grip. "Matthew Dumont made me stand still while he stuck his hand into my underwear and gloated about how I could do nothing to stop him. Not then, not later, not ever. Yes, that was sexual assault. If anyone ever did that to you, I'd tear their heart out of their chest. If anyone ever *tried* to do that to you, I'd tear their heart out of their chest."

Upon hearing the words, Marco stared at the table. "You're right. I've been hard on you. I'm sorry."

I jumped to my feet. "No, you have not been 'hard' on me. You looked me in the eye and told me you wished that I'd lost my hard-earned position on this team and had to stay with Matthew, who bragged how much he was going to enjoy raping me."

Marco rubbed his forehead. "I... I understand why you're so upset, but... you would've been—"

"*Married*? Is that what you were going to say?"

I hurled the ruined fork at the wall. Everyone jumped.

"So even though I never would have wanted it, and I probably would have been screaming and begging him to stop, it would've been okay because your uncle said we were married? Wake *up*!"

I threw my spoon at the wall next, tears suddenly streaming down my cheeks. Ember covered her mouth.

"Marco, look me in the eye and tell me that's not rape! Tell me that I don't have a right to be upset! Tell me I should've just laid down and shut up! Say it to me! *Say it*!"

Marco slowly stood and faced me. "Jill..."

I clenched my fists. "You said that I wasn't a victim because I wasn't sold to the Westerners. But you know what? I feel like a victim. I feel like my father abandoned me and my elders betrayed me. I feel like you and everyone else are expecting me to just swallow this and smile because I'm Battlecry. You said those words to me, Marco. That is not being 'hard' on me. You get so angry at us when you think we're treating you like a child, but if you want to be treated like a man, you have to own the words you say. You. Said. That."

Marco blinked once, swallowed, and said, "I... I don't know what to say to you now except that I'm sorry, and I understand if you don't forgive me."

I took in the sight of my cousin: sunken eyes, pale face, and horrified realization of the damage he'd caused.

But my anger was not mollified. How many times had Marco twisted a knife in my low moments? How many times had he mocked my pain or derided my decisions?

I took a step back from him, the truth washing over me. "No."

Ember reached out to me, but I slapped her hand away.

I didn't take my eyes off Marco's contrite face. "I'm not forgiving you. Not this time. You really are just like all the other camp men."

Marco bowed his head.

I did not stay to see what other effect my words had. I left the kitchen, a rushing sound in my ears, and hurried into my bedroom, where I fell onto my bed. There were no tears, no dry sobs, nothing. Just the drifting emptiness of losing another pillar. Marco was not the principles, but he was *Marco*, my faithful friend and a source of endless levity in my otherwise dismal life.

Had been. He was just another face now.

Someone knocked on my door. "Jilly?"

Marco's quiet voice cut through my hostility, but I didn't move. Instead, I pulled my pillow over my head.

"I'm sorry," he said, his voice breaking. "I'm so sorry. Please talk to me."

Dean wanted me to focus on my anger and harness it. I could do that, as I'd done so many times before. And right now, I had a lot of it. I could open my door and bombard him with such fury that he'd be a changed person. I could reduce him to dust, a whimpering remnant of the man he was now.

Or you could practice the seventh principle, kindness.

I gasped into the pillow. I *was* brainwashed. Here I was, facing a problem, and my mind automatically defaulted to one of the freaking principles.

"Jilly, please. I love you. Open the door so we can talk."

Be patient. Be sincere. Be virtuous. Be everything Patrick wasn't, Jill. You swore you would be the best leader you could be. What would Patrick do in this situation, and what is the opposite of that?

He would've destroyed Marco.

I took a deep breath. My pillow smelled musty. The shed that had sheltered Marco and me for several weeks had smelled musty, too. I'd enjoyed my quiet life with him then, even though we'd had to work sunup to sundown to scrounge a few dollars and the odd meal. We'd laughed and joked as we'd labored in the sun, content in each other's presence.

Though he'd been nothing more than a chatty nuisance when we were children, he'd quietly slipped into the spot in my heart that Gregory's departure had left behind. He'd come to Saint Catherine with me. He'd been the first to leave the team and find me.

He'd been the first to call me his leader. When it seemed as though the sky was falling, and nothing would ever be the same, he'd called me his leader and said he'd follow me.

No. Don't forgive him. He doesn't deserve it.

Invisible hands in my heart tried to grasp at the antipathy there, but it slipped through the fingers like water. Just as I was unable to feel joy anymore, so was I unable to reject my cousin. My heart could not handle that kind of loss.

I sat up. "Marco, you can come in." The door creaked open. Marco shuffled inside, his eyes never meeting mine. "Why don't you sit down."

He sat, still not looking at me. "I suck."

"Yeah, sometimes. I do, too."

"You don't."

"Yeah, I do. And you know who also sucks? Gregory."

Marco's head jerked up, his mouth a perfect O. "He—"

I held up a finger. "Don't get mad at me for saying it, 'cause it's true."

Marco stared at me for another second, then laughed quietly to himself. "Yeah, he does." He started to laugh harder. "Oh good gosh, he really does."

I gathered my hair and draped it over my shoulder, stroking it while I thought. "I don't think I'm going to try to be friends with him anymore. He's too far gone."

"Why not?" Marco said sadly. "If we just keep trying..."

I held out my hand to Marco, who took it in his own warm one. "No. I've had an image of him in my head for four years, but he's not that boy anymore. I saw that today. We've been replaced, and the quicker we accept that, the easier it'll be. Besides, I have another younger brother. I need to work out my problems with him because... because I care about my relationship with him more than I care about my relationship with Gregory."

I expected Marco to look away, or stare at me in shock, or say something typically Marco-ish. I did not expect him to suddenly grab me and hug me so tightly that my spine hurt.

He held me for a long time, never saying a word. Being in his unnaturally hot embrace wasn't comfortable, nor was the scratchy feeling of his hair against my cheek desirable. Yet I could not make myself pull away.

Marco finally released me and spoke in a rush. "You've always been my bossy, cool, intimidating older cousin. You were the big one. I was the little one. But when you said all that back there," he said, jerking his head toward the kitchen, "I saw myself differently. I'm a grown-ass man. I should've stepped in to protect you after the tribunal."

His face hardened. "You wouldn't have let anyone do to me what Matthew did to you. I've always been able to count on that. And I realized in the space of, like, five seconds that not only can you not say the same of me, but that I'd stood there and said I'd wished Matthew had attacked you, just because I was angry and confused.

That wasn't true. I've said a lot of terrible things and meant them, but that wasn't true."

"I know, and I forgive you." I pecked his cheek. "Let's start again."

An internal iceberg fractured and split, relieving a psychological weight of which I'd been unaware.

He patted my hand. "I'm going to be better. But this is hard, and I'm going to need help working through all the crap the elders taught us. Hearing you lay out what a marriage with Matthew would've meant, though... that was like being hit with a hammer. I couldn't help but picture it. I wanted to jump into my mind and kick his head in. It was so obviously wrong."

"Don't tell Benjamin, okay?" I twisted my hands in the blankets. "I don't want him to know."

He bit his lip, suddenly pensive. "I won't. But I'm not giving up on Greg."

"That's your prerogative. I'm going to finish dinner." I swung my legs onto the floor.

We walked back to the kitchen, where Ember and Reid were still seated at the table.

"Is everything okay?" Ember asked hesitantly.

I picked up Marco's fork, since mine was still on the other side of the room where I'd hurled it. He rolled his eyes but did not comment.

I smiled at Ember. "Yeah, we're fine." While I searched for a new subject for us to talk about, I took a bite of my corn and beans, which were unusually delicious. Apparently, Dean's powers affected both the appearance and taste of plants. "Did you guys know that Dean can play the harmonica?"

"Yep, I knew that. He has a clarinet, too," Marco said brightly. "According to some of the Sentinels, he'd love it if you asked to play it."

Ember kicked him under the table, but I frowned—I didn't know how to play the clarinet, and I had no idea why Dean would think I did.

Reid just sipped his water. "If you're going to repeat that to Benjamin, tell me beforehand so I can be there to watch."

The conversation turned to banter. I ate my cold dinner, not minding the temperature of the food. Right then I craved the intimacy from my little battle family, the three people who'd suffered with me under Patrick and followed me into the unknown. They'd seen me at my worst, when I'd cowered as Patrick advanced on me, and they'd watched me rise to new heights. These three, and Benjamin, were the most important people in my life.

Nobody talked about the raid, nor did Ember comment on the offensive meat on our plates. I shared my new knowledge about herbal remedies, which they all thought was fascinating. Reid vowed to buy only fresh herbs from then on, which were usually more potent than their dried forms.

"Do you think Benjamin knows more herbal remedies?" Ember asked, looking at the lone empty chair. "I'm sure he'd love to hear about traditional medicines."

I sipped my water. "You'll have to ask him yourself. I don't really want to talk to him right now."

Reid gathered up the empty plates. "It's odd that he cares so much about us killing people." His eyes darted toward Ember. "All of us have killed in the line of duty."

Ember closed her eyes and took a breath. "We're not soldiers, Reid. We kill as a last resort, with the value of human life at the—"

"Forefront of our decisions, yes, I *know*. You've only reminded me a dozen times."

Though I'd heard them shout at each other only a few hours before, it was still odd to hear Reid use that tone with Ember. He'd long struck me as the epitome of a gentleman—soft-spoken, polite, and considerate to women and men alike. Even before we'd overthrown Patrick, he'd never been anything but kind to me.

"If I've reminded you a dozen times," Ember growled, "it's because you keep forgetting."

Marco and I left Ember and Reid to their shouting.

Even though it was barely evening, we got ready for bed, because the Sentinels had to leave before midnight for the raid.

I'd just slipped under my blankets when Marco came into my room and sat at the foot of the bed. I sat up. "Hey."

His shoulder slumped. "Hey." He rubbed the back of his head. "Are you ready for the raid?"

"Honestly? No." Ember's shouted words echoed around the back of my mind, swirling with images of Gregory, Dean, and other Sentinels who'd been brutalized by the Westerners. "I guess I'm just not comfortable with killing people this way."

"Really? Reid did just point out that you've killed lots of people."

I heaved a sigh. "Yeah, I know. But it was always in self-defense or as a last resort. Even when the Destructor was blowing people up, we aimed to take him alive."

Marco's mouth twisted while he thought. "Maybe... maybe we're looking at this from the viewpoint of superheroes? And we shouldn't anymore? I don't know what we are."

I massaged my eyelids. "Maybe. I don't know what we are anymore, either. We're not superheroes, but I don't think any of the other Sentinels think we're one of them."

Ember's enraged voice interrupted us. "Don't you dare come back into this house tomorrow if that's how you feel about human life!"

Reid was quick to respond. "Why the hell would I ever want to come back to this house if I can't even protect my family without you tearing my head off?"

I winced. "Let's try to get some sleep."

Marco stood, then stooped down and kissed my forehead before hurrying out of the room. I set my watch's alarm for twenty-three hundred and closed my eyes.

The last thing I heard before falling asleep was ugly shouts coming from the kitchen mixed with the pleasant twittering of a small bird outside my window.

Then my watch beeped, and I sat up.

It was time for my first raid.

27

R eid's eyes glowed soft white. I pulled out my gun. We hid in the branches of a large pine, the spicy scent surrounding us.

I peered through the sticky needles and held my breath.

The ground shook for several seconds, toppling most of the twenty-five Westerners where they stood in their forested encampment. A wolf streaked past us, its fangs bared.

My team and I surged forward, ready for the kill. On the other side of the small camp, half a dozen Sentinels flooded the camp, guns drawn.

My brain took in the scene in lurches and lulls. I didn't hear the gunfire around me, nor did I wince at the anguished cries of the dying. Their fear and horror did not penetrate my heart.

Instead, I felt the cool metal in my hand, enjoying its weight. I smelled my warm breath inside the neck gaiter that concealed half of my face. The frozen earth was solid and dependable under my boots. The crisp early morning breeze played with a small lock of hair that had slipped out of my bun.

For one brief second, I asked myself if I was ready to abandon my superhero way of thinking and embrace what it meant to be a

Sentinel. A tiny, Benjamin-like voice tried to rise up, but I remembered Dean's advice to let my anger and hate become my fuel.

I hated the camps.

I hated the elders.

I hated what it meant to be a superhero, a peon of the camps that had hurt us so much.

I hated it all.

My hate solidified in my chest. The leaden sensation did not reach my feet, which were lighter than ever before as I ran into the clearing.

A Westerner crawled out of his fallen tent. I shot him in the head, just like I should've killed Patrick when he'd first beaten me.

A second man raised his hand to me and my throat closed. I shot his hand, and then his forehead. He'd tried to choke me with his mind, as Patrick had done so many times. My finger moved of its own volition as I shot him many more times than necessary.

Another man swiped at me with a knife as long as my hand. I blocked his attack and brought down my gun against his temple, relishing the crunch, which was similar to the sound Matthew's shin had made when I'd stepped on it. When he dropped, I shot him in the back of the head, just like the Westerners had done to the people who were supposed to replace Benjamin and Isabel.

A fourth Westerner shot at me from behind a large pine, missing by inches. I simply raised my gun and shot him in the forehead, ensuring that my eyes, visible above my neck gaiter, were the last things he ever saw.

There was silence in the dark clearing.

"Is everyone alive?" Dean asked.

Before I could answer, a man grabbed me from behind and pulled me close to him, a knife in his hand.

Without thinking I twisted and tossed him over my shoulder, then plunged my own knife into his neck. He twitched, then stilled.

I kneeled next to his corpse and tried to still my ragged breathing. Matthew had pulled me close to him, too. Matthew hadn't had a knife, but he might as well have held one to my throat while he... he...

The Sentinels cheered. The raid was over.

Two Sentinels ran over to me and patted me on the back, murmuring words of amazement that I had performed so well. A third Sentinel kicked the man I'd just killed, pure contempt in his eyes. It took me a second to realize that it was Gregory.

Slowly, so slowly, my vision widened, and my sense of time came back. I wasn't able to immediately gauge how long the attack had lasted. For all I knew, I'd been fighting for an hour, but the pre-dawn shade of blue above me hadn't lightened. Had it only been a few minutes?

I holstered my gun and gave my head a little shake.

Bodies were everywhere. Westerners littered the ground, their limbs bent at unnatural angles. Many bore bloody holes in their chests and faces. One of them lacked a head. The flesh of the head-less corpse smelled of cooked meat—Marco's doing, no doubt. I stepped over a man with a significant amount of neck missing and searched for the rest of my team.

Marco and Reid were in the center of the camp, examining a gash on Reid's arm by the warm light of an orb in Marco's hand. Reid dabbed at it with a cloth and winced.

I ran up to him. "Did one of them get you?"

Reid shook his head in disbelief. "I fell, and one of them jumped on me. Marco blasted the guy, so I'm okay."

"I'm fine, too," Marco said. "I wish I'd been able to kill more."

I pulled down my neck gaiter. "I killed five. That was... that was intense."

"How are you feeling?" Marco asked. "I know you don't like it when you have to kill people."

I glanced over at Dean, who was lining up the bodies on the ground. I looked back at Marco. "I'm fine. I'm going to go help Dean."

The leaden weight in my chest hadn't dissipated, but I didn't want to worry them. Perhaps if I set myself to a useful task like corpse disposal, I'd feel better.

I hurried over to Dean and picked up a still-warm corpse with little effort. "Here, let me." I dropped it on the ground next to the others. The man couldn't have been older than twenty.

The leaden weight descended into my stomach and mutated into nausea.

"How was your first raid?" Dean asked, elbowing me. "I told all the guys about the bet."

"You're an ass," I said, laughing with feigned mirth. "A stupid one. Now everyone is going to watch you lose." We finished lining up the bodies. "Want me to get Reid to help with burial?"

"Oh, yeah. That saves us a lot of time," Dean said, thoughtful. He waved at Reid, who hurried over. "Hey, Reid, we need a grave."

Reid's eyes glowed again, and he clenched his fist, staring intently at the ground beneath the bodies. A pit appeared, similar to the unfortunate lion pit from before the tribunal, and the bodies descended into the ground. After he'd lowered them about six feet, he swiped the air. Dirt fell onto the bodies, leaving nothing but a small depression in the ground.

"Lots of practice?" Dean asked, impressed.

"Tons. Though not just Westerners. I was the guy who buried everyone back home."

"Your life is depressing," Marco said. He wandered over to Gregory, who was speaking with Antonio. Gregory and Antonio paused in conversation to greet Marco, then continued their conversation.

Marco hung around the edge, unable to engage them.

I turned back to Dean. "Let's go back to camp and see who won that bet."

CHRISTIANA HADN'T JOINED the raiding party, so we walked back to our temporary camp on foot, hiking up and down foothills as the sun crested in the east.

The day was cloudless and freezing, and the prairie wind

whipped around us, cutting through my clothes. I shivered and pulled my neck gaiter up over my nose. A lone songbird flittered around above us, its yellow-orange belly making it appear as though it was a tiny ball of fire. Its plumage was familiar to me, though I could not place where I'd seen it before.

Reid and Marco flanked me, saying nothing. Every once in a while, Marco would turn to look behind us, where Gregory and Antonio were still conversing. He'd drop his head and turn away.

After the fourth time, I put my hand on his shoulder. "Do you want to talk about anything?"

"Antonio is a tool," Marco growled. "Why is Gregory friends with him? I bet he's the one saying all the nasty stuff about superheroes. He's a bad influence."

Reid and I exchanged quick glances.

"You know, I need to practice sparring," Reid said. "We haven't done any in a while. Wanna do that tonight?"

"Yeah, whatever," Marco muttered.

Reid sighed, and I shook my head sadly. "You should offer to teach Gregory some moves sometime," I suggested. "He was at the lesson yesterday. He might be more open to learning from you if Antonio isn't watching."

"Gregory doesn't want to learn what 'self-righteous bullies' learn," Marco spat. "I offered to coach him after Reid broke your nose. He called us that. He called *me* that."

"Gregory has issues," I said. "He's bitter and he's having trouble reconciling people he loves with the ideology he hates. That's why I decided to wait for him to come to me. He needs to come to the conclusion that we're not evil himself."

"But we were best friends!" Marco burst out. "There was a time when I didn't have any secrets from him. We used to play superheroes together when we were kids. I would be Apollo and he'd be..."

Marco let out a bitter laugh.

"He was Sentinel, because of his super eyesight. God, I'd forgotten that until just now. Sentinel." He kicked a rock. "The sun god and the sentinel. I guess we both got our wishes."

"SETTLE DOWN!" Dean called, beckoning for the small raiding party to come closer.

We were standing in the middle of the tiny cluster of tents we'd set up for the raid. "It's the moment of reckoning. I'm sure all of you remember me telling you about the little bet I made with Jillian." They hooted and hollered as Dean faced me. "All right, Battlecry, fess up. On your honor, how many did you kill?"

The corners of my mouth twitched. "Five."

"One was with a knife, though," Gregory said icily. "I saw you. The terms were that you had to shoot them, like an *actual* Sentinel."

"Okay, four then. God forbid I should use my knife to protect myself in a rear attack. Anybody with an hour of self-defense training will tell you—"

"How many did you kill?" Graham asked Dean.

"Five," Dean said with a little smile. "All headshots."

Damn it.

The Sentinels whooped and high-fived Dean.

I covered my eyes for a moment, riding out the embarrassment, then shook hands with Dean. "You won, fair and square. What do I have to do?"

Everyone watched Dean while he thought. I expected his usual smirk and an announcement of an exquisite humiliation, but instead his expression remained unusually serious.

"You don't have to do anything. You were right—you were attacked from behind and a knife made more sense. I wouldn't have wanted you to risk your life for the bet, so I'm letting you off the hook."

There were a few disappointed groans. "Um, okay," I said, taken aback. "If that's what you want."

The grumbling Sentinels dispersed to their tents. Dean looked over his shoulder to where Gregory and Antonio were speaking. "Gregory, come here."

Gregory waved Antonio on and walked up to us. "Yes?"

Dean's expression turned stern. "I'm concerned about the attitude you've been showing Jillian and her team. You implied back there that we are defined by our use of firearms, but that's never been true. We use guns because not all of us have powers, and most of the powers we have are impractical in battle. Nor do we always want to get up close to the Westerners. *Actual* Sentinels can appreciate the value in many forms of offense and defense. That's why I seized the opportunity to have superheroes working with us."

Gregory made a face. "They're not superheroes anymore. They're Sentinels now."

Marco stepped up. "No, you know what? I'm a damned superhero, Greg. Maybe I don't work for the camps anymore, but I'm not going to just turn my back on who I am just because I'm pissed at the elders."

"You can't go back," Gregory said through gritted teeth. "You left the camps. You're no more of a superhero than I am. You're just like me—camp trash that got thrown out."

"*Enough!*" Dean yelled. Gregory and Marco jumped. "Gregory, go cool off."

Gregory stormed away, joining Antonio and disappearing into their tent after one last furious look at us. I turned to ask Marco if he was all right, but he had already dashed into our tent. I knew to give him time before speaking to him. Reid, on the other hand, followed him into the tent.

"That was ugly," I said with a sigh. The wind blew again, and I shivered. "I'm going to go get some firewood. Wanna come with me?"

"Sure," Dean said. While we walked toward a line of trees at the edge of a nearby creek, he turned to me. "I thought Gregory would get over his resentment when he worked side by side with you guys, but there's more going on there than I thought." He sighed. "He's told me so much about the fierce sister he loved. I hoped he'd see you in battle and remember that you're the same person even though you're a superhero now."

"He's different than I remember him, but I hadn't thought that maybe we're different than how he remembers us. We must be so disappointing. You said so yourself."

We'd reached the trees. Instead of collecting firewood, Dean faced me. "No." He placed his hand on my shoulder and gave it a squeeze. "You're not. I was only teasing you to get a reaction when I said you were a disappointment. You traveled across the country and into the wilderness to find Benjamin and Isabel. That's exactly what I expected from Battlecry."

There was a quiet moment as we gazed at each other, the wind blowing wisps of my hair around.

"Dean?"

"Yeah?"

"Why did you call off the bet?" I gently removed his hand from my shoulder. "You *are* cocky, and I know you had something in mind when you issued the challenge."

Dean's brow furrowed. "I wasn't lying. I wouldn't have wanted you to risk your life to win a bet." All traces of his normal cavalier attitude were gone. "I'm actually surprised you didn't."

I looked down at the dead leaves on the ground. "When the man grabbed me from behind, it triggered a memory of when Matthew... of Matthew," I said quietly. "And instinct kicked in. My instincts are to use knives."

The corners of his eyes crinkled. "I'll never tell someone to go against their instincts in battle. For what it's worth, I liked watching you with the knife." He pulled down his neck gaiter and I did the same. "But what you said about Matthew... that's the other reason I didn't hold you to the bet."

"What does Matthew have to do with any of this?" A spiky ball of fear rolled down my spine.

Sadness settled on Dean. "If I won the bet, I was going to make you kiss me. But when you told me about Matthew, there was no way I was going to make you do it. I think you've had enough of that kind of thing."

I stood rooted to the earth. Dean wanted to make me kiss him? *Why?*

That wouldn't have been embarrassing, just silly and weird. The Sentinels would've laughed and whistled, and then forgotten about it.

Marco and Reid wouldn't have approved, and maybe even told Benjamin, but what could I do? A bet was a bet, and I'd lost.

I took in Dean's wistful expression and knew the answer to my question. "You know I'm with Benjamin." My voice was hardly above a whisper.

"Are you? Because all you've done since you've arrived here is fight. I know I'm not the only one who's noticed."

"We're going through a rough patch, though I don't know how we're going to get past it." I hated the truth.

As I spoke, I pictured Benjamin in the chemical lab, a gun in his hand. Berenice was on the floor.

The image swirled and changed to Benjamin's barb in the tent, the words he'd spat at me, the request for five minutes of peace from having to "deal" with me and my stupid network of superheroes.

I closed my eyes against the onslaught of pain but was unable to stop it. He'd rolled his eyes at me when I tried to tell him about Matthew. *Matthew.*

Dean took a small step closer. "I understand. If there's anything I can do to help, just tell me."

Something in me gave way.

Without a word, I pulled Dean close and kissed him, wrapping my arms around his broad shoulders. His lips parted, and I felt his breath in my mouth, and the pleasant pressure of his piercings against my lips.

He returned my passion eagerly, pressing himself close and relaxing into the moment. His hands traveled down to my waist. I moaned, wanting more.

For one second, I was sitting by the campfire before the tribunal, and his hands were Benjamin's.

I ran my hands through Dean's black hair, eliciting a breathy gasp from him. He unwound my bun and loosened my hair, tangling his fingers in it and causing pleasurable sensations to shoot through my body.

I was by the fire again, kissing Benjamin passionately, enjoying how he tugged on my hair.

Suddenly I was up against a tree, shoved against the rough bark by Dean's comforting, masculine weight. Our hands seemed to be everywhere at once while we explored each other. The temperature underneath my fleece had risen to an uncomfortable level.

I lifted a shaking hand to my fleece's zipper.

Fantasies and possibilities flitted through my mind: going to Dean's house, tearing each other's clothes off, the night of pleasure and relaxation, his hands on my body that I'd invited and welcomed. He'd eagerly accept my offer to be my first.

Our liaison would crush Benjamin, even more than he'd be crushed if he knew that we were kissing. Maybe then he'd understand how I felt when he'd rolled his eyes at me.

As I began to slowly unzip my fleece, I pulled my mouth away a fraction of an inch and inhaled, preparing to ask him the question to which he'd never say no. Dean never said no to me.

He breathed my name.

His voice was not Benjamin's.

I broke away from him, blinking rapidly and panting. "We're getting carried away. The guys will wonder where we've gone. Go back to the camp and I'll get the firewood."

Dean put a hand on his heaving chest, then nodded. "You're right. I'll see you there." He dashed toward the camp and disappeared over the hill.

I collapsed to my knees, letting the tears fall. They turned into sobs. I leaned back against a pine tree, crying freely.

What was *wrong* with me? Why had I kissed Dean? I barely knew him. What had spurred me to cheat on my boyfriend with a man I'd met less than a week before? What had spurred me to cheat on my boyfriend, period?

I sniffed and wiped my nose. Maybe what I'd done wasn't so bad. I'd kissed Dean because Benjamin hadn't been receptive to my attempt to talk about Matthew.

Because he's jealous of Dean.

The thought, almost peaceful in its simplicity, flowed through my mind. I'd been too angry with Benjamin's reticence to be honest to focus on the real reason he'd grown cold and distant in the medical building. Benjamin had no way of knowing that I hadn't even thought of pursuing Dean. He'd seen the rose and assumed the worst.

The worst had just happened, unless Benjamin thought Dean and I were sleeping together.

A hysterical, nervous giggle escaped me at the thought. I didn't want to sleep with Dean—not really. He could provide a moment's pleasure and comfort, I was sure, and would be more than willing to go to bed with me. He was handsome, brave, friendly, and displayed a lust for action and adventure that I shared.

But I couldn't even kiss him without fantasizing about Benjamin. I loved Benjamin. I loved him, and I wanted to be with him.

But he might not want to be with you when he hears about what you just did.

I stood on shaking legs and collected firewood, all the while figuring out how I was going to tell Benjamin about my infidelity.

28

I crawled into bed and put my pillow over my head to block out Ember and Reid's shouts in the living room. They'd been yelling at each other for fifteen minutes.

"—and I just want to be able to do what I feel is right without my girlfriend getting on my case! I shouldn't have to have your permission to do every little thing!"

"This isn't a little thing, Reid! This is abandoning your vows to protect Saint Catherine so you can play soldier!"

"You think this is a game?"

"Sure, why not! You think our relationship is a game! Why not killing Westerners, too?"

"How can you say that?"

"How can *you* say that I'm the center of your world and that you want to spend the rest of your life with me, and then just drop everything for revenge?"

"This isn't revenge, it's justice!"

"That is bull, and you know it!"

"They'll never stop, Ember! They'll never stop taking our people and killing us! I'm trying to protect you!"

"No, you're trying to make yourself *feel better!*" Ember's voice grew shrill.

I sat up in bed, my face in my hands. There was no way I was going to sleep.

"I hate it here, Reid! I hate the Sentinels! I hate that you're a different person when you're around them! And I *hate* that everything you said to me before the tribunal suddenly doesn't matter now that you can kill Westerners all day long!"

"You're just mad because your powers aren't working," Reid growled. "That's what this is about. You feel powerless, and you're taking it out on me."

Ember's voice grew dangerously quiet. "Oh, is that it? Thank you for explaining to me how I *really* feel. So, I'm upset that I'm power-less, huh? Well, there's one thing I can still do."

I bit my lip, knowing what was coming. "Don't do it," I whispered into the dark.

"We're over, Reid. I'm sick of this."

He gasped. "Ember, no. Please."

"Get out of my sight."

"Ember, please!"

"I said leave. You said you wanted freedom to murder people without your girlfriend getting on your case, right? Well, you've got it. I'm not your girlfriend anymore. Go butcher people to your heart's content."

"Sweetheart! *Please!*"

Ember burst into our bedroom and slammed the door behind her. She threw herself on her bed and began to sob.

I waited a few seconds, then walked over to her and kneeled next to her in the dark. I didn't know what to say.

"Did I just do that?" she asked between sobs.

I stroked her hand. "Yes."

"Do you think he hates me now?"

"No. Reid loves you. He will always love you."

She sobbed harder, unable to speak for several minutes. I held her hand, tears slipping down my own face and dripping off my chin. There was so much pain in the house now.

She finally hiccupped and wiped her nose. "That's what he said the night before the tribunal. We went on a walk, remember? It was cold, so he made a little shelter for us. He held me and promised to protect me. He said he'd always love me and that he wanted to spend the rest of his life with me." Her body shook as tears flowed anew. "We made love," she whispered. "It was our first time. He told me afterward that all he wanted from life was to be with me. Now all he wants is revenge. I hate the Sentinels."

She began to sob again, curling into a ball underneath the sheets.

I pushed her over in the bed and laid down next to her. "Benjamin and I are going to break up tomorrow, too. We can be miserable together." It was the only thing I could think of that might make her feel better.

"Why?" she squeaked.

"I kissed Dean today."

"You're a moron, Jill."

"I know."

I held her while she cried herself to sleep, then let myself close my eyes and drift off into troubled dreams.

I awoke to the sound of gunfire.

"GET UP! GET UP!" Marco sprinted into our room and yanked back the covers. "Get your weapons! Now!"

Before I could even rub my eyes and ask what was going on, a bottle with a flaming cloth attached to it crashed through our window, shattering on the floor and spreading accelerant over the hardwood. A blaze sprung up immediately.

Ember and I screamed and jumped out of bed, edging along the wall and dashing out of the bedroom.

Reid fled his room, pulling on a jacket. "What's going on?" He grabbed Ember. "Are you okay?"

I pulled them away from the doorway. "We have to get out of the house!"

As I said the words, bullets tore through the walls and windows. Our room was already engulfed in flames. Outside, the terrified screams of women and children mixed with the angry yells of men.

Above it all, gunfire pierced the scene.

I looked around frantically. "Where's Benjamin?"

"Infirmary!" Marco shouted.

A hellacious *whoosh* told me that the ceiling was on fire.

The four of us rushed out of the house.

Armed men ran in every direction, shooting wildly at the residents. Nearly every building was on fire, the flames reflected in the broken glass all over the ground. Next to our house, small, bloody footprints led off into the forest.

A man across the street grabbed a tiny boy, while another dragged a hysterical woman toward a truck idling in the trees.

"They're taking captives! Stop them!" I screamed.

Marco's eyes glowed yellow and he raised his hand, releasing a beam of heat at the truck. The beam cut through the grill, melting the engine block. He rushed toward the man.

I grabbed Ember's hand and sprinted toward the infirmary, ducking behind trees and buildings. I had to get to Benjamin. I'd defend him against the Westerners with my life.

Two men wrestled a blonde woman to the ground twenty feet from us and pulled a burlap sack over her head. I shoved Ember behind a tree and hurled my knife into one of the men's heads, then threw myself on the other one, breaking his neck with a simple twist.

I pulled the bag off and gasped—it was Eleanor.

"Go!" she yelled. "Help the others!"

I jumped up and ran back to Ember. "We need to get inside!" Ember shouted. "There's too many of them!"

I agreed. There was an unknown number of Westerners in Liberty, and while I wanted to get a machine gun from the armory and start fighting back, I had to consider Ember and Benjamin's safety. We were thirty yards from the infirmary. One good dash and we'd be reasonably safe, and then I could protect them both from the marauders.

An explosion in a nearby house blasted Ember and me several feet forward, directly into the middle of the street.

We tumbled over and over in the beaten snow and gravel, coming to rest in a disoriented, bruised pile. I pressed my hand to the warm trickle inching down my face. My ear was bleeding.

In the distance, a man yelled, "That's them!"

The world went dark as a burlap sack was shoved over my head.

I screamed and thrashed against my attacker. I couldn't see where he was or how many of them there were, but I heard Ember struggling. I reached for my knife, but it was gone. Without a weapon, I groped around wildly for anything I could reach, and settled for jamming my elbow into a muscular abdomen repeatedly. The man grunted but didn't let go.

Warm hands lifted up the side of my shirt and pressed cold metal points into my skin.

Every muscle in my body constricted at once, ripping an agonized scream from my throat. I fell to the ground, my limbs jerking uncontrollably. Nearby I heard the sharp buzzing of the Taser followed by Ember's high scream.

Someone grabbed me under my arms and began to drag me down the road.

A few feet away, the zipping of a bullet ended in the sound of a body hitting the ground. A wet, hollow pop above me concluded with a heavy thud next to me.

I lay on my side in the middle of the snow-covered road, my muscles not responding to my brain's commands. All around me, the night was torn apart by screams of terror and pain.

Cracking, splintering crashes began to join the pandemonium. Houses were collapsing.

With stiff, jerky movements I sat up and pulled off the sack. Spots floated in my blurry vision as I fell into a crawl and dragged an unconscious Ember by the hand to the side of the road, in front of a smoldering shell that used to be a house. Its occupants were nowhere in sight.

"Ember, wake up," I croaked, shaking her. "Wake up. We need to get inside."

The ground trembled. Elsewhere, Reid was battling the Westerners he hated so much. I tried to rise and join him, but my legs would not respond. My bare feet burned, though I could not tell if it was from the below-freezing temperature or a side effect of electrocution. They were bleeding. I watched the blood ooze from the cuts with remote fascination.

Trucks and vans began to race away down the road, their revving engines loud and powerful as they passed us. Men leaned out of the windows and shot at random targets, yelling and whooping. Some tossed yet more burning bottles.

My shoulder exploded in crippling agony. I fell backwards, warm blood flowing in the soft snow beneath me, and gazed up at the full moon overhead as it shone through the clouds. Snow swirled down in gentle spirals.

It was so quiet.

29

I sat up with a gasp.

I was on the floor of the main building, which had miraculously survived the raid, surrounded by three dozen or so blinking and confused people. Several Sentinels walked up and down the rows, offering water to the people on the floor.

Next to me, Ember sat up and rubbed her head. "What happened?"

Benjamin blurred up to us, his face gaunt. "I thought you weren't going to wake up," he said, handing us water bottles. "I healed you both minutes ago. It doesn't usually take that long."

I poked my shoulder through the neat little hole in the cloth. "Was I shot?"

"Yeah," he said, his voice raspy. "And electrocuted. And your feet were torn up. You'd lost a lot of blood and you both had Taser burns." He reached out to touch my face, then pulled his hand away.

I pushed myself to my feet, then helped Ember up. "How many casualties?"

"Fourteen dead. Ten missing. No injuries, but a lot of the kids are psychologically scarred for life, and I can't do anything about that." He pointed to a little boy who was huddled in the corner, rocking back and forth without blinking. "Aiden's dad was killed in front of him, and his mom was dragged away."

"Where's Marco and Reid?" I asked, working to not growl the words. I would have my revenge against the Westerners, but first I needed to make sure my team was safe.

"Marco was shot three times, but he's fine now. Reid got burned, but besides some missing hair, he's good. I made sure of it. They're both in the other room. Reid's been talking nonstop about you," he said to Ember. "He thought you were dead when they brought you in and, uh, kinda had a breakdown."

Ember gasped and ran off to the little room off to the side.

Before I could help myself, I threw my arms around Benjamin, who froze, then returned the tight embrace. He stroked my hair, which was sticky and matted with blood.

"I thought you were dead, too," he whispered. "I was the one who found you in the snow in front of the infirmary. You were coming to protect me, weren't you?"

I inhaled the smoky, salty smell of his neck. "Yes. I thought they were going to try to take you again."

"I wasn't sure if you cared anymore," he said quietly. "But I do. I always will."

I pulled away and looked at him. Though his face was smudged with soot, it seemed to me that there had never been a more hand-some man to grace the earth. I trailed a finger down his cheek. He closed his eyes, his breaths slowing and deepening. When my finger passed over his lips, they parted slightly.

Our intimacy reminded me of the last intimate moment I'd had.

"We need to talk," I whispered. "About Dean."

His eyes flew open. "What happened?"

His tense question made me look down. Benjamin was sharp enough to sense that something had "happened," and for the first time I couldn't deny it.

I couldn't meet his eyes. "Later. In private."

He grabbed my hand. "Tell me what happened." His tense words held a vein of fear.

"Jillian! You're okay!"

I broke away from Benjamin and turned around to watch Dean hurry toward us. His clothes were tattered and burnt, hanging off him like rags.

"Yes, I'm okay. Benjamin healed me."

Instead of answering, Dean swept me up into a deep kiss.

There was no warmth in my stomach, no fluttering in my chest, just shock and horror that Benjamin was watching the fruit of my terrible mistake.

Dean let go and looked me up and down. "As soon as we regroup, we're going to plan a counterattack. They took Graham and Antonio, as well as some of the non-Sentinels. Get your team."

I nodded, dumbstruck, and slowly looked around for Benjamin.

He was gone.

30

T wo days passed.

The main building, the armory, the school, the infirmary, and eight houses had survived the attack. All other buildings had been burned to the ground. Patches of red snow were soon covered by fresh snowfall, hiding the signs of the recent violence.

Seventy-five people had lived in Liberty before the attack. Nearly a third of them were now dead or taken captive. The remaining residents were hobbled by grief and despair, and rebuilding efforts were slow. There were few spare construction supplies on hand, and further hindering the reconstruction efforts was the fact that most able-bodied men were desperate for revenge and only wanted to rescue their friends. Repairing a town did not satisfy this hunger.

Meanwhile, my team was splintering down the middle, and I could do nothing to stop it.

The morning after Dean's passionate kiss, Benjamin would not speak to me, or even look at me. He moved into the infirmary's quarters, which had two beds for the medical team Liberty had always hoped to bring in.

Upon hearing that there was a second bed, Reid joined him. Ember cried for hours but did not ask him to come back.

Marco, Ember, and I moved into the armory along with several other Sentinels, leaving the more comfortable main building and school for the civilians.

Gregory was more irascible than ever, terrified that Antonio, a recently rescued slave, would be punished for his activities with the Sentinels. When Marco vowed to help him find Antonio, Gregory screamed that he didn't need a superhero's help to find his "brother."

Marco didn't speak much after that.

With that weight on my shoulders, I began to help salvage efforts on the second day after the attack. Before I began, Dean pulled me aside and told me to search for one thing only: the safe containing JM-104.

"It was in my house," he said, throwing a worried glance at the blackened, ashy wreckage he'd once called home. "I can't find it. Keep the news to yourself, though. I don't want to start a panic."

Thankfully, he was so busy with reconstruction that we'd barely had time to speak apart from that moment.

I tossed a crumbling beam aside and scoured the charcoaled floor for anything resembling a safe. Besides wood and remaining bits of furniture and hardware, there was nothing recognizable. I pushed more debris to the side and cleared the foundation, but the safe wasn't there.

I walked all around the yard, feeling around in the foot-deep snow for a metal box. Nothing. I looked behind trees and bushes in nearby yards, remembering the blast that had tossed Ember and me to the ground, thinking that perhaps an explosion had thrown the safe, too.

After an hour, I had to conclude that the safe was not to be found.

The snow, which had been falling lightly all morning, began to thicken and swirl in the rising wind. A snowstorm was moving in, which would hamper the search. After one final sweep of the area, I hurried down the street to the armory, where most of the Sentinels had already retired because of the storm.

Marco and Ember were in the main building, spending time with several children who'd lost one or both parents. Reid was checking the new earthen fortifications around the perimeter of Liberty.

I pushed open the armory's door and was greeted by the sight of Benjamin attending to four flu-sufferers on cots in the corner. He gave me a hard stare, then turned back to John Carl, Zander, Gabe, and a man I thought might be named Jonathan.

Dean was in the corner, speaking in hushed tones to Ken. They both looked worried.

I joined them. "Any luck?" Dean asked.

"No," I said, my voice low. "It's not there. I searched the entire area."

Dean swore. "I don't understand where it could've gone."

I failed to see the great mystery here. The answer was obvious. "Dean, they probably took it. This was a raid, right? They stole the most valuable things in the camp. I'm amazed they didn't plunder the armory, too."

"No, that doesn't make sense. Few people even know that we had JM-104. I don't tell everyone about it because of stuff like this. Your brother doesn't know, for example. The Westerners couldn't have known we had it."

I shook my head. "But they knew where Liberty was. They brought enough trucks to take nearly everyone here, so they knew how many people we had. Obviously, they have some kind of intelligence network. If they knew that, we have to assume they knew about the JM-104."

There was a long pause. "Are you suggesting espionage?" Ken asked. "I trust everyone here."

I took a deep breath. "The way I see it, the JM-104 was taken even though it was a secret, and the Westerners knew where this place was and how many people were here, even though Liberty is secret. It might be time to consider that you have a leak, or possibly even a mole. Goodness knows the Westerners are desperate enough to plant one."

The three of us gazed at the gathered Sentinels, who were sitting and talking quietly throughout the armory. I knew that Dean and

Ken were thinking what I was thinking—that any of them could've been the leak, and there was no way to know who.

Except there was.

"Ember will find out," I said. "If we can get Christiana away from Ember, we can use telepathy to pick the minds of everyone here and find out who the leak is."

"I hate the prospect of invading my men's privacy like that," Dean said. "But that is a good idea."

"Back off, Judd!"

My brother's furious yell echoed around the armory. All heads turned toward Gregory and Judd in the far corner, who were facing each other with clenched fists.

"No! It's your fault they got so many people! If you'd actually been where you were supposed to be that night—"

"The building was on fire, idiot! What the hell was I supposed to do?"

I walked toward Gregory and Judd. "What's going on here?"

"Oh, great, the clearing barrel is here to lecture us," Judd said, rolling his eyes. "What are you going to do, tell me I violated some principle?"

People began to gather around at a safe distance.

I crossed my arms but kept my face blank. "Is it the Sentinel way to make ridiculous accusations about your comrades?" I looked at Gregory. "I'm glad you didn't die. I wouldn't have wanted that."

"I don't care what you want," Gregory said. "Go away. This has nothing to do with you."

My chest throbbed, but I shrugged. "You're my brother. If someone is yelling at you and accusing you of—"

"This has nothing to do with you, Jill! Just get out of my face!"

There was a beat.

"Fine. See you around, Gregory."

I turned away to go back to Dean and Ken. Under his breath, Judd muttered a slur that even *I* never used.

I whirled around. "What did you just call me?"

"You heard me," he mumbled. "Nobody wants you and your team

here. Just do us all a favor and go back to whatever ghetto city you came from and leave us to do the real work."

I opened my mouth to call him a particularly nasty name in return.

Judd drew his handgun and pointed it at me.

For a fraction of a second, all I saw was the barrel of his gun, two feet from my face. My instincts screamed at me to disarm him, but I couldn't make my hand move. If he shot me, I'd never feel a thing.

Benjamin slammed Judd into the wall. He pinned him there with his forearm against his chest. "Drop your weapon. Now."

Judd dropped his handgun to the floor.

Benjamin released him, a scowl marring his handsome face. "Now get *far* away from me." Judd sidled along the wall toward the crowd, staring wide-eyed at Benjamin.

Benjamin turned to me, still scowling. "Are you okay?"

"Yes," I said, still stunned that Judd had drawn his weapon over mere words—but more so that I hadn't stopped him.

"Good." He faced the crowd, his eyes sparking with anger. "Let me make something very clear to all of you." His voice grew louder and carried over the crowd. "If any of you so much as look at a member of my team the wrong way, not only will I withhold medical help when you need it, I will hurt you. Don't let the red cross on my uniform fool you. I am neither your friend, nor an easy target. You do *not* want to cross me."

"You can't do that," one of the Sentinels protested. "You have to provide medical help."

Benjamin narrowed his eyes, looking more dangerous than I'd ever seen him. "You seem to be laboring under a misapprehension. Despite what your leader would have you believe, I am not a doctor. I took no oath other than a promise to serve and protect the people of Saint Catherine. Nobody—not Jillian, not Dean, not God Himself— can make me heal someone without my consent. Do I *make myself clear*?"

His shout echoed around the armory. The Sentinels nodded, dumbstruck.

He turned to me. "The four of you can come to me any time for healing, but I'd appreciate if some of you didn't unless it's truly life-threatening."

I understood the meaning of his cold words perfectly.

He stormed back to the flu patients.

The crowd dispersed, but Dean crossed the room and grabbed Judd. "Get your weapon and give it to me."

Judd had the sense to surrender his gun without protest. "Here," he muttered.

Dean unloaded it. "You're not going to join us on the next raid. You're not getting this back until you understand not to point a gun at anything you don't intend to shoot."

Judd stared at me with obvious hatred. "Right. Superheroes are our friends."

31

That night, I laid on my cot and stared up at the ceiling.

Next to me, on their own cots, Ember and Marco slept peacefully, their dreams seemingly undisturbed by memories of Patrick, Matthew, Benjamin, and Judd. The armory was freezing, but my woolen blankets and thick winter gear were enough to keep out the cold. My internal tremor had nothing to do with the temperature.

I pulled the blankets up to my chin, the walls pressing down on me. I needed to get out of the confining armory and feel the wind on my face.

I swung my feet on the floor and pulled up my neck gaiter, then walked silently past the sleeping forms of Dean and Ken, who flanked the door. I pushed it open and slipped through, shutting it softly behind me.

The snowstorm whirled around me, burying Liberty in soft snow drifts. I staggered through the snow, unsure of where I was going. I was so tired and cold, but I didn't want to go back to the armory. I didn't want to see Dean or Judd or Gregory, or any other Sentinel.

I just wanted to go home.

But where was home for me? Benjamin had sworn an oath to serve and protect Saint Catherine, as had I, but Saint Catherine was dangerous for us now. It would be where the strike team would begin their search for us rogue superheroes.

We weren't even really superheroes anymore, despite what the Sentinels said. We weren't anything or anyone. Just as I'd warned Benjamin, we'd left the camps and now we were drifting in limbo.

I wandered into the tree line, where the snow wasn't so deep. It was quiet except for a faint, omnipresent crackle of the snow touching down. I trudged away from Liberty, able to see my way in the forest thanks to the full moon's light reflecting off the snow, which appeared blue in the light.

I reached a high earthen wall—Reid's fortification. I ran my gloved hand over it. Though it was compacted dirt, it was as hard as stone. As steel.

I was trapped by another wall.

I fell to my knees, resting my forehead against the cold wall. I had no tears left to cry. I had nothing left inside me, nothing but the emptiness left behind by the principles, and the anger that constantly filled the emptiness, then drained away, then filled it again. The cycle burned every time, but I didn't know how to stop it.

The principles had never burned.

"The first principle, cautiousness," I whispered. "I... I will use judgment in hazardous situations. The second principle, deference. I will yield to the will of the authorities over me." The familiar words and definitions coursed through my mind, bringing a sense of peace I hadn't felt in weeks. "The third principle, decisiveness. I will... I will..."

I will choose a course of action when required and see it through.

The third principle was where I'd failed. I'd let my team be bounced around by the winds of change and chance. I hadn't made a decision about our future and seen it through. We could've gone back to Saint Catherine, we could've firmly decided to stay with the Sentinels, or we could've forged ahead into the unknown. I had no idea what I should've chosen. Isabel needed to be rescued, but that wasn't a reason to live. That wasn't my entire life's *purpose*.

What would my grandmother have done?

I sat against the wall and dropped my hands into my lap. I had no idea what Jillian St. James, the first Battlecry, would've done. All anybody ever remembered about her was that she'd led her team and been murdered. I liked to imagine that my double namesake had been fierce and proud, but I didn't know for sure.

I did know quite a bit about *her* grandmother, my great-great-grandmother Christina St. James, such as the fact that she'd gone public with her powers during World War I, the first Super to do so.

Christina had been the quiet, demure wife of a nice man, and the mother of six children, when she'd received word that her eldest son had been captured by the Germans. She'd flown across the Atlantic —the only known Super capable of flight—and stormed the prison camp, unafraid of bullets or bombs because she was also invulnerable to harm.

Following the almost immediate surrender of the Central Powers, the American people had been eager to learn more about the woman who could fight armies. Soon others came forward with their amazing gifts, and the first superhero teams were formed.

Christina had compiled the first list of principles, guidelines for how we should conduct ourselves. Garrett Williamson had "fixed" the guidelines decades later and added rule after rule about how we should live our lives. One of the first rules was that women couldn't be leaders because they were too emotional.

For the first time since taking over my team, I couldn't fully disagree with him. I was such a failure, in every possible way. I couldn't sleep because I had nightmares about people who were no longer in my life. I had flashbacks about them during combat. I'd ruined my relationship with Benjamin. I couldn't make Marco happy. I had no idea how to help Ember and Reid. I had no purpose.

I longed to be a machine, unburdened by memories of Patrick's abuse and Matthew's hands.

No, that wasn't what I longed for.

More than anything, I wanted sleep. Deep sleep. I wanted to fall asleep and never wake up, never have to see the hate in my brother's eyes and the betrayal in Benjamin's. I wasn't even cold anymore. If I sat out here long enough, I would fall asleep. It would be peaceful. I'd dream about Matthew for a little while, and then I wouldn't dream.

I closed my eyes and slowed my breathing. I pretended that the snowstorm was creating a soft blanket of snow around me. I wasn't sad. I had no future to mourn.

Warm hands lifted my chin up.

I cracked open my eyelids, which were stiff with cold.

"Jill?" Marco was kneeling next to me. "Jill, please look at me. We need to go inside." His voice sounded indistinct and far away, like a badly-tuned radio.

I didn't move. I was so tired. Marco looked over his shoulder and yelled something, but I couldn't focus on his words. The whole world wavered, as if I were under water. Why couldn't he just let me sleep?

A white face wreathed in red appeared, and then suddenly I was standing up, moving through the forest. They were helping me walk, though I could not feel my feet. Liberty neared, and then we were in the clearing, headed for the main building.

A gloved hand opened the door and warm air gushed out. People were sleeping on the carpet.

"Set her down by the heater," Marco instructed. "We need to warm her up. Can you get some warm clothes and a drink, please?"

Marco took my gloves off and grasped my hands in his. I couldn't feel them, nor could I move my mouth to tell him so. Instead, I admired the stark contrast of our skin tones, his pretty sepia against my bone white. My hands weren't always so pale—what had happened?

Ember gently tipped a salty, warm beverage down my throat. It snaked through me, heating my insides in a way that was painful and pleasant at the same time. I began to shiver.

"Good, that means she's warming up," Marco said. "Put the heated blanket around her."

The room finally came into focus and I noticed how hard I was shaking. "More, please," I whispered.

Ember handed me the steaming cup, her eyes wide. "Why were

you out in the snow? We woke up and followed your tracks. What were you doing walking around in a snowstorm?"

"I want to sleep," I mumbled.

"So stay in your cot," Marco said, incredulous. "If you sleep out in the snow, you'll... die..." Sad realization dawned on his face. "Jill, what happened?"

Ember stroked my hand, which ached down to the bones. "Please talk to us. You keep saying you're alright, but you're not. You're just not. You weren't doing well before the tribunal, but now it's so much worse."

I couldn't find the words to express why I'd sat down in the snow and waited to slip away. How could I begin to explain emotions that even I didn't fully understand? It wasn't one thing, or even a combination of things. It wasn't Benjamin's dishonesty, Gregory's rejection, Patrick's tortured last breaths, or the lingering memory of Matthew's fingers. It wasn't the anger and pain that choked me. It wasn't even the betrayal of the elders.

It was something else, something insidious and all-consuming.

It was running my hand along the wall and realizing that no matter how far I ran, how hard I fought, I was trapped. I would always be trapped. I was a lion in a zoo, a predator bred in captivity, on display for the American people.

Temporary sleep provided no relief, when I could get it. In my dreams, Patrick beat me, or Matthew assaulted me, ignoring my screams and pleas. I was powerless and afraid, and I was tired of being powerless and afraid. Death was the only option.

Ember cradled my head in her hands. "I've read about mental illnesses." Her eyes were large and kind. "There's a disease where you can't be happy, called depression. I... I think you should talk to Benjamin about it. Talking to people about how you feel is one of the ways people deal with it."

"I'm not sick," I mumbled. "And Benjamin doesn't want to talk to me unless it's life-threatening."

"You were going to let yourself die, and this isn't the first time you've thought about it. Remember your promise to Benjamin on the way to the tribunal? You said you'd keep yourself alive. He'd want to know."

I drew my knees to my chest. "He doesn't want to know. I've tried to talk to him, and he got angry about Dean."

"Benjamin is extremely jealous of Dean," Ember said. "And you need to be honest with him about what happened between you two. But Benjamin loves you, and he wants to be with you. You need to talk to him, even if he's being a butthead."

Marco looked confused. "Wait, what happened between you and Dean? Is that why Benjamin moved into the infirmary?"

"I was angry at Benjamin, so I kissed Dean. And then Dean kissed me in front of Benjamin after the attack."

Marco let out a long breath. "Wow. Why didn't you just shoot him?"

His mention of gunshots dislodged something inside me, and tears began to fall. Ember held me while I cried and shook, unable to rid myself of the memory of Judd's gun, and the men I'd killed during the raid several days before. I'd become someone else during the raid, someone I was terrified to be again.

"Aw, Jill, please don't cry," Marco pleaded. "I'm sorry. I didn't mean it like that."

"You say a lot of things that hurt, actually," Ember said sternly. "Like when you made fun of Jill for wanting to jump off the bridge last summer, or when you said that what Matthew did to her wasn't as bad as what Patrick did to me."

Marco clasped his hands in his lap. "I already apologized, and I really meant it. We talked about it and everything. I don't want to be the bad guy anymore, but I just don't see why Jill can't just let these things go and move on. Patrick's dead and she'll never see Matthew again."

"I don't know how to move on," I said, still crying.

"I talked to Reid about my attack," Ember said, stroking my hair. "He was willing to listen as much as I needed him to. It always helped, and now I don't have nightmares anymore. Talking to someone doesn't make you weak. Is that what you're worried about? Appearing weak?"

I nodded.

Marco drew me into a hug. "I'm sorry. I'm so sorry." He murmured sweet words into my ear that eventually caused my crying to slow. My cousin hadn't talked to me like that since we thought Gregory had died.

The three of us sat on the floor in the corner of the main building for an hour. Ember tried to persuade me to talk to Benjamin, but I wouldn't budge. He didn't want to see me, and I was unwilling to share such intimate information with someone who was withholding information from me.

Marco promised to speak to Benjamin about my disinterest in Dean, though he didn't hold out much hope.

"He probably thinks you and Dean are doing it," he said as we walked back to the armory. The snowy town glowed silver in the moonlight. "God, Jill, he's so in love with you, it's hard to be around him sometimes. When he gets started about how *brave* you are, and how *pretty* you are, and how glad he is that he met you, and how you changed his life, blah blah blah, it drives me up the wall. And then Reid jumps in about you, Ember..."

"Let's go back to bed now," Ember said, pushing open the door to the armory. "We can talk about this later."

We laid back down in our cots and pulled the blankets around ourselves. I felt a little better, as if I'd shed a burden.

But once again I stared up at the ceiling, wishing for sleep.

And then I woke up, warm and rested.

"Hey," Dean said, tying his boots. "You were sleeping hard. Good thing, too. I need to work out a plan with you and Ember about how we're going to find that information we talked about yesterday." He glanced at the other Sentinels, who were still waking up. "I want this done as quickly and quietly as possible."

"Understood." I sat up and stepped into my boots, then leaned toward Dean. "But first we need to talk about something."

32

Ember sat in a folding chair across from Jonathan, whose red nose and watery eyes made him appear as if he were sad to be in the little tent with us. However, when Ember extended her hands toward his, he grinned and took them in his own.

I resisted the urge to roll my eyes; all the Sentinels had been more than willing to let Ember ask them questions. Christiana had driven several miles outside of Liberty, so we could interview them.

Dean stood behind Jonathan. I stood behind Ember. Occasionally Dean would glance at me, disappointment evident on his face, but other than that he gave no indication that we'd had a short, unhappy conversation before beginning the interrogations.

I'd led him outside behind the armory and explained that I was dating Benjamin and I'd used Dean to make myself feel better, and then apologized for taking advantage of his feelings. When I'd asked for forgiveness and a new start, Dean had insisted that I hadn't taken advantage of him, a reaction that didn't surprise me one bit.

He'd asked for one last kiss, but I'd held a finger up to his lips. "No, Dean. I cheated on Benjamin once, and that's enough for a lifetime."

"What do you see in him?"

"There aren't enough hours in the day to answer that question."

We'd assured each other that we'd move on from whatever it was that had happened, and that it wouldn't affect our professional inter-actions. So far, Dean had kept his side of the promise. I liked to think that I had, too. We both supervised Ember's time with each Sentinel, asking questions as needed.

In the tent, Dean repeated the same words he'd said to the last two dozen people.

"Jonathan, Ember is going to look through your memories of the days before the attack. You're not in trouble, but we want everyone's account, and this is the best way to get it."

"You're at the range with your friends," Ember said in soothing tones as she led him into a trance. "You all have a competition to see who's the best shooter, but you know you'll win. They're all high-fiving you. Look, your mother is watching. She's so proud of you. She's so happy you rescued her. She's safe now."

A peaceful smile spread across Jonathan's face. Dean had told me that Jonathan's mother had been murdered years before at one of the Westerner compounds.

Ember stroked his hand. "Jonathan, did anything strange or unusual happen at Liberty recently? Something you couldn't explain?"

"Yes," Jonathan said, his voice airy and far away. "I caught Graham in the armory. He was loading boxes of ammunition into a duffel."

"What?" Dean asked, straightening. "Tell us more."

"Tell me about that," Ember said.

"I went to the armory to see if I'd left my neck gaiter there. Graham was putting ammunition in the duffel. I startled him, and he dropped a box. He said he was reorganizing the cabinet, but he didn't clean up the bullets. I thought he looked nervous, and I told Antonio later that day. Antonio said he'd talk to Graham about it, and then Dean. We thought Graham might be stealing bullets."

"Is that all?" Ember asked.

"I saw the doc behind the infirmary a few days ago. He was upset. His teammate was trying to console him."

"Okay, we're done," I said quickly, pushing Jonathan's hand out of Ember's. "Thank you, Jonathan."

Jonathan blinked, then looked around. "Oh my God, did I fall asleep? I'm sorry. Man, this flu is—"

Dean patted his shoulder. "You did good. We got the information we needed. Go back to the armory and tell the others that we're finished."

Jonathan left the tent.

Dean closed his eyes, breathing heavily. "Antonio should've come straight to me." He banged his fist against a tent pole. "Graham. It was Graham. I'll kill him myself."

"How long have you known Graham?" I asked. "And come to think of it, what's his power?"

"Graham has perfect recall. Useful for a spy," he said through gritted teeth. "We've known him for a year. We rescued him from a sorting station. He was so eager to fight with us." He slammed his fist into the tent pole again. "It was all a set up. He must've been working with the Westerners the whole time."

"That's not right," Ember said slowly. "You killed the people at that sorting station, right?"

"Yeah. A dozen."

I followed Ember's line of thought. "I know people make sacrifices for a greater cause, but would the Westerners sacrifice a dozen of their own to plant one guy? They're going through a population crisis, right? That's extreme."

He rubbed his eyelids. "These are the Westerners. They redefine extreme. I wouldn't put it past them."

I couldn't disagree with that assessment. "So, Graham stole the JM-104 and passed information on you to the Westerners. What's our next move?"

"We meet up with Andrew's team in two days and move against the compounds. The smaller one first, then the leaders' compound."

"Did Graham know about that plan?" I asked. "I recall you mentioning the plans about the compounds on the first day I met you."

Dean looked up at me, pained. "Yes, he knew."

"Then we can't do that. We need a new plan."

33

My team and I stood in a small circle in the snow, deep in the trees. It was the one place we could find where we were sure we wouldn't be overheard.

"Dean wants to attack the largest compound first," I said. "They won't be expecting an attack, and he's positive Isabel is there."

Marco pounded a fist into his other hand. "There's no question that we'll be helping. When do we leave?"

"Tentatively, in forty-eight hours. Graham's intelligence is that we'll attack the smaller compound on a different day, so we're changing. But we're not going to have Andrew's team with us, which means we'll be attacking the larger compound with half the manpower. We're going to need Ember and Benjamin this time around."

"If you think I'm going to shoot anyone..." Benjamin began.

"No, don't think you're going to shoot anyone. You can serve in any capacity you want, but mostly I just want you there as our combat medic. Ember, Christiana is going to go to Andrew's team, freeing up your telepathy. That way everyone has an animal telepath."

"I can do that," she said. "I've missed serving."

"So have I," I said. "That's why I turned in my gun today. Marco, Reid, we're back to being full superheroes. No firearms."

"What? Why?" Reid asked.

"Because we're not Sentinels. We're superheroes. I don't know all that the name entails anymore, but something has gone wrong recently, and part of it is because we joined a team we were never meant to be on. We're assisting the Sentinels and freeing the slaves at the large compound, but after that, I intend to go back to Saint Catherine. That's where this started, and that's where this will end."

"And after that?" Benjamin said. "What happens when a strike team shows up?"

"I find that unlikely," I said evenly. "Since I'll be going to the FBI as soon as we get home."

Marco startled. "What? What does any of this have to do with them?"

I stared Benjamin straight in the eye. "I read a book once about the Civil War. At the end, Congress passed the thirteenth amendment, abolishing slavery. The Westerners don't profess any allegiance to the federal government, but the camps do. They've used the allies to lobby for us in Congress, even. I'm going to tell the federal government everything. The slavery, the deaths, the cult, the abuse, all of it. I doubt Washington will want to be associated with them after this. In fact, I expect that the camps will be officially dismantled for what they've done."

"Why are you looking at me like that?" Benjamin asked. "I know you know about the Civil War."

I took a deep breath. "Because we will probably be called to testify before Congress, and we'll certainly be at the center of the investigation. On top of that, I bet the FBI will be just one of many federal agencies involved. The ATF will be called because of all the weapons, and the DOJ will get involved if for no other reason than the camps are technically part of them. I can see the Marshals getting involved if someone decides to run for it. This is going to be huge. I'm giving you a heads-up."

Benjamin's eyes tightened. "I see."

His sullen expression made my chest throb painfully. "If you want to temporarily leave the team... or... permanently leave the team, I'd understand why."

I needed to give Benjamin a chance to leave with grace.

Marco gasped. "What? No, don't leave. You're the medic. You're the most valuable member of the team."

"I'll have to think about it," Benjamin said. "But now that I've found Eleanor, I won't be alone. It might be easier for everyone if I left. A federal investigation might turn ugly if I'm on the team."

"No, you can't leave!" Marco's voice rose. "There's been enough change!"

"We'll talk about this later," I said. "Everyone, let's go to bed."

Benjamin looked at me again, his hard eyes tinged with hurt, but said nothing. He trudged away toward the infirmary.

Marco and Reid headed toward the armory, leaving Ember alone with me in the twilight, surrounded by silent, swirling snow.

"Jill, it doesn't have to end like this."

I stared at the infirmary through the trees. "Yes, it does. I don't know what he's done, but I know he doesn't want the feds involved. I'm giving him a chance to both get away from me and protect himself." Tears froze on my eyelashes.

"For the last time, *talk* to him! You need to talk to him about how you're feeling! I don't have my telepathy right now, but I know you're both hurting. This is stupid, Jill. You're both being stupid."

I glared at her. "He made it clear to me that he doesn't want me to approach him unless I'm actively dying. I... I don't want to die anymore, but I'm not even kind of ready to talk to him. He won't tell me the truth, so why should I tell him anything about how I'm feeling? How can we have a relationship when it's that uneven?" Tears flowed harder. I was going to lose Benjamin, if I hadn't already.

Above us, a songbird's call rang through the forest, its melancholic song underlining my own sorrow.

"Do you trust me?"

I sniffed. "What?"

"Do you trust me?"

"Of course I trust you. I trust you with my life."

"Then close your eyes and hold out your arm."

Though I was confused, I obeyed, closing my eyes and extending my right hand. Her soft hand took mine and turned it wrist-up.

Before I could ask her what she was doing, a fiery pain coursed through my wrist and my eyes flew open.

Ember held up her knife, my blood dripping down the blade. She'd sliced a three-inch gash in the vein.

"Ember!" I clutched my wrist. Blood flowed freely through my fingers. "Wh...why?"

"Well, well, look at that. You've got a life-threatening injury. It just so happens that there's a healer right across the street. He'll take of it."

I lurched away from her, wide-eyed and grasping my blood-soaked wrist.

34

The infirmary was locked. I pounded on the door with my good hand, already dizzy.

"Benjamin," I wheezed. "Please."

I looked behind me and saw a steady red trail leading out of the woods to where I was standing. I was going to kill Ember. Well, I would if I survived, which wasn't guaranteed since Benjamin still hadn't opened the damn door. How fast did people exsanguinate? I pounded on the door again. "Benjamin!"

I heard the deadbolt turn and Benjamin opened the door, his face still hard. "What?" His eyes traveled downward to my wrist. "Holy crap!" He grabbed my hand.

The relief was instantaneous—the dizziness ebbed as my wrist sealed itself, the pain fading into nothing. "Thank you," I breathed, rubbing my wrist.

"What the hell happened? Did you slit your wrist?"

I examined the smooth skin. "No, Ember did."

He narrowed his eyes at me. "What?"

"Ember slit my wrist with her knife."

He gave his head a little shake. "I'm missing something here."

"Do you have any medical books?" I looked up from my wrist. I didn't feel like talking about Ember's inane plan. How would I even begin to explain why I was bleeding on the porch?

"Medical books?"

"Yeah. Do you have any?"

"Um, a few. Which one do you need?"

"I want to look up a disease Ember told me about. She says I'm sick."

"Jillian, if you're sick, you can come to me. I *am* your medic. You don't need Ember or a book to diagnose you."

"Just let me see the books."

He sighed and stepped aside, pointing to a small bookshelf at the far end of the building.

I strode into the empty back room and studied the spines of the books. They bore names that I couldn't understand or pronounce. I frowned and pulled one out, then pushed it back. I wanted to find a book about depression, but without knowing which book to choose, I couldn't find one without asking for Benjamin's help.

"What sickness does Ember think you have?" Benjamin asked from the far end of the room.

"Mind your own business," I muttered. I wasn't sure why I was so angry at Benjamin. Minutes before I'd been crying over him.

"I'm your medic. If you're sick, it's definitely my business."

I spun around. "And I'm your leader! If you've fought and tried to kill superheroes, it's definitely *my* business!"

He wrenched open the front door so hard it banged against the wall. "Get out. Just get out."

The anger swung back to sadness and tears began to flow again. "Why won't you talk to me? I love you. I'm not going to kick you off the team or think that you're a psychopath. I just want to know the truth. All I have ever asked from you is for the truth."

Benjamin stared at me. "You love me?" His voice had dropped to a whisper.

"Yes!" My teeth began to chatter from the force of my emotions. "I couldn't say it before. I realized it after the tribunal, but you were already gone."

"What happened after the tribunal?" he asked, still quiet. "I asked Marco about Matthew the night I walked in on you guys yelling at each other. He wouldn't tell me anything. I thought about asking Reid, but I think I'd rather hear it from you."

"No," I said, backing away. "No. We're talking about you, not me." I collided with the wall and wiped tears from my face with the back of my hand. "This is not about me." I set my jaw. "I'm leaving. Goodbye."

"What sickness do you have?" Benjamin asked sadly. "The flu is going around. It's probably that."

I didn't answer. Without pausing to look at him, I strode past him toward the front door. I slammed the door behind me and walked down the steps, stopping at the bottom. The trail of blood I'd left behind me was still visible, an angry scarlet ribbon in the snow.

I gazed at it for a long moment, then walked back up the steps and turned the doorknob.

Benjamin was sitting on the edge of one of the hospital beds, staring at the floor. He looked up and rose partially when I came in. "Jillian?"

I sat down next to him and held out my hand. He accepted it without hesitation.

It was time.

"At the tribunal, the elders said Reid was guilty of dereliction of duty and sentenced him to fifty lashes. That probably would've killed him."

Benjamin gasped. "Why—"

I held up my hand. "I begged them to change their minds. They did, and they said Reid could lead. But I had to leave the team and marry Matthew. If I caused trouble, they'd reverse their decision." My hand brushed my neck. "Matthew made me throw the necklace in the creek."

He covered his mouth with his free hand. "That's awful. I'm so sorry."

"And then... and then Matthew described all the things he'd do to me on our wedding night. He was going to cause me as much pain as possible. It was obscene." My voice dropped to a whisper. "He looked forward to it."

No tears fell, but the words tumbled out of me. "While he was describing it, he molested me. It was so much worse than the time when he and I were courting." I began to shake. "I couldn't stop him. I just stood there, wishing I were dead and wondering where you were."

I finally looked at Benjamin, whose mouth was open. "I've been telling myself that I need to get over it and that it's not as bad as what happened to Ember, but I can't. Ember says it was just as bad, but I just *stood* there. I have nightmares about it. For a while I thought it was my fault because I could fight back and didn't, but now I—I just don't know, I didn't realize I could fight back because I was in a cult, and I just feel so angry and sad all the time and—"

Benjamin tilted my head up with his hand. "Why didn't you tell me this?" He looked broken.

"Because you got angry at me before the tribunal for not fighting back against my father and the elders. I thought you'd get angry at me again for not fighting back against Matthew."

Benjamin made a choked gasping noise and then blurred to the far side of the room, where he leaned against the wall with one arm, breathing raggedly. He spun around, stricken. "You thought I'd get mad at you for being sexually assaulted?"

"Well, yeah. You screamed at me about being brainwashed because I wouldn't leave the cult, right? I didn't realize I could leave the cult before the tribunal. I didn't realize I could leave the cult after the tribunal. What's the difference?"

Benjamin's eyes darted back and forth while he processed what I was saying. "You... really thought..." He looked up at me, still horrified. "I messed up. I can't believe you thought I'd be mad at you. And Ember's right. What Matthew did was just as bad as what Patrick did." He sank onto another hospital bed.

I walked to his side and sat next to him again. "I know now that we were in a cult. I sort of understand that it's not my fault. It took a while to sink in, but I get it."

His eyes were damp. "What finally convinced you?"

"Dean."

Benjamin flinched.

I shook my head. "Don't get upset. It's not like that. Dean explained that we were in a cult, and I was able to accept it because he didn't make me feel like absolute crap when he was saying it. But... I do need to talk to you about Dean."

He averted his eyes. "You're together now. I gathered that when you kissed." He hid his face in his hands. "I screwed it up between us. I don't blame you for going with him. I deserve this. I'm not mad, I swear."

"No, we're not together." It was my turn to tilt his head up, and I pressed my forehead to his. "I was trying to tell you about Matthew right before you got angry about the rose. I was so upset with you because of that, I kissed him after the raid. But all I could think about was you. He thought it meant something, but I told him today that it didn't. There's nothing between us. I don't want Dean, sweetheart. I just want you, if you'll take me back. I'm so sorry for kissing him." My lips brushed his. "I love you."

He gave me a desperate kiss. "You're not going to love me anymore when I tell you the truth about Baltimore. You're not going to want to take *me* back."

"Please tell me," I begged. "I can't stand any more secrets."

He hid his face in his hands again. "I'm not the heroic man you think I am. I made you think that, and I'm sorry." He looked up at me. "I'm so sorry, Jillian. I'm so sorry that you had to find out from Artemis. I never wanted you to know."

I stroked his cheek. "Know what?"

Benjamin jumped up and leaned against the wall, hugging himself tightly and gazing out the window. He was still shaking.

"There are dozens of supervillain families, but the oldest ones have specialties. The Henseys are assassins and hitmen. The Edges will traffic anything you want. The Sniders are arms dealers, but also dip into cybercrime. The Rowes are thieves and kidnappers. The Peery family produces terrorists. The Trents are..." He took a deep breath. "We're information dealers. Hacking, spying, corporate espionage. Whatever information you want, we can get. It's been like this for nearly a century."

"Is that what you were doing when Marco and I caught you and Beau?"

"Yeah. Working for the Howards to find JM-104 is the bread and butter of every supervillain family. Mom and Dad were chasing a lead on the formula at the bank the day we met. The night you caught me and Beau, we were there taking samples of some compound for testing. We do that a lot—always looking to see what Bell is cooking in case it's more JM-104. I never knew it could take away our powers, though. We don't ask questions."

"That's not so bad," I said gently. "I figured that much, actually. That's not even particularly grotesque. Why did you feel that you had to hide that from me?"

"Jillian, we're *information* dealers." His voice had grown cold and he looked at me, his eyes veiled. "And my family will use any means possible to get information. That includes 'enhanced interrogation.'"

There was an interminable pause.

"You mean torture."

"Yes. If someone is unwilling to part with information, we're the ones to call. Over the years, my family has interrogated dozens, even hundreds of people, all for a price. There was only one time when the Trents took it upon themselves to question someone without being hired to do so."

His words had taken on an odd tone. I tilted my head to the side. "Who, sweetie?"

He winced. "I'm not sweet. Nothing about this is sweet."

"Benjamin, please stop being evasive. Who was it?"

He hugged himself. "Your grandmother's team met their ends in my grandfather's basement."

Benjamin and I stared at each other for an eternity while his words sunk into my brain one by one.

I stood abruptly and strode to the other end of the room, pausing at a windowsill. I stared out at the snow, unable to name the emotion that threatened to overtake me. Disgust? Fear? Wonder at the sheer irony of our relationship? I brushed my fingers through the dust on the sill, picking my words. I loved Benjamin, and he hadn't killed my grandmother. But his family was responsible for the cult, in a way. That hurt.

Without looking away from the snow, I said, "Have you ever tortured someone?"

He laughed without humor. "Oh no, that was Beau's job. Beau and my parents, and sometimes the Rowe twins, because they're sociopaths who enjoy it. Eleanor got out early and became a professional student, then disappeared out west. I was only called in at the end, or when things went too far."

"To kill them?" Somehow, I could see Benjamin as the angel of mercy, or death, depending on how I chose to view it.

"No. To heal them."

I turned around, not bothering to hide my horror. "Making the torture—"

"Last forever, or until my family got what they wanted and finally put the poor bastard out of his or her misery. It could go on for weeks. It often did, because of me."

I moved to go to his side, but his expression darkened so much I stepped back. For the first time since meeting Benjamin Trent, I felt as if I were in the company of a supervillain. "There's more, isn't there?"

"Yes." He looked back out the window. "I was the one who healed them, and eventually I asked to be the one to kill them. I comforted myself that in killing them, I was giving them the mercy that I'd denied them by extending the torture. With that reasoning, killing became easy. A snapped neck here, a bullet there, all in the name of mercy.

"Then I started killing people on jobs, but only if they shot first, attacked first. Then it was because they might be a threat, and the responsible thing was to mitigate the threat. I began to get along with my family better. I began to enjoy the jobs we did, caring less and less about the people who got hurt. I didn't realize it at the time, but when

I began to justify the lives I ended, I began to justify every crime I committed. It was so easy, Jillian.

"I stopped daydreaming about being a superhero because, hey, that was never going to happen. Now I realize that I subconsciously didn't see myself as a hero, or even good. I still admired you all, though. I kept reading the books and hanging out on the forums, pretending that I wasn't covered in blood. I told myself that if I ever faced a superhero, I'd run instead of fight."

He heaved a sigh. "And then, one night about two years ago, Beau, Eleanor, and I were on a job in Baltimore. I'd started carrying a sidearm a few months before that. All the Trent kids were trained to shoot from the time we could pull a trigger, but I'd never cared for them. But I was packing heat that night, and then I saw Artemis holding Eleanor." He finally looked at me. "I didn't even think about shooting her. I just *did*. One second she was holding Eleanor, the next, she was on the ground and I was holding the gun.

"I never even thought about it. That's how numb to killing I was. I tried to murder a superhero who wasn't even trying to hurt me or Eleanor. I knew she was just going to detain my sister, but she was an inconvenience, so she had to go. That was the worst moment of my life—the moment I realized that no matter how much I lied to myself, I was nothing more than a killer who needed to be stopped. I was the reason superheroes exist." He covered his eyes. "And then you told me that not only did you know about that night, but you'd found out from my *victim*."

I bit my lip. Benjamin technically wasn't different than any other supervillain, but my brain rejected the idea, unable to connect his name with the word "murderer."

Perhaps it was because I, too, was covered in blood.

"And the Westerners?"

"It was me or them. And during the attack a few days ago, it was you and Ember or them. Four shots, four kills."

"I'm waiting," I said softly.

His brow furrowed. "For what?"

"For the revelation that's supposed to make me not love you anymore."

His jaw dropped. "Jillian, I'm a murderer!"

"I have a trail of blood behind me, too," I whispered, the scarlet snow fresh in my mind. "And unlike you, I enjoyed every minute of it. I beat Patrick to death. I was going to torture Matthew to death. I almost killed Peter, but the thought of you stopped me. But then after we started fighting and everything fell apart, Dean told me to focus on the anger and pain and let it fuel me. I killed the Westerners in the sorting station while imagining that they were all the people I hate.

"I can tell myself all day long that each one of those deaths or near-deaths was justified, and maybe they were. But when I'm in pain, I cause others pain. I was cruel to Patrick and Matthew and Peter, making me no better than they are. When I was angry at you, I kissed Dean and almost asked him to have sex with me, knowing it would destroy you if you ever found out. In that way, I'm just like every other superhero leader who has caused pain to punish their team."

"You're *not* like them. You're not."

"Yes, I am."

Benjamin was in front of me in an instant, his nose touching mine. "Don't say that. Don't."

"I still love you," I breathed. "I can't believe you still love me after all I've said and done."

"Why do you love me, though? I'll never understand."

I lifted his palm to my mouth and kissed it. "I love these gentle hands. These healing hands." I entwined my fingers with his. "You can kill and destroy with them, but you've chosen to heal and build." I placed my other hand on his chest. "This heart. Your beautiful heart." I looked into his eyes. "You saw the girl in the café and sat down next to her. You healed her. You've been healing her ever since." I kissed his eyelids.

"You're not disgusted by me?"

"No, sweetheart. I just wanted you to be honest with me. That's what I always wanted."

Benjamin broke away. "That's it? You're just going to look the other way? If I were someone else, you wouldn't. I'm a murderer. That means something, Jillian."

"You're on my team. You're my family. That means something more."

Benjamin turned his back to me. "No, I'm not your family. I'm always going to be a Trent. *They're* my family, and I can't get away from them. God, I get that now. Talking to you has helped me see it. Did Eleanor tell you that she wanted to recruit me into the Sentinels to be their medic? That's why she came to Saint Catherine last June. Her whole ex-boyfriend thing was just a dumb story she cooked up. Apparently, she and Dean had a fight about a stupid decision he'd made, and she got mad and decided to go get me. She told me the euthanasia-and-lube-rack stuff because, as you've pointed out, I'm an arrogant ass who—"

"Yes, she told me. She told me everything."

He snorted. "I'll never get away from them. They're going to come back one day and give me what's coming to me. We're all murderers, and we all have violent ends coming. Even Eleanor, though I hope she's able to escape it."

"What are you getting at?" I asked cautiously.

He turned back to me. "I love you, but I'm not staying on the team, for everyone's protection. I've been thinking about this since I found out that you knew about Artemis. My past will always come back to find me. And you were right, my presence on the team will complicate any federal investigation. It's better if I just go."

It was the first time he'd said he loved me, and it had been followed by a "but."

His fear of his family and their revenge overshadowed his love for me. His terror on the roof of the school in August made more sense now, as did his request to the police to fake his death. I'd wondered what could make brave Benjamin Trent run and hide from his family, and now that I knew he was afraid of the torments they had in store, I understood. He loved me, but he feared his family more.

What could I do to show him that I was never going to allow him to face his family's wrath alone? What would convince him that I would defend my teammate, and the man I loved, to my last breath?

I had just one idea.

"To my last breath," I murmured to myself.

"Sorry, what?"

Instead of answering, I stood up and walked to a glass cabinet. I opened it and pulled out a roll of gauze. Benjamin quickly scanned my body. "Are you bleeding? What's wrong?"

I walked up to him and held up my hand.

He hesitated, then touched his palm to mine. I began to wind the gauze around our hands.

"Jillian?"

"From this moment, to my last breath, I swear to stand by your side and defend you," I said quietly, continuing to wind the gauze.

Benjamin stared at our hands. His expression melted from confusion to comprehension. "Jillian..."

"I will be faithful to you," I continued.

"I will be faithful to you," he repeated, barely more than a whisper.

"And united in spirit and strength."

"And united in spirit and strength."

I finished winding the gauze. "You're on my team. You're my *family*. That means something more."

"Did we just get married?" He was staring at our hands, awestruck.

"Superhero married. I know it doesn't mean anything to you, but it does to me. You're a Trent, right? Well, the way I see it, I'm a Trent now, too. I love you, and I'm not going to let you face your family alone. I am your family now, and I think you'll find that the others are ready and willing to fight for you."

Benjamin slowly unwound the gauze, leaving our hands together long after he was done. "I won't leave," he said finally, entwining our fingers again. "I'm not going anywhere. And it does mean something to me. I love you, Jillian Trent."

There was no "but."

A candle flame of happiness burst into being in my heart, illuminating the dark cavity to which I'd become accustomed. I threw my arms around him and kissed him with renewed passion. He embraced me with equal fervor, kissing me as he'd never kissed me before.

I pulled away from him and tugged off my shirt, blushing a little. "I know I can say no. So can you. But now I'm saying yes."

Instead of pushing me away, he smiled shyly and reached out to me.

35

I lay next to Benjamin as he slept, his arm draped across my waist under the blanket. Listening to his slow, even breathing, I wondered if he was dreaming.

I'd dreamed of Matthew. Twice in the night I'd woken up from a nightmare, the aching emptiness in my chest painful and numbing at the same time, the candle's flame extinguished by the force of the nightmares.

Now, as the milky light of the midwinter sunrise streamed in through the white curtains, I curled up under the covers of the narrow bed and berated myself for my lack of gratitude. I'd ended my weird dalliance with Dean. I'd reconciled with Benjamin and even married him—sort of—and then we'd consummated our marriage. We would assault the Westerner compound, then my team would return to Saint Catherine. Things were falling into place.

So why was I still sad?

Benjamin began to stir. He groaned, and his fingers brushed my back. "Good morning, Mrs. Trent."

"Morning," I whispered.

He propped himself up on his elbow. "Hey, what's wrong?"

"Nothing. I just don't feel good."

Benjamin tenderly pulled me onto my back, so we could face each other. "You never told me what sickness Ember thought you had. You don't look like you have the flu. What are your symptoms?"

"Ember says I have depression."

Benjamin paused, then sat up, the sheet falling away from his bare chest. "Why does she think you're depressed?" He sounded concerned.

I couldn't meet his eyes. "Two nights ago, I walked out into the snowstorm. I wanted to die out there. Marco and Ember saved me. We talked about how I was feeling, and I didn't want to die anymore. But Ember says I'm depressed."

Benjamin looked at me without speaking for a long time. Finally, he brushed a lock of hair out of my face. "That was right after I said that I didn't want you to come to me for healing unless you were dying."

"That's not why I walked out into the snow. I don't really know why. I think I felt stuck and seeing Reid's wall was the last straw. I was tired, and I wanted to sleep. I couldn't talk to you. Ember and Reid broke up."

Benjamin blinked several times and looked down. "When we go back to Saint Catherine, would you consider seeing a therapist? There are therapists who are trained to help people get out of cults and... and how to cope with being a sexual assault survivor." He stroked my hair again. "I will never forgive myself for not listening to you when you needed me. I'll make sure you get the help you need."

"Really?" Could someone help me be happy? How did that work?

I sat up, and he ignored my nakedness, keeping his eyes on my face. I lifted my hand to his face and he kissed my outstretched palm.

An angry pounding on the front door made us both jump. We scrambled out of bed and pulled our clothes on. "Dang, what time is it?" Benjamin mumbled, glancing at the wall clock. "It's only seven."

"Benny! Open up!" Eleanor's furious voice grated against my ears. I hadn't really talked to her since she'd yelled at me several days before, and I had no desire for her to ruin my morning.

Benjamin blurred out of the room and opened the door. "El," he said, nonchalant. "What's up?"

"Have you seen Jillian? She didn't return to the armory last night. Marco asked me to search for her."

"I'm right here, Eleanor." I pulled down my shirt and walked out of the bedroom.

Eleanor stared at me, her eyes traveling up and down my body as she took in my bare feet, rumpled clothes, and messy hair. Her face slowly turned red.

"You *screwed my brother*?" she hissed. "Is stealing Dean not good enough for you? You had to take Benjamin, too?"

Benjamin opened his mouth to protest, but I held up my hand. "First of all, chick, I did not steal Dean, so don't bring it up again. Second of all..."

Her words had just clicked.

I pecked Benjamin on the cheek. "Sweetie, can you give me a moment alone with Eleanor, please?" Benjamin nodded and returned to the bedroom. I crossed my arms and faced Eleanor. "Be honest with me. Are you angry that I brought Benjamin into my world, or are you angry that Dean likes me?"

The pieces had just fallen into place and a very silly picture had taken form.

Eleanor had been cold to me since I'd entered the Sentinel camp, and I could believe that she was upset her brother had been taken captive, which ultimately stemmed from his position on my team. I knew a sister's concern for her little brother, and I could respect that.

But her open hostility had begun when I'd said that Dean was going to tell me about the Sentinels and the JM-104, despite him not even knowing me. He'd canceled plans to speak to Eleanor about something, and even assigned her to a different jeep so he could sit next to me. She'd referred to him as her "ex-boyfriend" in the little cover story she'd concocted last summer even though, by her own admission, they'd never dated.

As Ember had said, Eleanor wasn't really angry about my "fake" personality. Eleanor was angry that I was apparently playing with the heart of a second man she cared about.

Eleanor's eyes widened. "What are you talking about?"

"I'm talking about the fact that you were nice to me in Saint Catherine, but you've been horrible to me in the Rockies. I don't think you're a terrible person, and I don't think you faked being nice last summer. I *do* think that you struggle to handle situations that you can't control with your powers, like Dean's crush on me and my relationship with your brother. So, are you angry that I brought Benjamin into my world, where he's always wanted to be, or are you angry that Dean likes me?"

I already knew the answer. Eleanor, quiet and subtle, probably had no clue how to win over an exuberant man like Dean. I'd blown in like a tornado and ruined everything.

Eleanor's lip quivered, but she lifted her nose in the air. "Right now, I'm angry that you're playing both of them."

I shook my head. "No, I'm not. I told Dean yesterday that there's nothing between us, and since Benjamin and I got married last night, there never will be." I stuck out my hand. "Hi, I'm Jillian Trent, the sister you never had and probably never wanted."

"You got married?" Eleanor's face was priceless.

"Yes. It was a superhero ceremony. Binding of the hands, vows, all that."

"You're married." She was still staring at me as though I'd grown a second head.

"Yes."

"You married my brother."

"Yes," I said slowly. "Because I love *him*."

A confused little frown crossed her face. "But... you're both so young."

I sighed. "Oh, come on. Twenty-one isn't *that* young. It felt right. And I do love him, Eleanor. I'll treat him right, I promise."

She studied me for a moment longer, a wisp of sadness in her large, hazel eyes. "You must really hate me."

"Hate you? No. Spent a little while being scared of you? Sure. Now that I know what you learned growing up, it makes sense that you went with the torture route. That comes naturally to you, doesn't it?"

Eleanor looked down. "Yeah."

"Me too. I'd like to talk about it with you sometime."

I did, too. I wanted to start over with Eleanor, this powerful woman to whom I was now related. Not only could she prove to be an important ally, she might be a friend, if she could ever let go of the idea that I'd stolen Dean.

Eleanor rushed toward me and wrapped her arms around me. "I always wanted a sister. And I'm sorry I called you brainwashed. And yelled at you."

"I deserved it," I said, my voice muffled by her jacket. "But don't tell anyone we got married, okay? We want to tell them."

She backed away and smiled at me, her eyes tearing up. "I'll just go tell your team I found you. I wish I could tell you that you can relax here for a while, but we're loading up in two hours. A storm is moving in that'll make transportation almost impossible if we're still on the mountain, so we're leaving a day early. I can't alter the weather."

Her voice had taken on the sweet, lilting quality that I remembered from our first meeting. This was the Eleanor I knew and liked, who wasn't eaten up by jealousy and fear.

"I understand. We'll be out in a minute."

"Benny!" she called. "Get out here!"

Benjamin opened the door, now fully dressed in his superhero combat medic uniform. He eyed Eleanor with distinct wariness. "Hey, El."

She gathered him into a hug and rubbed his back. "Congratulations. Be blessed."

Benjamin patted her back. "Can you raise the chances of us being happy?"

Eleanor shook her head and wiped her eyes. "No. That's on you."

With that, she hurried out the door into the snow and made her way toward the armory.

Benjamin took my hand in his and we walked back to the

bedroom to finish getting dressed. After we were in our winter gear, he gave me a long kiss, and we shut the door of the infirmary behind us and headed to the armory to meet with the rest of our team.

It was time to begin preparations for battle.

36

"Dean, let me give the briefing."

We were in the armory, standing off to one side while the rest of the Sentinels cleaned their weapons and counted bullets. I faced Dean with a hand on my hip.

He blinked at me. "What? Why?"

"Because while you respect me, some of your men don't, and they're going to work with my team whether they like it or not. If I give the briefing, it'll establish that they have to listen to me."

"That's unorthodox."

"Have you *met me*?"

He gave me a crooked grin. "Yeah, I have. And I'm glad I did."

"So, what do you say? It's your team, so it's your call."

"Okay. The way I see it, this is a joint superhero and Sentinel operation anyway, so it stands that you should be giving some orders. Some of the guys could use a crash course in dealing with super-heroes." He glanced over at Judd, who'd been reissued his weapon in light of the new mission.

I clapped him on the shoulder and joined my team in another part of the room.

Ember grinned at me. "Benjamin said you two made up. I'm so glad."

"You're psychotic," I said, holding up my wrist. "But thank you. Did Benjamin tell you anything else about last night?"

"No," Reid cut in, clearly fighting a smirk. "And I don't really want to hear about anything else, because when I went into the infirmary to go to bed last night, the bedroom door was locked and there were some interesting noises coming from inside." He gave Benjamin a significant look. "You'd better have done that on *your* bed, pal."

Ember blushed, but Marco pinched the bridge of his nose. "Aw, come on, man. I did not need that mental image."

Benjamin winked at me. "I thought you'd like to tell them the big news."

Marco looked up and squinted at me. "Out with it. Are you pregnant? Is that why you're back together?"

I merely smiled. "I suggest you pay close attention during the brief."

Reid and Ember gave us looks of playful suspicion, but I wouldn't say anymore.

A few minutes later, Dean called the room around him and told everyone to pull out a pen and paper.

"All right, Sentinels, listen up. We're doing something unlike we've ever done before. Most of us have raided compounds, but we've never had a superhero team on our side. Battlecry and her team will work with us tomorrow, providing offensive power, cover, and medical." He looked each Sentinel in the eyes. "If anyone here has a problem serving alongside superheroes, the door is behind you. The main part of the brief will be delivered by Battlecry. Pay attention."

Several Sentinels uncapped their pens, poised for notes.

I stood in the center of the circle and directed all attention to the detailed whiteboard diagram of the largest known Westerner compound, in which two hundred and fifty people lived. Around me, twenty-three Sentinels either stood or kneeled, ready for my part of the brief. It was not often that I gave operation orders on this scale.

I took a deep breath and pulled my shoulders back.

"I'm Jillian Trent, codename Battlecry, leader of the superhero team that will be working alongside your unit for this mission. Prepare to copy. Please hold all questions until the end." I pointed to the surrounding area. "This is the situation."

Dean, Marco, Ember, and Reid's mouths fell open. Benjamin beamed.

I quickly explained the weather, terrain, and the known activities in and around the compound, on which Dean had briefed me earlier. I moved on to the description of the friendly forces—my team.

"I will lead Tank and Helios on the north side of the compound, where the wall is weakest. Firelight will be stationed here," I said, pointing to a small hill that contained a copse of trees. "Positioned with Luke, who will provide cover for her while she directs local fauna. Mercury will attend to injuries as needed."

I raised my voice to grab people's attention. "This is our mission: The Sentinels and my team will attack the enemy compound at zero two thirty at the coordinates listed on the diagram to liberate forty-eight known captives. I say again," I said, speaking even louder, infusing as much strength as I could into my words as I repeated our mission.

I continued to speak, falling into the role forbidden to me by Garrett Williamson so many years before. I assigned tasks to each squad, explaining their jobs and the concept of each operation.

The Sentinels glanced at me every few seconds, then wrote notes on their pads, their eyes communicating not hatred, but confidence. Though I was a despised superhero, they trusted me to lead them, along with Dean, into enemy territory with unknown variables. I wanted to.

As I explained the rules of engagement with the Westerners—order to surrender, shoot if they did not—I recalled a quiet evening many months before.

Marco and I had researched Benjamin and his siblings, and during our research we'd found a picture of Christina St. James, the woman who'd stormed a prison camp, walking through the gates and batting away bullets and grenades.

On that fateful day almost exactly a century before, she'd never heard the word "superhero." She hadn't yet devised the principles, nor given herself a codename and uniform. She was just Christina St. James, and she was going to liberate the prisoners or die trying. She'd done so in a time when not only did women not lead nearly anything, but they weren't even allowed to vote.

She hadn't cared. They'd taken her family and she was going to do something about it.

I was her direct descendant. I'd compared myself to her on the night I'd taken my oath to be the leader of my team. Had I kept my vows? I'd tried to. But there, in the armory tucked in the middle of the Rockies, I felt the mantle of the legacy that had been handed down to me, mother to daughter, for one hundred years.

Though I was giving tactical orders, I was not a soldier.

Though I was surrounded by Dean's men, I was not a Sentinel.

I was a superhero.

The hollow ache in my chest began to hurt a little less.

37

Inch by inch the Sentinels and my team moved to our positions. The overcast sky obscured any natural light, but none of us dared turn on a red-lens headlamp. We were in sight of the largest Westerner compound, which appeared to me as a fortress in the gloom. High walls surrounded a village of houses, community buildings, and small gardens. Around the compound, fallow fields spread out for a quarter of a mile.

Dean had spent the first fifteen years of his life in such fields. Now, to my left, he gripped a tree, visibly shaking with anticipation of liberating more slaves.

I hardly dared to breathe.

Dean turned to Ember, who stood on his other side. She nodded once and peered through the thick branches of a conifer. I could make out her face—surprised, then alarmed.

She caught my eye. *I can't hear anyone in the compound.*

I closed my eyes and listened to the faint sounds of life in the compound: a cough, a toilet flushing, a baby's hungry cry. *I hear lots of people.*

Ember lightly punched the tree and let out a whispered curse. *There must be some other animal telepath. I'm beginning to hate them.*

I pinched the bridge of my nose while I thought. If Ember could not hear the thoughts of the Westerners, her role in the fight was greatly diminished. We wouldn't be fighting blind, exactly, but the fighting teams would have a much harder time. My job was fairly simple—find the slaves—but the Sentinels needed to know where the Westerners were. All of us were relying on Ember to direct them to where they were required most.

Ember caught my eye. *Change in plan?*

There wasn't enough time to come up with a new plan, especially since I didn't know who or what was responsible for Ember's power failure this time. *No change in the plan. You'll stay here with Luke.*

We were in the copse of trees that we'd decided upon during battle planning. It was pitch black out, and we weren't especially close to the compound. She'd be safe here, but I'd make sure her cover, a moody Sentinel named Luke, guarded her even if she wasn't playing a major role anymore.

I put my lips to Dean's ear and whispered the new development. He nodded once.

I checked my watch. The attack would begin in one minute. Spread out around the compound, Sentinels and superheroes alike were strategically placed in groves of trees and in low areas, out of sight. All of us waited for Reid's signal, which would be unmistakable.

The plan was solid. The Sentinels had raided the Westerners countless times. Though they'd never attacked a compound of this size, my team would provide the offensive power required.

So why could I not shake the feeling that something was terribly wrong? I glanced at Ember, whose powers had been snuffed out immediately before they were most needed.

My stomach curled. Something wasn't right. This wasn't a coincidence.

Dean's watch beeped.

I took one last calm breath and willed myself to settle into a cool, calculating mentality devoid of emotion. I would not be a mindless killer, but I *was* a trained warrior. We'd storm the compound and surprise the Westerners in their sleep.

The ground began to shake. Large, sharp cracking noises in the distance were followed by the deafening crashes of walls falling to the ground. Within the compound, men yelled for their comrades to prepare for battle.

Dean and I surged forward with the rest of the Sentinels.

Gunfire and muzzle flashes lit up the night, but they weren't from Sentinel weapons.

The Westerners had been waiting for us.

Enormous stadium lights around the perimeter of the compound blasted on, temporarily blinding me. Dozens of men were lining up behind the rocks of the fallen compound wall, aiming automatic weapons at the highly-visible Sentinels who rushed at them from all directions. Bullets whizzed around me while Sentinels fell.

Benjamin ran to each fallen Sentinel and healed him, allowing them to jump up and continue the assault.

I opened my mouth to order Reid to provide cover.

He was one step ahead of me. A wall of dirt flew up between the Sentinels and the Westerners, hardening to rock with a loud crackle. My second-in-command was several yards to my right, his eyes glowing ghoulishly, psychokinetically pushing the wall of dirt in front of him.

The wall of earth moved slowly across the field like a broom, and then I heard shouts of horror as it reached the ruined wall and the shooters on it. All at once the earthen wall collapsed onto the men, crushing them in dirt and rocks. For a few seconds, there were no gunshots. We scrambled over the dirt, stones, and bricks. I could barely hear anything over the sound of my panting.

I was the first one over the pile. When I reached the top, I took one look at what awaited us and ducked down for cover. "*Tank!* Earthquake! Now!"

Reid fell to his knees and slammed his fists into the ground. As his hands struck the earth, the ground began to shake, harder and deeper than I'd ever felt it move beneath my feet. I tumbled down the little dirt hill he'd made, but the ground did not stop quaking.

Around me, Sentinels shouted and fell, but all of them landed safely in the field.

In the compound, buildings began to collapse. As I'd hoped, many of them collapsed on the snipers and crew-served weapons that had been set up. In the brief second I'd looked over the hill, I'd counted at least five snipers lying in wait for us and dozens of men crouched behind barricades with various assault weapons and handguns.

Buildings left and right collapsed with deafening roars. Power-lines began to fall, their lines swinging and snapping everywhere, threatening everything around them. There was a high, metallic screech, and then another. The stadium lights tumbled to the ground, crashing onto wreckage in the compound.

There was a loud explosion followed by a flash of light, and then the familiar crackling of flames. I peeked over the dirt and saw a tremendous inferno rising up from one of the stadium lights. Men everywhere were laying on the ground, trapped under fallen buildings.

"Sentinels! Now!" Dean's deep voice had taken on a quality I'd never heard before—threatening and compelling at the same time.

The Sentinels regained their footing and expertly cleared the downed wall. They flooded into the spooky, dusty, half-lit compound, their weapons drawn. Shouted orders to surrender filled the night, followed by a steady barrage of gunfire. Bullets flew everywhere, rico-cheting off the walls of buildings.

I ducked and twisted to avoid falling bricks, always searching for signs of the slaves. They were here. They had to be.

The flames spread to another building, and then another. The terrific *whoosh* they made began to overtake the sounds of warfare. I heard no screams from within, though. There were plenty of men within the compound, but where were the women and children? The slaves?

Beneath the din was another sound that I struggled to make out

—a buzzing, perhaps. Yes, it was definitely buzzing, and growing louder. I pressed myself against the fractured wall of a house and focused on the strange noise. Electricity? Lawn mowers?

My heart began to pound harder. I knew the sound from my childhood, specifically the summer that the seventeen-year cicadas had crawled out of the ground and didn't leave for weeks. Every day that they'd been out had been filled with the endless, brain-splitting drone of insect wings.

I looked up, my mouth falling open in horror.

What little light there was in the compound was extinguished as thousands—no, millions—of locusts descended from the pitch-black sky. Sentinel, superhero, and Westerner alike stopped their war, too busy batting and swinging at the enormous insects to worry about combatants.

I stumbled along the ruined street, nearly blind from the swarm. They landed on every inch of me and tried to climb into my mouth, but I kept it shut. I bumped into walls and tripped over a corpse, unable to focus on anything but the two-inch-long bugs and the endless din they made. What was going on? Why were locusts swarming in January? How?

After a minute, I walked into the closed door of one of the few standing buildings, which appeared to be a small shed. I groped around for a doorknob and turned it, forcing the lock. With a gasp I shoved it open and slammed it shut behind me. Without pausing to see what was inside I shook my limbs to rid myself of the locusts and frantically combed my hair.

"Don't tell me *you're* the whore that Ben turned traitor for. Gotta say, you're hotter in your pictures than you are in real life."

I jerked my head toward the speaker.

The shed, which was dimly illuminated by a camping lantern, contained just one folding table and chair. A young woman, probably in her mid-teens, sat on the chair, her legs up on the table and her arm draped over the back. She tossed her thick brown hair and smiled crookedly at me, though her eyes contained no mirth.

I straightened. Whoever she was, she wasn't a Westerner. Her knowledge and dim opinion of Benjamin's defection pointed to one conclusion: supervillain.

I suppressed the urge to hurl my knife into her throat. If supervillains were in the compound, then there was far more going on here than we knew. We needed this woman, whoever she was.

"Who are you?" I asked, my voice like ice.

"As if I'd tell you." As she spoke, a locust fluttered away from my hair and landed on her outstretched index finger. She made a cooing noise and raised her hand, from where it flew away to a darkened corner of the room.

Suddenly, she plunged her hand into her pocket and pulled out a tiny pink handgun.

I lunged at her and tackled her to the floor. "You just did," I hissed, before punching her once in the temple. She crumpled like a paper bag and lay still. Her name wasn't important to me, just her role in the fight.

I stood up and panted for a few moments. While I caught my breath, I reviewed the events of the raid thus far: Ember's power disappearing, the Westerners knowing about our attack, the supervillain controlling the locusts. For the second time, I couldn't help but feel that something was very wrong. Why was this young woman here? Her youth and sloppiness when attacking me hinted that she wasn't a trained fighter.

Perhaps she'd been hired to provide a distraction. Yes, that made more sense. I could believe that evil had partnered with evil in the form of a Westerner-supervillain alliance. However, the locusts hadn't discriminated against anyone outside, nor had they tried to harm me. If she had allied with the Westerners, she'd done a terrible job.

I needed to get the slaves, get my team, and get out of here. If supervillains were here, this fight was going to turn nasty in ways we hadn't anticipated.

Outside, gunfire filled the night once more. I crouched as low as I could, cracked open the door, and peeked out into the darkness.

It wasn't so dark anymore. Now that the locusts had no mistress, they'd either landed on the ground to be trampled or had flown away. Fires from the fallen stadium lights were spreading throughout the compound. Men ran here and there in the dark, smoky air, some waving weapons like madmen, but others ran with more intent. I had no idea where my team was.

Ember? Can you hear me?

I'm helping Benjamin find injured people. My powers just came back on.

I grinned. My guess about the locust woman had been correct. *Where are the slaves?*

I slipped out through the door and pressed myself against the wall of the shed, looking back and forth for anybody I recognized. Above the loud pounding of my heart, I could hear furious shouts from Sentinels as they battled their former captors.

The slaves are in a basement room!

A piece of wall exploded inches above my head as a bullet pierced it. After a quick dash, I ducked and huddled in a rocky corner of another destroyed building. Three corpses littered the floor inside, their weapons scattered around them. *Ember, where's the basement door?*

I don't know. They can hear the battle, though. They know the Sentinels are here for them and they want to join the fight. She slipped out of my mind, and then back in. *The Westerners' women and children are in another basement room. They've been told that the Sentinels will, uh, be indecent to them if they're taken captive. Some of the women are thinking about killing themselves and their children.*

I was going to liberate the slaves or die trying, and nobody was committing needless suicide if I could help it. I just had to figure out where everyone was. Still crouching, I peered past the crumbling edge of the wall and tried to find any building that looked as if it might be used for storing slaves.

A female figure walked through a wall and sprinted across the street. She disappeared through another wall.

I stood, suddenly unafraid of bullets.

Alysia Rowe was in the compound, and if she was here, then surely her brother Will was, too. My nails dug into my palms as I remembered how he'd used his lion puppets to play with me before they'd mauled me in Reid's pit. Wherever Alysia was, Will was sure to be.

But why were they here? Possibilities raced through my mind, but none of them made sense. I was sure there was little of value in the compound for them to steal. Alysia wasn't engaging anybody. The only scenario that made sense was Benjamin's prediction weeks before that the supervillains were going to deliberately wreak havoc to harass, intimidate, and hinder my team. They'd probably somehow been alerted that we were aiding the Sentinels. God only knew how many supervillains had chomped at the bit to offer the Westerners aid in the fight.

They were going to pay, active war zone be damned. I needed to take down the Rowe twins and all their cronies before I could successfully liberate anyone.

I sprinted down the street toward the building Alysia had entered. Bullets whizzed around me, and once I crashed to the ground, a grenade exploded nearby. After the stone and burning bits of material finished raining on me, I jumped up and kept running. I vaulted over an upturned car and skidded to a halt outside the building, which appeared to be a house. I crashed through the door and was greeted by the barrel of a handgun.

Alysia Rowe's bullet collided with my bulletproof vest with the force of a truck, blasting me backwards into the wall. My head hit the bricks with an alarming *thunk*, but I kept my eyes open.

High on adrenaline, I threw my knife at her left leg without so much as a swear word. She screamed and dropped her handgun. I lurched toward her and kicked the gun across the room, then kneeled down and grabbed the lanky brunette by her neck. She gurgled a little and clawed at my gloved hands.

"Hello, Alysia." I squeezed her throat as I picked her up. "I'm Jillian Trent. My husband has told me all about you." I threw her across the room into a large television, which crashed to the ground. "Couldn't quite make yourself go through that, eh?"

Alysia pulled out my knife and struggled to her feet. "Trent?" she said, disbelief coloring every line of her face. "He married a super-hero? Oh, girl, you've made a *big* mistake."

I threw another knife, but this time it sailed right through her.

I sized her up, calculating the best way to attack. Perhaps she was like Patrick, whose powers had required concentration to use. I'd surprised her with my first knife, and now I just had to figure out how to surprise her again.

Before I could attack, the door burst open and half a dozen Westerners rushed toward us. I screamed in fury and tackled them, much as I had the Sentinels in the shipping container not so long before. They fell to the floor in the same kind of confused pile.

I spun around to see if Alysia was there. She wasn't. I punched each Westerner into unconsciousness, then jumped up and dashed out of the house.

The gun battle had ended. The fight to rescue people from the flames had just begun.

Fire engulfed half of the compound. All around me, men sprinted up and down the street with their injured comrades slung over their shoulders. Nearby, in a burning building, a man screamed in terror and agony as flames engulfed him. His screams grew more hysterical until they abruptly ceased.

I ran the other direction. If I could just reach Ember, I could tell her to ask the slaves to make noise. My sensitive ears would hear them. *Ember Ember Ember Ember Ember...*

There was no reply.

I skidded to a halt at a dead-end street. All around me, blazes raged and Westerners ran past me, either not noticing the superhero or not caring anymore. Tiny, floating sparks made my eyes water, and the air was becoming difficult to breathe despite the constant breeze that moved some of the smoke and fed the flames.

Ember Ember Ember Ember Ember Ember Ember...
Silence.

I wasn't going to stand around and wonder what had happened to Ember—not while supervillains roamed around us. I turned and ran back the way I'd come, toward the fallen wall. As I ran, I scanned for anyone I recognized. In the smoky distance, I thought I saw Marco digging people out of wreckage, but the smoke thickened and hid him.

Ember Ember Ember Ember Ember Ember where are you? Please answer!

The ground shook for a moment and tossed me onto the rubble-strewn street. I crawled to my knees and then jumped up, wobbling slightly. I saw an overturned folding chair in the middle of the street and realized that the locust woman was probably awake and blocking Ember's telepathy again. I rushed to the shed in which I'd left her.

The shed was completely engulfed in fire. I looked through the fiery doorway and saw no corpse. She was blocking Ember's telepathy again, but I couldn't make myself calm down. Something was very, *very* wrong.

In the distance, beyond the ruined walls of the compound, a man's inhuman, terrified shrieks mixed with the rough barking of dogs. Cold fear sloshed in my stomach.

I reached the dirt blockade and ran up it. Without breaking stride, I jumped to the bottom, where I immediately tripped over a dead Sentinel. I squinted at the copse of trees in the distance.

"*Ember!*" The scream ripped out of my throat of its own volition.

I began to sprint.

Ember was pressing herself against a tree as two mangy, growling timber wolves surrounded her with their fangs bared. One of them had a strange protrusion jutting out of his head: her knife. Will Rowe was nearby.

In front of her, two more wolves were in the last stages of tearing Luke apart. His limbs and other body parts were scattered everywhere.

"Will! Show yourself!" I shouted into the darkness. "Come out so I can kick your ass like I did your sister's!"

Ember looked up, her tearstained face visible in the darkness, and held out a hand. "No, Battlecry, don't! They can't die!"

All at once the four wolves turned and ran toward me. Hideous, deep barks ripped out of their muzzles. Instead of fear, a thrill of rage coursed through me. How *dare* Will terrorize Ember?

When the wolves reached me, I seized the closest one's neck and swung it like a sack of potatoes into its pack mate. The two others jumped on me.

I fell backwards under their weight and shoved them off, kicking furiously at any wolf I could. Blood dripped down my forehead into my eyes, but I brushed off the remote pain in my scalp and swiped at one of the wolves' legs with my largest knife.

The blade cut through muscle and sinew and stopped at the bone. Without hesitating, I grabbed the wolf's leg and snapped off the rest, crippling it. Will would have a hard time using a three-legged puppet.

The wolf fell limp. The other sank their fangs into my arms and legs, tearing away chunks of cloth and the flesh beneath.

I screamed, but I did not stop slicing at the wolves. One by one, I removed paws or larger parts of legs. The last wolf, whose entire leg was bent like the letter L, let out a weak huff before falling to the ground, finally "dead."

I limped to Ember, who was shaking violently. Blood flowed down my limbs, my face, and the back of my neck. Ember ran up to me and helped me to the base of the tree, where she forced me to sit.

"Get Benjamin," I gasped.

"He's beyond my reach right now. I can't contact anyone in the compound. I'm sorry, I'm so sorry." She wiped at her eyes. "The wolves came out of nowhere, and I couldn't talk to them. I thought it was my telepathy failing, but I threw the knife and they just..." A sob wracked her body. "They just attacked Luke. I could hear his thoughts while he died."

She covered her mouth with her hand to stifle a whimper, my blood dripping off her fingers.

I guided her hand back to my bleeding scalp. "It's okay," I murmured. "We'll avenge all of them."

While she tried to stop the bleeding, I leaned my head against the tree for a moment, then gazed out at the compound in the distance.

The Westerner compound was entirely in flames. Around the walls, men waged war with their weapons, but some with their bare hands. Small explosions threw burning debris in the air which rained down on them, leaving fiery trails in the fields where it landed. I could not tell if the raid was a success or a failure, nor could I make out any distinct person in the fray.

I closed my eyes, cool fatigue creeping up my legs. It had been a long time since I'd been this injured, but I wasn't terribly concerned. We had Benjamin.

"Oh my God."

Ember's whisper made me open my eyes. She was staring behind the tree, wide-eyed and paler than I'd ever seen her. She took her hand off my head and reached for her knife. "Don't speak," she whispered, barely audible. "Close your eyes."

She took my hand. *Pretend to be dead. Beau Trent and another man are coming our way. They plan to kill you and take me. Graham told them that I can help them find the JM-104.*

It took every ounce of self-control I possessed to not jump to my feet.

So, Graham had been working for the supervillain families, not the Westerners. That made sense. A dozen Westerners had died at the sorting station from which he'd been "rescued," and it was always the prerogative of the supervillains to look for the JM-104. And now the Trents were aware of Ember's incredible power. I remembered Graham's excited ramblings about how useful she'd be in the search. He wasn't wrong.

Could it be that the entire supervillain mess during the battle was about capturing Ember?

Beau's almost here. Slow your breathing. No matter what I say, do not move. Quiet footfalls in the forest behind us became louder, announcing the presence of a third person. I bowed my head and slowed my breathing, trying to remain as still and dead-looking as possible.

Ember stroked my face. "Jill, please wake up," she begged. "Please." She began to cry delicate tears. She gasped, then shook me.

"Jill! Wake up! It's Beau Trent!" She began to cry harder. I didn't think she was acting anymore. "Wake up!" *Oh my God. They have the vial of JM-104 that Graham stole. They're going to use it on me.*

"Good job, Will. She's finally dead."

Beau's deep voice came from behind us. I remained as limp as possible, straining to hear any sound that would help me when I finally attacked. A little beyond him, another person approached. Will Rowe, I recalled, was Beau's best friend. What a team.

Beau came to a halt, just to my left. "Hello, pretty." His voice was low and even.

Ember scrambled backwards. "What do you want?"

"If Graham was telling the truth about you, you already know." He was still quiet. He stopped walking next to me. "You're coming with us."

"The hell I am," Ember growled.

"I'm sorry, you seem to think that was a request."

I heard Ember unsheathe her knife.

Will inhaled. "Beau."

"I will stick this in my neck before I go anywhere with you to be your tool," she spat. "I don't know what Graham told you about me, but I'm a superhero. I go down fighting."

Beau chuckled. "I like a fighter." I heard the skin-on-cloth sound of Beau pulling something out of his pocket. "I wonder how much fight you'll have in you with this coursing through your veins."

I heard Ember take a step back. "I won't be much use to you with that in me, dumbass."

"It's a three-week dose." His smile was evident in his voice. "You won't be able to call for help or know where we're taking you. And three weeks is more than long enough to give us time to persuade you to help us, if you're still reluctant. I have a lot of practice in that area."

"No." Her voice was trembling. "Nobody can make me tell them information I don't want to."

"Challenge accepted," Beau said.

I slashed at Beau's leg with my remaining knife.

Beau fell with a shout. Before Will could rush to his friend's aid, I hurled the knife at his leg. It sunk into his thigh, close to where I'd stabbed his sister. He collapsed with a howl of pain.

I whipped around and looked at Ember. "Run!"

She obeyed.

I tussled with Beau for a few seconds. I tried desperately to squeeze his throat enough to knock him out, but my bloody hands made my grasp slippery. Even as I tried to kill him, I was struck by how much he looked like Benjamin.

Instead of clawing at my hands, he groped around blindly next to him, his metal hand glinting eerily in the low light. The tiny vial lay on the forest floor a fraction of an inch out of his reach.

I lunged at it. My fingers curled around the small bottle. I'd die before I let Beau have it again. I just needed to get the bottle and destroy it, and then he'd have no way to—

There was a click and a hiss.

My high scream shattered the relative quiet of the forest.

I'd been mauled by lions and wolves, but I'd never felt anything like JM-104 as it licked its way through my veins and arteries, burning me as it went. I fell backwards and thrashed, unable to escape the mind-bending agony of my powers leaving me. It was everywhere, in every inch of my body. My vision seemed to constrict as it lessened to that of a normal human. My limbs, already shredded, became limp and heavy as my strength was reduced to an average woman's.

I fell onto my back and gasped for breath.

Beau pushed himself up and leered at me. "If you scream like that again, I might need a cigarette."

"Damn it!" Will yelled. "She used up the bottle! What the hell are we going to tell your mom?"

"Calm down," Beau drawled. "We can honestly tell her that we killed my brother's girlfriend. That'll make her happy." He put his metal hand around my throat.

"Wife," I growled.

"What?" Beau hissed. He pulled his hand away. "What did you just say?"

"Brother's wife."

Beau grabbed me by the front of my shirt and hoisted me to my feet, his hazel eyes nearly sparking with rage. Blood flowed down my fingers. "My brother married one of *your* kind?"

I nodded, unused to the effort the action required.

Beau's furious eyes darted all around my face, as if he were searching for the lie.

I gave him a weak grin. "Got a wedding gift for your new sister?"

Beau began to shake. "I should've killed you in the warehouse," he whispered.

I looked over his shoulder and saw two tiny white lights behind him.

My knee collided with his groin. He dropped me, and I caught myself before I fell. Beau was doubled over, allowing me to hobble away. Will was still on the ground, unable to overcome the pain from the knife in his leg.

"Weakling," I called to him as I passed him.

Reid ran up to me, his eyes a flat shade of white. "Ember got in touch with me," he said, panting. "She said you were in trouble."

I pointed a finger at the men. "Trap them. Don't let them go. That's your one job."

The ground trembled, and then the dirt beneath Beau and Will seemed to collapse as if a drain were under them. In seconds they were buried up to their necks. Beau shouted curses at us, but Will merely muttered ridiculous, graphic threats of what he'd do when he got his hands on me. I didn't look at Beau as I limped past him. I planted one foot in front of the other and willed my heavy, aching body to move. I slowly walked in the direction Ember had gone. *Ember Ember Ember Ember...*

I'm here. I'm hiding in the forest.

I need Benjamin. Find him.

Will do.

I thought I heard someone running through the brush, but I wasn't sure. I wasn't sure about anything I heard anymore.

I fell to my knees and took deep breaths. The forest smelled different than it had just minutes before. I'd always been able to differentiate the various odors that made up any space, manmade or natural. Now, instead of pine sap, dirt, animal droppings, water, leaves, and the thousand other parts of a forest, I just smelled "forest". It was one broad smell, blended together like a slurry in my weak nose.

If I survived to see the sunrise, would I be able to see all the colors? The night was so black now, so devoid of the shadowy grays and blues that usually made up a night to me.

Benjamin appeared a few feet away. I hadn't heard him. "Jillian, where are you?"

"I'm here," I croaked.

Benjamin dashed to me and touched my face. My wounds healed, and the pain faded, but still the weakness remained. When he hoisted me to my feet, my legs shook, and I had to lean against him.

He examined me. "What's wrong? What happened?"

"Beau and Will are here. They meant to inject Ember with JM-104. I got it instead."

Benjamin was stunned into silence for several seconds. "Where are they?" His voice was like steel.

"Back there. Reid is guarding them." He moved to go to Reid, but I caught his hand. "Don't. Go help the Sentinels."

"What are you going to do? You don't have your powers anymore."

"I'll find Ember and stay with her."

He nodded and disappeared into the darkness. My weak sight combined with the dark made it appear as though he'd teleported. *Ember, where are you?*

I'm coming back toward the trees.

I crashed through the forest, my uniform catching onto branches and thorns. At the edge of the grove, Ember slammed into me and we embraced for a moment.

I pushed her away. "Are you okay?"

"Yes," she said, panting. "What happened? I was so busy trying to contact Reid that I didn't listen in on you."

"I accidentally injected myself with JM-104."

As the words left me they seemed to take my adrenaline, shock, and horror with them. I started to giggle, and then I was on the ground, laughing uncontrollably.

Tears streamed down my cheeks as I laughed, and I could no longer name the emotion that I felt. Perhaps I'd lost the ability to differentiate the feelings in me as well as the sights and smells around me.

Ember kneeled next to me, somber. "You can't fight now, can you?"

After my laughter subsided, I looked at the compound. The burning had died down. The smoldering buildings glowed red and orange in places, but there were few active flames left. Sentinels and Westerners swarmed the grounds around the compound, still fighting. The sounds of their weapons were fainter than I remembered them being at this distance.

"I can't fight like I used to," I said. "But we're still going to free the slaves. I'm still Battlecry."

"How?"

I tapped my temple. "Tell me where they are, and we'll get to them."

Ember bit her lip but nodded. "I'll need to get into the compound."

I grabbed her hand. "Let's go."

38

My confidence evaporated as we ran toward the compound. Each step was a labor, a conscious effort to lift my heavy leg and plant it in front of me. Every few seconds, I'd rub my eyes in a vain effort to rid them of the invisible veil that clouded my vision and robbed me of the sharp clarity I'd always had. I even instinctually batted at my ears once or twice to clear away whatever it was that muffled every sound. Though I could feel nothing in my nose, I might as well have been pinching it shut. How did my team live like this every day? How did anybody?

Ember and I approached the fighting and threw ourselves to the ground behind a slight hill, propping ourselves up on our elbows. She turned to me. "Any ideas?"

I squinted into the darkness but could see nothing besides muzzle flashes and the glow of the compound. I growled and slammed my fist into the ground. Pain shot up my hand. Three weeks couldn't pass fast enough. "Can you contact Marco? We're going to need help."

She nodded and closed her eyes. "He's nearby," she murmured. There was a long pause, and then she smiled. "He's on his way."

I chewed on my lip. "Is this what it's like to be you?"

Ember shot me a surprised look. "What do you mean?"

"I'm not used to needing, well, an escort in dangerous areas."

I thought Ember might have a sarcastic comment, but instead she just nodded. "Yeah, this is what it's like to be me. Imagine how I felt when my uncle told me that I was being released into service even though I was a telepath with no actual fight training. I was terrified."

"He probably decided that a telepath was too much of a risk to have around with all this JM-104 bull. I bet you were always slated for service, but he couldn't just put you into the trainee group without people wondering why. And then he decided that he could make his son happy and get rid of you at the same time."

Ember made a noise of disgust. "So he just sent me onto the streets. Thanks a lot, Uncle." Her expression softened. "But it wasn't so bad. You've always looked out for me."

I elbowed her. "I'd be a crappy sort of friend if I didn't."

She patted my arm. "We're all going to do the same for you, you know. Nothing's changed. I can hear your thoughts. You think the best part of you is gone, but you're more than your powers. We all love you, and we'll help you through this."

I had to look away. Where would I have been without people like Ember in my life?

Ember lifted her chin. "Here he comes."

I couldn't see Marco until he was nearly on top of us. He sprinted through the field and dove on the ground next to Ember and me. "I'm here," he said between panting breaths. "What's going on?"

"Ember and I are going to find and free the slaves. We need cover."

"*You* need cover?"

I massaged my temples. "Long story short, I don't have powers right now. Just make sure we're safe as we go through, okay?"

I was certain I saw Marco's confused frown, but he jumped up and helped us to our feet. "Alright, let's go. There's a section of wall on the far side of the compound where there aren't many Westerners, and most of the fire has died down. I suggest we go in there."

"Lead the way," I said.

He snorted. "Okay, Battlecry."

We hurried behind him in the dark, ducking down periodically and winding our way around hillocks and behind trees. He led us through the smoky darkness toward the far side of the compound. Marco was correct—there were less men on the opposite side, and the glow of fire had diminished to the point where I could barely see anything.

Underneath the shock and horror of losing my powers, an old thrill lurked, ready to seize upon this new challenge and conquer it. I needed to be Battlecry.

We laid on the ground again. Marco pointed ahead of us to a hole in the wall that had been blasted away. "There. That's where we'll go in. What do you need after that?"

"We're going to find the slaves," I said. "We still don't know where the basement entrance is. The Westerner women and children are somewhere else in the compound. They're next."

I was formulating a plan about how I'd approach the latter group. If Ember had been correct, delicacy would be required to avoid an unspeakable tragedy.

Ember rubbed her temples. "My telepathy..." She looked up and shouted a foul word. Immediately after she'd spoken, the horribly-familiar buzz of locusts returned. Two seconds later, they fell on us by the thousands.

"Marco! Blast them!" I screamed, my face nearly pressed to the ground. I could feel the locusts crawl on the back of my neck and down my back. The sensations of their tiny feet on my skin felt just as terrible as the first time. That didn't seem fair, somehow.

Marco jumped to his feet. "Get as low as you can!"

There was a slight rippling sound as the sun's energy flowed out of him. The air around us heated up, and then locusts began to rain down on Ember and me, their dead carcasses bouncing a little as they hit the ground and our heads. Finally, the storm of locusts ceased. I lifted my head and could make out thousands of dead locusts around us in the field.

"Let's go," Marco said, pulling us to our feet again. "I killed all the ones around here, but they'll be back."

We ran to the hole in the wall and clambered through. I landed roughly on the other side and leaned against the rough cement to catch my breath.

"In the center of the compound," Ember said suddenly. "I've told the slaves who I am, and that they need to make noise. They're in the center of the compound, I think. The locust telepath is gone."

"Then what are we waiting for?" I said.

We began to work our way around twisted, crumbling wreckage. The temperature inside the destroyed compound was well above one hundred degrees, causing me to sweat beneath my heavy winter uniform. More than once, we had to stop to push a burned beam out of our path, leading to a complete collapse of the structure. Every time that happened, we threw ourselves to the ground in case roaming Westerners came to investigate, but none ever came.

The compound was largely devoid of people, the fires having forced most of the fighting to the outside of the walls. However, I wasn't positive that we were alone. I wagered it was approaching zero four, but still the cloudy sky remained dark, obscuring my ability to scan for enemies.

We crouched behind a shattered wall and surveyed the center of the compound, which appeared to have been a large building similar to the main building in Liberty. Even though the fires had only recently abated, two armed men prowled around the space, no doubt on alert for Sentinels and superheroes attempting to do exactly what we were doing.

"Ember, what are they thinking?" I whispered.

"They're jumpy. If we approach directly, they'll shoot us without a second thought."

Marco flexed his fingers. "I might have one good heat blast left. Without the sun..."

I gently pushed his hand down. "No, we're trying to do this the superhero way. What we need is a diversion."

"Can I help?"

All three of us froze.

Isabel St. James shimmered in the air next to us, appearing out of the dark like a beautiful mirage. Her hair had been cut short, and she wore a plain, sack-like dress that fell to her ankles, but even my weak eyes could see the familiar face. She was smiling, but the St. James sparkle was gone.

Marco could not speak for several seconds. He and Isabel stared at each other, until suddenly Marco seized his sister and hugged her fiercely, his entire body shaking as he sobbed in silent relief. Isabel embraced him, crying and hiding her face in his neck.

Ember and I both had to avert our eyes from the emotional reunion.

Finally, Isabel broke away from her brother, her eyes leaking a bit. She spoke in a low voice. "Last night I heard some of the Westerners talking about an attack on the compound. They knew superheroes would be there, and I figured it was you guys. When they rounded us up, I disappeared." She flickered out of sight for a second. "There was so much chaos that nobody noticed I was gone. I stayed low until the locusts came, and then I ran into the fields. Then I heard Marco." She wiped her eyes.

Marco hugged his sister again, still lost for words.

"This is probably a stupid question, but are you okay?" I asked Isabel.

Isabel nodded and gulped. "I'm good at staying out of sight. I was smacked around a little bit, but nothing serious. I promise. I probably would've run away, but I don't know where we are, and it's so cold."

"I'll make them pay for every time they touched you," Marco growled. "Nobody hurts my little sisters and gets away with it."

Isabel sniffed. "How about you let the others out? They're down in the root cellar. The wives and kids are in the tornado shelter."

"You said you could create a diversion?" I asked, glancing at the armed men in the distance.

Isabel nodded fervently. "Yeah. What do you need?"

I thought for a moment. "Marco, do you have any light left?"

"Lots."

"Isabel, can you get everyone to look in one direction?"

"Yeah."

"Good. Marco, when they're all looking at Isabel, blind them. It'll be just like the warehouse."

"It had better be nothing like the warehouse, Jill."

I smacked his shoulder. "Isabel, Marco, go."

They scurried off, away from Ember and me.

Ember turned to me. "I didn't hear her," she said quietly. "She was literally right next to us at the end, and I didn't hear her."

There was a rough yank on my hair. I cried out as I was pulled backwards a few feet onto my back, allowing me to see who had so roughly manhandled me: the locust woman.

She glared at me and brandished a small knife. "Hi," she spat. "You're dead."

The two sentries by the main building shouted something.

My foot met her knee with as much force as I could muster. She shrieked and fell to the ground. Ember and I jumped on her. Ember pried the knife out of her hand and tossed it to the side while I kneeled on the bug telepath's chest and punched her once, twice, three times in the face. Each punch caused an unfamiliar pain in my fingers, but I did not stop until she was unconscious once more.

"Hands up! We'll shoot!"

The two sentries had heard our fight. I swore under my breath but raised my hands. Next to me, Ember did the same. She caught my eye, and in the dim light I thought I saw her smirk at me.

"Are you Sentinels?" one of the men asked us. The barrel of his M-16 was pressed into the back of my head.

"They're women," his partner pointed out.

"Aren't you observant," Isabel said.

I heard the two men turn around.

There was a tremendous flash followed by the distinct sound of a fist meeting flesh. The sentries fell to the ground, and I grabbed one of their weapons. I spun it around and slammed the butt of the weapon into the side of the first sentry's head, and then the second. When they were still, I hastily unloaded the magazine and scattered the bullets inside the ashy ruins of a nearby building.

The four of us ran to the large husk of the main building and found the heavy metal trap door that led to the root cellar. I breathed a silent thanks to the sky that the lock was neither combination nor key, but a simple bolt and nut.

Men shouted in the distance. "They're in the main building!"

Bullets began to fly around us.

"Stop them!"

"They're letting the slaves out!"

Ember, Isabel, and Marco laid on the ground while I fumbled with the bolt and nut. I was on my hands and knees, shaking from adrenaline and anticipation.

"Sentinels are coming," Ember gasped. "I called them."

A bullet whizzed past my head, ruffling my hair.

I finished unwinding the wing nut and threw it, then grabbed the bolt.

"*Stop her!*"

I tossed the bolt aside and threw open the trap door.

39

The slaves quickly overwhelmed the remaining Westerners.

As much as I wanted to aid in the fighting, I realized that I would be of little help in the melee. The four of us were pushed to the edges of the compound, where we clambered through the hole in which we'd entered. When we were certain that we weren't at risk of being ambushed, we peered through the hole and watched the violence.

Years of pent-up anger and oppression poured forth from the dozens of captives.

The Sentinels could not stop the men, women, teenagers, and even a few elderly people as they stormed through the twisted wreckage, trampling and killing their former oppressors.

As we watched, a teenage boy dressed in rags beat a man to death with a rock. Terrified screams and pleas for mercy filled the twilight air, mixing with the shouts from the Sentinels for the Westerners to surrender. There were no more gunshots, only the yells of anger and fear, not unlike the night Benjamin and Isabel had disappeared.

There was little we could do. I did not wish to send any of my team into the compound. Ember and I could not fight, Marco was out of power and tired on top of it, Benjamin was less skilled than Marco and needed elsewhere, and Reid was still guarding Beau and Will.

All we could do was watch as the Westerners reaped the whirlwind.

In the distance, partially concealed behind the shell of a building, a young slave fought tooth and nail with a Westerner. The young man lost his footing and fell, at which point his foe reached down and twisted the young man's neck, breaking it. I was grateful that I could not hear the snap.

The Westerners, who now numbered only in the teens, surrendered within ten minutes.

One by one they fell to the ground and raised their hands, calling for mercy. The remaining Sentinels swarmed the compound with their weapons up, ordering the few survivors to kneel with their hands on their heads and cross their ankles. A few Sentinels had to order the freed slaves to stand back and not attack.

I put a hand on Ember's shoulder. "Go find Dean. I need you to listen to the people who surrendered and make sure they're not planning escape or an attack, and then we're going to find the women and children."

Isabel cleared her throat. "I can take you to them."

"Then lead the way, Chameleon. That'll be your codename."

"Oh, *hell* no," Marco muttered.

I caught Marco's eye and gave him a soft smile. "Let her have her moment."

Marco relaxed and nodded. Isabel let out a nervous giggle, then we all climbed through the hole in the wall once more.

Ember sprinted toward Dean, who was standing at the far end of the main street. Isabel took Marco and me by the hand and led us down a smaller peripheral street that ended in a set of large metal double doors set into the ground.

As we hurried down the street, we passed the glassy-eyed corpse of Jonathan, the Sentinel who'd told us about Graham's treachery. A few feet from him, Judd's body lay spread out over a large piece of concrete. I took a moment to close Jonathan's eyes and move Judd's body to a more dignified position. As I crossed Judd's arms, a murmured whisper of forgiveness escaped my lips.

When I was done, Marco, Isabel, and I ran to the shelter where the women and children were hiding.

Marco moved to open the doors, but I held up a hand. "Let me do this." I lowered my voice. "Isabel, I need you to be invisible behind me."

He stood back, and I hauled open the doors with a grunt of effort. They opened to reveal an earthen stairwell, at the bottom of which I heard frightened shrieks and cries.

I calmly walked down the stairs into the dim subterranean room, little swirls of dust rising up with every step. I didn't turn around, but I trusted that Isabel was there. When I reached the bottom, my eyes adjusted to the darkness. Women and children were huddled around the edges of the room, many in their pajamas. A tiny girl clutched a doll to her chest, then burst into terrified sobs.

One of the women, who appeared to be not much older than me, approached me with hard caution. "What happened? Are you a Sentinel?"

I straightened and looked her in the eye. "I'm not a Sentinel," I said loudly, though I did not take my eyes off the woman. "I'm a superhero. My team is in the compound with the Sentinels. Your men have surrendered to them."

Several of the women began to weep. The young woman's face hardened. "And what will happen to us, superhero? We've heard about what they do to survivors."

I put my hands on my hips. "You've been lied to. I'm going to make sure you're treated with dignity and respect. The Sentinels have better things to do than torment you, like go home to their own families and live their lives." A few women exchanged confused glances. "However, you're all going to have to cooperate. If you consider fighting back or causing trouble, not only will I know beforehand that you're planning it," I said, tapping my temple, "but I will have no qualms when one of the Sentinels actually does shoot you. If you attack me or one of my teammates, I will personally kill you. These

are the terms, do you understand? Surrender or face the consequences."

"We're not soldiers," a mother insisted. "We're women and children. We're not dangerous."

I gave her my iciest glare. "I'm not a soldier, either. But I think
you'll find that I'm one of the most dangerous people you'll ever have
the misfortune to meet. I dare you to put that to the test." I turned
around and began walking up the stairs.

"And what's your name, superhero?" the young woman asked
with a sneer. "Who should we say treated us so well?"

I looked over my shoulder. "My name is Battlecry. I'm the woman
who pissed everyone off."

I walked up the stairs into the sunrise.

40

As the women and children climbed out of the shelter and lined up in lines and rows to be counted and identified, I hurried to find Ember, so she could listen in on their thoughts. Marco and Isabel stayed behind to supervise the Sentinels, whose presence made several of the women visibly panicked. Ember was standing next to Dean in another corner of the compound.

As I neared, however, I saw that I'd been wrong—the man was in fact John Carl, one of the Sentinels who'd loaded Marco into the truck at the sorting station when we'd first met them.

John Carl saw me approach and beckoned me over. "We need your help," he said, urgently. "Several men are missing."

"Who?" Cold worry sloshed in my stomach.

"Dean, Judd, Jonathan, Ken, Gabe, and Gregory."

I covered my mouth, momentarily overcome by emotion. "Judd and Jonathan are dead," I said finally. "Their bodies are near the storm shelter where the women and children were."

John Carl's brown eyes, the only visible part of his face, conveyed his sadness. "Oh. Did you see any of the others?"

"No. Ember and I will find them. Where's Benjamin?"

"Doc is looking for survivors already, over on the north side." He pointed with his pen to the far side of the compound.

I thanked John Carl and we began to work our way through the destroyed settlement, keeping an eye out for survivors or corpses.

When we were halfway through the compound, Ember grabbed my hand. "It's Dean."

She was staring to her right at a collapsed building. We moved at the same time, grabbing beams and still-hot pieces of wood in unison and shoving them aside. The form of a man took shape in the charcoal and splinters.

Dean was lying on his stomach under a heavy piece of wood, unconscious and horribly still. With strength I didn't know I had, I lifted the final beam with a yell and let it crash to the side. I gently turned him over and gasped. "I'll get Benjamin," Ember said quietly.

Dean's handsome face had been burned nearly beyond recognition. His once pale, slightly weathered skin was now red, black, and oozing. Much of his thick black hair was gone. The horrible stench of burned flesh emanated from him.

As I looked down at the formerly-handsome man whom I'd once considered a relationship with, tears began to fall. But why was I crying? Benjamin could heal him in an instant. His hair would take a while to grow back, but his face would go back to be the same lovely face as before.

There was a slight puff of air. Benjamin was there.

He kneeled next to me, his forehead wrinkled in deep concern. "There's no need to cry, sweetheart," he murmured. "I'll heal him." He pressed his fingertips to Dean's ruined forehead.

Like always, the splotchy red and black burns melted away to smooth skin. The oozing merely left behind yellowish, flaky residue. Dean inhaled, frowned, and then groaned.

"Hi, Dean," I said, my high voice breaking.

Benjamin's eyes flickered up at me, sadness lingering in them.

Dean opened his eyes. "Hi, you," he croaked. He grinned, but the effect was slightly different from the lack of piercings, which I assumed had been lost when he'd been burned. He turned his head slightly and saw Benjamin, whose face had gone blank. "Thanks, Ben. I really owe you one."

"No problem," Benjamin replied in a tight voice.

I helped Dean sit up, then gave him my stocking cap. "You need this more than I do right now. Don't look in a mirror for a while, okay?"

Dean put on the cap and gave me a wide grin. "Glad to see you still look as great as ever." He stood up and dusted off his uniform. "If you'll excuse me, I need to go see who's alive. I assume we won?" He craned his neck and looked around. "We're not being paraded through the streets, I mean."

"We won. John Carl is over there. We're looking for survivors."

He nodded once at Benjamin and me, then rushed off.

I turned to ask Ember where we should go next, but she'd moved away from Benjamin and me to the other side of the road. She caught my eye and gave a significant look at Benjamin, who was standing with his hands in his pockets. There was a certain hardness to his expression.

"What's wrong?" I already knew the answer, though.

Benjamin wouldn't look me in the eye. "You were so upset about Dean."

I sighed. I didn't want to have this conversation here, but it seemed like I was going to have to whether or not I liked it. "Yes, I was."

Benjamin kicked a pebble. "What do you see in him? I know you said there was nothing going on between you, but—"

"Benjamin, please look at me."

He did.

I took a deep breath. "When I said that there was nothing going on between Dean and me, I meant it. When I said that I only wanted to know the truth about your past, *I meant it*. You need to start trusting me." I took one of his hands out of his pocket. "Yes, I was upset that Dean had gotten hurt because..."

My words failed me as a great pain encompassed my chest. I cleared my throat. "Because, for a little while, Dean filled the role in my life that you weren't. So yes, I feel some affection for him. But I still married you."

As I spoke, guilt blew through me. Now that the dust had settled, figuratively and literally, it occurred to me that I'd never asked Benjamin whether he'd wanted to marry me.

In the heat of the moment I'd bound our hands and promised myself to him, but what if he'd never wanted that from me? What if he'd been so moved by my grand display that he'd simply gone along with it, relieved that I wasn't going to call the feds?

On top of all that, we *were* young. Twenty-one was hardly an unusual marriage age in the camps, but what if Benjamin thought I'd stolen his wild youth from him? I knew the civilian phrase "ball and chain." Did he now think of himself as imprisoned by, and to, me?

I cleared my throat again. "However, if... if you don't want to be married to me, I'm willing to, well, pretend that it didn't happen. There weren't any witnesses, so I'm not really sure it was a real marriage."

Benjamin's face went from morose to shocked. "What are you talking about?"

"Well, I never asked you, and we are pretty young, I guess. And half of the drama of our recent life has been about people coercing us into situations."

"And the other half was...?"

"Superhero politics and militia crap. But that's not the point. Do you want to be married or not?" The words came out more annoyed than anything else.

His eyes darted toward Dean in the distance. "There was really nothing between you?"

I couldn't be angry at him for doubting me, because I *had* kissed Dean, who was clearly holding a torch for me. "Dean will get over his crush. On my part, I kissed him because I was upset at you and just wanted some comfort. I never encouraged him until that moment. I don't know what to say beyond that, except that I made a mistake I won't make again, I'm sorry, and I love you. I want to be married to you, but only if you want to be married to me. And if we're going to be married, I need you to trust me."

There was a beat, and then Benjamin swept me into a deep kiss. After he broke away, he said, "Marry me?"

Ember threw a piece of charcoal at our heads from across the road. "Really? Here? *Now*? Everyone already thinks you're married anyway. Shut the hell up and start looking for survivors."

After an amused exchanged glance, we rejoined Ember in the search.

We quickly found Gregory, alive and furious, under more wreckage. Over the next hour, we located and found the rest of the injured Sentinels.

WHILE I CLEARED away wood and burnt furniture, a fluffy, orange-bottomed songbird fluttered overhead, then landed delicately on a piece of charred wood near me. I paused in my labors, studying the bird as it studied me. It looked familiar.

I finally remembered where I'd seen it: on the wall at Baltimore-Washington International Airport.

A Baltimore oriole in the Rockies? How odd.

I quirked my eyebrow at the pretty little bird. "Aren't you a little far from home? Though I guess I'm not one to talk, since I'm from Georgia." I took a swig from my canteen and waved my hand at it. "Go back to Maryland, puffball. You don't belong with us superheroes."

The bird didn't fly away... but it did turn its head and looked at Benjamin, who was working across the street.

I frowned. "Wh—"

It took flight.

I shrugged and went back to work.

41

One by one we laid the bodies of the fallen Sentinels onto white sheets.

Ken, one of the men who'd escaped slavery with Dean, had been shot in the initial assault on the compound. I'd tripped over his body while I'd rushed to aid Ember. Gabe Spivak and three others had been killed by a collapsing building. Bobby, Judd, and Jonathan, we surmised, had been killed during the main battle while I'd fought the locust woman and Alysia. Antonio had been the slave whose neck had been snapped by the Westerner.

Gregory found his body.

I could only watch as my brother fell to his knees and screamed in despair when he discovered his best friend's remains. All heads turned and stared as he picked up Antonio's corpse and wept, unashamed of his emotions. Gregory carried the body to the long line of the dead and placed it, with great tenderness, on a sheet, crying all the while.

I kneeled down opposite him and gazed at Antonio's face. He looked peaceful in a way he never had in life.

Gregory bowed his face to the ground. "My brother," he groaned. "He was my brother."

Marco kneeled next to me. "I'm so sorry, Greg."

Gregory jerked his head up, his bloodshot eyes full of rage. "I don't want your 'sorry'. It doesn't mean *anything* to me."

Marco simply watched Gregory mourn for a minute. "I know how you feel," he said softly.

Gregory laughed mirthlessly. "How could you possibly know how I feel? Tell me about the time one of your precious superhero teammates died in battle, *Helios*. Or should it be Apollo? Because what you guys do is just a game. This is the real world."

Marco took my hand in his. "I am privileged to have never lost a teammate in battle," he said, still gentle. "But four years ago the Westerners murdered someone who was like a brother to me."

Gregory's fury twisted into derision. "I'm alive, moron. Antonio is actually dead."

Marco gave Gregory a pitying smile. "I'm truly sorry for your loss, Sentinel."

Marco planted a soft kiss on my hand and helped me to my feet. We left Gregory to his grief and joined Ember and Benjamin by a small campfire near the wall, in the sparse shade of a tall tree.

Above us, the silly little oriole twittered pleasantly. The sun had risen completely, but snow had started to fall from the overcast sky. Now that the adrenaline of the raid had died down, I was freezing. I shivered violently until Marco threw his arm around my shoulders.

"Where's Reid?" he asked, scanning all around us. "Is he okay?"

"He's fine," Ember said. "He's still guarding Will and Beau." She closed her eyes for a minute. "Your brother is such a creep, Benjamin."

Benjamin wrinkled his nose. "Lady, you are preaching to the choir. What is it this time?"

Ember massaged her temples. "Beau's been telling Reid what he'll do to me when he eventually captures me. He wants a reaction out of Reid." Her eyes went unfocused, then she laughed. "Oh please, Beau. Patrick was more creative than that."

Her laughter suddenly stopped.

She leaned toward all of us, and we copied her. When she spoke, her voice was low and tense. "Everyone, laugh like I just said something funny."

We instantly cracked up. She caught my eye. *Get Dean. Now. Act casual. Tell him to act casual.*

I yawned and stretched. "Guys, I'm going to go check on the schedule. I'll be right back." I walked over toward Dean, who was kneeling with John Carl next to a slave's mangled corpse. They were trying to identify the unfortunate man.

I kneeled next to Dean and whispered in his ear, "Ember needs you immediately. Act like nothing's wrong."

My tone must have carried the urgency, because he stood up and checked his watch, his usual smirk on his face. "No problem, Jill." Behind the humor was a hint of concern. "Any updates on that?"

I shrugged. "That's all I heard, but feel free to ask her yourself."

He laughed and punched my shoulder. "I'll be right back," he told John Carl, who was watching us with a confused expression.

We walked back to the campfire, where they were talking about a movie we'd all seen a few months before—an unusually light topic for post-battle. Ember watched us approach and became the essence of bashfulness, ducking her head and peeking coyly through her eyelashes at Dean. She locked eyes with him.

Dean blinked in surprise, then relaxed. "I wish you'd told me earlier," he said tenderly, holding out his arms to her. "There was no reason to hide it. I feel the same way."

Ember threw herself in his arms and kissed him with shocking passion.

What...?

Without warning, Dean shoved her aside, drew his handgun, and fired at the songbird in the tree above us.

There was a high scream as a middle-aged woman fell out of the tree and landed on the hard ground with a tremendous thud. Her arm was bleeding, but she was able to grab something out of her pocket and shove it in her mouth.

Ember dashed up to the woman. "Think about your secrets," she hissed. Ember grabbed the woman's face and scowled at her. *"When's the attack?"* She shook the woman roughly. "Answer me, damn it!" Ember gasped and dropped the woman, who had begun to twitch. "No," she breathed. "Oh God, no."

The woman's eyes rolled back, and foam bubbled out of her mouth. Within seconds she fell backwards, as dead as Antonio.

Ember kicked the woman's body repeatedly. "Damn it! *Damn it!*"

I pulled Ember away from her desecration. "What? Ember, what is it?!"

Ember's fury turned to naked fear. "She's been spying on us since we were in the sorting station. I don't know what she told the forbidden families about us, but I heard one thing. They planned an attack on Chattahoochee."

Marco and Benjamin were at our sides in moments. "When?" I demanded. "We have to warn them!"

Ember shook her head, tears spilling over. "It was last night."

42

T he ancient truck, taken from the compound, screeched to a
halt at the NO TRESPASSING sign. The gate was open.

Benjamin shoved the gear stick into park and we hopped out of
the truck. Without a word, we grabbed onto Reid and clung to him
like a life preserver. There was a small rumble, and then we flew up
into the deep blue mid-afternoon sky and began to soar north over
the woods.

Far in the distance, the steel wall of Chattahoochee stuck out of
the canopy like a razor. Beyond it, Fort Mountain stood, eternally
watching over the camp.

The freezing wind made my eyes water, but it also woke me up.
We hadn't eaten since before the raid, which had ended nearly eighteen hours before. Upon hearing that there'd been a supervillain
attack on my childhood home, I'd ordered my team to drop everything and find a vehicle. Reid had been called away from Will and
Beau, leaving them buried up to their necks in the woods. Dean
promised to watch over Isabel, who'd flat-out refused to return to
Chattahoochee.

Benjamin had driven the entire way from southern Montana to
Georgia, only stopping for gas. The shadows under his eyes were

darker than the rest of ours, but as we neared the steel wall, I saw the anger on his face. His old family had just attacked his new family.

Ember also displayed signs of deep exhaustion, as she'd stayed awake the whole time in the front seat, acting as a police scanner while Benjamin raced down the interstate highways at speeds well above one hundred miles per hour.

We landed in the main meadow with a dusty thud. I took a moment to get my bearings, then slowly looked around.

No hut or shelter had survived the attack. Shredded clothes and items were everywhere, most of them unrecognizable. Trees were broken, tossed all over the field. At a moment's glance I could not guess what powers had been used, but clearly there had been a show of great force.

"Marco?" my Aunt Grace called from the edge of the trees. I squinted and thought I saw many people in the shadows of the forest. Aunt Grace sprinted toward us. "Marco! Sweetheart!"

Marco rushed to greet his mother. "Mom, what happened? We heard there'd been an attack."

Aunt Grace fell to her knees and began to sob, hugging Marco all the while. The rest of us watched from a respectful distance.

"They came in the night," she moaned. "They came in the night and started killing people. The trainees fought them off, but they killed so many people."

Marco removed his mother's arms from his neck. "Where's Dad? Where are the girls? Are they okay?"

Aunt Grace tried to compose herself, but a moment later she hid her face in her hands and began to sob anew.

Ember covered her mouth, tears sparkling in the corner of her eyes. "Oh *no*. How horrible."

"What is it?" I said, spinning around to find my family. Where were my little cousins? My uncle? My own parents and siblings?

Instead of answering, Ember ran up to Marco and pulled him away from his mother. "Come with me, Marco. Come now."

Marco's eyes darted back and forth between Ember and his wailing mother. "Why? What happened? Mom, *where is everyone?*"

"All the survivors are in the woods," Ember said. "Ma'am, I'll tell him. Benjamin, a lot of people need healing."

Benjamin blurred away to the edge of the forest. Reid helped my aunt to her feet and offered his arm as he walked her toward the forest.

Marco's breathing had become ragged. "Ember, tell me what is going on right now. Where's my family?" His voice was shaking.

Ember took his hands in her own, his lip quivering. "Melissa, Caroline, and Adora were killed in the attack. Mrs. Trent killed them. It was very quick. They probably didn't feel anything."

Marco collapsed into Ember's arms.

———

I SURVEYED THE BLOODY, oddly shaped corpses that had yet to be buried.

I could see that my mother-in-law was responsible for at least half of the deaths. I remembered the last time I'd seen her, in August of the previous year. After she'd accused me of somehow forcing Benjamin to join my team, Marco had killed her husband right in front of her before threatening to do the same to Beau.

As I peeled back the cloth that covered the partial corpses of seven-year-old Melissa, nine-year-old Adora, and thirteen-year-old Caroline, all of which lacked heads and shoulders, I couldn't help but feel that these particular murders had been personal.

After delivering the terrible news, Ember had guided Marco to a shady tree nearby. She sat with him for more than an hour, telling him stories of where civilians believed good people went when they died. I still didn't know what I believed about such things, but if such places existed, surely my littlest cousins were there. My chest throbbed to think of them eternally young and carefree, safe from the heinous designs of evil people.

Allison had been shot in the head. She'd been holding my infant niece, whose name I'd had to ask for: Meredith. Allison had been fleeing across the creek when she'd been shot, so Meredith fell from her arms into the water and drowned.

Next to their corpses, Samuel Dumont's lifeless body bore the unmistakable signs of a fatal beating. Sarah Spivak, Lark's sister, had told me that Samuel had died defending his wife and child.

Beyond their bodies lay the remains of Stephen Monroe, whom I now knew had been Dean's cousin.

At the end of the tragic line lay the corpses of Sidney Dufresne, Ella St. James, the entire Saur family, and my father.

I stood over my father's body for a long moment, feeling nothing but the vague guilt over feeling nothing.

Set apart from the main line of bodies lay the small bodies of the eight trainees who'd died in combat. Noah St. James's corpse headed the line, which ended with Heather, the tiny girl with whom I'd spoken before demonstrating a kick attack. Her hair was still in pigtails. All of them would be burned on a pyre, the traditional funeral rite of superheroes. Their pyres stood half-constructed at the far end of the field.

As I sat on my knees next to the grim row, Marco's father came up to me. Tracks from earlier tears were still on his cheeks, visible in the low light from the campfire. He offered me a hand and I took it, standing up and facing him.

"Could you describe the people who attacked the camp?" I asked. "My team is going after them."

"Maybe. The woman who killed my daughters disintegrated them."

"I already know who that is," I said quietly. "Anybody else?"

"You'll have to ask the others. There was so much confusion. It was in the middle of the night, people were running everywhere and screaming. I didn't realize the children were gone until I saw that witch reach for their faces." He turned away from me, his shoulders shaking.

I put a hand on his back. "Uncle, I can't bring them back, but I can tell you that Isabel is alive and safe. We found her, and Benjamin, too.

She's in Wyoming right now with people who've promised to look after her."

Uncle Howard spun around. "Why is she in Wyoming? What happened that night? You never told us, you just ran off."

"Before I answer that, tell me one thing: where's your brother?" I meant Elder St. James, but I could not make myself use the honorific.

"Thomas died," Howard said without emotion. "So did his wife, Theresa. The woman who killed my daughters completely destroyed their bodies. I saw it happen. There's nothing left to bury. My nephew Eli came from Oconee a few hours before you arrived. He's the new Elder St. James. His new homestead is about a quarter mile into the woods." He pointed to the area of woods in question.

"I need to speak with him about Isabel. I want you to be there. In fact, I want anyone who's ever lost a family member to the Westerners to be there. Can you round them up?"

"Yes," he said, confused. "Give me ten minutes and I'll have the word out."

I turned and walked into the dark forest.

At first, there was no indication that people lived in the trees, but soon enough I began to see pin pricks of fires in the distance. I wanted to hurry but could not see my way in the dark. Twice I tripped over logs.

When I finally reached the huddles of people, I saw that Benjamin was busy healing injuries. The line of the injured was far greater than last time.

I leaned against a tree and watched as my husband patiently placed his hands on men, women, and children. Though he was exhausted, he never betrayed any negative emotion or desire to take a break. Person after person came forward to receive healing, and he just smiled and spoke a few words with each of them.

Matthew reached the front of the line. His hand and leg were heavily bandaged, and he leaned on a crude wooden crutch. I drew back into the shadows, suddenly hyperaware of my lack of powers.

I could not hear them, but I could see them well in the firelight.

Benjamin's face showed no emotion as he said something to

Matthew. The way his mouth moved made me think it was a question.

Matthew seemed surprised at what Benjamin had asked. He inclined his head forward, confusion playing across his face.

Benjamin whispered something into Matthew's ear.

Matthew gasped and staggered backwards. His leg gave way, and he fell with a yell.

Benjamin's only response was a small smile and a dark gleam in his eyes that I'd never seen before.

Matthew limped away, throwing one terrified glance behind him before disappearing into the trees. I was tempted to ask Benjamin what he'd said to Matthew but decided that I'd let him have that secret.

A little girl stepped forward and held out her arm, which was wrapped in a bloody bandage. Benjamin's face smoothed over, and he lifted her hand and pecked it as a gentleman would a grand lady's. She threw her arms around his neck and covered him in sloppy kisses.

I turned away from the scene and continued to look for Eli St. James.

Before I could go ten feet, Uncle Howard rushed up to me. "Jillian, the people you wanted are meeting next to Eli's shelter. Whatever you have to say, you should say it now." His voice was tight.

I followed him through the trees to a crude hut. A man in his early thirties stood in the middle of a small crowd of onlookers, my mother among them. I did not greet her. I wasn't here for pleasantries.

"Eli," I said as I approached him.

Eli let out a long-suffering sigh. "It's Elder St. James, now."

"No, you're Eli to me."

The crowd went quiet.

"What is this about, Jillian?" He didn't show any anger, but I detected a note of impatience. He'd heard about me, no doubt.

"This is about your father, and the rest of the elders, selling people to the Westerners. Or did you not notice Benjamin back there? I'm sure you heard about the healer who died in the attack. That's him."

Eli didn't speak for several seconds. "Do you have proof? That is a very serious accusation."

I kept my voice even. "My team not only tracked down Benjamin and Isabel, we found several former inhabitants of this camp who'd been sold by your father, and more who'd been sold by other elders. One of them was my brother Gregory."

My mother screamed. "Gregory's *alive?*"

I didn't look at her. Instead, I took a step toward Eli, who didn't move. "I'm not going to ask you whether you knew about the slave trade, because you'll deny it, and I won't believe you. Instead, I'll ask you this: what are you going to do when I call the FBI and start the investigation?"

Even my team didn't know that I wasn't showing my full hand. I'd spent much of the drive back to Georgia planning my next move. Alerting the FBI was just the beginning.

I had to hand it to Eli—he was able to maintain composure in a way his father never had. He appeared to think about my question for a moment, his lips pursing. "I'll work with them. I'll tell them everything my father ever told me."

"And my team? Technically, we're rogues. What are you going to do about that?"

Eli gestured toward the gathered people. "Let these people be witnesses. You have my word that your team can return to Saint Catherine and serve in peace. We have no quarrel with you. As the elder of this camp, I hereby declare my father's judgment at the tribunal null and void."

"Good move."

Eli didn't say anything, but some ugly emotion shimmered in his eye for the briefest second.

I turned on my heel and walked into the trees. Marco and Ember met me there, joining me as I strode toward Benjamin's line.

"He's lying," Ember said quietly.

"I know. What's he planning?"

"Nothing yet. He just knows that we're too troublesome to have around."

"Then we'll be ready," Marco said.

I stopped walking and put a hand on Marco's shoulder. "Yes, we'll be ready. But the Trents won't, nor will the people who helped them. We've been on the defensive with these people for too long. As soon as we go back to Saint Catherine and get settled again, we're going after them. And then we're going after the JM-104. It's over. It's all over. We're getting justice."

Marco's eyes filled with tears again. "But why did they kill my sisters? What did they want?"

I'd asked myself the same question when I'd uncovered Melissa's tiny body. "I don't know. I think it was revenge for killing Mr. Trent."

Marco let out a long breath. "I'm not angry at Benjamin. I don't know if you were worried about that, but I'm not."

"I know. Have you talked to him since finding out about your sisters?"

"No. I didn't really know what to say."

"How about, 'Help me find the bastards who did this?'"

Benjamin walked up to the three of us, Reid close behind.

He smiled sadly at Marco. "From what I can tell, my mom and about five others stormed the camp a little after midnight. They killed fairly randomly, but everyone agrees that they definitely came here for a purpose. After they murdered your aunt and uncle, they ran off. No offense, but I can guarantee you that the trainees didn't actually fight them off. A bunch of kid heroes wouldn't scare my old crowd."

"You think maybe they wanted to make a statement by killing the highest elder?" I asked. "That's why they killed my grandma and videotaped her death, right? To make a statement."

Benjamin's eyes tightened. "I was always told that Grandpa killed Battlecry and her team because they wouldn't give details about the camps. I think they were planning some kind of invasion. But yes, the tape was a statement."

Reid swore. "What? Your *grandpa* killed Battlecry?"

"Yes," Benjamin said, looking down. "I'm sorry for not being honest about it with all of you when we met."

"We'll definitely talk about this later," I said in pacifying tones.

Reid's unsurprising outburst reminded me that I'd never shared Benjamin's revelations with my team. As far as they knew, he'd only ever killed the two Westerners right before meeting the Sentinels. We'd have to sit down and discuss his past when we got home.

"What's the plan in the meantime?" Reid asked, glancing once at Benjamin. "I've been asked to bury the bodies."

"Do that," I said. "And then we're leaving."

43

W e arrived at our headquarters at nearly zero one and slept for twelve hours.

Benjamin had disappeared into his bedroom while I walked into mine, but when I woke up in the early afternoon, he was lying next to me, unclothed and sound asleep. I'd woken with a headache and aching joints, but instead of climbing out of bed and finding some painkillers, I laid back down and watched him breathe in and out, letting his warm breath waft over my face. While he breathed, I thought about our marriage.

What did marriage mean to me? To him? What did it take to make a marriage work? I suspected that the examples of marriage I'd seen growing up weren't what Benjamin would call ideal, but then again, I didn't think his parents had had a healthy marriage, either.

We'd have to find out on our own what made a happy, stable relationship. Perhaps I'd married him in haste, but I was devoted to him. To us. Our youth would not hurt us. Though supervillains prowled around us and the elders schemed against us, we would stay together.

Benjamin inhaled deeply and slowly opened his eyes. He smiled. "This is the best way to wake up."

I poked his nose. "Good dreams?"

He grinned, his sleepiness lending it an adorable quality. "About our wedding night, so heck yeah."

I rubbed my chin. "Show me again how that went. I forgot."

He laughed and pulled the blanket over our heads.

An hour later, the five of us sat at our round kitchen table. Reid quietly poured mugs of steaming coffee and pushed them toward each one of us. I sipped on the bitter drink and let it warm my stomach, but it couldn't quite make my headache or joint pain abate.

I reached behind me and grabbed the bottle of ibuprofen from the turntable on the island and popped two of the pills into my mouth.

After I swallowed them, I gave my head a little shake. "Okay, guys. We've got some stuff we need to talk about. I'll go first."

My team politely folded their arms on the table.

"First off, since I won't have powers for about nineteen more days, Reid will be mission leader for anything out of the house. Reid, do you have any problem with that?"

"No. That's fine."

I sipped my coffee. "Good. Next thing. Beau and Will made it clear that they were after Ember. From now on, Ember will be accompanied by either Marco or Reid when you guys leave the house. No exceptions. Ember, stay alert. I don't know what happened to those two men specifically, but we have to assume that any number of supervillains will try again."

Now that I thought about it, unless Dean had freed them, there was no way Beau or Will could have extracted themselves from the ground. Alysia was still running around, but she couldn't have known they were there.

Yet, I felt a curl of unease as I thought about them. If there was one thing the slavery conspiracy had taught me, it was that nobody was really dead unless there was an identifiable body or multiple witnesses.

Ember laid her head on her arms. "I hate being a telepath," she grumbled into the wood. "I never asked for this."

"I know," I said softly. "We'll stop them, Em. I promise."

Reid reached across the table to hold Ember's hand, but she shot him a look so hateful that he recoiled.

He placed his hand in his lap and stared at the woodgrain for a moment before lifting his head and staring blankly at Benjamin. "I'd like to know a little more about what you said regarding your grandfather and the first Battlecry."

Benjamin's fingers clenched his mug. "I have a long rap sheet. It's a bit longer than I made it out to be when I met you guys. I... I've killed people. A lot of people. Jillian and I talked about it back at Liberty, but I understand now that I need to be honest with all of you."

Marco, Ember, and Reid exchanged glances.

Marco leaned toward Benjamin. "You're going to help us catch the people who broke into Chattahoochee, right?"

"Of course," Benjamin said, shocked.

"Actually, as soon as my powers are back, we're going after all the forbidden families," I said. "It's not going to be easy, and we're going to be itinerant for a while. But the attack on the camp proved that they're getting bolder, so we have to get bolder, too. Benjamin is our biggest asset in this fight. We need him. Are there any objections?"

Marco crossed his arms and looked around the table at all of us. "He's served on the team for months, helped rescue slaves, and he's our biggest source of information on the forbidden families anyone could possibly have. Oh, and he's, you know, married to Jill. If anyone has a reason he shouldn't be on the team, I'd love to hear it."

Reid rubbed the back of his neck. "I wish you'd told us. Don't get me wrong, I'm not mad. I get why you didn't say anything in the beginning, but all the months you've lived with us..."

Benjamin blushed deep scarlet.

Ember picked her head up, her eyes suddenly gentle. "Oh, Benjamin. What am I going to do with you? You're such a puppy."

Benjamin scratched at the table's surface. "I always wanted to be a superhero," he said, barely audible. "And then I met you guys and it was like I had the family I'd always wanted. Brothers who weren't sociopaths, and a sister who was my age, unlike Eleanor." He finally looked at me. "And I had you. Wouldn't you hide the awful truth about yourself, too?"

"Perhaps," I said. "But somewhere along the way you convinced yourself that we were going to turn you in if we found out. I still don't understand why."

"It's what I deserve," he mumbled. He went back to picking at the table.

I folded my hands in front of me. "Deserve? Maybe. But if we're talking about what we deserve, then Marco, Reid, and I deserve to do prison time for joining an unauthorized militia and killing people. I deserve to lose leadership of this team for being a brat more times than I can count. And I deserve to be dumped for kissing Dean." I inclined my head toward Benjamin, who was now staring at me, wide-eyed. "We don't always get what we deserve."

Benjamin's eyes shimmered, but he didn't reply.

I drained my mug and put it on the table with a hard clink. "Later today I'm going to make an appointment with the local FBI field office, as well as a therapy appointment. I'll also be calling a press conference, and I'd like you guys to be there with me."

"A press conference?" Ember said. "Why?"

I poured myself more coffee. "I'm going to scare the crap out of the elders."

Benjamin smirked. "How so? Announce that you're going to college?"

Instead of being annoyed at his mocking question, I let myself laugh. The elders *would* be scared of me going to college.

I'd come across a short proverb in one of the many books on my bookshelf upstairs: knowledge is power. I hadn't quite understood it when I read it months before, but now I did. I'd defeated Patrick in the library with my knowledge of electricity.

Now, months later, I would defeat the forbidden families with the knowledge Benjamin had about their abilities and methods. I knew I'd been raised in a cult, and so I could begin to extricate myself. I knew I had a sickness called depression, and thus I could take steps to overcome it.

I knew my ancestresses had led teams into the heat of battle, and I could, too.

I reached my hand into the center of the table. They all put their hands on mine. "I've got something I need to say."

It was time to share some of my power.

44

At noon the next day, I stood behind the thick blue velvet curtain that divided my team from the throng of reporters in the auditorium in City Hall. I didn't dare peek out at the crowd, which contained representatives from all the major news networks, plus every local one. They were all waiting for me to appear. I didn't want to cause unnecessary pandemonium by showing my face early.

Ember brushed a lock of hair out of my face. She'd put my hair up into a chignon earlier, but my constant fidgeting had messed it up a bit.

"Stop worrying," she said. "You'll be fine."

"I'm going to be sick," I groaned. "Why did I do this?"

Behind my clammy forehead, a headache prickled. It hadn't gone away since yesterday.

"Because you're a badass," Benjamin said, handing me a glass of water. "Don't forget it."

"We'll be right beside you," Reid said.

I sipped on my water, but it didn't make me feel better. I looked up at Benjamin. "You wouldn't happen to have anti-nausea medication on you, would you?"

Marco pointed at me. "I knew it. You *are* pregnant."

Benjamin looked quickly between Marco and me.

I rolled my eyes. "No, I'm not. Will you let that idea go, please?"

Marco squinted at me. "How can you know for sure? You keep having sex."

"Well, see, sometimes when a woman experiences a huge shock to the system like, say, being injected with JM-104, it triggers an early period. Now, a period is the part of the menstrual cycle where—"

"Oh, God, *stop*," Marco said, holding up his hands. "Forget I said anything." He pressed a hand to his stomach. "Ugh, now I don't feel good."

A short woman poked her head into the small waiting area where we were standing. "Miss Battlecry, it's time."

I set my glass on the table and threw back my shoulders. *I can do this. I can do this. I have to do this. There's no backing out, now.*

My team and I stepped out from behind the curtain.

At least twenty-five reporters and journalists were crammed into the small space, most of them holding microphones or cameras. A few of them carried recorders. When we walked out, a hush fell on the crowd.

I took my place behind the podium. My team stood behind me, and though I did not check to see, I was certain they were standing straight and tall with smooth faces. Respectable. Strong.

I stood up straighter.

"I'd like to thank you all for coming on such short notice," I began, my voice surprisingly calm. "I know this is an unusual act for a superhero. We're not known for speaking openly to the media. In fact, one of the things I'm going to talk to you about today is why we're not known for our relationship with the media."

The reporters murmured to each other. I gazed over the crowd, catching their eyes and smiling ever so lightly. A few of the people returned the expression, their curiosity no doubt battling their professional demeanor.

"Though I'm addressing you, and by extension the American people, my message today is not for civilians, but for all superhero teams serving across the country."

Quite a few eyebrows shot up.

"Many of my fellow superheroes will not be allowed to watch this broadcast. Perhaps it is because your leader won't allow you to watch live television. More likely it is because I'm Battlecry, the woman who dared to command a team. As you all know, I have committed a crime, so to speak, by doing so."

Jaws dropped.

"If you're still allowed to watch me, listen carefully to what I'm about to tell you."

The crowd fell silent as I began explaining to my fellow brothers and sisters in service how the elders had used poverty, ignorance, abuse, and fear to control the most powerful people in the world.

I told them about the tribunal, where a man had been tortured for daring to love someone the elders couldn't control, and how they'd tried to marginalize me for standing up to them. Several reporters' faces grew grim when I described how I'd been sexually assaulted, unable to fight back because of my overwhelming belief that I could not.

Then I began to describe how the elders had sold our friends and family into slavery.

"One of my teammates was sold to the compounds. Their sale was based on the erroneous belief that we would not investigate their supposed death," I said, struggling not to growl the words. "During the investigation we uncovered proof that not only had the elders sold our friend, but that they'd been selling children for decades. I am currently working with the Federal Bureau of Investigation to put a stop to the human trafficking. I urge every superhero watching this to speak to your local field office and tell them what you know about the so-called Westerner attacks. Any information you have is valuable."

I relaxed my grip on the edge of the podium.

"Some of you will not believe me because I'm a woman. Others of you won't believe me because it is easier to think that I'm lying. But I know that out there, across the country, there are superheroes who are tired of living in fear. You're tired of being told that you can't speak, can't think, can't learn. You're tired of the cult. Yes, you were raised in a cult. It's very possible you don't even know what that word means because the elders do not want you to have the power that knowledge gives."

I took a deep breath and looked directly into a camera.

"If you need help, the heroes of Saint Catherine are ready to give it."

Reporters yelled questions for me, but we refused comment and went backstage.

We collected our things and headed out a small side hallway and out into an alley that bordered City Hall. As we passed the news vans parked out front, I took a moment to remember our lives in our old base camp, before Benjamin had joined the team. We'd been with Patrick then. We'd sometimes sit in the living room and watch the news, hooting when we saw ourselves on the screen.

Were there teams that were now having an uncomfortable conversation about what the recalcitrant Battlecry had said? Were there young heroes and heroines examining their lives? Perhaps they'd never heard of me, the news of my rebellion having been kept from them. As long as they did not know they could rebel, they would never try.

Who is she, they might ask each other.

I'd asked myself the same question once. I hadn't been able to answer. I passed the tinted window of a parked car and saw my reflection. Who was I?

Unlike last time, the answer came easily.

I was the woman who'd pissed everyone off. I was the woman who'd done the unthinkable. I was the woman who'd issued a rallying shout to the troops: *rise up, fight back, take what's yours.*

I was Battlecry.

ONE WEEK LATER

My phone rang as I walked up the brick steps of our headquarters. The ring tone wasn't any of the four I'd assigned to my teammates, so with a bit of curiosity I pulled out my phone and looked at the screen. The unfamiliar number was from Wyoming.

I dropped the shopping bag I was holding and sat on the steps, already having an idea who was calling. There was only one person in Wyoming who would ever want to call me. "Hello?"

"Benny!" My sister's annoyingly high voice grated against my ear. "I got your message right after you sent it, but there's no service on the mountain. I couldn't call you back until now."

"Hi, El."

"Why so dismal? You're a married man. You should be delirious with joy."

I pinched the bridge of my nose. "Do you really want to know what's going on in my life, or did you have a reason for calling me?"

I knew I sounded rude, but I had things to do. I checked my watch. I'd give her five minutes. Eleanor and I were on okay terms, but I was still rankled by how she'd treated Jillian upon hearing about our arguments, as well as miffed that she'd lied to me for years about her activities in Colorado. I *hated* liars.

Of course, that was probably one of the big reasons I struggled to like myself.

"I actually did have a reason for calling you. I wanted to tell you that the raid against the other compound was a success, mostly because I was there."

"I'm glad to hear it."

"Oh, come on, Benny. You wanted the Westerners to lose as much as anyone. Dean was just saying…"

I leaned back on my free arm and looked up at the night sky. I didn't know which constellations hung above me, and as Eleanor chattered about raids in distant states, I idly wondered if Jillian did.

She was as dedicated a crime fighter as anyone else, but when she started on an explanation of the heavenly bodies and their movements, a guy would think that she was a professor of astronomy. Her face would light up and she'd babble excitedly about whatever it was I'd asked her about.

The night before it had been the Kuiper belt, planetoids, and why Pluto actually wasn't a planet. Her enthusiasm for astronomy was beautiful.

"Benny? Still there?"

"Oh, sorry. What was that?"

"I asked you how everyone is doing," she said, gentle. "I saw the broadcast."

I sighed. "We could be better. Jillian's had a nasty flu for a week and there's no signs of her getting well. Marco is handling his sisters' deaths as well as can be expected, I guess. He's been sad, but he and I talk a lot, and I think it's helping. He just recovered from a stomach bug. Ember and Reid are still broken up. They can't be in the same room anymore without arguing, though Ember caught Marco's stomach bug and she's been laid up for a few days."

"I'm sorry to hear that. I wish I could help, but from this distance…"

"Don't worry about it. Jill and Ember will get better, Marco will heal, and Ember and Reid were meant to be together. They just need some time to cool off." As I spoke, a young black woman walked past our house. Her hair was pulled back into a thick braid much like Isabel's had been when I'd met her. "How's Isabel settling in?"

"Isabel is adjusting. She was almost inconsolable when she found out about her sisters, but lots of the younger Sentinels are more than happy to offer their shoulders to cry on. She's very popular. She's moved in with Gregory's family, the Welches. He won't admit it, but he likes having a familiar face from Georgia nearby."

"And how are the Sentinels doing?" I was trying for politeness but ended in sarcasm.

"Dean is fine. We have dinner together every night, so we can discuss Liberty's finances. It was my idea. I told him I wouldn't take no for an answer." She sounded almost sheepish. "I could've knocked him over with a feather."

I rubbed my forehead. "Over dinner? That kinda sounds like a date."

Dean wouldn't move on from my wife to my sister, would he? *Would* he? I slumped forward, resting my elbows on my knees in near-defeat. Would I ever be rid of that guy?

Eleanor's sing-song *mmhmm* did nothing to quell my unease. However, she changed the subject. "What happened with Beau and Will?"

I straightened. "We left them in the woods by the compound. Tell me Dean captured them or killed them or something."

There was a long silence on the other end of the phone. "No... no, Dean never mentioned them, actually. Did you guys give him directions about handling them?"

I swore under my breath. "No. We ran off in such a hurry that I never thought about it. We were all exhausted and freaking out about the attack." I gazed up at the stars again. "If nobody ever found them, they're dead by now."

Though Beau was my brother, the mere idea of his death brought nothing but relief. I knew without a doubt that he'd meant every one of his threats against Ember.

"Maybe," Eleanor said, her tone dark. "But even I've never been that lucky. Consider them alive, armed, and pissed off. Watch over Ember, because if they come back for her, it won't be pretty."

I pictured my friend, slight and delicate, trying to fight off my brother and his lackey. The image made my stomach turn, but it also kindled a surge of protectiveness. Beau had failed in his plan, forewarning us of all future attempts. That would be his downfall.

"I will," I promised. "How are you doing, El? Seriously." My protective instinct covered all of my sisters.

"I'm fine. I'm sorry about everything that happened here. Please give Jill my love and hug all the others."

"Love you."

"Love you, too."

She hung up.

I slipped my phone back in my pocket and grabbed the shopping bag. I typed in my entrance code and scanned my fingerprints, then quietly walked into the darkened living room. The light from the kitchen cast a yellow beam onto the couch, illuminating Ember's sleeping form. Next to her, on the floor, a large bowl contained the vomited remains of whatever she'd eaten that day.

I placed my hand on her thin shoulder. "Hey, Ember," I whispered.

She groaned and opened her eyes. "Wha...?"

I fished out the small box of nausea medication I'd bought for her, since she'd ran through my supply in the sick bay. "I got this for you," I said quietly, placing it in her hands. "I'll get some water."

She gave me a weak smile and closed her eyes again.

I walked into the kitchen, where I was immediately assaulted by the overpowering, astringent odor of oregano. Reid had stuffed a thick bouquet of the herb into a little jar with water on the bottom, and the cutting board on the counter bore both the green-stained marks of frequent use as well as a small knife covered in tiny bits of leaves.

I filled Ember's glass with water from the pitcher in the fridge, which was next to yet more bouquets of oregano.

When Jillian had returned from the press conference a week

before, she'd asked Reid to make her oregano tea, of all things. Marco, Ember, and Reid hadn't shown any surprise or confusion at the bizarre request, and when I politely asked my wife if she actually was pregnant and whether this was merely the first strange craving, the four of them had launched into simultaneous, enthusiastic explanations about herbal remedies.

Days later, I still had no idea where they'd learned about them, but now I had to cross-reference every medication I gave them to make sure there weren't any relative contraindications with the herbs they insisted I "prescribe."

I shook my head. Never a dull moment for the heroes of Saint Catherine, oh no.

But I had to admit that as strange as their sudden interest in herbal remedies was, I was relieved that Jillian wasn't pregnant. Not because I wasn't ready to be a father—I liked babies—but because if the baby were mine, it would be too early in her pregnancy for symptoms to present. However, if the baby were someone else's...

No. I trust her. Nothing happened.

I placed Ember's water on a coaster on the coffee table. She was already asleep again. I walked upstairs to Jillian's and my room, where I could hear her and Reid speaking in low voices. I leaned against the wall and waited for them to finish.

Reid had started to stop by Jillian's bedside with growing frequency this last week, but only when I wasn't there. A few times I'd overheard snatches of conversation: "Matthew," "Ember," "make up."

I'd concluded that Reid felt guilty about what had happened after the tribunal, and he wanted advice about Ember, with whom he desired to make up.

He and Jillian had endured a terrible ordeal at the tribunal that I had not been able to share, and I supposed that he felt Ember's best friend might be the better source of advice than, say, Marco or me. I couldn't blame him. As far as I knew, Marco had never had a girlfriend, and I was stupid enough about women that I'd basically driven my girlfriend into the arms of another man.

Why was I not threatened by Reid's intimacy with my wife, but had been driven out of my mind with jealousy by Dean?

By the pure facts alone, Reid should've been the bigger threat to me: tall, good-looking, from the same background as Jillian, and he already enjoyed a close relationship with her. Jillian had endured a sexual assault, and threats of more, to keep him safe. Even if he'd been Ember's shadow until recently, a blind person could see that Jillian loved Reid.

But it was Dean who got under my skin. Dean, with his *joie de vivre* and his stupid lip piercings that made him look like an alternative fashion model. Dean, with his militia and All-American let's-go-free-the-slaves mission. Dean, who was brave enough to not just escape his tormenters, but to face them repeatedly in battle. Dean, who'd comforted my wife in her darkest hours and had, if only for a moment, carried her heart in his hands.

Dean was everything I wasn't: optimistic, compelling, courageous, and sensitive. I'd detected some of that in the first hour I'd known him, and if we'd met under different circumstances, I probably would've asked to be the Sentinel medic. I didn't approve of their methods of dealing with the Westerners, but it would've been like being a superhero *and* an Army nurse.

Yet Jillian had chosen me. I'd told her every nasty thing about my past, and she'd still chosen me. I smiled despite myself; I'd spend the rest of my life trying to earn that honor.

The door creaked open and Reid walked out, an empty mug in his hands. He held up the mug. "Just bringing her some more."

I thanked him and then walked into the bedroom. Jillian was propped up on a thick stack of pillows, tissues and books scattered all around her on the blankets. On her bedside table, a ripped box of over-the-counter flu medication lay half-empty next to a water bottle. Her tablet displayed our team's fan forums.

Jillian grinned at me. "Welcome back," she croaked.

I sat down on the edge of the bed. "I'm sorry I took so long. I had to stop at the drugstore on the way home to pick up more medication for Ember."

"Still barfing everywhere?"

"She's getting it all in the bowl now. That's an improvement."

Jillian started to laugh, but was cut off by several deep, chesty coughs that racked her body.

I handed her the water bottle. She tried to sip, but another sudden cough made her choke on the water. I reached out and held her while she sputtered, enjoying the feeling of her warm body in my arms. As muscular as she was, she was still soft. Touching her had quickly become my favorite pastime.

When she was done, she leaned back into her pillows. "Why is this flu so bad? Do you think it's that swine flu?"

"No, I'm sure you have the same bug everyone else had. I'll bet anything that the JM-104 has suppressed your immune system, at least to a degree. You have to watch out that you don't get overtired or stressed. Flu can turn into pneumonia."

Jillian sighed. "Fun. I hope Reuben is okay. If he's got a suppressed immune system, he's gonna have to make sure he doesn't get gangrene. Do you think you could fly up to Baltimore and heal him?"

I took her hand in mine and kissed her knuckles. "Even if Artemis didn't kill me on sight, I wouldn't. I just found out that Beau and Will weren't captured by the Sentinels. We have to assume that they're going to try to take Ember again. I'm going to be here when they do."

Jillian swore. "That's my fault. *Damn it, that's my fault.* I hope my powers are back when they return so I can kick their asses properly."

I stroked a lock of hair that had escaped her loose ponytail. "Stop it. Remember what Erica said at your appointment? You can't blame yourself for everything that goes wrong."

I'd convinced Jillian to reschedule her meeting with the FBI agents, which had been set for a few hours after the press conference. However, the next day I'd driven her to her new therapist's office myself. Erica, a kind and impeccably professional licensed therapist, hadn't expressed any discomfort when sneezing, coughing Jillian sat down for their first appointment.

Jillian fidgeted with her ponytail. "But some things are my fault. If I'd—"

I leaned forward and touched my nose to hers. "Please stop."

"Okay," she whispered.

I kissed her, wishing that all her worries could flow into me through the kiss. She melted into the kiss, humming happily. Though desire stirred in my belly, I broke away before things got carried away.

I did let myself eye her bosom, which strained against the thin fabric of her shirt. However, as much as I wanted to rip off my buxom wife's delightfully snug t-shirt and yoga pants, I had to take her health into consideration. Right now, that meant letting her rest, and not letting her berate herself to death.

I pulled a small box out of my pocket.

She cocked her head. "What's that?"

"If you promise not to blame yourself for Will and Beau, I'll give you something pretty."

A curious little smile lit up her face. "I like pretty things. I promise."

I opened the box. Inside, a delicate silver heart pendant gleamed in the light of her bedside lamp. Two delicate gemstones sparkled blue and green. I lifted the bright pendant from its velvet box and held it up. "To replace your other one. I thought there might be too many negative memories attached to the first design, so I had this one made."

Jillian stared at the necklace, slowly extending her hand to stroke it. "What type of stones are they?" I could see the necklace reflected in her eyes.

"They're our birthstones. Peridot, for you, and blue topaz, for me."

Jillian leaned forward and gathered her ponytail up, so I could hook the necklace on. I did, and she leaned back, allowing me to see how it rested. It sat just below her collarbone, drawing the eye to her stunning décolletage.

Jillian drew her knees up to her chest, her eyes watery. "Thank you. It's even prettier than the J necklace. I didn't think that was possible." She blinked several times, and then tears began to fall. She wiped at her face furiously. "I hate him," she said, her voice cracking on the last word. "You shouldn't have had to buy me a new one."

I gathered Jillian in my arms and rubbed her back. "It was my pleasure. And he will never hurt you again. He'll never hurt anyone again."

I'd made sure Matthew Dumont would spend the rest of his life looking over his shoulder.

He'd been so adorably confused when I asked him if I could tell him a secret. Nothing could have prepared him for what I'd whispered into his ear: *My real name is Benjamin Trent. I'm a murderer. You're my next victim.*

In the week since, I'd tried to make myself feel guilty about revealing my true identity and threatening to kill him. But every time I did, I recalled Jillian's dull, broken gaze as she'd described how Matthew had assaulted her. The more I thought about it, the more I felt that I'd done a public service.

Jillian touched her necklace, the tears already slowing. "Aren't rings more common?"

"I thought about getting us rings, but we work with our hands so much, a necklace made more sense. Would you like me to wear one?"

I hadn't meant the question as a joke, but Jillian started laughing through her tears. "No, that's fine," she wheezed. "I think it looks better on me. I'll put this back on after I've had a shower, though." She unhooked the clasp and carefully placed the chain on her bedside table.

I rubbed my chin, pretending to be lost in thought. "If a necklace and a ring are out... a tattoo on my chest, then. 'J and B Forever.'"

Jillian fell back into the pillows and giggled. I took off my uniform and draped it over the desk chair, then crawled into bed next to her, shoving aside quite a few tissues and one ridiculous-looking bodice ripper. I reached over to turn out the light while Jillian snuggled next to me. Soon her breathing slowed and deepened, and she was asleep.

I laid in the dark, staring up at the dozens of tiny glow-in-the-dark stars she'd glued to the ceiling. They were the stars of the previous

June first's night sky—her "lucky stars," she'd called them, because we'd met on that day.

The last thought I had before I fell asleep was that it was I who was the lucky one.

"Ben, wake up." Reid's urgent whisper pulled me from pleasant dreams.

I sat up and wiped sleep from my eyes. Jillian was still asleep next to me. "What's up?" I whispered back. When my eyes focused, I saw that Reid was fully dressed.

"There's been a bombing. Captain Nguyen needs us down by the docks as soon as possible."

I checked my watch on the nightstand. It was a quarter past two. Who the heck would bomb a dock in the middle of the night? "Okay. Give me less than five."

He hurried out of the room, and I got out of bed, careful not to wake Jillian. I hastily pulled on my clothes.

Just as I was walking out of our room, Jillian's sleepy voice called, "Benj-min?"

I was at her side in a fraction of a second. "We got a call from the police. There's been a bombing across town."

Jillian propped herself up on her arm. "Okay," she mumbled, clearly still half asleep. She was suddenly seized by a violent coughing fit. When she stopped, she cleared her throat. "Can you just put a full kettle on the stove before you go? I'll make myself some more tea in a little while."

I kissed her forehead. "Of course. I'll see you in a few hours."

I walked back to the doorway, pausing for one last look at my wife. She was already dozing, her arm draped over her flat stomach. Flu or not, she was the most beautiful woman I'd ever seen. *And she wants me.*

I met Ember, Marco, and Reid in the kitchen, where I quickly filled the kettle. Ember still looked sickly, but Jillian's rule was firm: Ember had to be near Marco or Reid at all times.

We rushed out of the house. For the first time since returning to Saint Catherine, Reid ordered us to hold on to him while he directed a large piece of rock beneath our feet out of the ground.

"This is the best way to travel, if you ask me," he said as we rose up into the air.

I watched the white and orange lights of Saint Catherine spread out underneath us like a glowing patchwork that ended abruptly at the Atlantic Ocean. The Georgian city's winter breeze was almost balmy as it blew past us, and I found that I couldn't disagree with him.

I dashed around the site of the explosion for at least the twentieth time in an hour, searching everywhere for survivors, corpses, or even pieces of corpses. Around me, my team scoured the blast zone for the same.

Ember, never more than an arm's length away from Marco, sat down on a large piece of rubble. *I don't think there's anyone here. Maybe I can't hear anyone because they're dead, but I haven't found any bodies. I've asked the flies, and they don't smell any meat other than us.*

I joined Marco and Ember in the middle of the wreckage. "I don't get it, though," I said, running a hand through my hair, a nervous hangover from when it was longer. "Why would someone bomb an empty dock?" I nodded toward the partially destroyed abandoned warehouse nearby. "There wasn't anyone here to kill, nor anything in storage to sabotage."

"Vandalism?" Reid suggested as he floated down from his platform from which he'd searched aerially. "Someone owns the dock, right?"

"The city, I presume," I said, looking around. "But the bomb was a big one, which points to some sophistication. I just can't see going to the trouble of creating a decent bomb and just blowing it up in the middle of nowhere."

Reid threw up his hands. "You got me. That's for the cops to figure out. If there's nobody to rescue, our job here is done."

Marco raised his hand one more time, the ball of light casting a warm glow over the dark carnage.

The lack of casualties was comforting, but something about the scene was weird. The way we all stood there, looking around for people to help, made me feel vulnerable in a way I couldn't quite explain.

I wanted Ember to get inside. It wasn't right for her to be exposed like this for so long.

"Ember, is anyone watching us?" I asked.

She closed her eyes. "No. The only people nearby are the cops."

"Okay." But I was still uneasy. I strained to explain why the dock had been targeted. Perhaps a shipment was coming in and someone didn't want it to arrive. Or maybe some sick terrorist group had decided to test a bomb on infrastructure but didn't feel the need to kill people as they did so.

Reid beckoned Captain Nguyen over and quickly gave our report. The police officer thanked him and gave us our all clear. Reid gathered us around and flew us up into the air again.

From our vantage point, I could see that the bomb had been very powerful indeed; the blast zone radiated out five hundred yards. The bomb itself had been placed in the middle of the empty dock. But *why*?

We began the breezy flight home. The peaceful picture of the city offered by our altitude hid the truth: Saint Catherine had been in upheaval since Jillian's press conference. There'd been demonstrations in front of the mayor's office every day since the broadcast.

Each evening, the national news networks reported on protests in other superhero cities. The Seattle, San Francisco, Chicago, and Tallahassee teams had been asked to leave. We'd received many requests for interviews, but Jillian had refused them all until after the inevitable court cases. The federal government had vowed to move against the Westerners, as well as summoned the elders to Washington.

My wife had started something that couldn't be stopped. I was hopeful that the nature of superheroism would change for the better at the end of it all, but between now and then stood the herculean task of taking down my family, and all families like mine. I didn't know if I'd be alive to see the end of it all.

As we flew over a quiet neighborhood near our home, Ember gasped. "Reid, land! Now!"

Reid obeyed without question. We dropped to the ground so quickly my stomach fluttered, landing with a hard impact. Ember whipped around and stared at a small playground behind us.

A man was walking toward us from the playground, barely visible in the darkness. Reid, Marco, and I moved to shield Ember at the same time.

As the man approached, he pulled down his black hood, revealing a black mask, which he also removed. He passed under the light of a streetlamp, allowing me to see his face. I breathed a sigh of relief.

He was no older than me, and obviously a relative of Reid's—they had the same distinct Fischer jaw, long face, and gray eyes. Everything he wore, from his solid hooded jacket to his combat boots, was black. I counted four large knives strapped to his legs and arms. I was reminded of a ninja.

Reid squinted, then gasped. "Raphael?"

Raphael strode up to us, looking over his shoulder once. "Where's your leader?" he asked urgently.

"I'm mission leader right now," Reid said. "Why are you here? I didn't know you were in service yet."

Raphael glanced over his shoulder again, breathing hard. "I don't have time to waste. Six hours ago, the Baltimore team murdered their leader, Imperator. The elders have ordered my team to execute them."

Reid's jaw fell open. "You're on a strike team?"

Raphael checked behind him once more. "Not right now. Buck

asked me to recuse myself because of my relation to Reuben. But listen to me, all of you." His eyes darted across our faces. "You're next. There's been no official order. It won't be a public hit. But Elder Lloyd made it clear that after Baltimore, it's you guys. That news broadcast was your death knell."

Before anyone could say anything, Raphael glanced behind him again. "I don't think anyone followed me, but I can't stay." He gave Reid a brief hug. "Get your leader and run for your lives. If you fight my team, you will not win. That's a promise."

"Go," Reid said, giving him a gentle push. "Be safe."

Raphael nodded and sprinted back into the shadows of the playground.

When he was out of sight, Reid gathered us together. "We're getting Jill and leaving. I'm sure she'll agree with that plan. We'll warn the Baltimore team, too."

I was also sure she'd agree. I had no idea how to process what we'd just heard, but I knew Jillian would order us to get into the nearest car and drive very far, very fast.

We flew up into the air and over the houses, landing in front of our house less than five minutes later. Ember put a hand to her forehead. "Jill's safe. She's asleep..."

Ember threw out her arm, barring us from passing her.

Did she sense Beau on the street? I reached for my newly-assigned weapon, an extendable baton. "What?" I demanded. "What is it?"

"That's not Jill."

I was at the front door immediately. As my trembling fingers entered my code, I saw that the front door's wooden panels were swirled and warped in a way they hadn't been ninety minutes before.

The door clicked open, and I burst inside. "Jillian! *Jillian!*" I ran upstairs to our room. The bed was empty. So were the bathrooms and the other bedrooms.

"Benjamin!" Ember's terrified voice came from the kitchen.

I was there in an instant, freezing in the doorway when I saw what my team crowded around—a body on the floor. My heart seemed to stop beating as I walked up to the unconscious person, then started again when I saw that it wasn't Jillian.

It was Graham.

Reid's kitchen knife was wedged between two of his ribs. Ember held up a shaking hand. "Don't heal him. Just touch my hand." Her voice was trembling as hard as she was. "He's dying. I'll show you his final memories."

We touched her hand.

An explosion of color and sound assaulted my mind as she contacted Graham, and then we were in the same kitchen, but standing in the doorway, approaching Jillian as she cut oregano for her tea. The kitchen clock read 2:45.

I could feel Graham's annoyance that she wasn't asleep in bed and his certainty that he could sneak up on her. A floorboard in the living room creaked.

Graham internally cursed Beau, who was behind him.

Jillian spun around and shrieked. She jumped on Graham, plunging the knife into his chest. Graham fell, and the memory tilted a little as his vision changed from straight on to looking up from the floor. The steady pulse of pain from his chest colored the memories.

Beau and Will ran in and tackled Jillian, who screamed and struggled underneath their weight. Without her powers, they were easily able to pull her arms behind her back and handcuff her.

I couldn't even cry out in my mind, so overwhelmed was I by what I was seeing.

Will hauled her to her feet, so she was facing Beau. Behind Beau, Alysia wandered into the kitchen. She perched on the kitchen table and crossed her legs. She was holding a small black plastic bag.

"Hello again," Beau said, his quiet voice laced with a world of fury.

"You are never going to get Ember," Jillian growled. She spat at his feet.

Beau merely tilted his head to the side. "Ember? Who said anything about Ember?"

Jillian stilled. "What do you want?" Her voice was cold.

"You know where the JM-104 is," Beau said, tracing little patterns on her cheek. She jerked her head away from his metal hand, but he caught her chin. "My friends checked out your lead in Chattahoochee, but they didn't find anything. You're going to tell us what you know."

My heart rate increased.

Jillian's eyes grew wide. Over the memory, Graham's recollection of Jillian's words in the jeep weeks before played behind my eyes. *"...I know where it is at Chattahoochee..."*

Jillian stared at Beau for a long moment. "I'm not telling you anything," she said finally.

Beau's lips curled in a small smile. "I was hoping you'd say that. Alysia, if you would. I don't want her waking the neighbors."

His words kindled cold dread in my stomach.

Alysia smirked and removed a roll of duct tape from the bag. She tore off a small piece and placed it over Jillian's mouth, cutting off her protest.

Beau grinned at Jillian before grabbing the neckline of her t-shirt and tearing her shirt straight down the front. Jillian tried to squirm away from Beau, but Will held her firmly in place.

My brother walked over to the stove, where the tea kettle was steaming away. Nobody spoke as he poured out the boiling water into the sink, steam rising up as he did so.

He turned around, kettle in hand. "Are you going to tell me where the JM-104 is?"

Jillian's eyes were locked on the kettle. She shook her head.

Beau nodded at Will, who grabbed Jillian's hair and yanked her head back, stretching out her torso.

"Don't do it, Beau," I whispered. "Please."

Beau pressed the bottom of the kettle to Jillian's smooth stomach.

My wife's high, muffled scream made Alysia and Will burst into hysterical laughter. Tears streamed down Jillian's face as Beau removed the kettle and placed it back on the burner. "Are you going to tell me where the JM-104 is?"

Jillian shook her head.

Beau slapped the perfectly round red burn, eliciting another muffled scream. "Last chance."

Jillian shook her head again, still crying.

Beau glared at Will. "Get her out of here."

Will dragged Jillian out of the kitchen, Alysia close behind and still laughing.

Graham made a little noise. "Help," he whimpered.

Beau kneeled next to him, his face impassive. "You're already dead. Dealing with your corpse will just slow us down."

Graham's horror, betrayal, and fear overtook him, clouding the memory.

And then we were out of his head, kneeling next to the dying man and hyperventilating. Marco dashed to the sink and threw up.

I was frozen in place, unable to let go of Ember's hand. In my worst nightmares, I had never imagined that Beau would've come back for Jillian. From the stunned expressions around me, I gathered that nobody else had, either.

In an instant, my mind snapped back into work, calculating what I'd just witnessed.

Jillian didn't know where the JM-104 was—I was certain of this. She'd refused to say anything to Beau because the only alternative, admitting ignorance, would've meant her death... *if* he believed her, which wasn't guaranteed. I knew my brother better than anyone. If he'd decided that Jillian knew where the serum was, then nothing would dissuade him.

A tiny voice in the recesses of my mind suggested that Beau didn't actually care about JM-104. This was his chance to take revenge on me by proxy. He was capable of atrocity when it was purely business. What would he do when it was personal?

No. If this was solely about revenge, he would've let me know that he'd taken my wife. He didn't know that I knew he had her, which was my first and best advantage. He believed he had time to draw out the interrogations. I lifted my head up, hope rising in my chest. His worst methods would also have to be his final ones, because I wasn't there to heal the injuries—and if I worked fast, he wouldn't have time to carry out the worst methods.

My nails dug into my palms so hard they drew blood. I'd show him injuries. I'd show him injuries unlike any he'd ever seen. I, too, was a Trent. He'd obviously forgotten that.

"He's gone," Ember said, dropping Graham's hand.

There was silence in the kitchen for several seconds.

Reid stood up. "We're going after her. We leave in five minutes. The bomb must have been a diversion. Marco, Ember, get supplies. Benjamin, where do you think they'll take her?"

Ember and Marco ran out of the room.

I climbed to my feet, fire spreading through my veins. "We're going to Baltimore."

Reid opened the back door and picked up Graham's corpse. "Baltimore? I'm going to need your help with this mission. You know these people better than any of us. Where in Baltimore? We're going to need to stake out the location and come up with a plan."

"No, they're going to Annapolis. But we're going to Baltimore first."

Reid froze. "What do you mean?"

I walked up to him and gave him a hard stare. "What I mean is that we're going to Baltimore and warning your brother's team about the attack, then both teams are going to go to Annapolis to rescue Jillian and finally put my family in the ground. Jillian was right: it's *over*."

Instead of a stern rebuke for giving the orders, Reid's eyes glowed white. A hole appeared in the backyard and he stepped outside to dump Graham's body. The grave smoothed over in seconds.

He came back inside and crossed his arms. "The Baltimore team doesn't like you."

"I know."

"They probably won't trust you."

"I know."

"We're going to have to fight some of the most dangerous, highly-trained killers on the planet before we can even begin to figure out how to save Jill."

"I know."

"Then let's go." He strode past me into the house.

I ran up the stairs in less than a second. I grabbed Jillian's necklace from the nightstand and shoved it into its velvet box, which I put into my pocket. She'd wear it soon. My heart pounded in my chest as I gathered Jillian's knives and uniform. She'd wear them soon, too. We'd fight the strike team, storm my old house, and rescue Jillian. She was going to be okay.

But for every hopeful thought, though, a thousand images of Beau's victims raced through my mind, an obscene film reel of blood, pain, and violence. No matter what Beau did, Jillian wouldn't fare well. She was sick and powerless. It could easily get out of hand...

No. Not this time. She's a fighter.

I glanced at Jillian's tablet, which still displayed our team's fan forums. Every thread started in the last week was about Jillian's speech. Countless people had expressed their admiration of my wife, who'd stood up against her abusers and dared them to challenge her. She'd thrown down the gauntlet in front of three hundred million people.

My hand closed around the hilt of Jillian's favorite knife. As with the elders and Jillian, the fight between Beau and Jillian wasn't going to be about brute strength, but a battle of wills.

Battlecry would win.

I ran down the stairs and met my team. We all looked at each other for a second, confidence evident on everyone's face.

Reid opened the door. "Lead the way."

ACKNOWLEDGMENTS

Writing *Battlecry* was hard—but writing *Sentinel* was much harder. Thanks are in order, because I never would've been able to do this without the support of my friends and family.

First and foremost, I'm grateful to God for blessing and guiding my career. Similarly, thank you to everyone who prayed for me, and continues to pray for me. Special shout-outs to the Tumblr Catholic community and the Young & Wild Catholic Mama Facebook group.

After that, of course... Alex. I never would've gotten this far without you at my side to encourage me and prod me in the right direction. I love you.

I must thank my Scribophile critique team, especially: Alan Billing, Renee Harvey, J.S. Dewes, Ada Hardy, and Katie Acosta. Additionally, many thanks go to the ladies of Enclave: Monika Holabird, Emily Gorman, Katherine Bueche, and Ryann Muree.

A HUGE thank you goes out to Christiana Dodge, the real queen of the horses. Where would I be without my equine technical advisor? Because of your help, my horse scenes are so much better. From one writer to another: just write. Write anything and everything that makes you happy. Read a lot. Dream big. The best time to start is now.

Never, ever, ever, *ever* be ashamed of being a bookworm and a dreamer.

Many thanks to Erica Sartwell, who helped me deal with the tough areas of my life as I was writing *Sentinel*. I wouldn't have named Jill's therapist anything else.

And of course, more thanks to Sarah Gonzales, who has been at my side since the beginning.

ABOUT THE AUTHOR

Emerald Dodge lives in Maryland with her husband, Alex, and their two sons. Emerald and Alex enjoy playing with their children, date nights, hosting dinner parties for their friends, and watching movies. They are a Navy family and look forward to traveling around the nation and meeting new people. When she's not writing, Emerald likes to cook, bake, go to Mass, pray the rosary, and FaceTime with her relatives.

Her favorite social media platform for interacting with fans is Tumblr. Message her on her Tumblr page!